OBSCURA

JOE HART

THOMAS & MERCER

Published by Thomas & Mercer, Seattle

www.apub.com

Amazon, the Amazon logo, and Thomas & Mercer are trademarks of Amazon.com, Inc., or its affiliates.

ISBN-13: 9781503949898 (hardcover)
ISBN-10: 1503949893 (hardcover)
ISBN-13: 9781503949881 (paperback)
ISBN-10: 1503949885 (paperback)

Front cover design by M.S. Corley

Back cover design by Ray Lundgren

Printed in the United States of America

First edition

OBSCURA

SHORT STORIES

"The Line Unseen"
"The Edge of Life"
"Outpost"
"And the Sea Called Her Name"

COMICS

The Last Sacrifice

To all those who have lost their pasts—may we remember for you.

ONE

Now

"Ten, nine, eight, seven . . ."

The voice inside Gillian's helmet reverberated in her skull as the shuttle shook to life around her.

She braced herself, every muscle tense. Straining.

Overwhelming panic flooded her, thickened with regret. What the hell was she doing here? She wasn't an astronaut. Wasn't ready for this.

Gillian reached to her right, finding Birk's gloved hand, and squeezed it. He squeezed back.

"Six, five, four . . ."

"Ignition."

The shaking took on new life, rattling her teeth in their sockets.

"Three, two, one."

The g-force shoved her backward in her seat and forward at the same time, the velocity something alive as the shuttle roared. Carson was still speaking in her earpiece, but she couldn't understand him.

Everything was speed.

Pressure.

She heard someone moaning and realized it was Birk. She tightened her grip on him even as his slackened. Had he passed out? Concern was overridden by a new wave of force from behind and the sensation of someone stacking weight plates on her chest.

She had felt it before. The terror of losing all control.

They were leaving the ground.

TWO

Eight Years Before

They almost always held hands when they drove somewhere together, but tonight they weren't.

It usually didn't matter if they were on their way to a romantic dinner or running to their local grocery store for a late-night snack; they held hands. It was something spawned early in their relationship, a cute and exciting thing that gradually became a sentimental comfort. Kent would set his hand, palm up, on the console between them, and Gillian would lace her fingers in his. Six years of marriage had only entrenched the routine.

But tonight he hadn't reached for her as they pulled out of the restaurant's parking lot onto the highway.

Gillian looked across the Tahoe to where Kent sat in the driver's seat. The clean lines of his features sharpened then muted in the wash of streetlamps they passed. What was he thinking? She had wondered this a lot recently, almost obsessively.

There were differences with him, subtle but there.

He would end his sentences in the middle, as if another thought overrode the current one, his face going slack, eyes distant. When she asked what was wrong, he would return to himself immediately, asking what he'd been saying, and after jumpstarting his memory, he'd be off again. But it wasn't only the hitches in conversation. Last week when she'd got off shift early at the hospital, radiology being strangely quiet for a Monday afternoon, she came home to find Kent standing in the living room, gaze fixed on a fly crawling along the wall. She'd thought he was trying to swat it, but then the insect had taken flight and buzzed past her into the kitchen, and Kent remained motionless.

She'd watched him for several eternal minutes, a tingling unease building exponentially, before clearing her throat, which brought him out of the fugue. He'd smiled and come to greet her like normal, but there had been a strange expression on his face when he first turned around.

Almost like he hadn't recognized her.

In the hours she'd lain awake on the nights since, she wondered how long he'd been standing there before she came home.

He was different, and she wondered if maybe it wasn't because he noticed she was different now too.

Gillian cleared her throat. "You were quiet tonight."

"Mmm?" Kent replied, not looking at her.

"I said you were quiet tonight."

"Was I?"

"Yes. You've been quiet for the last few days."

"Sorry. Been busy with work. The new client . . ."

She waited for him to say the client's name, willed him to say it, tension growing in her with each passing second. Kent cocked his head, as if hearing a distant sound, then relaxed again.

"Intersect," she said, barely able to get the name out.

"What?"

"The new client, Intersect Inc."

"Yeah. What about them?"

Something in Gillian's stomach plunged. It dropped deep inside her, deeper than she'd thought any feeling could go. A needling memory returned from earlier that day, the subject of an article she'd read in a recent med journal one of the physicians had left in the break room. The appearance of a new neurological disorder always made waves in the medical community, but this one was different. Losian's, they were calling it, and it wasn't only the symptoms that were terrifying; it was the susceptible population. The disease could strike anyone.

And now, riding in the car with the dark outlines of trees scrolling by beside the highway, a horrifying possibility formed like a bridge connecting over a gap.

"What's today's date?" she asked before she could stop herself.

"Today?" Kent said.

"The date today, what is it?"

A small smile formed at the corner of his mouth. "Don't you know?"

"I forgot."

"Well, it's . . ." He glanced at the dashboard before returning his eyes to the road. "It's seven forty-five."

The fear on the other side of the barrier she'd been constructing over the last few weeks burst through, consuming her.

This wasn't happening. Not to her husband. Not to their life.

She thought she might be sick for the second time that day.

"I think we need to make an appointment for you."

"Hmm?"

"An appointment. Tomorrow . . . we need to get you into Dr. Danner."

"What? Why? I feel fine."

"You just told me it was seven forty-five."

"Yeah?"

"I asked you what the date was."

At last his gaze left the road and found hers.

And she saw he was afraid.

Just as quickly, the fear curdled to anger.

"I'm fine. I've been stressed out with the new client. They want all their IT done by the end of the month and . . . and . . ." She watched the shadow of his jaw clench in the glare of another car's headlights. "And what's his name asked me to help finish his basement too next week."

"Greg," Gillian said. "Your brother's name is Greg."

His face slackened. The anger left his eyes, its presence there like some alien parasite. She had seen him truly furious only twice in the years of their relationship.

Gillian reached a trembling hand out to touch his shoulder. It was warm and solid beneath her fingers, reassuring. Her husband—he was still there beside her. But was he really?

Stop. Keep it together.

"Honey, I think there's something wrong with your memory. We need to go get it checked to be sure. I can oversee the tests and I'll read them myself. But we have to have you see someone because this is start-ing to scare me." She paused, unsure whether she was going to say the next part or if she should wait. She stood on a swaying high wire with solid ground nowhere in sight. "And I need you. We need you. Honey, I'm preg—"

It was in the moment she felt the passenger-side wheels leave the highway that she recognized the blankness of his stare for what it was.

Grass hissed beneath the undercarriage, and she yelled, reaching for the wheel that turned in his loose hands.

I should've been holding his hand, she thought before the ditch sloped sharply away and the Tahoe rolled.

◆ ◆ ◆

Gillian came to on her side.

There was glass embedded in her cheek. When she raised her head, tinkling pieces dropped away to the roof of the Tahoe she lay on. And there was something wrong with everything outside the broken window: the whole world was turned on its head. Her door was shaped like a "V," and a tree was lodged in its center.

She managed to lever her upper body away from the mangled door and the tree that shouldn't have been there before the pain hit.

It was a hurricane that swept over her in an instant, almost all of it radiating from her right leg, and when she looked, she wished she hadn't.

Because legs weren't supposed to bend that way. Or that many times.

Gillian sobbed Kent's name, even as the sound of a siren began to rise somewhere in the night. She looked through the tears that fractured her gaze, seeing him dangling from his seat belt beside her. He moved his head slightly, and a drop of blood ran upward from the tip of his nose toward his forehead, catching the light of some approaching vehicle so that she could see through it, how red it was. How red everything was.

And as her consciousness slipped away like silk being drawn through weak fingers, the siren in the distance became the heartbreaking cry of a baby.

THREE

"Two Gs," Carson said.

Gillian wondered briefly what their speed was, but the thought was swept aside as the shuttle became a tuning fork around them.

It was going to shake apart.

As violently as she was pressed into her seat, the vibration still managed to rattle her.

Her fillings hummed, and her vision doubled before straightening again.

Tinsel, who had been silent until now, sitting in front and to her right, made a high-pitched wheeze. "How long does this last?" the analyst managed.

"A few more minutes. You'll be fine," Lien Zhou, the command pilot, said brusquely.

"Three Gs," Carson intoned.

How the hell did he sound so calm? He'd done this twice before, she reminded herself. With effort, she managed to turn her head to the left and look out the viewing port, catching a burst of color there.

Flames engulfed the shuttle, obscuring the view of everything outside the window.

FOUR

Two Months Before

She was thankful there was no one else in the lab attached to her office when she received the email because she was able to release the scream without worry.

When Gillian's voice finished reverberating and faded away, she grasped the laptop and picked it up to throw it. She stood there at her cluttered desk filled with the last six years of her life's work, and the only thing that kept her from hurling the computer like a discus was the recent picture of Carrie on the corkboard above the mess.

The little girl had Kent's blue eyes and her own nose and chin. The delicate cheekbones and light-brown hair were an amalgam of them both. Kent had lived long enough to see her born but not long enough to see the beautiful girl she'd grown to be.

Gillian set the laptop down with a sigh and scanned the email again.

It was sad that she was almost used to a few words taking away all hope.

She read through the lines, read between them. Each was more vague than the last and sprinkled with handy deflecting phrases like "deferred allocation of funds" and "referendum on hold until further notice."

So here it was at last. The day she feared would come. The culmination of her failings.

The seed of panic that had been planted at last month's Senate meeting sprouted another root. She could feel it growing inside her, trying to blossom into the kind of sorrow she hadn't truly felt in years.

Gone. Everything slipping away.

Gillian gritted her teeth, using an old meditation tactic she'd picked up in one of the countless self-help books she'd read after . . . just after. She closed her eyes and pictured a tumultuous sea, the waves crashing against one another, dark clouds roiling overhead, the water angry. Hungry. She imagined it all slowly calming, a gradual easing of weather until the surface of the ocean was flat as a mirror.

Quiet. Nothing disturbing the water.

She opened her eyes to the email, and immediately the sea in her mind was replaced with the image of the prescription bottle in the back of her bottom desk drawer.

The little pills inside. Their rattle always soothing her more than any meditation could. How easily she'd fallen back into the habit, after working so hard to leave it behind.

The door to the lab outside her office opened, and she came back to herself, wondering how long she'd been sitting there.

Gillian straightened a pile of reports on her desk as a lumbering shadow slid across the floor outside her doorway before its owner appeared.

Birk Lindqvist, the largest man she had ever met. If he weren't clean-shaven, Thor's hammer would have looked perfectly at home in one massive hand. Besides being a modern-day Viking, he was also the most brilliant postgraduate who had ever set foot in her lab.

"Doctor, I brought a muffin for you from the cafeteria. I mistook it for chocolate chip, but it is raisin, so I apologize." His native tongue's lilt was still discernable despite six years in the university's dialect melting pot. The huge Swede stepped into her office holding out a paper bag that looked comically small in his hand.

Gillian took the muffin from him and smiled. "You didn't have to, Birk."

"I was passing through, so . . ." He shrugged. "What's wrong, Doctor?"

"Nothing. I was just doing a little cleaning."

"You never clean."

"Not true, I rearranged my bookshelf last week," she said, gesturing to the stacks piled so precariously a stiff wind might topple them all to the floor.

"Yes, of course," Birk said, raising one eyebrow as he studied the shelf.

"That sounded almost insolent, and I don't accept insolence from postgrads like yourself."

"Will you accept it when I have my master's?"

"Absolutely. There's an unwritten rule that advanced-degree holders have to endure disrespect from one another. In fact, it's encouraged."

Birk smiled. "Then I cannot wait."

"Yes, well, until then, let's get to work, shall we?"

She tried making her way past him, but he stood his ground, blocking her path to the lab. "Doctor, I've worked with you for nearly four years now. I've eaten at your home, watched after your daughter, and when the time comes for Justin and me to be married, you will be our guest of honor. You are an open novel. So please, tell me what's wrong."

"An open book." She corrected the idiom automatically before letting her head droop forward, all the weight of the recent months falling on her at once. Lie or truth? It was an easy choice; he would find out soon enough. "Our funding's been cut. I just got the email from the committee a few minutes ago. We have enough for one more month."

When she glanced back up at him, the surprise and outrage she expected in his face weren't there. Instead, he merely nodded. "I had guessed it would be soon."

"How?"

"I overheard you speaking with one of the committee members a few months ago before you addressed the Senate. It did not sound encouraging."

"So you're not only insolent but an eavesdropper too." Her attempt at humor had the opposite effect, and a sad weariness settled over her. "I'm sorry, I won't be able to pay your salary this month. I'll need to put it all toward the lab. I'll completely understand if you need to take another position." The mere thought of continuing the research in Birk's absence was more than daunting. It was blackly disheartening.

"Doctor, I've been returning my pay to the general fund for the last three months. I'll be here to the end." He smiled again, tipping his head to one side in his customary fashion.

The tears that sprang to her eyes were so sudden they caught her off guard. She wiped the first that fell away before it could travel more than an inch down her cheek and choked out a short laugh. "You're too good, Birk. Someday someone's going to take advantage of you. You know that, right?"

"Maybe it isn't that I'm a good person, but that my fiancé is very rich."

She laughed in earnest this time and embraced him, which was like hugging a towering oak tree. He patted her back once. "It will be all right, Doctor."

When he released her, she swallowed several times until the knot in her throat unraveled enough for her to speak. "Okay, let's go ahead with the trial. Maybe we'll get lucky and prove those bastards on the Hill wrong. Then they won't have a choice about funding."

"I think luck will have nothing to do with it," Birk said, moving out into the lab to don a clean coverall. She followed him, doing the same, all the while trying to keep the email from derailing her. If she could take a hydro right now, that would give her the clarity she needed. It would help her focus. She paused midway across the lab, turning back to her office.

The familiar gnawing began at the back of her mind. Whispers of how nice it would be to swallow one of the little pills, everything around her taking on a sharpened shine, how easy it would be to concentrate if she were surrounded by the narco-glow.

No. She didn't need it. She could work through a day without relying on the pills.

But later at home, it might be nice to have one.

Stop it.

Gillian took a deep breath and finished prepping to enter the portion of the lab separated by a sterile barrier and governed by air-filtration units that controlled humidity, pressure, and temperature. The whispers faded as she stepped up to the entry beside Birk.

"Ready, Doctor?"

"Ready."

The clean space wasn't large, barely fifteen feet by twelve, just enough to house the monitoring equipment, an array of touchscreens, and the table in the center holding the Plexiglas cage with the open top.

Gillian took a deep breath, letting everything fall away. There was no room for anxiety or worry here, no space for doubt. Only concentration and will.

"Recording on," she said, moving to the center table. One of the screens in the corner of the room lit up. "May 6, 2028, eleven fifty a.m. Neural plasticity light trial number fifty-four in regards to Losian's disease. This is Dr. Gillian Ryan assisted by Birk Lindqvist." She nodded to Birk, who crossed the room to the small cage. "Subject is male

Rattus norvegicus, or common brown rat. Expression of neural channel rhodopsins is at sufficient levels for trial to commence. Trial fifty-four variable is a luciferase dose increase of .6 milliliters."

Birk approached the table, cupping the small brown rat in his hands. It was groggy, head barely moving.

"Luciferin compound injected at eleven a.m. for sufficient cranial absorption. Sedative administered at eleven thirty-three a.m.," Birk said, lowering the rat into the bottom of the cage where a small harness awaited. He settled the rodent quickly, positioning it as if it were standing on all four of its feet, head extended out. "Affixing neural bioelectroencephal monitor as well as injection line into cranial port." Birk threaded a miniscule wire into the metallic port poking up through the animal's fur at the top of its skull with a few deft movements before giving Gillian a nod.

She eyed the docile rat through the clear cage, making sure everything was in place.

Her heart rate began to climb.

What if this was it? The moment she'd been waiting, dreaming, hoping for.

What if?

She swallowed, stifling the excitement that had begun to build. It could easily be as disappointing as the last trials had been.

Or it could be the answer. Salvation.

She studied the nearest monitor. "Vitals are all stable. Proceeding to trial."

Her finger hovered over the "Execute" square on the screen. Touched it.

There was a quiet humming from the machine beside her. "Injection of luciferase initiated," she said quietly, and after a brief delay, the next display in line came alive with pulsing movement.

It was like watching a hundred thousand fireworks.

The biomonitor was a combination of electrical and light-sensitive apparatus and software, all tied together into a 3-D imaging computation. And right now she was looking at the partially sedated rat's thoughts.

Each time she saw the inner workings of a mind, it threw her. No matter if it was a PET scan of an eighty-year-old Kansas woman's brain or an MRI of a five-week-old lab mouse, the unreality of observing what made up another being's thoughts was transfixing in a way she could never articulate. She supposed it was the intimacy of it: she was seeing what made a person or animal who or what they were.

Their thoughts. Emotions. Memories. Everything that culminated in the truest sense of their identity—it was all there on the screen before her.

Even though the rat was barely conscious, many of its dendrites, axons, and interceding synapses remained active. She could see these as flitting glimmers of light where the luciferin and luciferase were reacting to create a deep-blue bioluminescent glow throughout the rat's brain. And where the chemicals joined, the neurons began to fire.

First thousands.

Then millions.

It was working.

"Pyramidal neurons active . . . and inhibiting neurons are now firing," she said quietly, tearing her gaze away from the screen to look at Birk, who stared at a second monitor.

He nodded once. "Light-plasticity target engaged." He touched a control screen as Gillian brought her attention back to the display.

More and more of the rat's brain was becoming active. The cerebellum, hindbrain, midbrain, and olfactory structure.

But her focus was on none of them.

"Come on. Come on," she whispered, willing it to work. Willing it to play out how she'd dreamed of it happening.

"Bioluminescence approaching hippocampal region," Birk said.

Gillian watched the glow spread, firing neurons in its path, billions of synapses triggered by the compound, her hypothesis being proven true before her. She caught a prayer on her lips and, even in her state of excitement, banished it away.

The first portion of the rat's hippocampus lit up, light flaring in millions of connections.

Then nothing.

Patches of darkness knitted with erratic stabs of brightness, like a lightning storm at midnight.

The compound flowed through the rat's hippocampus, but the majority of the area remained black and unresponsive.

The hope inside her folded, collapsing in on itself like the house of cards it was.

Gillian looked down at her hands and found them balled into fists. With enormous effort she unclenched them.

"Inhibiting neurons preventing full excitation of the hippocampus," Birk said. Gillian stared at the floor before reaching up to shut off the injection system. She moved away from the array of screens, not giving the rat a glance as she left the clean room.

Outside she tore at her coverall, unable to get it from her body fast enough. She was drowning, her lungs filling up. She needed a pill. Right now. Not later.

Now.

She made it to her office doorway and physically stopped herself from going any farther. Hands on either side of the doorjamb, she let her chin rest on her breastbone. The expected tears didn't come; the frustration and anger were too much and wouldn't allow any to form.

"It's okay, Doctor," Birk said from behind her.

"No. No, it's not, Birk," she said.

"I apologize. I misspoke."

She felt a scream building in her like a steam whistle, but just as quickly the rage deflated, leaving the customary emptiness she was used to.

"Take the afternoon," she said, still not facing him. She heard him shuffle around the lab for a moment before one of his large hands rested on her shoulder.

"I meant we are going to find the solution. We will try a different amount of luciferin. Perhaps—"

"It's all right. Just . . . just take the afternoon. Let's start early tomorrow."

His hand left her shoulder after a final squeeze, and she listened to him exit the lab. When all was quiet again, save the soft hush of the air circulation and occasional beep of one of the many machines, she stepped fully into her office and raised her head.

She looked at the clutter of her desk. The notes scribbled hastily in her messy scrawl. The journal articles marking the gradual uptick in cases of Losian's, named for the first child who had died, Charles Losian. He had been ten.

It all mocked her.

Gillian stepped forward and cleared her desk with one swoop of her arm.

Even as everything fell to the floor, she was turning toward the bookshelf. Tomes flew and struck the wall; one of the heaviest, an analysis on new neural radiological studies, left a dent in the Sheetrock. She spun again, tearing papers from the walls and corkboard, even her degree, which she held for a split second before sailing it to the farthest corner.

Glass tinkled, and it was this sound that stopped her cold.

Glass shattering, the feeling of it embedded in her cheek.

She brought a hand up automatically and felt the telltale scars there: small upraised patches of flesh, a horror story in braille.

All at once her legs wouldn't hold her, and she slumped to the floor, pressing her back against the wall, feeling the solidity of it, grounding herself in the present as the past tried to draw over her like a dark veil.

She stifled a quiet moan, covering her mouth as the tears came. Why wasn't the compound working? What had she missed? Why wasn't she smart enough to find it?

Why had any of this happened?

But there would never be solace or an answer for that last one.

She looked around the office, half admiring the destruction she'd wrought. *On the bright side, it doesn't look that much different than before.*

A sob emerged in the form of a laugh, and she let it play out. She laughed until she was crying again and her stomach ached. She was sure her tenure would be revoked by the end of the day if the dean or a member of the board were to walk in here right now, but what did it really matter? She'd be gone in a month anyhow.

The thought was enough to sober her. Because it did matter. Time mattered.

Every second.

FIVE

Now

So this is how I go. Burnt up on the way out of the atmosphere.

She closed her eyes, waiting for the heat to consume her in a hungry maw of fire. A piece of handy information came back to her then. Frank, her trainer at NASA, had mentioned the main rockets burned fuel at a temperature up to six thousand degrees Fahrenheit. So maybe she wouldn't even feel it.

The vehicle shook again, the hardest it had so far, and she released a breathless cry.

"We're okay," Carson said in her ear. "Everything's a go."

Gillian opened her eyes. In the fire's place was a collage of smoke and a blue she could only guess was the ocean thousands of feet below. Carrie was somewhere down there. The thought made her stomach flip in a poisonous somersault. A second later the pressure on her body increased, flattening her farther into the seat.

"Three point five Gs," Carson said, and now she could hear the strain in his voice.

The shuttle rocked, and there was a popping sound, like both of her ears equalizing at once.

She was going to die from the velocity. It was too much.

Another wrenching shudder.

Consciousness was ebbing, dark clouds growing at the corners of her vision.

No. She'd trained for this. She should be fine. But the assurances did nothing to keep away the creeping shadows invading her eyes.

Gillian held on to the last image of her daughter, the feeling of her small body hugged close, the smell of her hair, even as everything else faded away.

SIX

Two Months Before

Traffic was light that early in the day, and the sky was overcast, a threat of rain on the horizon.

After Gillian left the lab and picked up Carrie, they made good time on 494 East toward their neighborhood a dozen miles outside Minneapolis, where most days the increasingly common clouds of smog drifted north and there was less need to wear the white pollution masks many in the city had taken to donning outdoors.

When Gillian saw the blinking sign advertising ice cream in a waffle cone, she pulled into the drive-through. Carrie accepted the double scoop of Blue Moon with a quiet thank-you. Every so often Gillian looked in the mirror, watching her daughter nibble half-heartedly at the treat while she gazed out her window at the passing landscape.

Mrs. Seaton, the manager at the day care where Carrie spent Gillian's lab hours, had said she'd been distant today. Dispirited. And when Gillian had questioned Carrie as they left the fenced-in parking lot through the manned security checkpoint, the girl had shrugged, not meeting her eyes.

As they made their way closer to home, Gillian returned to the conversation she'd had with her sister the week before. It had been their usual back-and-forth—Katrina checking in on how Carrie was and how the research was progressing, then pivoting smoothly into the topic of them coming to visit.

We have plenty of room, and you haven't been down in over a year, Kat had said, a hint of the adolescent whine still lingering from their childhood.

Been a little busy. Besides, you need your rest. Won't be too long and you'll be up all night cleaning up puke and shitty diapers.

Kat had laughed. *I clean up puke and shitty diapers at the hospital every day. This'll be like going on vacation.*

You say that now.

Seriously, Gill, think about taking a break and coming down, even for a few days. I wanna spoil my niece, and she loves the beach. You can drink all the margaritas you want, and I'll just smell them on the way by. Maybe you could pick up some college beach bum and educate him on the ways of an older woman.

It had been Gillian's turn to laugh. *I'll think about it.*

But they'd both hung up knowing she wouldn't. There was too much at stake to take a vacation.

A train blocked their path a mile from their neighborhood, and Gillian let her mind float again, bumping off thoughts like a vessel drifting through wreckage-strewn waters. And all the while the need for one of the hydros grew.

Some graffiti on a train car caught her eye. *Saul Gone*, it said in hurried letters, as if the artist had been forced to rush through their work, perhaps by approaching law enforcement. She pondered the phrase. Was it referring to the popular TV show from years ago? She and Kent had never missed an episode. And Saul was definitely gone now; there was no question about that. Or maybe the artist had just been lamenting an existential truth. *It's all gone.* Or it soon will be. She supposed the statement could be applied to last month's devastating landslides in Peru and China because of heavy rainfall. Or maybe it was referring to the last of the Arctic ice, which scientists were saying would vanish completely in the next five years. She guessed it didn't matter what it was. Everything eventually ended.

Maybe she needed to stop watching the Weather Channel.

"Momma? I'm sorry I was bad."

Gillian blinked and came back to herself. "What, honey? Why would you say that?"

"Because Mrs. Seaton looked angry today after the fuzzies. I didn't mean to forget."

"The fuzzies" was how Carrie had first described the fugue states she sometimes fell into. They had been watching an old TV show where the character's television had turned to static, and Carrie had said that's what it felt like when she had a lapse.

The first time she tried to reply, Gillian's voice didn't work. "You had the fuzzies today?"

"Yes. A little bit. I think I fell down and skinned my hand. I think Mrs. Seaton was mad."

"You don't need to be sorry, darling. You didn't do anything wrong."

"Because I'm sick?"

"Yes. But we're going to make you better. Momma's going to make you better."

"Because you're smart."

"That's right. And because you're strong."

"And I won't go away like Daddy?"

The last car of the train clattered past, and the guard arms rose before them. Gillian pressed the accelerator and kept her eyes straight ahead until she could speak again. "No, honey, you won't go away. I won't let you."

By the time they entered their neighborhood and pulled into their driveway, she was trembling so badly, all she could think was, *Get Carrie inside, get a pill, and make some coffee. Everything will be clearer after that. Everything will make more sense.*

But as they pulled to a stop before the double garage, her attention was drawn to the person seated on their front steps. He rose as she shut off the car.

"Who's that man on our porch, Momma?"

Gillian stared at him, unable to separate the emotions that rushed through her. "An old friend, honey. A very old friend."

SEVEN

Gillian shut the back door of the house behind Carrie, watching her jog to the middle of the yard.

A second later, Sadie, the girl from next door, rushed over to meet her, their voices high with excitement as they walked to Carrie's play set in the farthest corner. Gillian had been reluctant to let her play outside after the incident at day care, but when Carrie had asked, there had been genuine excitement in her voice, and it was one of the few things able to lift Gillian's spirits. Besides, she wasn't sure she wanted Carrie to hear the conversation that was about to take place.

She watched the two girls for another moment before moving back through the house. She paused in the doorway to the kitchen, gathering herself and fighting the urge to turn down the hall to the left to grab a pill first. Instead, she moved forward past the man seated in the chair at the table.

"Thanks for letting me in," Carson LeCroix said.

Gillian stopped at the sink, picking up the clean coffeepot before turning to face him.

Carson was much the same as the last time she'd seen him: hair still dark and curly without so much as a hint of gray, a few more lines around his mouth, and he'd maintained the swimmer's physique he'd had in college. If anything the years had given him a distinguished appearance, as if age and experience had only enhanced who he truly was. Unbidden, the image of him nude in her dorm-room bed came even as she brushed it away, but not before she recalled the sensation of him inside her.

"It's the polite thing to do, right?" she said, busying herself with fixing coffee. "Was I supposed to chase you off the porch with a broom?"

"Guess I wouldn't have blamed you. We didn't exactly part on the best terms. It was my fault how everything turned out."

Gillian hesitated as she set the pot percolating. Finally she turned to him again, leaning back against the counter. "That was a long time ago."

"Still, it's bothered me all these years. I wanted to say I'm sorry."

"Didn't know 'sorry' was in your vocabulary."

He looked down at the table and half smiled, not in the cocksure way she remembered from college when he knew he was the smartest person in the room. No, now the smile looked genuine, and a little sad. They were silent for a moment before he tipped his head in the direction of the backyard. "She's a beautiful little girl."

"Light of my life."

"What grade is she in?"

"Second. But I'm homeschooling her with the help of a private tutor. Her condition makes school hard."

"Must be tough."

Gillian sighed. "Carson, what are you doing here?"

He paused, shifting in his chair. "I've been following your work ever since your accident. The change of focus and the progress you've made—it's brilliant."

"I can't say I've been oblivious to your career either. You're still at NASA?"

"I am."

"So again, what interest does an astronaut have in a neural radiologist?"

He gazed at her in the same unflinching way he had when they were together, radiating a confidence she later learned was rooted in selfishness. "Tell me a little about your research."

"You said you were following my work."

"Still would like to hear it from the source."

The coffeepot chirped, and she poured a cup for each of them. Carson held his palms to the mug as she settled into the chair across the table. "With Losian's disease the central cause is neurofibrillary tangles, basically clumped proteins within a brain cell. The tangles in turn cause neuron loss. Most of the neurons affected are in the hippocampal region of the brain, which consolidates spatial navigation, converts short-term memories to long-term, deals with emotion, that type of thing."

"So it basically makes you who you are."

"Yes."

"You said in one article you think the increase in pollution could be the cause of the tangles?"

"Along with genetic factors. Like diabetes, some people are genetically predisposed, and some develop it due to a variety of factors. With Losian's the exact toxins or chemicals are still a mystery, but we think it could trigger a genetic variant that's passed down through generations." She stopped, her eyes flicking to the backyard where Carrie played.

"So your goal is to . . ."

"Fire every neuron in the human brain at once. The substrates we use react and trigger neural activity. With the imaging we'd then be able to pinpoint exactly which neurons are damaged. It's the first step in fixing the problem."

"And you're close."

Gillian fidgeted with her mug. "Yes. Yes, we are."

"But not close enough for Congress."

She huffed a laugh. "Until you have a solution wrapped up in a bow and delivered on a platter, it's never close enough for politicians. I'm guessing you saw the last address?"

"I did. You really think Losian's will eventually overshadow Alzheimer's?"

"Yes. The models we're using are . . . they're frightening. If the rise in cases continues, Losian's will be by far the most prominent dementia in the world. But it won't matter until one of them or a member of their family gets it. Then, suddenly, it'll be a concern." She turned her mug around on the table. It had been Kent's favorite.

"I'm sorry about your husband. And your daughter. I can't imagine—"

"No offense, Carson, but I'm tired of hearing people tell me they 'can't imagine' what we've gone through. You may as well say, 'I'm glad I don't know what it's like.' Spare me the sympathy, I know that's not why you're here."

If her outburst unsettled him, he didn't show it. Instead, he took a long drink from his coffee before saying, "I know you lost your funding."

Gillian flinched. "How—"

"I work with people who hear about things before they happen."

She shook her head, took a deep breath.

"Look, before you go off half-cocked like you always did, hear me out," Carson said.

"Such flattery. How can I resist?"

"Please. Five minutes."

She brought the cup to her mouth and tried to keep her hand steady. "Go ahead."

Carson leaned forward, the familiar intensity in his face unchanged by the passage of years. "NASA is working on something big. Very big. It will have major ramifications not only globally, but eventually within your field."

Despite her irritation, her interest spiked. "What is it?"

"If I told you, you wouldn't believe it. You need to see it yourself. All I can say is, it will be revolutionary in terms of travel."

"Very dramatic."

"Trust me."

"So how does this relate to my funding?"

Carson's jaw worked from side to side as he settled back in his chair, a tic she recalled from college when something perturbed him. "There's been some unpleasant incidences—neurological side effects, I'd guess you'd call them—that are bogging down the project. These issues are directly in your area of expertise. We want you to come work for us. It would require some . . . training."

"Training? As in?"

"Space. You'd be going to space for six months."

Gillian smiled and rose from the table, then dumped the rest of her coffee in the sink. "You're kidding."

"Absolutely serious."

"You want me to go to space."

"Yes."

"For six months."

"Give or take."

"That's ludicrous. I'm not an astronaut."

"That's where the training comes in. You'd be given a fast-track overview and be added to the mission as a consultant. We do our thing and fly the shuttle, you do yours and help us iron out these kinks."

"I appreciate the job offer, but I have more important and pressing matters to attend to at the moment."

"Like finding new funding?"

She glared at him. "Among other things, yes. Besides, there's no way I could leave Carrie for that long."

"What would you say if I told you in your downtime you could continue your research?"

"Tempting, but not tempting enough to blast off into space and leave my daughter here. Come on, Carson, what did you expect me to say?"

"What if I told you I could guarantee funding if you accepted?"

She watched him, waited for a tell that would reveal his true intentions. "For how long?"

"Indefinitely."

"Indefinitely," she repeated, the word feeling foreign on her tongue.

"Yes. That's how important this is."

Gillian shifted in place. "But why me? There's got to be a dozen other specialists that are more qualified."

"Now you're being humble, and it doesn't become you. Be honest, there's no one in neural radiology that's made the progress you have. Your development of the imaging and neuron analysis technique was a major breakthrough."

"The technology was already there, I just made some observations."

"That led to what almost every neurological institute is utilizing today."

"A lot of good it did me."

"But you said yourself, if it wasn't for the lower occurrence percentages of Losian's, you'd have all the funding you need. If this was an epidemic, you'd be the number-one resource of the medical community."

"But it's not yet!" She stepped away from the counter, every nerve in her body hot with anger. "It's rare and it comes out of nowhere and destroys who you are." She opened her mouth to continue but caught movement past Carson's shoulder.

Carrie stood on the back stoop. The door was cracked open an inch, and as Gillian watched, Carrie stepped back, pulling it shut, and gestured to Sadie, who shrugged as they walked away from the house.

She felt the anger die out at once, a flame dipped in water.

Gillian sighed, running a hand across her forehead and into her hair. "Listen, this isn't a good time. I'm sorry your project's having issues, but I'm not your solution. I can't be."

"I know you're tired of sympathy, but what I'm saying is this: you've seen hell, and you're not out of it yet. You need what I can give you, and I need the most brilliant person in the field, bottom line." He stood and crossed the kitchen, placing his empty cup on the counter along with a business card. "Do me a favor and consider it for her."

She tried to say something to his back as he left the room, tried to ask if he really thought she was doing any of this for herself. But her energy was gone, sapped by the day's failings to the point that all she wanted to do was lie down in a dark room and weep.

The front door snapped shut, and she listened to Carson's rental pull away down the street. As the sound faded, another took its place, like a tornado siren slowly winding up to full volume. It was coming from their backyard.

Screaming.

Carrie was screaming.

EIGHT

A light rain had started falling.

It wet her skin as Gillian sprinted across the yard to where Carrie was standing, head thrown back, eyes squeezed shut, another throat-tearing scream coming from her open mouth.

Sadie was crouched several feet away, hands clamped over her ears, twin trails of tears running down her red face.

Then Gillian was holding Carrie, pulling her close as she thrashed against her.

"Stop, honey. It's okay, you're okay."

Carrie shrieked again, and it was like trying to hold on to a wildcat. Gillian eased them both to the ground, getting a better grip around her daughter's waist as a small fist struck the side of her chin.

"Shhhh, shhhh, it's okay. You're all right, honey. Calm down."

Carrie's entire body flexed, seizurelike, before gradually relaxing.

Sadie's back door opened and closed as her father stepped outside, his hand shielding his eyes as he hurried toward them.

"Is everything all right?" he asked, scooping his crying daughter into his arms. "Should I call someone?"

"No, no, we're fine, Dan," Gillian managed, rocking Carrie gently in her lap. The girl's gaze was unfocused, and a small string of saliva hung from her lower lip.

"She was like a statue and then started screaming," Sadie said into her father's shoulder. "For no reason."

"Shush, Sadie," Dan said, frowning, turning away.

Gillian brushed Carrie's hair back from her brow, the rain starting to soak through both their clothes as the girl's eyelids fluttered.

"Momma?"

"I'm here, baby."

"What happened?"

"You're okay. Let's get you inside."

She got them both to their feet, one arm holding Carrie tightly to keep her from falling. They were almost to their back steps when Gillian heard Sadie say, "I don't want to play with her anymore," in a muffled voice. Gillian resisted looking at them as they disappeared into their home, Dan hushing his daughter again.

Inside she stripped Carrie out of her wet clothes and wrapped her in a blanket before settling her into the couch. Already the girl's eyes were closing, completely exhausted from the episode.

"The fuzzies," Carrie said in almost a whisper.

"Yeah. It was. You rest now, okay?"

Carrie nodded, snuggling farther into the cushions. "Forever?" she asked.

Gillian struggled, making sure her voice wouldn't break when she spoke. "Forever."

The exchange had begun when Carrie asked Gillian how long forever was. She had responded with "That's how long I'll love you." And over the years, it had been whittled down to the two words, call and response, question and answer, their weight far beyond their few syllables.

Gillian watched the slow rise and fall of Carrie's chest, and within a minute her breathing was steady and deep.

She reached out and brushed her fingertips down her daughter's cheek, overwhelmed by a mixture of love and terror. It was so powerful, it felt like the wind had been struck from her, and her eyes began to burn. Two lapses in one day. This was the first time that had ever happened. She was getting worse.

Blinking, Gillian spread another light blanket over Carrie's sleeping form and glanced out at their backyard. The spring rain continued to fall, and already the sprouting grass looked greener, more alive. Nature moving forward, always onward, the natural order of things. She turned back to gaze at Carrie again.

Except my little girl is going in reverse. Losing more and more of herself each day.

Gillian drew in a shaking breath and headed for the bathroom, her fingers already feeling the safety cap of the pill bottle, but halfway down the hall, she stopped.

Kent's office door was open, just a little.

She reached out and grasped the knob, meaning to pull it shut, but instead stepped inside.

It was an average-size office with a desk in one corner beside the only window. It was also basically unchanged from when he had spent his hours here running the small IT business he had built from the ground up. There were still pictures on the desk of herself and Carrie, covered in dust and slightly faded. And she knew somewhere on the laptop beside them was a novel Kent had been working on for some time. It was half-finished like so many things he'd left behind: several IT contracts, the landscaping along the front of the house, the Sheetrock in the basement.

And their life together.

She gazed at the objects in the room. Everything from before his death looked different now. It was one of the many oddities of losing someone that close. The most mundane things became hypnotizing. A notepad transformed into a well of memories. A lamp now something that brought tears to her eyes. Losing someone didn't mean they really went away. His ghost was everywhere she looked.

Without meaning to, she propelled herself down the hall and into the bathroom, where she flung open the medicine cabinet. She fumbled for the pill bottle and dropped it twice before getting it open.

One. No, two. Two pills on her tongue and pounded down by a glass of water before she leaned into the wall to steady herself. Sometimes she wondered if the hydrocodone was the only thing that kept her going. And to think she'd refused anything more potent than acetaminophen while she was recovering from the crash in fear it would affect the baby.

The pain she'd endured. It was almost too much for her to think about.

But after she'd given birth, it had been a different story. Back then her leg had hurt all the time, so she'd given in to taking the narcotics. A little over a year after the accident, on the day Carrie turned six months old, she had buried Kent. Losian's had finished its work with him, and she'd watched the man she'd built her life with lowered into the ground and covered up as if he'd never been. After that she'd begun prescribing the medication to herself as chronic-pain management, which was partially true, but the physical pain was nothing compared to the gaping hole in her life. Afterward, the struggle to get clean had taken every ounce of her will. But her sobriety had fallen apart like a sandcastle at high tide with Carrie's diagnosis.

Now she couldn't go a day without at least one pill.

She gave herself a glance in the mirror but looked away almost at once. All she saw anymore were the scars, inside and out. She took several deep breaths and made a list of people she needed to call. There were a few sources she could tap for potential extension of funds.

She would push through this. It was a molehill compared with the mountain she was attempting to move.

But what about Carson and the offer? Indefinite funding.

Carson came here for Carson, no matter what he said. He's always looked out for himself first, and this time's no different.

But indefinite funding.

No.

She straightened. There had to be some other option. The thought of leaving Carrie for even a week sent a roiling wave of sickness through her. She'd find someone who would say yes, and she wouldn't stop until she did.

Gillian made herself look at the mirror. "There's always another way."

♦   ♦   ♦

She walked down the hospital hallway, everything too bright, corners and edges of walls and counters sharpened to blades. The far end of the corridor held a square of pure light she knew was a window, though it made her vision blur to look directly at it. But more than the ethereal quality of her surroundings, it was the lack of stiffness in her leg that told her this was a dream rather than reality.

The doorway came into view beside her, and she turned into it.

Kent rested in the bed, his head and shoulders propped up on a mound of pillows. His eyes were open, and he stared out the window across the room.

She felt the same elation as she had that day seeing him awake. The doctors had assured her that his consciousness at this stage would be seldom and fleeting. She couldn't hear the words she spoke as she neared the side of the bed, but she felt the happiness in them even as her eyes found the table on the opposite side, the bandage scissors atop it left by a careless nurse who had put in a new IV for him only minutes ago.

As she stepped into his line of view, his eyes traveled up to her face and settled there. No life in them. No recognition.

His lips worked, but no sound came out.

He blinked, one hand reaching out to her. She grasped his fingers even as terror began to rise within her.

Because she remembered this. She knew what would happen next.

She tried to pull away, but already his other arm was moving toward the table, and his hand grasped the scissors.

They flashed toward her in an arc she could think of only as fatal. He was going to kill her.

She turned at the last second, and the scissor blades buried themselves in the hollow of her shoulder below her clavicle.

The pain was molten.

It boiled down through her arm and up into her skull, giving her a shot of adrenaline so powerful she yanked away from him and fell to her back, dragging him out of bed at the same time.

There was an electric red spreading down the front of her shirt, and her left arm wasn't working like it should have been.

She scrabbled backward, kicking her feet on the tile floor like a dying crab. He was crawling after her, pulling himself along the floor to finish what he'd started, but when she looked at him fully, it wasn't Kent who approached on all fours like a feral animal.

It was Carrie.

There was blood on her daughter's face, and when she opened her mouth, the final words Kent had ever spoken came out.

"Who are you?"

◆　◆　◆

Gillian came up out of the dream to her own shriek. She stifled it with a hand while her other rubbed at the dimpled scar on her shoulder where Kent had stabbed her.

She sat up and placed her feet on the cool hardwood floor, letting the cold soak in.

A dream. The dream. Nightmare. Memory. Whatever you wanted to call it. She hadn't had it in over six months and had been almost sure it was done plaguing her. But this time it was different.

It had never been Carrie before.

Her stomach lurched at the image of Carrie's beautiful face speckled with blood, her words echoing in Gillian's ears even now in the empty room, fully awake.

Who are you?

She stood up and paced out into the hallway. Across from her room, Carrie's door was wide open. She stood there, watching her small form tucked beneath the blankets, listening to the gentle breaths for nearly five minutes before walking down the hall and into the kitchen.

The windows were graying with dawn, pale light nudging shadows into the corners. It was still early, early enough for her to go back to bed, but the thought of closing her eyes again was revolting.

Gillian crossed the room, passing the notepad on the table with the names and numbers she'd carefully drawn a line of defeat through after each phone call the prior afternoon, and stopped at the garbage beside the counter. She hesitated, rubbing the old wound on her shoulder before opening the lid of the garbage can and digging inside.

Carson's card had fallen near a banana peel and the coffee grounds from earlier. She brushed it off, looking at the number near the bottom. Then she went to find her phone.

NASA transcript of Discovery VI disaster press conference.
Office of Space Flights, Cape Canaveral, FL.
Spokesperson: Anderson W. Jones, Deputy Administrator.
Introduction: Erin Fulson, Associate Administrator.
August 21, 2028.

E. Fulson: *Hello, everyone. Thank you first and foremost for all of the heartfelt support during this tragic time. We appreciate all the condolences, as do the affected families and loved ones of the mission. Now I'll turn the microphone over to Deputy Administrator Jones, and he will explain the situation to the best of our current knowledge. Please hold all questions until he is finished speaking, and at that point he will answer as many as he can.*
A. W. Jones: *Thank you, Erin. Good evening, everyone. I address you all tonight with a heavy heart. As many of you already know, the latest NASA mission, Discovery VI, has suffered catastrophic failure. At two p.m. Eastern time, mission control in Houston received a distress call from astronaut and medical consultant Dr. Gillian Ryan. Shortly thereafter, all communication was lost. The initial launch and docking of the shuttle was textbook with no indication of any mechanical and/or human error. At this time we have assembled a special investigative task force to collect and analyze all data available to determine the cause of this tragedy. NASA and its associates are heartbroken but remain steadfast in honoring those who were lost as well as reaching a conclusion as to why this happened. I'll take a couple questions now from . . .* [Indistinguishable/people speaking over one another.]

David Fryburg—MSNBC: *Sir, can you comment on the exact nature of the Discovery VI mission?*

A. W. Jones: *It was a routine flight rendezvousing with the United Nations Space Station. The crew had several priorities, but the essential operation was that of medical research.*

Cynthia Carpenter—FOX News: *Mr. Jones, what can you tell us about the information coming out of several Russian news outlets concerning a type of "space sickness" on the UNSS?*

A. W. Jones: *Those are unsubstantiated claims, and as of now I am unaware of any reported illness on the Explorer Ten or the space station.*

Lisa Prenetti—CNN: *As far as the personnel involved, do you have a firm casualty count yet?*

A. W. Jones: *At this point I cannot give you the names or even the number of the other men and women involved in the mission, but there were no survivors. No more questions.*

NINE

Gillian picked up the sweating glass of chilly water and repositioned it on the table, interconnecting the tenth ring of condensation.

The glare of a passing car's windshield on the freeway outside the office building swept the room and was gone, causing her to glance up at the concrete and tarred paths outside in the growing Florida sun. Immediately her gaze was pulled to the massive US flag painted down the side of the towering structure across several streets and parking lots. The NASA vehicle-assembly building loomed over the otherwise flat landscape in all its blockish glory. She'd been told by the overly talkative receptionist who'd led her to the conference room that the vehicle-assembly building was over 520 feet tall, the largest one-story building in the world.

Interesting, but not really enough to stay entranced for however much longer Carson intended to keep her waiting. And she was sure the room's views were no accident either—another tactic to impress her in order to get what he wanted.

It was funny. She hadn't thought of him in years, yet he had entered her life again just as smoothly and in the same way he'd exited: by putting himself first. They'd met when she'd been a sophomore at the university, a shared mathematics class and fate placing them a desk apart. There had always been an undercurrent to everything in their relationship, skewed toward what he needed or wanted. Mostly it was harmless: his knowledge of culinary arts meant he picked the restaurants they ate at, and the social circles he traveled in dictated what nights they went out or stayed in. Even their lovemaking had been slanted by his need to always see her, look her in the eye as he sweated above her. And it had been his ambition that broke them apart—an opportunity at a military college out of state where he could pursue his love of flight. He had expected her to transfer with him, and when she hadn't, that had been it. A break so clean and quick it was like they had never been together in the first place.

But now he was back. Wanting something. Needing it.

She drummed her nails on the tabletop as the air-conditioning whispered that she should've taken two hydros instead of one this morning. What was she doing here? She'd been crazy to whisk Carrie off to Florida, even though there'd been no cost since Carson had sent a vehicle and they'd flown on a private jet, which Carrie had adored, but Gillian knew it for what it was: another of his wooing attempts. Of course, it didn't hurt that Kat had been overjoyed to see them, settling them into the spacious spare room on the second floor of the sprawling home overlooking a white strip of Daytona Beach that she and her husband, Steve, shared.

But honestly, Gillian knew the reason they'd come here.

Even now the dream with Carrie superimposed in Kent's place lurked in Gillian's mind like a stealthy predator, the memory sending a slither of nausea through her stomach each time it reared its head.

Who are you?

That's why she was sitting in this conference room. Because she would do anything to never hear Carrie say those words.

The door opened to her left, and a compact man wearing a gray suit entered. Everything about him was trim, from his manicured receding hairline to the way he walked in an efficient line directly to the end of the table. Behind him Carson appeared, dressed much more relaxed in a pair of jeans and a dark-blue polo.

"Gillian, sorry to keep you waiting," Carson said, coming over to her. He held out his hand, and she shook it, the formality amusing her. "This is Gregory Tinsel. He's the head project coordinator and investment manager who'll also be joining the mission."

Tinsel inclined his head but made no move to greet her as Carson had. "Good to meet you." A faint French accent clipped his words.

"You too. Tinsel, like the decoration?"

Carson laughed. "A decoration overly concerned with the bottom line."

A look of exasperation crossed Tinsel's face, and Gillian wondered how long ago Carson had found his needling point. "Spelled the same, yes." And he offered no more before sitting.

Carson settled into a seat to her right, placing a tablet between them on the table. "Thanks for coming. You don't know what it means to all of us here. We couldn't—"

"I haven't agreed to anything yet," she said, cutting him off.

"But the necessary nondisclosure agreements have been signed," Tinsel said.

"Yes."

Tinsel sniffed, relaxing in his chair, and Gillian decided that her initial dislike of him was well founded.

"I think once you see what I'm about to show you, your mind will be made up," Carson continued. "Are you familiar with the term 'absolute zero'?"

Gillian nodded. "The coldest possible temperature, right?"

"Zero Kelvin or right around minus four hundred and sixty degrees Fahrenheit."

"Cold."

"That's an understatement."

"But if I remember right, it's kind of a paradox, isn't it? You can't ever actually reach absolute zero."

"Exactly," Carson said, tapping the table with one finger. "Bringing a particle down to that temperature reduces its movement to nearly nothing, but there's still movement, so in turn, there's heat."

"Which prevents reaching absolute zero."

"Right. No laboratory or scientist has ever been able to get closer than a billionth of a degree." He swiped the tablet and pushed it toward her. The screen held graphs of data along with partitioned numerals below in rows her eyes flowed over. "These are files from Dr. Eric Ander, a physicist out of Cambridge who's been working independently for the last fifteen years."

"Rhodium?" she asked.

"That's the element he began with for the trials," Carson said, leaning forward to touch the screen. She could smell his cologne and feel some of the heat of his skin against hers, but Gillian ignored the sensations and focused on the numbers. "Nearly eleven years ago, Ander managed to bring five billion particles of rhodium down closer to absolute zero than anyone had before. On that scale it was a niche science, but it was only a stepping stone for much more remarkable things."

"Impressive."

Carson smiled, touching the screen again. "That's nothing."

A video began to play.

It had been shot from what appeared to be a security camera, albeit in high definition, from the corner of a large room. Almost directly below the camera was a long, clear tube large enough for a person to lie in comfortably, with a port open at the closest end. Opposite the opening, the tube was attached to a towering dark box with several thick cables growing from its base and trailing out of the frame. A short distance away, a duplicate setup filled the rest of the room. There was a brief span without movement before a man entered the scene.

He was tall and thin and completely nude. His shoulder blades were two prominent wings of bone, and his dimpled spine led down to sagging middle-aged buttocks.

Gillian frowned, glancing at Carson, who tipped his head toward the screen with a *just watch* motion. She returned her gaze to the tablet as the man crawled inside the first tube and turned onto his back, the angle and reflected light thankfully obscuring his genitalia. From what she could see, he was sallow-faced with a disarray of gray hair sprouting from his head.

The man lay motionless for several seconds before the hatch at his feet swung closed, moving with an automated speed that confirmed her suspicions that he was working alone. Even though the video was soundless, she could hear the hiss in her mind as two jets of air rushed from the hatch.

"Is that a vacuum?" she asked, unable to look away.

"Yes."

"But what the hell's he doing? That's—"

"Keep watching."

The jetted air tapered off, and for thirty seconds, according to the tracking numbers at the bottom of the screen, nothing happened.

Then everything changed.

There was a brightening of the chamber around the man, who continued to lie still, hands at his sides. It became incandescent, flooding the screen white before a flash brighter still bleached everything from view. The video remained blank as Gillian watched, leaning forward.

Slowly, definition crept back in from the edges.

The walls, floor, black boxes, and tubes. But there was something wrong . . .

"Oh my God," she said, despite herself.

The first tube was empty.

Her brain stuttered, tripping over itself to explain what she was seeing, before she noticed the second tube. The man lay within it, exactly as he had prior to the flash.

Within seconds, the hatch to the second tube swung open, and he began to stir, groggily reaching out to trace the walls of his enclosure before scooting to the opening. He sat there in the port, gazing at the floor, then glanced over at the first tube, which was still sealed. Slowly, his head lowered, and by the way his shoulders began to tremble, Gillian knew he was weeping.

The video ended, the tablet going blank.

She swallowed, spit gelatinous in her drying mouth. She wanted to tap the screen and watch the video over again but instead sat back in her seat and looked at Carson, who beamed.

"I know that wasn't . . . but it looked like—"

"Yes," Tinsel said, drawing her attention to the end of the table where he smiled, sharklike. "You just witnessed the very first instance of human teleportation."

TEN

They gave her several minutes to gain her bearings and to also watch the video twice more.

When it had ended for the second time, she tried to find all the words she wanted to say but instead merely asked, "How?"

Carson laughed. "The key was absolute zero. See, the problem that's been facing teleportation, or shifting as Dr. Ander likes to call it, was the Heisenberg uncertainty principal—basically it's impossible to know both the position and the velocity of a particle at the same time. If you don't know where each and every particle is that makes up an object, or person in this case, as well as its momentum, you can't transmit and re-create it somewhere else. By truly reaching absolute zero, the movement of an electron slows to nothing and can be calculated."

Gillian blinked, taking in what he had said. "That's stopping time."

Carson grimaced. "Time's a loop, so that's an oversimplification, but—"

"But for the man in the video, that's exactly what happened. Every atom in his body was stilled for a fraction of a second."

"Right."

"Again, how?"

Obscura

"The tubes on the video are Dr. Ander's design. They contain a three hundred sixty–degree array of lasers, something he calls a photon net. Contrary to what people think, lasers can cool atoms by slowing their electrons' movement. This technique used with the vacuum of the tube, a strong magnetic field, and a short blast of radiation is the perfect combination." Carson smiled. "Unbelievable, right?"

"Unbelievable," she repeated, drawing a line through the water rings on the table with her finger. "But there's trillions of atoms in the human body. How do you calculate and account for every one of them?"

"The big black boxes attached to the tubes? They're quantum computers. Traditional computers deal with data in sequential ones and zeros. Quantum computers use ones, zeros, or both simultaneously."

"It's the absolute cutting edge of technology," Tinsel chimed in. His unsettling smile was gone, stagnant voice back in its groove. "Quantum computing will be the standard soon."

Gillian nodded, focusing again on Carson, who took a drink from her water glass, daring her with his eyes to challenge him. He was in his element now, grandeur and spectacle his best friends. Instead of commenting on the water, she pressed on. "How does the reconstruction work?"

"The second quantum computer interprets the information sent from its counterpart. That much data transmitted along a farther distance than the few feet separating the two chambers in the video would result in an obvious delay. But either way, the information is the exact composition of a human body, and using the same photon net, the second computer rearranges all the necessary elements into order." Carson ticked off his fingers. "Oxygen, carbon, hydrogen, nitrogen, calcium, phosphorus . . . you get the idea."

She did. But comprehending said idea (not to mention what she'd seen with her own eyes) was like placing an ocean in a thimble: it wouldn't fit, the notion overflowing each time she tried. "How do you know this isn't a hoax? The video could've easily been faked. There's any number of other explanations for this."

49

"Gillian." Carson's voice lowered an octave. "The man in the video is Dr. Ander. I watched him perform the experiment in person. It's real. Trust me."

She shook her head. "Okay, for the sake of argument, let's say I believe you. What does any of this have to do with me?"

Carson's face darkened, the excitement dimming. "I'll let Greg walk you through the specifics."

"I've asked you not to call me that," Tinsel said before shifting his attention to her. "Do you recall several NASA launches over the past six years?"

"Was it something to do with the space station?"

"Yes, but not the old beast that's been up there for decades. A new, fully updated version with the very latest technology, funded by the United Nations. It was launched in portions and assembled before being put into . . . orbit, one of the central reasons being the video you just watched. Undoubtedly the breakthrough Ander made will eventually have applications in space such as interstellar travel, and since a portion of his grants came from NASA, we chose to utilize the new station for trials and research away from prying eyes, so to speak." Tinsel licked his colorless lips. "Since the tests began, though, there have been . . . complications."

"Complications?"

"This project was originally designed to transport materials, but from the moment we realized we could teleport complex things, its application to human travel became a priority. Recently subjects participating in the trials have reported disorientation, slight memory loss, and bouts of irritation among a few other complaints."

"Losian's," Gillian said, shooting a glance at Carson.

"Obviously we don't know for sure, and we have no idea if the technology is the cause or if there is another factor at play. The earliest trial subjects haven't reported anything unusual." Tinsel leaned forward. "It very well could be the disease, but billions of dollars and years of research are at stake here, so we need to be sure. It's my job to evaluate whether this whole thing continues to move forward or is shut down and brought back to Earth for further study." He examined her, and at that moment, he could've been any number of male colleagues at a neurological seminar where she was presenting. Disdainful. Dismissive. "Honestly, Dr. Ryan, I'm doubtful you'll be able to shed any further light on what's happening. We've already had the best minds working on this without a single solid answer."

She bristled. "Then why exactly am I sitting here listening to you?"

"Because Mr. LeCroix has complete faith in your work." The rise of his eyebrows completed the rest of his thought: *I, however, do not.*

"Let's not get ahead of ourselves," Carson said, motioning in Tinsel's direction. "Like you said, we have no idea what the causes are, and that's where you come in, Gillian. You're the leading mind concerning Losian's. We want you to examine everyone and see if you can explain what and why it's happening. Anything you need would be provided."

She tamped down her anger. "Why do we have to go up there? Haven't they been brought back to Earth?"

She watched Carson and Tinsel share a look, quick and furtive, before Carson said, "The work they're doing is vitally important, and it's complicated. Bringing everyone back would destroy years of planning and billions of dollars in investment across many countries. The issues, whatever the cause, aren't stopping the objective. So we go to them."

"I could oversee testing and do full-time consulting from here. You could send someone else, another radiologist who's just as qualified."

Carson shook his head. "There's no one utilizing the same approaches you are, and besides that we need someone there who can interpret the data in real time and help make decisions."

"But for six months? Why so long?"

"We're allowing for hang-ups and roadblocks. All the typical tests like CT scans and MRIs have shown nothing, so we're anticipating a solution will take some time. Trust me, we've tried solving the problems with every source we have already. We need you."

The sun seemed to brighten outside, and a strange weakness invaded her limbs. Was she really considering this? Leaving Carrie for six months? The thought of not being able to hug her daughter, to read to her at night, to tell her she loved her whenever she wanted, sent a sickening lurch through her stomach.

And what if her condition worsened while she was away? What if Carrie didn't know her when she returned?

"I think I need some air," she managed to say.

"Sure. Through the door and down the right hall is a balcony," Carson said, standing up as she left the table. Tinsel remained where he was, drawing his phone from his pocket as she passed.

The spring Florida heat was a stifling wall as she stepped outside, and another wave of weakness passed over her. The continually shifting climate was all the more apparent here in the South, the peak-heat points of certain days making it unsafe to even venture outside.

She made it to the railing and gripped it, steadying herself. It wasn't only the thought of leaving Carrie that had done this to her. She'd just witnessed a man vanishing from one place and appearing in another. The breakthrough was unprecedented, something that came along perhaps every thousand years or so. The applications to everyday life were staggering.

Behind her the door opened, and a moment later Carson matched her pose at the railing. He didn't look at her but instead followed her view to the vehicle-assembly building.

"Did I ever tell you I always dreamed of going to space?" he asked.

"I knew that was your end goal, yeah."

"But I mean since I was a kid. My dad took me to an astronomy club when I was five. My mother had bought him a cheap telescope along with dues to the club for a year for his birthday, even though he'd only mentioned in passing he thought stargazing was interesting." Carson smiled. "Anyway, he didn't take to it, but for me it was over the second I put my eye to the telescope." He glanced up as though he could see through the ocean of blue sky above them to the stars waiting beyond. "Something so much bigger than me, but I was a part of it. I knew I had to go out there someday."

"And now you have."

"Twice. And the promise of going again is as exciting as it was the first time." He brought his gaze back to her. "Come with me. Help us. Please."

"Carson, Ander's breakthrough is incredible, and I'm really pleased for you and everyone involved, but—"

"Tour the lab with me. One of the original two transports Ander built is still on campus. Come on, where's the fearless woman who faced down Dr. Childs in Biology 1 when he tried mansplaining to her?"

She smiled. "That was a long time ago."

"Even so, I don't think the good doctor ever forgot it. I know I didn't."

Gillian sighed. "Look, I really appreciate you flying us down here and for the opportunity, but I can't leave my daughter." Her throat began to draw shut. "She's getting worse. She might have four years, maybe less, and I can't justify the time away from her. Those days are . . ." Her voice failed her, and she had to look away. "I would never get them back."

Carson was quiet for a time before placing a hand over hers. The contact was unexpected and, though she tried to ignore it, stirring. "There's another aspect of all this you haven't considered, and it concerns Carrie."

"What's that?"

"The application to medicine. What Ander's transport does is map the body, right? Every atom of every cell. Every single cell, Gillian."

She stared at him, unsure if he meant what she thought he did. "So the damaged neurons, the tangles—"

Carson squeezed her hand. "If you help us determine what's wrong with the system, there's a possibility the neurons damaged by Losian's could be deleted while shifting. You could save her."

NASA-transcribed audio files in reference to Mission Discovery VI disaster. Required personal entries for Dr. Gillian Josephine Ryan, age thirty-seven, neurological consultant. Inaudible or unknown words are labeled as such. File #179081. May 27, 2028.

[Static and quiet breathing for ten seconds.]

I still feel really strange doing this.

I've recorded audio logs before, but they've all been for notations on research. So it's weird just talking to myself, but Carson said it's a must for everyone who's riding that glorified missile into space. Sorry, Carson, or whoever is listening to this. I'm told the audio files will only be reviewed if I die. So if I'm dead, it's all your fault, Carson.

Recording yourself is supposed to help you cope with feelings and focus on your objective—what you've learned so far. For the record, there are numerous studies that writing is more cognitively linked to focus and memory than speaking, but what do I know? Neurology is not psychology.

So what are my objectives? If I'm being honest, I decided I was going by the time I left the first meeting with Carson and Tinsel, but I didn't let it sink in until I got back to my sister's house. Carrie was out on the beach playing in the sand. She was making little concentric rings around where she was sitting, like the ripples when a rock is dropped in a pool. In that instant I knew I had to go. Sacrificing six months with her is going to be like losing a limb, but if I don't and I can't find funding, then . . . [Inaudible.] I need to stop that. I'm going to figure out what's wrong with the crew. It's the only way I can help Carrie.

For a second when Carson was talking about what Ander's machines actually do, I thought I had a simple solution: If every atom and cell was mapped during teleportation, why couldn't we write a program to scan the data from those who are being affected to see if there are any neurological tangles present in their brains? Apparently too simple. Carson said none of the data is recorded after re-atomization, given the enormous amount of storage it would require. And now that shifting could actually be causing the problems, they don't want to risk sending anyone else through the machines.

That's why they need me up there so desperately. I'm closer than anyone to pinpointing which neurons are affected in a living brain. Close to a breakthrough—I can feel it—but I need more time. And as much as I hate it, the time will have to be spent away from Carrie.

So I accepted their offer on the contingency that if there's an emergency here, I'll be able to come home immediately on the shuttle. Carson agreed. So if something happens, I can be back within twenty-four hours. It's a small comfort, but it's there just in case. And it'll help that I'll be able to talk to Carrie every day through NASA's uplinks. Won't be the same as being here, of course, but . . .

[Long pause.]

I've been going over the files of the station's crew who've been affected. Whatever's happening to them is eerily similar to Losian's. Mostly the complaints are fairly mild, but two cases are extreme. Severe memory loss, irrational outbursts of anger, extended trancelike states. I've compared these two with all the others and can't find any significant differences in their work habits, diet, or other available information. It's . . . strange. If it is Losian's, this is the first case of group onset, which doesn't fit the disease's MO. It's not infectious, it's a genetic anomaly caused by a pollutant or inherited. So unless the crew's been exposed to a high concentration of the same pollutant, Losian's doesn't truly fit. And there's something else that's been bothering me: the names of the two extreme cases have been redacted. Not sure what the reasoning behind that is. I'll have to ask Carson.

So there it is. We leave in four days. The last couple weeks of training have been tough. I'm on a crash course in being an astronaut, even though Frank, my instructor, has reassured me I won't have to fly the shuttle. He said they have simpletons like Carson to do that. I like Frank. I've spent hours underwater in my space suit and did zero-gravity training today on an airplane. Still sick. Could only drink some water for din—

[Sound of a door opening. Man's voice—inaudible.]

[Gillian—inaudible.]

[Door closes.]

So thankful that Birk's coming with me. I don't know what I'd do without a research assistant. Besides that, I'll have someone I completely trust with me. Carson and Tinsel did not like the idea of adding Birk to the mission—I mean it really pissed Tinsel off, which was a bonus—but I'm glad it's all settled now. I had to weather an angry call from Justin as payment, though. Never heard Birk's fiancé that pissed before, but I assured him I'd bring his sweetie back to him in one piece. I told him he should be thankful Birk's so huge, all he has to do if he misses him is go outside at night and look up. Justin didn't think it was as funny as I did.

Then again, I might not be laughing for too long either. A question-naire I filled out asked if I was on any medications, so I was honest. Carson cleared the meds along with the titanium plate still in my leg, even though I'm guessing both of those things would typically be a real deal breaker for the mission. I'm beginning to wonder how much pull Carson actually has. It's nice he's going to bat for me, but also a little unsettling. I'm almost expecting to get a call any minute saying I'm not cleared for the mission. In any case, Carson is . . . he's come a long way since college.

Anyway, I made a promise to myself—I'm getting off the hydro after I get back. I packed enough for six months, and it was a chore getting that many, believe me. I'm going to try easing off them during the mission to reduce withdrawals when I come home. By the time I come back to Earth, I'll be coming back to Earth. Haha, that was an addiction joke. I have to do

it, though. It's something I've meant to do for years now, and I know I can because I've done it before. But addiction is the ultimate procrastinator. It's always "we'll get clean tomorrow, today you need it" or "this weekend's going to be tough, shoot for next week." This is a real chance for me to help Carrie, and I can't screw it up. I need to be coherent. Concentration and will.
[Long pause.]

I guess that's it. We're going to space.

So strange to say that. And as daunting as it all is, for the first time in years, I'm rejuvenated. Maybe even hopeful about the potential outcome. This could be the best thing that ever happened to us.

Oh, and we've been studying Ander's early lab trial videos and notes. When he first moved on to living organisms, he used rodents and . . . [Gagging.] *I can't go into it now, not with the vertigo. I'll be sick.*
[End of recording.]

◆ ◆ ◆

File #179082. May 29, 2028.

Two days.

Counting down. Always counting in my head. Everything's become the second hand on the clock. Three more breakfasts with Carrie. Two more bedtime stories. One more afternoon at the beach.
[Long sigh.]

It's . . . beyond hard. Carrie asked today if I was going away forever like Daddy. Because, she said, that's where he was, right? Up in the stars somewhere? And wouldn't I stay there if I saw him?
[Inaudible. Recording pauses. Resumes.]

I told her that nothing would keep me from coming back and I'd be there above her all the time like her own personal star, looking down. I don't know if she believed me. I know I didn't always believe my dad when he would leave on a business trip. He'd say he'd come home safe and to trust in

Jesus in the meantime. But kids get scared. Then you grow up, and you're still scared.

[Clears throat.]

Anyway. Yeah, Birk and I have been watching Ander's trial videos. I have to hand it to the man, he's absolutely brilliant. Even with my rudimentary understanding of quantum mechanics, this guy blows me away. He's either brave or foolish since he used himself as the first human trial. He went ahead with it when he had no idea if it would work on a person. I mean, this is beyond typical science, this is . . . Frankenstein stuff. It'll be very interesting to meet him when we get to the station; he's been up there for over a year along with his son, Orrin, who from what I've read is some kind of military hero. Guess success runs in the family . . .

On another note, I've finally found Birk's weakness. Not to mix body-part analogies, but as unbelievably strong and smart as he is, his inner ear is his Achilles' heel. He did a second run in the plane with zero gravity, and now I know why they call it the vomit comet. I heard him about twenty minutes ago throwing up in the bathroom again, and his flight was six hours ago. I'm worried he won't do well in space and offered to let him go home. He wouldn't even let me finish the sentence. I love the guy. Just hope he doesn't hurt himself on my account.

[Long silence.]

Frank said something strange today. He was talking about long-term space travel and the effects on the human body. Then he said something about how stasis will be key to reduce those effects. I asked him what he meant, and he got this strange look on his face and said, "I mean, in theory, if you had to travel farther, it would be useful." Then he changed the subject.

Gave me a weird feeling.

I'm being paranoid, I know. It's the stress of leaving. I'm seeing bad omens everywhere I look. [Laughs.] *Wow, I need some sleep.*

[End of recording.]

◆　◆　◆

File #179083. May 31, 2028.

[Inaudible.]

Launch day. It's ten hours before I leave Earth, but that's not what I'm dreading.

What I'm terrified of is holding the little girl in the bedroom next door while she cries and clings to me and begs me not to go. She's not coming to the launch. If something goes wrong like the Challenger *mission . . . I . . .* [Inaudible.] *I thought I could do this, but now . . .*

Carrie had a lapse yesterday. I was at Kennedy, and Kat didn't tell me about it until I got home. I'm not sure if I'm grateful she can handle everything while I'm gone or supremely pissed off she kept me in the dark. Carrie was playing with Kat's dog (his name is Goat—don't ask), and after about thirty minutes outside, she rang the doorbell and asked Kat where her house was and why I wasn't there. She didn't remember my sister at all and didn't recognize the house we've been staying in for the last few weeks. [Deep breath.]

Katrina brought her inside and had her lie down, even though she was scared of being in a "stranger's" house. She fell asleep, and when she woke up, she was better. No screaming this time, but next time . . .

Kat assured me she was up to this, even with her being pregnant. She's strong and very capable, and I love my sister, but she's a lot like other people who've never had to deal with the challenges we have. I've lost track of how many times she's quoted Bible passages at me since we got here. And last night when she saw I was having a hard time calming down about Carrie's lapse, she handed me Mom's rosary and told me to take it with me when I left. I know I shouldn't have, but I was angry, and I asked her what she supposed God's purpose was for Losian's disease. In the great framework of the Almighty, why had my husband been taken from me, and why was my little girl now being pulled in the same direction? She looked like I'd slapped her.

If there's a God, he's like Eric Ander, and we're all the mice in his experiments, being turned inside out over and over again.

[Recording pauses. Resumes.]

I keep going back to the design Carrie was making on the beach the day I saw Ander shift for the first time, the concentric rings in the sand around her. I wonder if that's what I'm doing by leaving, creating waves that can't be called back.

[End of recording.]

ELEVEN

Now

The pressure vanished.

Gillian drew in a stuttering breath, consciousness coming back like a hammer to her temple. The weight was gone from her chest and extremities. In its place was an odd freedom she couldn't describe. And quiet. The roar of the engines became a memory.

Something moved out of the corner of her eye, and when she looked, a digital clipboard floated past, turning slowly end over end.

"Clear of atmosphere and main rocket is detached," Carson said. He turned slightly in his seat. "Can you grab that checklist that got away from me, Gillian?"

"Uh, yeah." She grasped the edge of the clipboard and pushed it toward him. The board glided across the space between them and into his waiting hand.

"Thanks."

She started laughing.

It wasn't conscious. Suddenly it was bubbling up from her like an untapped wellspring.

"Wild, isn't it?" Carson said. "Everyone laughs, you can't help it." She could hear the smile in his voice. "You can unhook here in a second if you want and get the full experience."

"Is that safe?"

"Completely. In fact, you can check on Birk and make sure he's okay. Think he lost consciousness shortly after ignition."

"From the acceleration?"

"I think it was nerves."

"Oh."

Gillian unhooked her seat harness, fumbling through the suit's thick gloves before managing to free herself. As soon as she was clear of the straps, true weightlessness took over, and she found herself beginning to float toward the front of the shuttle. She laughed again, pushing herself back before she invaded Carson and Lien's space. Gillian had met the command pilot only once before takeoff, and the other woman had been professional but cool in a way that cemented the impression that Gillian was the outsider.

Beyond the two pilots, the shuttle's windshield was a blanket of black, pinpricked with stars unwavering in their arctic brightness. She was looking at the universe for the first time without Earth's atmosphere impeding the view. A sense of awe nearly as powerful as seeing Carrie for the first time after she was born settled over her.

"Wow," was all she could say.

"Well put," Carson said.

"Approaching vector attained," Lien said, breaking the reverence of the moment.

Gillian tore her eyes from the view, maneuvering away from the forward cabin while avoiding Tinsel's gaze. The man stared straight ahead, his calm reasserted and belied only by his ashen complexion.

Birk began to blink behind the clear lens of his helmet as Gillian faced him, his eyes finding her. "You are . . . flying, Doctor."

She grinned. "Astute as ever. How do you feel?"

"The same as the weeks before this. Sick as a horse."

"Sick as a dog. Healthy as a horse," she said, patting his helmet lightly.

"Birk, the evacuation mouthpiece is at the base of your helmet. If you're going to be sick, put your lips around it and vomit into the opening. It'll keep your helmet from filling up," Carson said.

"Very couth," Lien said.

"I'm all manners."

Birk groaned and leaned his head forward, finding the mouthpiece as Gillian floated past him, squeezing his shoulder once as the sounds of his retching filled her earpiece. A fist of nausea gripped her as she drifted to the rear of the cabin, all sense of direction gone as the shuttle shifted around her. But the sensation didn't catch her by surprise; if nothing else, the hours spent in the parabolic flights had done their work preparing her for the assault on her system. She pulled herself even with the rear port window and looked out.

Earth filled up the entire viewing pane.

Its horizon was a blue-scribed line against the blackness of space, its surface mottled with clouds drifting in islands of white over oceans. Receding by the second was an unfamiliar coastline, the water around it an insane Caribbean aquamarine.

She found herself searching for Florida's coast.

Searching for where Carrie was.

Tears flooded her vision, blurring the surreal sight of the Earth falling away, of everything she loved fading.

This is how Kent felt, how Carrie must feel now. Everything familiar becoming indistinct.

She shook with a stifled sob, knowing the rest of the crew would hear. For several minutes it was all she could do to suppress the shuddering sorrow mingling with the raw beauty before her as silent tears gathered in her eyes.

"How's it look back there, Gillian?" Carson asked.

She cleared her throat. "Incredible."

"Nothing like it."

"No. I don't think there is."

Six months. Six months and I'll be home.

"Visual of EXPX confirmed," Lien said. "Docking sequence initiated. ETA fifteen minutes."

There was a brief pause before Carson said, "Gillian, you'll want to get hooked back in before we dock."

She guided herself to her seat, bumping into the compartment's roof several times before managing to settle in beside Birk, who was breathing deeply with his eyes shut. Nestled in the inky dark ahead of the shuttle was a sliver of light like a slit in space. As she clicked the last of her seat belts closed, the shape took on more definition.

The space station was sleek and narrow. What she could only assume was the front, if the facility had such a thing, was a dagger that grew steadily wider before fanning out in a spoke pattern supporting a circular structure encompassing the entire rear of the station. As she watched, patterns of windows glowing with light materialized down its side, and an image of a 747 taking off, people gazing out its portholes, flashed inexplicably through her mind.

The station continued to dwarf their shuttle until it filled the entire view, blotting out everything beyond it.

"Transferring from manual control to patterned docking protocol," Carson said. "Initializing paired rotation."

The shuttle jerked, shaking them in their seats as it turned slightly and flew alongside the rounded portion of the station. It was then that Gillian saw the circular motion of the wheel compared to the streamlined center of the facility.

"It's spinning?" she asked as another jolt shook the shuttle.

"The crew and research areas are, yes," Carson said, leaning forward to flip a switch on a control panel. "The rotation simulates gravity. It's not perfect, so it'll feel a bit strange for a while until we're acclimated."

"Acclimation," Birk said in a whisper. "What I wouldn't give for sweet acclimation."

They all chuckled as the rotation of the station and shuttle began to match.

The shuttle turned to its side, and the station slipped out of sight, the vastness of space taking center stage once more, hypnotizing Gillian in its infinity.

"Docking sequence commenced," Lien said. "Attachment in five, four, three, two—"

Her countdown was cut off by a hollow boom and a hard jerk to the right. The strap over Gillian's shoulders dug painfully through the suit.

"Little late there, Lien," Carson said. The comment was met with silence.

"Are we secure?" Tinsel asked.

"Yes. Let's unhook, and we'll get moving toward the docking module. We have gravity now, so use your handholds and the ladder at the rear of the crew compartment," Carson said.

As Gillian released the buckles on her seat once again, unease spiked over her like cool water amid a hot shower. She frowned. The launch had gone well. They were safely outside of Earth's atmosphere and attached to the station. Everything was going according to plan.

So what was bothering her?

She chocked the sensation up to nerves and helped Birk rise from his seat. The earlier weightlessness had vanished, leaving her weaving on her feet like a punch-drunk fighter. Carson flashed her a reassuring smile as he filed past her in the tight space. Lien followed close behind, avoiding her gaze.

They moved in a short line to the back of the crew compartment, where a nondescript set of bars led upward, if there was a direction in space. Carson climbed first with Lien going next. Tinsel followed while Gillian tried steadying Birk as the big man swayed in the artificial gravity.

"I think I can feel us spinning," Birk said, grasping the ladder as Tinsel's feet disappeared through a port above.

"Try not to think about it," Gillian said, keeping her hands on his suit's belt as he began to climb.

"Like the white bear."

"What?"

"Telling someone not to think of a white bear only makes them think of it more."

"Well, don't think of a polar bear either."

"Are you trying to distract me, Doctor?"

"Is it working?"

"No."

"Just go."

The port above the ladder was small enough that Birk had to reach one arm through and thread the rest of his torso afterward to enter the chamber beyond. The airlock itself was a featureless room barely tall enough for her to stand comfortably. When she'd cleared the port, Carson latched it and pointed to a row of long hooks attached to the airlock's wall.

"We'll leave our suits here. They'll only slow us down inside, and we won't need them unless we go back to the shuttle."

They removed their gear, placing the various articles on the hooks and below in designated lockers. Beneath their suits they all wore insulated blue coveralls, with a single zipper running from the lower right leg to the left shoulder. The interior of the shuttle had been almost sterilely cold, and she'd been thankful for the warmth of the coverall and suit, but now, beads of sweat were forming on her sides and back, the air stale and cloistering in the lock.

"Okay, everyone, we'll get you settled before we do a quick briefing. Follow me, and for now, don't touch anything," Carson said, stepping up to the wide door set in the end of the airlock. He scanned a small key card across a control panel, and the door slid open.

Gillian forgot to breathe as she stepped through the entry.

They stood in a long hallway stretching away in both directions. The walls were an off-white and looked like plastic, though she doubted they were. Radiance came from intermittent panels on the floor and sides of the hall, while above them the walls rose up and gradually came together nearly three stories overhead. It felt as if they were standing inside an enormous cone. Straight across from the airlock, a ladder climbed up to the pinnacle ceiling and ended at another port. The station's design was strangely unnerving. It was almost like trying to make sense of an optical illusion.

"Follow me, everyone," Carson said, motioning them to the left as he strode away. "As you noticed from our approach, the crew and research areas are circular, utilizing centripetal acceleration or centrifugal force to imitate gravity. It's about fifty percent of Earth's pull, so you'll be able to do things like this." Carson suddenly took two quick steps and leaped into the air. Instead of coming down immediately, he soared a dozen feet or more before landing. He grinned over his shoulder. "Kinda fun, but be careful, it can be disorienting."

"I'll say," Birk said, walking with a hand sliding along the nearest wall. "It feels like there's a sinkhole in the center of my skull."

"Don't worry," Gillian said, patting his arm. "All of my postgrads had that problem."

"It may be the lower gravity, but your jokes are less funny here, Doctor."

She smirked, keeping a hand on his elbow to steady him.

"The ship's central structure is zero gravity and can be accessed by any of the ladders you'll find along the wall," Carson continued. "On the opposite side are the crew laboratories as well as berths. Each door leads to a hallway for access to the rooms. As you probably noticed already, we're not walking on a rounded floor. To keep logistics and work habits in mind since this whole thing is like one big Ferris wheel, the inner construction of the wheel, as I like to call it, is squared off so the floors, rooms, and halls are all ninety-degree angles, except for where the hallways meet. These, you'll see, are gently curved for transition purposes from one quadrant to the next. Otherwise, when you came to the adjoining corridor, it would feel like you were meeting a wall before stepping onto it and walking up it. Which would be really weird."

Ahead the floor began curving in a strange upward direction that Gillian had trouble interpreting until she and Birk started walking on it.

She felt as if she should have been falling backward, but gravity pressed her firmly to the curve before the next hall flattened and stretched out before them.

"That was beyond wild," she said as a slight bout of vertigo swept over her and receded. Birk merely moaned.

"Hang in there, Birk," Carson threw over his shoulder. "Like I said, the wheel is divided into four sides, with Quad Four being Research; Three the galley and lounge areas; Two is Stasis and Control; and One, which we're in now, is personal quarters."

"I'm going to find Easton," Lien said, glancing at Carson, who nodded. Without giving them another look, she set off down the hallway, disappearing around one of the strange vertical corners a moment later.

Carson stepped up to a door mounted opposite another ladder, and it opened without a sound, sliding into the wall as he walked through. "Tinsel, you'll be in berth four. Birk, berth two, and Gillian, you're in five. You'll find a toiletry kit in the closet along with extra sets of clothes. There are windows in nearly all the rooms, but we typically keep the shutters down to avoid vertigo caused by visually registering the wheel's rotation. If you want to peek outside, do so at your own risk."

The new hallway was narrow, branching to the right and left in a "T" a dozen yards down from where they stood. Tinsel glanced around once, his color not yet fully returned, before grimacing and entering his room.

"I think I should lie down if possible," Birk said. His pallor had grayed considerably since they'd entered the airlock, and he swayed as if on the deck of a ship.

"Sure, right in here," Carson said, guiding the big man through the next doorway on the left. "Yours is around the corner, Gillian. Go ahead and get some rest if you'd like. I need to take care of a few things, but I'll wake you once we're ready for the briefing."

She took two steps down the corridor before stopping. "Carson?"

He glanced at her as Birk vanished into his berth and the door slid shut again.

"Where is everyone?" she asked.

"They're in Quad Four."

"Fifty-five people are all in one section?"

"Yeah."

She watched him, unease rippling through her again.

"Get some rest," he repeated, his smile frozen in place as he turned away and disappeared through the entrance to the main hallway.

She stayed rooted in place for nearly a minute. The walls seemed to absorb sound, and she mused she could hear the rush of blood in her veins if she listened intently enough. A sinking sensation that had nothing to do with the artificial gravity filled her stomach.

Something was wrong.

Stop it. You're nervous.

She let her breath leak out in a long sigh, then walked around the corner and found a doorway with an illuminated "5" over it.

The door whisked open as she approached.

The room was Spartan, with only a twin bed and a steel desk as furniture. A lanyard with a small gray square attached to the end was coiled on the desktop. A stool was positioned before the desk and bolted to the floor. Two doors adorned the opposite walls. One slid open, revealing a small closet complete with a half dozen jumpsuits identical to the one she wore, while the other led to a stainless-steel bathroom with a shower stall that looked as if it would have to be entered sideways.

As she took in the room, her fingers found the bottle in her pocket and opened it. Gillian glanced down at her palm, where two hydros had appeared magically in all their pale-pink glory.

It took actual physical restraint not to take them both. With sharp-edged regret, she slid one back inside the bottle and palmed the other into her mouth, snapping her head back and dry-swallowing in one motion.

She sighed, moving to the bed. It was firm, and the comforter on top was plush. She lay down, tucking one hand behind her head. A few hours ago, she'd been on Earth. Last night she'd kissed the crown of her daughter's head, the smell of her shampoo strong and sweet, then watched her fall asleep.

Gillian closed her eyes, willing the hydro to move its ass.

She should rest. She was tired, and no doubt the next twelve hours would be a whirlwind of action. They would be briefed, and she would meet the personnel who were working on—well, she didn't exactly know what they were working on besides Ander's transportation project. Carson had been cagey in his answers when she'd pressed him, so she'd assumed there might be some other government involvement he couldn't talk about, at least not until she was safely stowed away on the ship without any recourse or option for backing out.

Her eyes came open.

Ship.

Shit.

Carson had said "ship," not "station," when he was guiding them through the hall.

And the initials Lien used on the shuttle. EXPX. Not UNSS.

She sat up. That's why she had kept thinking of an airplane when she first saw the facility materializing out of the dark.

Because this wasn't a space station.

It was a ship.

A lurching sensation overcame her as if she were on a carnival ride that had just malfunctioned. She stood and moved around the end of the bed to the slim panel mounted in the wall, a single fingerhold grooved in the bottom. With a jerk she threw up the shutter covering the window.

Stars rotated past in a dazzling array. She adjusted her gaze and waited, what she was looking for coming into view a moment later.

Gillian watched for two more full rotations of the wheel before confirming what she already knew.

Earth was getting smaller.

They were moving swiftly away from it.

TWELVE

She found Carson in Quad Two.

She'd had to use the lanyard and key card attached to it on the door to stasis and control by waving it across a scanner outside before gaining entry. Inside, the room opened up to the full width of the wheel, which was considerable. One wall was composed of high-resolution screens that changed their displays every few seconds, flicking from the dark view of space, which she guessed was their trajectory, to a room filled with thick bundles of wires and circuit boards, to one of the many hallways. The rest of the area was filled with sleek banks of touchscreens on pedestal mounts with rolling chairs before them.

Carson sat at the farthest pedestal to the left.

His attention shot to her as soon as she cleared the door, almost like he was expecting and fearing her appearance.

Good.

As she closed on him, he stood, mouth already opening in defense, and it was all she could do not to ball up a fist and punch it shut again.

"Gillian, listen—"

"You fucking lied to me, Carson," she said, stabbing him in the chest with her index finger. "This isn't the station. It's a ship."

Carson deflated, looking at the floor before meeting her eyes again. "You're right. It is a ship. The *Explorer Ten*."

"That's a great name. I don't care. Let's go get suited back up."

"What are you talking about?"

"I'm talking about putting our suits back on, getting in the shuttle, and you taking me back to Earth. If you do that right now, I'll ask them to go easy on you when I file charges."

The door she had come through slid open, and a man she'd never seen before walked into the room. He had a square face matched with square glasses below neatly combed white hair. He hesitated, easily reading her expression.

"Sorry, I—"

"It's okay, Leo. We're just—" Carson started to say.

"Just leaving," Gillian finished, daring Carson to say differently.

"I'll be in the lounge if you need me," Leo said, backing out of the room.

When they were alone again, Carson sighed and sat down in his chair. "There's some things I need to fill you in on."

"Yeah, no shit."

"First, I wasn't really lying. There is a space station, and we are going to it, but it's not in orbit around Earth. It's in orbit around Mars."

She blinked. "Mars."

"It was launched in pieces disguised as deep-space probes and assembled in Mars's orbit. Look, it's complicated, and I wanted to go over all this at the briefing, but there's been an incident on the station— a death. A murder."

"This is all really intriguing, but I'm serious, Carson. You need to get out of that chair and take me back."

"Maybe you should sit down and we can talk."

"Maybe I should go get Birk and have him break your neck."

"Gillian, please. There's nothing I can do. I have my orders, and this is the mission. The ship's course is set. We've traveled nearly thirty thousand miles already."

She stared at him, anger boiling so black and thick within her, it was like she'd swallowed hot tar. "Listen to me carefully, Carson. I don't care who's dead and who did it. I don't care about your mission or what your superiors are going to say. The next words out of your mouth better be, 'Okay, Gillian. Let's go home.'"

"I'm sorry. I really am, but there's so much more riding on this than you know. You're desperately needed."

"My daughter needs me!" Her voice broke in the middle of the yell, and she hated how desperate she sounded. But the anger was distilling into something else now.

Panic.

Fear.

"I know that. Nothing's changed as far as the mission goes. We need your help, and the time frame is no different, six months is six months whether we're orbiting Earth or traveling to Mars."

"You know fucking well it's different."

"It was the only way I could get you to come along."

She imagined slapping him but was afraid if she did she wouldn't be able to stop.

Instead, she walked away, scanning her key card at the door, which opened, releasing her into the hall. The walls blurred, and she wiped away tears as she stalked around the vertical corner into the next corridor and through the doorway into Quad One. When she stopped before Birk's berth, it didn't whisk open like her own had earlier, and she waited before knocking a fist against it.

"Birk?" Nothing. No sounds of footsteps or stirring within. Only the close silence of the hall. She knocked again, calling his name louder this time. She tried pushing against the door, but it remained steadfast.

He must've locked it from the inside and was asleep. She raised her hand and resumed pounding on the door until her hand ached. "Damn it!"

She stepped back from the berth, breathing hard, sweat sticking hair to her forehead. What could she do? Stop the ship. But short of that, call for help. Yes. She could radio NASA and let them know what Carson had done.

She searched her memories of Frank's tutelage on comms. It had been brief and rudimentary. Everything he'd taught her had been concerning the shuttle's communications.

Okay, she had to get to the shuttle. As she started back down the hallway, the possibility that Carson was telling the truth about being unable to return to Earth gave her pause, her mind already doing the calculations.

It would be a little more than two months to Mars. Six round-trip. They wouldn't be orbiting just above Earth's atmosphere; they'd be flying millions of miles away. Away from Carrie.

"No," she said so quietly the word was nearly lost to her in the silence of the hall. Any semblance of control and comfort the hydro had given her was gone, smothered by an avalanche of dread. She couldn't be that far away from Carrie. What if something happened to her? There'd be no emergency return flight that would have her back on Earth in a matter of days. And what if something went wrong with the mission? There'd be no rescue from ground control. They'd be helpless, completely on their own. Carrie would be on her own.

She let out a small cry as the door to the main hall opened, and she nearly ran into Carson. He caught her by the arms as she tried pushing him away.

"What the hell are you doing?" she managed. She felt a wasplike sting in her shoulder and caught a glimpse of movement behind her, someone there as a strange film slid across her vision.

Tinsel. One of his hands grasping something. A syringe.

"What?" she said, her legs weakening. Folding.

Carson eased her down gently, his face eclipsing her vision, features wavering as if she were looking at him through an intense heat.

"I'm sorry, Gillian. I'm sorry."

She tried to form words, a threat, a curse, but her eyes slid closed, and darkness swallowed her whole.

THIRTEEN

Thudding pain from her leg.

It was the first sensation she became aware of. Gillian opened her eyes and saw a sheen of red. Beyond it the upside-down interior of their old Tahoe.

She was in the car again. In the crash.

Her leg was multijointed in all the wrong places. Blood, leaking from the gashes in her face, seeping into her mouth, into her hair.

She moaned, head throbbing in time with her leg. She tried to sit up, pulling herself sideways to avoid the crushed-in passenger door. But instead of the tree that had bashed it in, outside the broken window, there was nothing.

No. Not nothing. Lights.

Stars. Space. And something blue receding into darkness.

She blinked, eyes trying to roll away into unconsciousness again.

"Gillian."

The voice was clear and so close she nearly screamed.

Kent hung from his seat belt beside her, and she braced herself for what she knew she would see. But it wasn't Kent. It was Carson.

He wasn't fastened to the seat at all. He floated upside down, staring at her blankly. Blood dripped from his face in a metronomic rhythm, but instead of falling to the ceiling of the Tahoe, it floated away in crimson droplets, hanging like weightless rain.

"Thank you," he said, his voice oddly flat. "Thank you for your sacrifice." He pointed to her lower body, and she managed to raise her head and look down.

Blood pooled out from between her legs, soaking her jeans black.

"No," she whispered. "No, the baby. Carrie."

"Thank you."

"No! Carrie!"

Gillian.

Carson's voice changed as she tried to roll herself over.

Something snagged her shoulder, and she lashed out with a fist.

"Gillian, stop. You're all right. You're dreaming."

She opened her eyes, and everything spun for a sickening moment before locking into place.

She was lying on a narrow bed in a small, nearly featureless room, and a man stood over her. Not Carson. There was something vaguely familiar about him. Older, carefully parted hair, glasses. He held her shoulder gently, keeping her from rolling off the bed onto the floor.

"Where am I?" she asked.

"In your room."

"This isn't my room."

He frowned. "Do you feel like sitting up?"

"I feel like my head's underwater."

"It'll pass soon."

She managed to swing her legs over the side of the bed and sat, leaning over, trying not to be sick. The man walked to the bathroom, and she heard the tap running. He came back holding a plastic cup filled with water. "Here. This will help."

Gillian drank, stilling her shaking hand. When she was finished, she gave the cup to him.

"Thank you." *Leo.* She looked up at him. "Leo. Your name's Leo."

He smiled. "Leo Fuller, that's right. Glad it's coming back."

"And I'm . . ." The rush of memory was a dam breaking in her mind.

The launch.

The lies.

Carson and Tinsel drugging her.

And the sight of Earth retreating in the distance.

She sprung off the bed, triggering another wave of dizziness. The window shutter was down, and she flung it up.

Stars rotated past, speckling the dark like strewn diamonds. But that was all. No blue-white orb. Nothing but endless space.

She let her head drop, closing her eyes. "How long have I been out?"

Leo took his time answering. "Almost twenty-four hours."

Gillian slumped onto the foot of the bed.

The room began to tip, and Leo's hand was there again, steadying her.

"Whoa, it's okay. Moving too fast. I'm going to check your pulse, okay?" Soft fingers found her wrist and pressed there. "You're going to be fine, Gillian."

"My daughter . . . she's . . ."

"I know." Her head snapped around, and she yanked her wrist from him. Leo held his hands up. "I should clarify. I know, now. I was completely unaware of what you were told before and during your training. All the information I was given stated you were a consultant dedicated to the mission."

"Why should I believe that? Carson probably sent you in here."

"He did. But it was to make sure you were safe. I'm the flight medical officer. I'm disgusted that they did this, and I'll be more than happy to help file charges when we get back."

She watched him, trying to see any gap in his sincerity, but there was none. "So that's it."

Leo sighed and crossed to the stool bolted before the desk, then sat down heavily. "Yes. But to be honest, I'm not sure how far the charges will go even if they're filed."

"What do you mean?"

"Carson couldn't do this on his own. He had to get clearance from higher up. You can't wipe your ass at NASA without someone okaying it first."

She shook her head, the waterlogged quality less but still there. "This is unbelievable." Frank's slipup came back to her then. He had mistakenly mentioned stasis before correcting himself. "I need to contact NASA," she said.

"You could try. But I don't think it would do any good."

"Why?"

"Like I said, you'd be dealing with the people who gave Carson the okay to go through with this. They're not going to abort the mission now."

"You don't understand, my daughter is sick. I can't be that far away from her. It was bad enough when we were going to be in orbit."

"Believe me, Gillian, I'm pissed too, but I don't know what we can do till we return." He shrugged. "There's a briefing in a few minutes if you feel up to it."

The room swayed. "I'm going to throw up."

"Here, let me help." Leo held out his arm, and she steadied herself on it as she moved to the bathroom and shut the door.

Hot tears filled her eyes, and she trembled silently as they slipped down her face and fell into the stainless-steel basin. When she was able to see herself again, she glanced at the mirror.

"You're not giving up," she said in a low voice. She ran cold water into her hands and splashed her face until her skin buzzed. Then she dried off and opened the door.

Leo was sitting at the desk again, leaning forward, elbows on knees. Summoning courage she wasn't sure she had, she said, "Okay, let's go."

FOURTEEN

They found everyone in the lounge.

It was a long room with tall shades lining a wall that she guessed was composed of massive windows. To the left was a bar paired with six stools, and beside it padded bench seating ran below the shades for a dozen steps before ending at a kitchenette complete with stove, microwave, pantry, and dining table. A huge digital screen hung opposite the bench seating, and it was this the others, minus Birk, were watching.

Carson stood beside the screen and had been pointing at something on the display when she and Leo entered, some kind of complex diagram, but his arm dropped to his side when he saw her.

"Gillian, glad to see you up—"

"Save it," she said. "I'm going to say this once. Everyone who was complicit in what was done to me will be facing charges when we get back to Earth." She ran her gaze across Lien, who looked away, while Tinsel stared at her unblinking. A lanky man lounged at the far end of the seating away from the others, slowly chewing on a plastic toothpick. She pointed at Tinsel then Carson. "And if the two of you ever lay a hand on me again, you'll lose it."

"I know you're upset, but please listen to what we have to say," Carson said.

"What choice do I have?"

"You can leave the room at any time you'd like, but I hope you'll stay."

Gillian fixed him with a glare, pouring as much malice as she could into it before moving to an empty spot on the seating well away from Tinsel. Leo joined her, giving her a small nod as he sat.

The tall man raised a hand at Carson, who nodded in his direction. "Yes, Easton?"

Easton held up a small bottle of vodka. "This a dry meeting, sir?" Carson gave him a long withering stare. "Trying to ease the tension is all," he said, tucking the bottle away.

Carson glanced at the rest of them before taking a deep breath. "Okay. Everyone's aware of Dr. Ander's breakthrough along with the possible complications it's suffered." He touched the digital display, and the diagram vanished, replaced by a headshot of a middle-aged man smiling into the camera. His head was shaved, and he wore a manicured, graying goatee. "This is Dr. Ivan Pendrake. He was Ander's partner from the beginning on the research, a psychologist, highly regarded in the field. He was murdered three months ago."

By the crew's reactions, this was the first they'd heard about the death. All except Tinsel, whose expression remained unchanged.

"What happened?" Lien asked.

"He was found dead in his study on the station. A NASA biologist named Henry Diver killed him."

"Diver confessed?"

Carson paused. "He was found in the doctor's study with the body and attacked the person who opened the door."

"Why did he do it?" Leo asked.

"No apparent motive."

"No one's interrogated him?"

"Diver has been in a constant psychotic and incoherent state since the murder. He hasn't said anything relating to Pendrake's death."

Gillian wiped her sweat-slicked palms against the knees of her jumpsuit. She should've taken a pill before the meeting. "Diver was one of the severely affected patients, wasn't he?" she said.

Carson sighed. "Yes. He was."

"So you think the effects of teleportation drove him to kill Pendrake?" Leo asked.

"I didn't say that," Carson said. "We have no clue about what's causing the symptoms. It could be any number of things from environmental to a pathogen."

"But not everyone on the station is reporting symptoms, right?" Lien asked. "If it were a communicable disease, wouldn't they all be exposed in such a contained area?"

"Yes. And as of now, there hasn't been a quarantine established for the crew except for Diver and the other person who's in a critical state. You've all been briefed about the situation, but I'd like Dr. Ryan to say a few words about what we're dealing with concerning the possible side effects or disease." He looked at her. "If you would?"

Her first impulse was to refuse, to give him nothing, but that wouldn't turn the ship around or get her to Carrie any faster. She rose, facing the crew.

"From the reports I've studied, the two main physical complaints from the affected personnel are mild muscle tremors and general fatigue. The neurological symptoms are much more concerning. Fugues or extended trances, memory lapses, and occasional outbreaks of unprovoked anger have been recorded."

"Sounds a lot like Losian's," Leo said.

"It does."

"Do you think the teleportation, this shifting, could be somehow causing the neurofibrillary tangles that are associated with the disease?"

"I don't know. There's no way to tell for sure since the tangles are typically only diagnosed postmortem in an autopsy."

"We believe Gillian's research with bioluminescent neural scanning could be the key to correctly identifying what type of damage might be causing these symptoms," Carson said.

She ignored the comment. "The research isn't conclusive yet, so I really can't say anything one way or another."

"Does anyone have questions for Dr. Ryan?" Carson asked.

"I do," said Easton, who had been quiet up to this point. "Easton Sinclair, mission specialist, by the way. Didn't get a proper introduction before you were drugged and locked in your room." Gillian saw Carson and Lien shift uncomfortably, and in that moment, she liked Easton very much. "Correct me if I'm wrong, but doesn't everyone who travels through the mad scientist's machine essentially die the first time, and each time after?"

"We've gone over this," Carson said. "Extensively."

"I want to hear what Dr. Ryan has to say."

Gillian frowned. "In a sense, you're correct. Ander's technology causes the atoms that make up an individual to first freeze solid before being vaporized by radiation. They essentially cease to be. But to be fair, we aren't the atoms and cells we were born with; they're constantly being replaced by new and healthy material. By that logic, a person technically dies dozens of times over their lifespan."

"Fair enough," Easton said, leaning back against his seat. "If you don't believe in a soul." Carson made an exasperated sound, but Easton held her gaze.

"If you are reconstructed exactly as you were down to the last atom, then you are the same person," she said. "And I'd guess if a person has a soul, it gets rebuilt as well. If you believe in that sort of thing."

Easton placed the toothpick in the corner of his mouth and smiled, all the while continuing to watch her. "If you believe in that sort of thing," he echoed.

"Okay, any other questions relevant to the mission?" Carson asked.

"Yes," Gillian said. "Why is the space station orbiting Mars and not Earth? It can't just be for secrecy."

85

"It's classified."

"Just like kidnapping Birk and me was classified?"

"Gillian—"

"No, that's great. I'm torn away from my daughter, my life, to come help you with your little experiment, and now you won't even tell me the whole story."

"What a fucking mess," Easton said, flicking his toothpick across the kitchenette and into a waste bin.

The sentiment seemed to sum up the collective mood because Carson didn't say anything further. Instead, he took a deep breath and looked at the floor. "All I can say is you're all the very best. That's why you were handpicked for this mission." He let his gaze drift to Gillian. "Everyone should get some food and rest. In twelve hours we prep for stasis."

With that, everyone began to move. As Leo started to rise, Gillian put her hand on his arm. "Is stasis what I think it is?"

"Probably. It's basically a suspended state. Two and a half months until we rendezvous with the UNSS, so we'll be sleeping our way through the time."

She felt her brow crinkle as she glanced at Carson across the room pouring himself a cup of coffee. "Listen, I want to trust you, but you need to give me a reason."

Leo straightened and lowered his voice. "I promise to back up your story against Carson and Lien when we get back to Earth."

"Lien? So she knew I was being lied to?"

Leo hesitated. "Yes."

"That's why she was so standoffish. Makes sense." She considered his offer. "Not good enough."

"Why?"

"Because you could change your mind at the last minute. I'm sure you didn't get this far without jumping through some hoops. What keeps you from jumping through one more once we get back home?"

"I understand. What do you want?"

"Get me communication with Houston."

"I can do that, but like I said—"

"I know, it won't do me any good. But it might. And it will pave the way for charges if I record the transmissions."

He studied her for a minute before nodding. "Okay." Gillian relaxed, not aware until that point that she'd been holding her entire body tense. She could feel the tug of withdrawal on her system. An itchy craving that fluttered through her center as if a caged bird were trapped there. "When can you get me access to communication?"

"It's my shift in control in an hour."

"I'll see you then."

Leo exited the room, but as she began to follow, Carson headed toward her and grasped her elbow as she tried to step through the doorway. She jerked her arm free and shoved him backward a step. "Did you think I was joking about touching me again?"

"Gillian, I'm sorry. I am. About everything. You have to understand I didn't have a choice."

"You had a choice. You chose wrong."

"I don't think I did. I could have picked other neural radiologists for this that were less qualified, but I didn't. I chose you because you're the best, and despite what you think, I wanted to help you."

She stepped closer to him, their faces inches away. "I'm going to be millions of miles away from my daughter. Anything could happen to her, and there'd be nothing I could do about it. Does that mean anything to you?"

"If you help us get to the bottom of what's causing these symptoms, you'll have steady funding, and possibly a way to actually cure Losian's altogether. You can save her."

"I've been trying to save her for three years. I didn't need a gun pointed at my fucking head," she said, striding away from him before he could respond.

FIFTEEN

The halls were caustically silent as Gillian made her way to Birk's berth.

This time when she knocked, there was a murmur from within, and a few seconds later, the door slid away to reveal the postgrad standing on the other side, a blanket wrapped around his bare shoulders. He was no longer simply pale; a greenish cast had sprouted around the edges of his face and neck like mold.

"I'm dying," he said, turning away from her and returning to his bed.

"You're not dying." She followed him inside as the door hissed shut behind her.

He eased himself to the mattress, which groaned with his weight. There was a faint earthy smell in the room, and she noticed the open door to the bathroom.

"I'm sorry for the odor. The toilet and I have become . . . intimate. I can't keep anything down."

Birk's room was a clone of her own, and she settled herself into the stool by the desk. "Are you having any other symptoms besides nausea?"

"Vomiting."

"Besides that."

"Dying."

"You're not going to die, you're just not acclimating."

He gave her a look from beneath swollen eyelids. "And now it seems we will be acclimating on the way."

She sighed. "So you found out too, huh?"

"Yes."

"Who told you?"

"The medical officer."

"What did you do?"

"Went looking for you. When your door was locked and you didn't answer, I searched for Carson."

"What did he tell you?"

"Nothing. He wouldn't open his door either. I think it had something to do with me stating I was going to remove his head from his shoulders."

She smiled weakly. "I don't blame him for not opening up."

"All this aside, Doctor, why did you agree?"

"Agree to what?"

"This trip. It is so far away."

"I didn't agree." She paused. "They drugged me when I found out. That's why I didn't answer when you knocked."

"What?" In the next instant, Birk was striding past her toward the hall, the blanket falling to the floor. She stood up and grasped his arm almost as Carson had done to her only minutes ago.

"Stop," she said, but was pulled along for another two steps before Birk slowed.

"I'm going to make things right."

"No, you're going to hurt someone."

"That is what I meant."

"Birk, we're almost a million miles away from Earth already. They're not going to turn back."

A cold detachment entered his eyes. "I could . . . make them turn back."

"You could, but you might end up really hurting someone, and then *you'd* be facing charges when we got back instead of them."

"I'm okay with that."

"Well, I'm not. And I'm pretty sure Justin wouldn't be either."

"He would understand. This isn't right, Doctor."

"I know. But there really isn't another choice right now."

A shiver ran through him, muscles quivering as if it was taking everything in him to simply stand there.

"Here, you need to sit down before you fall down," she said, guiding him back to the bed.

"Nonsense. I'm fine." But when they reached the bed, Birk almost collapsed onto it and rolled to his back. His breathing came in shallow pants as he closed his eyes and moaned.

"What have you been eating?"

"Space crackers. Water. Some kind of protein mixture. Never been this ill before. I can feel the ship's rotation. Here," he said, bringing a hand to his temple. "I can feel the entire universe falling around me. Everything falling away." He was quiet for a time before licking his dry lips. "And something else."

"What?"

"I've been . . . hearing things."

"Like what?"

"I don't know. Things that should not be heard on this ship. Laughter."

Gillian felt her brow furrow. "Laughter? You mean like one of the other crew?"

"No. It came . . . came from the closet," he said.

She looked at the sliding door involuntarily, half expecting it to move as she watched.

"I know it's not possible, but I heard it. Also, I saw something," Birk said.

"What? What did you see?"

"A face."

"Where?"

"Outside," he said, gesturing at the shuttered window at the foot of the bed.

A rash of goose bumps spread across the back of Gillian's shoulders and down her arms. She tried to find something comforting to say, but what did you tell someone who was hallucinating?

"I think you're very tired," she finally managed.

"Yes. I've told myself that as well. But I wonder, Doctor, is it . . . could it be Losian's?" When he looked at her, there was a flicker of fear in his gaze.

"No. The onset isn't this sudden. You know that. Besides, hallucinations aren't a symptom. You're dehydrated and sleep deprived. That would make anyone see and hear things. Just rest. Would you like something to drink?"

"God no."

"Okay. Try to sleep."

"Can't. Too sick." But his voice was growing weaker.

Gillian placed a hand on his forehead and stroked back his hair. "I am sorry. It's my fault you're here."

His eyes opened to slits. "We have an old saying in Sweden. *Av skadan blir man vis.* It means, 'Injury makes you wise.' You did not do this, but we can learn from it, Doctor."

She tried to respond, but his breathing had already evened out, and a soft snore floated up to her as she stroked his hair back one last time.

Gillian sat at the foot of his bed for the better part of an hour, staring at a spot on the surgically clean floor, eyes unfocused, mind floating.

Guilt battered her, followed by anger before sharp-edged panic began to set in. She could feel it tearing at her, peeling away her defenses. The air was close in the room, and her hands tingled unpleasantly.

Before she knew it, she was opening the door to the hall, every thought centered on the pills waiting for her in her bathroom. She took less than two steps and bumped into someone walking the opposite way.

Tinsel.

He let out a grunt, and she held back a surprised cry, instead feeling heated anger return instantly at the sight of him. They were standing in almost the exact place where he had drugged her, shoved a needle in her arm, and watched her go out like a light.

"Pardon me, Dr. Ryan. Is your associate feeling any better?"

"Yes, much."

Tinsel smiled. "Good to hear."

All at once looking at the man was too much to bear. As much blame as Carson deserved, Tinsel had also known what was being done to her. And there was no remorse in his eyes whatsoever.

Without another glance at her, he walked away, stopping at the door to his berth before disappearing inside. She stared after him and finally turned toward her own room, a subtle unease slithering through her. Gillian fought down the slight tremors in her hands as she hurried to her berth and shook two of the small pills into her palm, and before another thought could give her pause, they were in her mouth and swallowed.

She stood, hands braced on the sink, breathing heavy. When she looked up at her reflection, an addict stared back.

She wanted to break the mirror, shatter her image. There was a strong urge to go back to Birk's room and wake him, tell him she'd changed her mind. *Yes, go hurt Carson and Tinsel and Lien, force whoever had the ability to turn this ship around to do so.* Because her baby was so far away and a little bit of her was disappearing even now, and if something happened . . .

She'd be gone like Kent.

The last thought was enough to send her to the floor, face held in both hands as it all came out of her.

The last few days. The pressure of training, of her decision to leave. But it went beyond that. All eight years of Kent's absence coursed free as she wept and a memory came unbidden. Their first day in the house, she and Kent carrying in box after box of their belongings, stopping to kiss every time they met each other in the hall until they'd succumbed and christened their new home right there on the hardwood floor. They'd lain there in the afterglow, blissfully unaware of the heartache barreling toward them. The pain of remembering now was so sharp, she was afraid it would cut her wide open. She'd never known that something as beautiful as what they'd had could hurt so much once it was gone.

"I'm so sorry, honey. So sorry," she whispered.

It was a long time before she could bring herself to stand. When she stepped out of the bathroom, the narco-glow was in full effect around her—everything made of knives, edges crisp and clear. She took a deep cleansing breath and settled her mind back into the groove the drug always provided.

I'm in a seriously bad place. What can I do?

Concentration and will.

The real question was, What was being asked of her?

Gillian sat on the edge of the bed and laced her fingers together. As much as she hated to admit it, Carson was right. If she could find out what was causing the station crew's symptoms and eliminate the possibility that shifting was the source, she could send Carrie through Ander's machine. The images of the rats Ander had first tested on returned to her, and she grimaced. The technology had come a long way since then, but the possibility of Carrie ending up like one of the twisted masses of bloody matter was horrifying. But the alternative was watching her slip away like Kent had.

She sighed and ran a hand through her hair, instinctively reached for her phone in her pocket, and nearly laughed. Her phone was on the nightstand in Kat's house. In any case, it would be a fancy paperweight here since she was pretty sure there wasn't coverage in this area.

The thought of making a call brought her to her feet. Leo would be in Quad Two now. Even if she couldn't get NASA to order Carson to turn the ship around, she could at least get the ball rolling on pressing charges against everyone who had lied to her.

Tinsel.

The nameless unease she'd felt before returned, this time clarifying and causing her to pause at the threshold of the berth. When they'd bumped into each other, Tinsel hadn't been coming from the direction of the main hall. He'd been traveling the other way.

From the direction of her room.

Gillian turned in a slow circle, glancing around the space. Was anything out of place? Anything missing? But what was there to take? Her extra jumpsuits? Besides the hydros, there wasn't anything else she'd—

She swallowed. Had he done something to the pills? Maybe to keep her compliant in her room? No. They'd seemed fine when she took them, and the rest of the bottle was still mostly full.

She rubbed a hand across her forehead, finding a thin film of sweat there. This was one way to break an addiction: Blast off to a space station where a mysterious murder has taken place and the workers are exhibiting signs of a life-threatening neurological disease. It's the newest in extreme treatment plans!

She sighed, trying to quell the frantic thoughts. *Quit worrying about Tinsel and Carson. You're not here for them anymore. You never really were. You're here for Carrie. You're here for your daughter.*

Gillian nodded to herself, the old mantra beginning to play on repeat in her mind as she let herself out of the room and strode down the hall.

Concentration and will. Concentration and will.

SIXTEEN

She found Leo sitting before one of the pedestal consoles reading a book.

As she neared, he set it aside, and she recognized the cover immediately, the cymbal-chiming monkey with dead eyes staring at her out of her own literary memory.

"*Skeleton Crew*, huh?" she asked, nodding toward the paperback.

Leo's face reddened as he stood. "My wife says I'm a grown man, a doctor, an astronaut, and I'm too damn old to be reading King's stuff, but I'm a fan through and through."

"Preaching to the choir," Gillian said, allowing a smile. "I've read everything of his."

Leo beamed at her. "Now we know we can trust each other." They both laughed a little before he motioned to the seat he'd vacated. "Sit down and I'll get comms fired up." She sat as Leo pivoted the pedestal toward him and began typing on the touchscreen. "It's about two a.m. in Houston, but someone is always awake. A word of warning, though: since the mission has clandestine features, all communication is routed through the command operatives in charge. We won't be getting mission control, it'll be someone else."

"And by someone else you mean . . ."

"Since the space station and everything around us has been funded partially by the UN, you'll be speaking to one of their representatives who's 'in the know.'"

"So not an actual human being."

"Not really. No." Leo squinted at the screen before turning it back to her. "We're recording and it's uplinking."

The monitor displayed a rotating half circle in its center. It spun, first hypnotizing, then sickening, until she felt as if she were no longer on the ship but lost in the spiraling crescent, everything falling away, as Birk had said.

The screen blazed to life, a man's face filling up its entirety. His blond hair was styled in a tight crew cut, and his sallow-skinned, hollow cheeks made him appear as if he were recovering from extreme starvation.

His face remained blank as he studied her across the massive distance of space before sitting back from his own screen. "Hello, Dr. Ryan."

She was so stunned by the stranger saying her name, she struggled for a moment before finding her voice. "Who are you?"

There was a short lag before he said, "My name is John. I'll be your communications liaison." His voice was deep and toneless.

"John. Got a last name?"

"Just John."

"All right, John, I'd like to file a formal complaint against Carson LeCroix, Lien Zhou, and Gregory Tinsel."

"I suppose this is concerning your new destination?"

Her eyes narrowed. "Yes."

"I'm your lifeline in case things go south. If there is a pertinent threat to the mission, I will act accordingly."

"So you're the broom sweeping everything under the rug."

"Let me put it this way: there is nothing, and I mean nothing, more important than the success of this undertaking."

Gillian felt her face flush, anger welling to the surface. "More important than lying to me, separating me from my daughter, who's ill?"

"Judging by the records I have, you volunteered. No one forced you."

"I didn't agree to this and you know it."

"I understand your frustration, but I'm afraid it's out of my hands."

She paused, trying to calm the fray of her thoughts. "I want to speak to my daughter and my sister. I need to tell them what happened."

"When the time comes, your sister will be informed that there's been a problem with the space station's comms and that we're working to get it fixed."

"I want to see my daughter." Her voice came out heavy and unfamiliar.

John looked to the left, not meeting her gaze. "I'm very sorry. That won't be possible. But as long as you do what you pledged and make this mission a success, you'll not only be a hero, you'll get to spend a long life with Carrie." John smiled, and it was a cold mockery of a grin. "Nice chatting, Dr. Ryan. Feel free to call again, the line's always open."

The display flickered to black, and for several seconds Gillian couldn't get herself to move.

He'd known Carrie's name.

The fact made her nauseous. When she managed to look at Leo, he was pale and frowning. His hand trembled when he touched her shoulder and squeezed. "I'm sorry, Gillian."

She swallowed. "It's not your fault. Thank you for this. I . . ." She trailed off, the throb of a headache beginning behind her left eye. Until that point, she had harbored the hope, small as it had been, that NASA would agree to turn the ship around and let her return to Earth, return to Carrie. But amid the simmering fear brought on by the conversation with John, there was a cold finality to the words she spoke to Leo.

"I'm trapped."

SEVENTEEN

Over seven miles a second.

Each breath, that much farther away.

In the early hours of what counted for morning, Gillian showered and dressed slowly in a fresh jumpsuit, all the while eyeing the bottle of pills in the bathroom. She'd resisted its pull, not without a fight, and settled onto the bed to wait, trying to meditate and calm the churning sea within her.

A chirp came from a small box near the door, followed by Carson's voice. "Gillian, it's time."

When she didn't respond, she heard him sigh and wondered what he'd do if she refused to leave the room. But there was no point in rebellion now. She'd made up her mind, and besides, Birk would be waiting for her.

She still couldn't get used to the quiet of the corridor, or any of the ship for that matter. It was like having cotton stuffed in her ears, every sound much softer than it should have been. When she rounded the corner near Birk's room, she saw he was already waiting for her outside. His eyes found hers, and she nearly faltered. They were red, the whites completely gone in a solid layer of ruptured blood vessels. His skin was chalk white, and a layer of sweat beaded near his temples.

"Oh God, you look terrible," she said, stopping before him.

"Always the confidence booster."

"I mean it. You need to have Leo look at you."

"He stopped by this morning."

"And?"

"He said at this point the best thing will be stasis. I have to agree. Anything to escape . . ." He shot a quick glance at the closed berth door.

"What?"

Birk struggled with something before dropping his gaze to the floor. "I saw my uncle Axel. He was standing in the bathroom doorway when I woke." His gaze flicked to hers and away again, and she noticed his accent was much thicker than before. "He beat me when I was a child. He knew that I was gay before I understood myself. He would strike me in places my . . . clothes covered, and I was terrified to tell anyone. My mother eventually realized what was happening and forbid him from our home. He died in a traffic collision ten years ago. But I saw him this morning, and he was . . . smiling at me."

Gillian tried to swallow the knot in her throat and placed a hand to Birk's forehead. "You have a fever."

He nodded, a tear slipping down the side of his nose. "I pray that is the cause."

"Come on," she said, leading him away from the door while giving it a last look.

When they entered Quad Two, she was struck by a wave of disorientation. The wall to the right of the doorway and control pedestals was gone, revealing another chamber with an arched ceiling extending back twenty yards. Along the hidden chamber's wall were a dozen rounded, coffinlike protrusions made from thick plastic, which angled away from the walking area before them. Seven of them were open, the top halves folded up, revealing a molded white interior in the general shape of a person. Carson stood before the closest one in a formfitting bodysuit, each muscle starkly defined through the thin material. He held a digital pad, and as they entered, his attention rose from the screen to them.

"Hi," he said, moving closer.

"Hey," Gillian returned. Birk remained silent, but she could feel anger rolling off him, and she noticed Carson stayed several paces out of the Swede's reach.

"Okay, the stasis units are all calibrated, and your suits are in the lockers opposite the units. Your names are on the foot of each one." He looked like he was about to say more when the door behind them opened, and Lien, followed by Easton and Leo, entered the room with Tinsel trailing behind. All of them wore the same type of suit as Carson, and Tinsel's appeared to be bothering him because he continued to pick and preen at his left sleeve even as the group gathered around them.

"Glad everyone's here," Carson said. "I was just running Gillian and Birk through stasis protocol. So once your suits are on, Leo will—"

"I won't need mine," Gillian said.

Silence flooded the room. Carson frowned and said, "What do you mean?"

"I'm not going into stasis."

"Gillian, listen. I know you're upset, and you have full right to be, but this isn't an option."

"It's how it's going to be."

"No. It's not. It's a full two and a half months before we reach the UNSS. That's seventy-five days of isolation."

"Thanks, Carson, I can count."

"You're not trained for it."

"Then you should have thought about that before you lied to me."

Carson blinked, his gaze roving over the rest of the group before he finally shrugged. "I'm sorry, it's not possible."

"You know what won't be possible? Determining exactly what's happening to the people on that station without my help. How am

I supposed to do that?" She stepped closer to him. "If you want me to help these people, I need to stay awake and work on the neuron-mapping procedure. What if the shifting turns out to be an utter failure and there's no application for my daughter? Right now all I have is time. You can't take two more months from me."

She stared into his eyes, daring him to contradict her. After several seconds of drawn silence, Carson looked away and gestured over her shoulder. "Leo, show her medical in case she hurts herself while we're asleep."

"You can show us both," Birk said, turning to follow her. "I am staying awake as well."

"You're too sick," Gillian said.

"I will be fine." But even as he spoke, he swayed slightly to one side.

She placed a hand on his arm. "You need to sleep. When you wake up, everything will be all right."

"Doctor—"

"Birk . . ." She squeezed his arm. "It's okay."

Defeated, Birk lowered his head.

"I'll be right back," she said.

Leo led her away from the group toward the opposite wall of the quad, and as she passed Tinsel, his gaze snagged hers, and he leaned in close, whispering as he did, "Make sure to ease off those pills slowly. I've heard withdrawal can be brutal." She froze, and he smiled. "Oh, and John's always there if you need to talk." He winked.

Gillian slammed her fist into the side of his head.

Tinsel went sprawling, trying to catch himself, and the room erupted in a chorus of shouts. Someone grabbed her from behind, and blind with rage, she nearly swung an elbow back at whoever it was before Leo began saying, "Hey, take it easy. Calm down."

Easton steadied Tinsel, who glared at her, one hand pressed to where she'd struck him. Carson stepped between the two groups, his arms outstretched. "What the fuck, Gillian? What the hell are you doing?"

She tried to form the words, but as she looked at Carson, a new anger overtook her. "Don't act like you don't know. You're both in on it."

"What are you talking about?"

"The guy I spoke to at mission control wouldn't let me talk to Carrie or Katrina."

Carson's face constricted in a frown. "You should have let me speak with them first. They're under orders not to allow any contact until you're fully briefed about the situation."

"And what is the situation?"

Instead of answering her, Carson turned to Tinsel. "What did you say to her?"

"To be careful during the trip. Then she went crazy."

"Liar," Gillian said.

"Stop it, both of you," Carson said. He glanced from one of them to the other for a moment before pressing the heels of his hands into his eyes. "Easton, Lien—get Tinsel and Mr. Lindqvist prepped. Leo, take her to medical."

Gillian watched Tinsel throw her another look of disdain before he was ushered away toward the waiting stasis chambers. She felt Leo touch the inside of her arm, and she jerked it away, not wanting anyone's hands on her. The receding adrenaline had left a dry, acidic taste in her mouth, as if she'd licked a nine-volt, and an irritating weakness in her muscles.

"Sorry," he said, motioning in the direction they'd been going when Tinsel had stopped her. "This way."

At the other end, the quad's wall, which looked seamless at first glance, opened in the center when Leo scanned his key card across a flush panel mounted to one side of the gap. "Anyone's key will open the med bay," he said, stepping inside a room half as large as the stasis area. There were two medical beds on the left flanked by stainless-steel cabinets, while the opposite side held a long counter hollowed at the far end by a deep sink.

"General first aid is there," Leo said, placing his hand on a low locker across from the first bed. "There's also kits on each outer corridor of the quads if you can't make it here. If you're in real trouble, you can wake one or all of us from stasis. The process takes nearly an hour, but don't hesitate if need be."

"How do I do that?"

"There's a command pad on the side of each unit. You just have to press the 'Wake' option. Everything else is automated." Leo studied her. "You're sure about this?"

She wasn't, but she couldn't let even the slightest hint of hesitation show through. If this was her only choice, she was going to make use of every second she had. Gillian summoned false composure and tried to smile. "I am."

Leo nodded and glanced at the floor. "I'm sorry about what happened in there. What did Tinsel say to you?"

"He . . ." She fumbled for a split second, almost mentioning something about the pills. "He said to call John if I needed to talk."

"Bastard," Leo grunted. "Never liked him."

"That makes two of us."

They were quiet for a moment before Leo straightened, talking almost to himself. "What else? All the food is stored in the lounge near the kitchenette. There's enough there for all of us for the entire round-trip journey and then some, so you won't starve. The flight systems are automated and locked, so there's no changing course in case you considered that."

"Don't worry, I won't try to turn us around. Probably end up driving us into an asteroid belt or something."

"Yeah, that would be particularly bad. There are instructions for how to contact Earth near the farthest console out there in control." He held up his hands. "I know you'll only be able to speak to that John or someone else like him, but if something happens, it's not only our hides on the line, it's theirs as well. We all have to answer to someone. Remember that."

"Thanks, Leo. I mean it."

"It's nothing. Wish I could do more."

"Really, I don't know how much time I'll be spending outside of the lab. I'll have more dedicated days than I've ever had before in one stretch."

"Just remember to take a break from time to time. I know you had a crash course before coming up here, but the psychological concerns of isolation in space are very real. The mind is an endless maze, and a person can easily get lost there."

She considered asking him then if he could give her some additional pills to get through the coming months but just as quickly dismissed the idea. It would be suspicious to ask for more when she still had so many. "Don't worry, I'll have plenty to keep myself busy with."

He gave her an appraising look before smiling. "I don't doubt you will. Come on, I'll show you around stasis, and you can say good night to everyone."

"I'm sure Tinsel will appreciate that."

Leo laughed as he passed her, and she was about to follow him out of the med bay when something caught her eye. It was a lighter area on the back wall of the room, and it took her a second to realize she was seeing another doorway set seamlessly into the partition.

"Coming?" Leo asked.

Gillian nodded, eyeing the sealed doorway before following him.

◆ ◆ ◆

Tinsel's and Lien's units were already closed, their names in neat block letters on a digital display at the foot of each pod. Easton was just climbing into his own, an IV trailing out from his left arm as he settled into place. He nodded at Gillian, his expression unreadable.

"The chemical compound introduced in the pods slows the metabolism, heart rate, breathing, everything to a fraction of normal levels," Leo said from beside her. "The next seventy-four days will be biologically equivalent to five for us."

"That's pretty amazing."

"Not the same as shifting, of course, but it will feel instantaneous."

"Do you dream?" she asked, pausing by the next waiting unit with Birk's name at its foot.

"Dream? Yes, many people report dreams and have higher recorded brain activity during stasis. Why?"

"It just seems like it would be eternity without dreaming."

A strange look crossed Leo's features before he smiled. "Let's get the necessities over with," he said, nodding toward Carson, who waited beside Birk in the middle of the room.

"I'd like to ask you to reconsider one more time," Carson said as she approached. "You should go into stasis. It's for the best."

"I'll be fine, thanks," she said, turning to Birk. The big man gave her such a miserable look, she nearly did reconsider. But she couldn't. She'd never be able to live with herself if she squandered the time and resources that were available to her just because she didn't want to be alone.

"Doctor. I'm sorry," Birk said.

"Sorry that you're sick? Stop it. This will make the trip go a little faster for you."

He dropped his eyes, looking as if he wanted to say something more, but if he did, she thought it would be the last straw that would break her tenuous will. She stood on her tiptoes and kissed him lightly on the cheek. His skin was chilly and rough with stubble.

"I'll see you soon," she said, stepping back.

Birk dipped his head once and turned away, then climbed into the pod with some effort. When he relaxed into the leaning position, he barely fit, his shoulders brushing the sides of the unit as Leo inserted an IV into one of his arms. A minute later the pod's lid lowered, and she lost sight of him behind the opaque shield.

Carson stood with his hands on his hips, eyes unfocused for several seconds before saying, "Leo, can you give us a minute?"

"Sure. I'll get my unit prepped."

When the older man had retreated to the far end of the room, Carson glanced at her. "I was hoping to have most of this cleared up by now, but there's a lot I can't tell you yet."

"You really haven't told me anything."

"No."

"Yet you're the reason I'm here."

"You're more right than you know."

"What do you mean?"

He worked his jaw. "I wasn't being gracious when I said you're the most brilliant in your field. There was another reason I chose you."

"Why?"

"Because of Carrie. I wanted to call you thousands of times after your husband passed away, but I could never get the courage to actually dial the number. And when I found out about Carrie's diagnosis, I came to see you at your lab but stopped outside the door and left before you saw me."

"What are you talking about?"

"I chose you for the mission not only because you're the best in your field, but because I thought maybe it could help Carrie." He paused. "Help you."

Carson opened his mouth to say more but then closed it. With a last look, he turned and climbed into his waiting stasis unit. Leo inserted the IV, and a moment later the pod sealed with a short hiss, and

Leo motioned her to follow him. They walked to his unit, and he settled himself inside and placed his own IV in his left arm with practiced ease.

"Remember what I said: take a break every once in a while. Relax and recharge your batteries. And if you need to, wake one of us. There's no shame in needing help," he said.

No shame in needing help. That was the slogan of every rehab clinic she'd ever considered checking in to before abandoning the idea. But shame was the cage that kept her from reaching out for help. Shame at not being strong enough to deal with what life had handed her. *I got news for you, Doc: when you're an addict, there's always shame.*

"I will," she said.

"And remember not to get lost in here." He tapped his temple once and pressed a button on the inner wall of the pod. "Godspeed," he said as the lid closed.

There was the familiar hiss of air, then silence.

She was alone.

EIGHTEEN

Alone.

Some words never fully encompass the true depth of their meaning. Some are so small, so insignificant, that what they represent dwarfs them into meaningless and trivial utterances.

"Death" is one.

"Alone" is another.

Gillian caught herself thinking this as she gazed out the window at the passing stars. She stood in the lab she'd spent almost every waking hour in since watching the crew go into stasis. How long had it been? Two days? Three? She'd already lost count. So many more to go. She nudged the thought away.

She sighed, facing into the room again. It had taken the better part of a day to get acclimated to the lab itself: finding where all the instruments were, bringing up her data on one of the many tablets, and organizing everything she would need to continue trials for the neural highlighting. There hadn't been much progress. For what seemed like the millionth time, she found herself wishing Birk was with her. Not only because his assistance was indispensable, but also to break the silence that surrounded her like a cocoon. She almost never talked to herself, but she had begun doing so every few hours just to brush back the quiet.

"Better get to it." Gillian moved to the nearest worktable and sat down before one of the digital displays holding data for the most recent trials she and Birk had completed on Earth. She read through the numbers three times, having to repeat the process because her eyes kept traveling to the entrance of the lab.

The doors to this part of the ship were different: they contained windows set halfway up their length. She supposed they were for people to assess whether any sensitive tests were taking place before entering.

Gillian brought her focus back to the chart and the notes Birk had made concerning the time lapse between pyramidal and inhibiting neuron activity, but slowly her gaze slid to the doors once again, almost anticipating the lurching fear that had gripped her the day before.

She had been sitting almost exactly where she was now, organizing vials needed for the bioluminescent trials, when a strange sensation invaded her.

All at once she'd registered what was wrong.

Someone was standing outside the lab doors.

She'd jerked her head up, a butterfly's wings in her heart. But there was no one there. For nearly a minute, she'd sat unmoving, watching the windows while letting the rational part of her mind coax the rest of it down off the ledge of panic.

You imagined it.

You're tense. Remember what Leo said about the mind.

Rationalizing it hadn't stopped her from moving carefully to the door and peering out, sure she would see someone standing there. The hall had been empty, of course, motionless, white, the same as when she'd walked there from her room. She'd tried to stop herself then; she really had, but no matter how much she reassured herself she was being absolutely foolish, her feet had carried her to stasis, where she verified through everyone's display that each pod was still occupied.

Afterward, she'd taken a hydro, brewed a strong cup of coffee, and sat at the table in the lounge sipping it and staring at the nearest wall. She hadn't actually seen anything. But her lizard brain strongly disagreed. Perhaps it was nerves or maybe some kind of delayed reaction to the environment—maybe it was a delayed onset of motion sickness like Birk had.

"Or maybe you're really losing it," she said to herself, coming back from the memory. Gillian stared at the doors for another moment before dismissing them, dismissing the incident. She had been stressed, still was, to be completely honest. And seeing something out of the corner of one's eye wasn't a rare event. It happened all the time.

"Happens all the time," she murmured, bringing her full attention back to the notes.

Audio file transcript—#179084. June 6, 2028.

I counted the remaining pills today.

Twice. I was having a hard time focusing in the lab, and I'd brought them there from my room, so I counted them to relax. I took two yesterday to concentrate and managed to get ready for a trial on one of the fifteen rats that were brought along in their little self-cleaning cages. Their food is also dispensed automatically into their bowls. When they hear the pellets fall, they come scurrying. Just like me and my pill bottle. Rattle, rattle.

I went a day without having anything and started to get the shakes by the end. Not good. Got a feeling I'm in for a pretty terrible ride when they're gone.
[Brief pause.]

There's this lie drugs or booze tells the person that's using them . . . or that they're using, if you want to be honest. It's the idea you can't function without them. A guy with terrible anxiety drinks Scotch at his desk all morning and manages to seal a deal with a big corporation? It was because he was relaxed. Then he gets thinking that it was the only reason he was able to do it. That it was all the booze and none of his talent. Life's a big flat-faced mountain we have to climb, and the wonderful substances are our climbing gear.
[Long sigh.]

Where was I going with this? Sleep maybe. I haven't been sleeping well. My room feels too small, and I wake up almost hyperventilating every time I'm in there. I tried napping on the couch in the lounge but

kept jolting awake every few minutes. I thought . . . I thought I kept hear-
ing something. A banging or thumping. I don't know. Maybe it's the ship
functioning, but I never heard it before. Although I can't be sure I actually
heard it or not.

I thought I'd be used to the isolation by now, but I'm not. I considered
using comms, even went so far as to look for Leo's instructions on how to do it
before remembering John's face and voice. I'd rather go the rest of my life with-
out speaking to another human being than hear one word from him again.
[Long pause. Muffled laugh.]

Leo. I had to laugh when I found where he'd left the instructions for
communications. They were written on a folded piece of paper tucked inside
his copy of Skeleton Crew. *I've forgotten a lot of the stories. Probably wasn't*
the best choice of reading material given my state of mind, but it passes the
time. Got to the one about teleportation last night. "The Jaunt," it's called.
Spoiler alert if I'm dead and anyone listening to this hasn't read it. It's in the
distant future, where teleportation is commonplace, and follows a man and
his family getting ready for a trip across the universe. The father's relating
the history behind how the technology came to be, how it was absolutely
necessary for people to be unconscious when they did it because everyone who
had been awake went insane and died immediately afterwards. The part
that stuck with me besides the ending, which I remembered enough of that
I decided not to read it again, was where a convicted murderer is given the
chance of a full pardon if he agrees to teleport awake. He does, and comes
out looking absolutely ancient on the other side and dies immediately after-
ward. Like an eternity passed for him in a matter of seconds.
[Clears throat.]

Yeah, I know—wonderful subject matter given what we're going
to be dealing with in a couple months. Regardless, it got me thinking.
What would it be like to stay awake while shifting? I know it's never been
attempted—the vacuum causes unconsciousness within a few seconds—but
how would it feel as every atom in your body slowed down and froze? What
would it be like for time to stop?

[Recording pauses. Resumes.]

I'm rambling. Need to be sleeping instead of talking to a recorder. Big day tomorrow, first neural bioluminescent trial in space! Congratulations to me! I'll celebrate with some shitty coffee and that caramel pudding stuff I'm sure isn't supposed to be pudding.

[Short pause.]

Carrie loves pudding.

[End of recording.]

◆ ◆ ◆

Audio file transcript—#179085. June 15, 2028.

I made a huge mistake coming here.

Not just because of the obvious reasons. Nine days and zero progress on the trials. I don't know what to do. I keep going back over and over the data, all of our notes, reading through every paper that's come out of the neurological community in the last three years.

Nothing. Nothing works.

It's the inhibiting neurons that are the problem, and it seems relegated to the hippocampus for some reason. They're shutting down the bioluminescent triggers before there's a clear picture. Without all of the neurons firing, we'll never be able to see where the neurofibrillary tangles are located. And if I can't find them . . .

[Indistinct.]

[Recording pauses. Resumes.]

I managed to get a few nights of good sleep. Had to take a pill beforehand, though. I get really edgy right before I drift off. It's beyond quiet. Haven't heard the sounds anymore. Maybe I imagined them too. Think I'm still anxious about what I thought I saw the other day. I know there wasn't someone watching me from outside the lab, but I've caught myself looking over my shoulder when I walk down the hallways. I half expect someone to be there, two steps behind me.

I'm starting to wonder if everything will fall apart. If I can't figure out how to fire the neurons, what will happen when we reach the space station? What use will I be? And even if I still get the funding once we get home, will it be any different? Right now I've got a fully equipped lab and all the time in the world, and I can't make any progress.

[Soft crying.]

I miss her. I miss Carrie. I miss our house, and I miss our walks and how she always pointed out things I would have never noticed.

I miss my life.

[End of recording.]

◆ ◆ ◆

Audio file transcript—#179086. June 27, 2028.

I saw someone today.

I was rounding the curve in the hallway near Quad Two and heard something. It was a shushing noise, and at the same time, I saw the door to the quad slide closed. I stopped so quickly, I nearly fell, and my heart felt like it was going to climb out from between my ribs.

I didn't know what to do, so I stood there for a few seconds before realizing someone must have woken up early from stasis.

I jogged down the hall and scanned in through the door, completely expecting to find Carson or maybe Easton sitting at one of the pedestals when I went inside.

But there was no one.

I went into medical, sure that they'd gone in there, maybe for some water or aspirin or something, but it was empty. I half ran to stasis and started checking all the units. Everyone was asleep and accounted for.

[Ragged breathing.]

So I guess I didn't actually see anyone. Just . . . saw the door closing. It could've been a malfunction. I went in and out of the quad a dozen times to check it.

Worked perfectly.

I went and sat in the lab after that for a couple hours, but I couldn't concentrate. Not even with the pills. I've been taking more of them than I should. Up to four a day now.

We'll be at the space station in less than seven weeks.

Still no progress.

One of the rats died. It looked natural. It wasn't even one I'd been using for trials. It was just lying on its side when I went into the lab. Maybe space didn't suit it. Maybe space doesn't suit anyone. We don't belong this far away from Earth.

I keep going back to what I know about the mind. The hippocampus. Memory, emotion, how we interpret our experiences and how we store them. What makes us who we are, and how delicate that is.

How it can just fade away and we become nothing. A shell. Something that eats and breathes until even that stops too.

[Rustling sound. Indistinct.]

There was something else. When I went into medical after seeing the door close, there was a smell. Something I couldn't name.

But I know I've smelled it before because for some reason it terrified me.

[End of recording.]

◆ ◆ ◆

Audio file transcript—#179087. July 4, 2028.

I dreamed about Kent last night.

We were on Mars. I can only assume it was Mars since I've never been there, but everything was red and desolate. I was following him across this horrible dead landscape. He was in a space suit, and I couldn't see his face, but I knew it was him. And I . . . I wasn't wearing one, but I could breathe. He led me to this huge depression, this enormous valley that was like a gaping wound, and he stood there on the edge before he looked back. And his face . . . it was . . . it . . . [Slurring. Indistinct.] *I couldn't stop him. He fell. No. He jumped.*

[Indistinct.]

[Recording pauses. Resumes.]

Fuck you, Tinsel. And fuck you, Carson. I don't care what you were thinking when you brought me here.

[Long silence.]

I haven't slept in days. Can't work. I'm in a cage every time I try to turn around and go in a different direction. Like the rats. Dead ends, everywhere. Feels like someone's watching. Eyes on me wherever I go in this ship.

[Soft crying.]

Today's the Fourth of July. I hope . . . I hope Kat brought Carrie to see the fireworks. She loves the fireworks. [Slurring. Indistinct.] *. . . she thinking? Does she think I'm gone? Gone like her daddy? Or does she not remember at all?*

[End of recording.]

NINETEEN

Gillian brought the morning's third cup of coffee to her lips.

This was the first day in almost a month that she wasn't high before noon. Caffeine swam through her system, and her nerves hummed like electric wires. Her head felt like a blacksmith's anvil, and her muscles were languid and waterlogged.

She felt like shit.

The last three weeks were a blur from the pills. Too many. She didn't know how much she'd taken on certain days. Her earlier weaning had given way to excess when she hadn't been able to make headway on the research.

And now she didn't know if she'd be able to make it to the space station before full-on withdrawals hit. Forty-eight days.

"Gonna be rough," she said to the empty lounge. She no longer felt self-conscious speaking aloud. It was second nature now. At times it felt like the only tether she had to reality, the sound of her voice and what she was saying. In the back of her mind, she knew she was actually managing the isolation fairly well, even with leaning harder on the drugs. She'd read enough psychological studies to know people could snap in much less time than she'd spent alone.

"Who says you haven't snapped already?" She shivered, noticing the familiar sensation of weight on her back and shoulders.

The feeling of being watched.

She knew it was the drugs or the paranoia that accompanied them, but that made it no less palpable. Even the sounds she heard could be chalked up to heightened imagination and the hydros wreaking havoc on her senses.

But what about the door closing by itself? What about the smell in medical?

Gillian raised the cup again, unwilling to think about those questions anymore, and realized it was empty. Maybe a little more coffee and she'd get to work. No. She needed to eat something. She'd lost weight in the last two months; her jumpsuit hung like a limp rag.

She left the table she'd been eating and drinking at alone for the last sixty-two days and went to the kitchenette. All of the crew's meals were separated on shelves into neat rows, the corresponding member's name below each stack. She'd thought it was strange at first that the prepackaged meals were segregated, but then it made sense. If an individual were consuming more than their fair share, it would be noticeable almost at once. Her own supply had barely dwindled.

One of the muscle tremors that had plagued her since decreasing the hydrocodone ran through her arm, and her hand bumped into the stack beside her own.

It toppled outward, spilling a dozen or more packs onto the floor. As she tried to catch them, she bumped a pile of her meals, and they fell too, bouncing off her feet and spinning away across the room.

"Damn it!" she cursed, the pack she'd grasped initially slipping free to fall amongst the others.

She stood there for a moment, on the verge of tears, her throat tightening before she looked at how many of the meals had escaped the storage unit. They were everywhere.

She broke into laughter.

The tears came then, forced out by the mirth that doubled her over in silent gales. It was laughter of the insane, cackling of the crazy, but it felt too good to stop.

"Oh fuck, look how many there are," she managed between breaths, which kick-started another round until her belly began to cramp. Slowly she knelt and started retrieving the meals, the thudding of her headache killing any more laughter. After collecting several handfuls, she went to place them back on the racks and realized the meals she'd spilled had been Birk's, and there was no way to tell her own from his. She read a few labels to confirm the packs were the same before placing them inside. She knew Birk hadn't eaten a lot before he'd gone into stasis, so she distributed them accordingly. Besides, what did it really matter? She'd been the only one consuming anything for the past two months.

Gillian eyed Carson's meals, imagining a number of creative experiments she could try on them. Then she saw Tinsel's.

"Could use them to soak up rat piss," she murmured, which tugged a giggle from her before she dismissed the idea. She finished cleaning up the rest of the packs and selected one, opening and warming it before settling down to eat.

She couldn't really complain about the food. Of the many things wrong with her situation, the food wasn't one of them. When she finished, she left Quad Three and headed for the lab but gradually slowed, running out of steam before turning the corner of the hall.

What was she going to do today that she hadn't done in all the days before? What was different now? The answer was simple.

Nothing.

Even with all the narco-glowing she'd been doing, there had been no epiphany, no breakthrough moment, no eureka! Science was the slow grind of facts and theories gradually milled down through tests and trials. And if you were talented and very, very lucky, you'd sift through everything to make a discovery. But even then it was normally a small step in the marathon of innovation.

Gillian sagged and leaned against a wall. Her hand went out, and she was surprised when it landed on the rung of one of the access ladders leading to the center of the ship. She considered its narrow length for a second before beginning to climb.

The weakness was even more pronounced with the extra effort of hoisting herself up the rungs. Her breathing became heavier, and her heart picked up its thudding rhythm in her eardrums.

At the top of the ladder was a simple port she scanned through, and pulled herself into a small rounded room that held a more typical doorway along one side. She scanned her key card again as the port near her feet closed slowly and locked.

There was a quiet clunk, and the entire room rotated counterclockwise before the door slid open.

An immense conical space opened up before her. It stretched away in an array of support girders, access panels, bundled wiring of every color, and ducts twisting and sprouting from one another like the roots of a massive tree. And even as she registered it all, she began to float.

Her feet left the floor, and she had to reach out and grasp the doorway to keep from bumping into the ceiling. She laughed, unable to help herself, and launched out into the open space of the ship.

Gillian glided past the cluttered walls, soaring fifty feet above what she'd call the floor of the craft. A crippling sense of vertigo came and went, the image of gravity suddenly returning and plummeting her to the solid girders below so vivid she sucked in a panicked breath.

But she didn't fall. She flew.

How many people had ever felt this? The utter freedom of true weightlessness was nearly overwhelming. This was how a young bird felt, leaving the nest and discovering it wasn't bound to gravity as it thought it had been.

It was how she'd felt being wheeled out of the obstetric wing, the new smell of Carrie's skin moments after her birth, the sharpness of colors and pain. The medical bed beneath her had glided down the hallway of the hospital, just as she was gliding now.

Carrie was a warm bundle in her arms, fast asleep. There had been a wrapping of painkillers as well as fatigue around her, but not in an unpleasant way. She felt as a soldier might who's made it through a skirmish alive along with the rest of their company.

Triumphant. Victorious. Satisfied.

The nurses had wheeled them through the halls and taken an elevator down to another room, and she still recalled exactly how she'd felt as they pushed them through the doorway.

Kent had been waiting there in a wheelchair, thick restraints across his legs and waist so he wouldn't get up and wander away. His gaze had lit on them both as they'd entered the room but just as quickly slid away, not recognizing her. Not registering his newborn child.

Her doctor had warned her this wasn't a good idea, but she'd insisted, dead set on introducing their daughter to Kent, whether he realized what was happening or not.

Her heart double-timed as the attendants wheeled him closer.

Their eyes met, and a flicker of recognition bloomed in his, the clouded confusion clearing away.

He'd reached for her. Out of instinct or something else, she never knew. And she'd grasped his hand. Held it, tears already forming, blurring her vision.

Gillian? What are you doing in bed, honey? What's wrong? He'd asked her the questions as if he'd seen her only minutes ago instead of almost a week. She couldn't answer, couldn't make herself form the words. In their place, she tilted Carrie up so he could fully see her through the swaddling of blankets.

He'd frozen, and for an instant she'd thought her doctor had been right. This was a mistake. Kent would recede now, the man she loved curling in on himself, leaving only anger behind. The rage would expand, and he would be dragged away from them again. A stranger furious at all around him, furious because nothing was familiar.

But that didn't happen.

Kent had reached out, stretching as far as he could while bound to the wheelchair, and brushed his fingertips across Carrie's cheek.

Gently. So gently.

He began to cry then, looking from her to the baby and back again.

I remember. I remember now. I remember.

Everything was in his voice. All the lost time between them since the accident and even before. He was there, fully and truly her husband. He was seeing his daughter for the first time.

And they were a family, if only for a moment.

She remembered everything.

Her eyes flew open, flinging the tears she was crying away in droplets like wobbling jewels.

That's it.

The revelation was a row of dominoes in her mind, one thought crashing into the next, the succession leading to a surety she felt in her bones.

Gillian twisted in midair, grasping the nearest support strut. She spun herself around and sprung from it, gliding in a straight line to the entrance.

Then she was inside, swiping her key to close the doors.

The room rotated, gravity returning so quickly she hit the floor and stumbled sideways. She was back in the centrifugal rotation. The hatch at her feet opened, and she clambered down the ladder, a righteous joy of discovery coursing through her.

"It's gotta be. It's the only answer," she said as she leaped from the ladder and sprinted down the hall toward Quad Four. She scanned in to the lab, barely pausing to put on the coverall before opening the closest rat's cage. The animal uttered a short squeak as she drew it free. The small fitting in its skull glinted in the harsh light, but it barely struggled as she brought it to the table.

"It's going to be okay. This won't hurt at all," she whispered, securing it with the small harness to the test tray. After withdrawing a fresh vial of luciferin compound from the nearby cooler, she injected it into the rat's cranial port. While the absorption took place, she turned on the recording equipment, attached the injection tube to the rat's port, and measured out the luciferase before loading in the injector capsule. This was second nature after all the other trials, but now there was a thrumming energy beneath her motions. There was true potential.

"You know, luciferin is named for Lucifer. It means 'light bringer.' Ironic, isn't it?" she said to the rat as she reset the trial program on the nearest touchscreen. "Maybe you can be a light bringer that lives up to the name." Gillian rechecked all the connections before going to the rat's cage and pulling its food pan free along with a handful of pellets from the dispenser. She noted the time and took a deep breath, pausing before reaching out to touch the screen. This was trial 188. Almost two hundred attempts, all of them failures. Doubt ate away at the confidence she'd felt only minutes before. Why would no anesthesia make a difference? Why would being awake and alert with an external stimulus present be the key?

Her jaw tightened even as the reservations tried to consume her. "Because we all remember," she said, and touched the screen's button.

The injector clicked, and the luciferase flowed through the tube into the rat's port.

Immediately its synapses began firing.

Thousands.

Millions.

She watched as the enzyme flowed across and into the rat's brain, igniting the neurons in a firestorm of action. The activity drew closer and closer to the hippocampus, and when it was seconds away from reaching it, Gillian moved to the rat, set its bowl in front of its nose, and sprinkled the pellets into it.

The distinctive tinkling sound filled the room, and the rat's ears perked. It squeaked once, straining against the harness to try to get to the food.

Gillian rushed back to the screen.

Her eyes widened, a hand coming to cover her open mouth.

The hippocampus lit up in waves, the neurons firing in succession, first the pyramidal then the inhibiting.

The entire portion of the brain was awash in the flaring bioluminescence. She watched, not daring to breathe, not daring to move, afraid anything she did would interrupt what was happening.

The luciferase continued through the last of the hippocampus and flowed away to other areas of the brain.

She'd done it.

She'd actually done it.

"It worked," she whispered, taking her hand from her mouth. "It worked." She wasn't doing it justice. "It worked!" she yelled as loudly as she could, her voice ricocheting off the lab walls. Exuberance beyond any chemical high she'd ever felt coursed through her. This was it, the moment she'd dreamed of. Not just a step forward like all the other progress.

A leap. A catapult.

The implications were too great to absorb all at once, but the realization she had when watching the neurons firing was like a pillar in her mind.

I can see what's wrong now with Carrie. I can find it.

And soon we'll be able to fix it.

She wanted to dance. Instead, she unhooked the rat from its harness and port. It immediately leaned over its dish and began eating.

"You deserve all that and more, you did amazing," she said, stroking the rat's fur. "You can have as much food as you want. You're going to be fat and famous, Lucifer." She laughed. "Might have to give the press a different name, but to me you'll always be the light bringer."

Gillian stood back and let him eat, turning to the screen and the data once again. It was all there, the key to mapping any irregularity in the brain, and it had been unlocked by memory itself. The hippocampus had always been a mystery: how it stored spatial memory, how its conversion of short-term to long-term memories worked, and what role emotion played amid it all. Who you were was shaped by your experiences and how you reacted to them as well as the emotions associated with those reactions.

But memories, they were what opened the door to what was stored inside. That's where the external stimuli came in. How many times had seeing something or smelling a scent brought back an experience from the past? For her, every time she walked through their home was an assault from before, when Kent had been alive and healthy and their life was something protected and filled with potential for the future. The memories were what had allowed the neural pathways to open like a gate for the bioluminescent imaging to work. In this case, it was the sound of the rat's food falling into its bowl, spurring pleasant memories of eating. The difference had been allowing the subject to be awake and aware.

All along the answer had been right in front of her.

A sense of accomplishment settled over her unlike any she'd felt before in her career. But with it came weakness and a tinge of nausea. Probably normal with all the excitement. Also, she hadn't had any hydro yet today.

"Just one," she said, forcing herself to turn away from the screen.

Gillian moved to the bottle of pills she'd begun keeping in the lab. She reached out but stopped her hand an inch from the small container.

The cap was loose.

It sat askew, one side higher than the other.

Had she forgotten to close it last night? No. She always snapped it down tight; hearing the childproofing click was ingrained.

She picked the bottle up and stopped breathing as the cap tipped off and fell to the floor.

Before she brought her shaking hand closer, before she shook the container, before she even picked it up, she knew.

The bottle was empty.

TWENTY

Gillian searched the entire ship.

She moved systematically from the airlock where the shuttle was docked through all the quads. One by one she went to each of the rooms and covered the areas she was most accustomed to before admitting to what she was doing.

Looking for someone.

She had to be honest with herself: this wasn't normal behavior.

It was textbook paranoia.

There was no one else on the ship besides the crew, who were all still in their stasis units (it was the very first of the four quads she had checked).

Gillian placed her back against the wall, feeling the silent hum that vibrated throughout the ship. What exactly was she doing? Hoping to flush out a secret passenger?

The thought was jarring. What if there was someone else on the crew that she hadn't been aware of? Someone who had come up to the ship on the prior trip with Leo and Easton? No, Leo would have mentioned them.

But what if he wasn't aware of them either?

She brushed the notion aside. She wasn't pulling herself out of the nosedive of conspiracy; she was angling into it. Where would it stop if she gave in to every possibility? It wouldn't. Every idea would seem reasonable, every outlandish thought holding a sliver of merit.

Maybe in your addled state you imagined how many pills there were. Maybe you did spill them, and the part of you that depends on them blocked it out, wasn't able to deal with the fact that you doomed yourself to hell. Because that's what withdrawal is going to be without tapering off or any type of treatment.

"Stop it," she said. Her voice sounded sick and flat in the hallway. She hadn't spilled them or taken all of them without knowing. It was impossible.

She pushed off from the wall and continued down the hallway, scanning in through every door she came to and briefly searching the room inside. The empty beds, tidy and unused; small bathrooms, a faint disinfectant scent hanging about them; and worst of all, the closets. Even though a person would be hard-pressed to fit inside them, there was room. She left them for last, drawing each open quickly while stepping back, a part of her expecting a hand to shoot out to grab her every time.

But there was no one.

She even went so far as to inspect the zero-gravity portion of the ship in case someone had doubled back behind her and was hiding there amongst the struts and cables, floating, waiting for her to tire and fall asleep so they could come creeping down the ladder to walk silently to where she lay—

Gillian pinched herself hard on the inner skin of her wrist. She had to stop. Stop imagining things. Get grounded. Stay focused.

Her hand found its way into the pocket of her jumpsuit, and she grasped the beaded string there.

She'd found her mother's rosary in her personal bag while digging for nonexistent extra pills in the bottom. Kat must've hidden it there after their squabble. Her sister's stubborn faith a stowaway now.

Gillian drew it out and pressed one wooden bead after another down into her fist with her thumb. How many times had she relied on these illusions for comfort? In its own way, religion was the greatest addiction. Where else could you receive encouragement for being kind and penitent? Where else could you absolve doubt and sin—any wrong-doing you committed—by speaking words that no one else had to hear? There was no other high like righteousness. But even as she mused, the prayers for each one of the beads automatically floated up in her mind. She hated to admit it, but the repetition was calming. And she needed calm. Needed rational thinking more than anything.

But it was becoming tougher because she wasn't suffering only from an unstable mind-set.

Even as she stowed the rosary back in her pocket and made her way toward the lounge, she noted the slight tremors that had been only occasional before were now almost constant. A new arrival was the nagging ache in her muscles that fleetingly swam from one area to another.

How many hours since she'd last taken a pill? Almost fifteen, maybe more? It was going to get worse from here on out. Best to get ready any way she cou—

Gillian paused near the lounge's doorway and nearly laughed before hurrying away toward Quad Two.

Upon entering medical, she began her search anew. This time for any type of opioid painkiller that was bound to be stocked for emergencies. As she opened and closed cabinet doors and rifled through well-organized drawers, a sense of calm settled over her. Regardless of how the pills had disappeared, she wouldn't have to suffer through withdrawal. It was a consolation. Small, but a consolation nonetheless.

By the time she searched the last cabinet, she was sweating.

Her heart beat at an irregular rhythm, and an irritating tingling danced across her fingertips as if she'd stayed out in the cold too long.

She slid her gaze across the two shelves inside. Cotton pads. Blue paper gowns. Rubber-soled slippers.

No drugs.

The closest she'd come to finding some were two bottles of Advil.

There had to be something here. Had to be. NASA wouldn't jettison seven people into space without proper medical supplies. They wouldn't leave Leo without the tools he needed in case someone sprained an ankle or broke an arm. They wouldn't—

Her eyes fell on a narrow panel set into the wall above the farthest countertop, a scan pad beside it. "They wouldn't leave them lying out in the open either," she said, moving to the square she could now see was sealed along one edge.

She brought her key card up and placed it before the scanner

It beeped and blazed a deep red before resetting.

Gillian tried again. And then again, her stomach curdling.

This was where the stronger drugs were kept; she could feel it, but her key card wouldn't open it. Probably only Leo's did, and she had watched him store it along with his regular jumpsuit in his secured locker across from the stasis units.

The elation she had felt with the breakthrough only hours ago was gone. In its place was a pulsing knot of dread.

After another minute of contemplating the sealed compartment, her legs insisted that she sit down, so she did, pressing her shoulders into the base of the bed across from the cabinets. She glanced at the nearly hidden doorway to her left, which she had spotted while Leo was giving her the tour all those days ago. But was it a door? There was no scan pad beside it, no visible handle. Probably an access panel to a service shaft. In any case, there was no way to check inside and see.

A prickling in her throat grew until her vision blurred. What was she going to do? She swung a fist down, pounding it against her knee until it throbbed in time with her eyesight.

Finally she covered her face and gave herself over to weeping, letting the fear drain out through her tears.

TWENTY-ONE

Whispers.

Someone was whispering. What they were saying was lost in the white noise of the susurrations, but Gillian could hear them. Hear them telling her something that wasn't . . . good. Like a warning.

She moaned, trying to respond, to ask them to say it louder even as she strained herself up out of sleep and into—

Vertigo so strong she gasped. Her eyes came open, and the room tilted, jackknifing in strange places as if the walls were hinged and flexing back and forth.

She vomited. She couldn't help it. The remains of her dinner spewed out as she leaned over the side of the padded bench in the lounge, stomach cramping so hard it was as if someone had kicked her.

She coughed, spitting out bile, slowly gathering the will to sit up. Her body was tingling everywhere, a funny-bone ache in every muscle. When she hoisted herself into a sitting position, another wave of dizziness crashed over her, and she closed her eyes, but there was no respite from the assault. She tipped forward, gagging again, but nothing came up.

"Oh God," she said. While she'd slept, her heart had relocated to the middle of her skull, and it beat at a poisonous tempo. Her mouth was full of acrid chalk, but even the thought of water made her stomach turn.

Gillian drew in a deep breath, slung her legs over the side of the bench, and stood as if she were on the pitching deck of a ship. Water. She had to drink. Keep hydrated. It was the only way she'd get through this, especially if this was a taste of things to come.

She made her way to the table, grabbed the bottle she'd been drinking from the night before, and shuffled to the tap. The stream of water was sandpaper to her eardrums, and she moaned again with the exquisite misery of all her senses. She brought the bottle to her lips and managed two small sips before her throat closed off and her stomach threatened mutiny.

This was hell.

There was no other word for it. She had to do something. Had to fix it. Had to escape.

"Think. Think. Think," she whispered, gripping the sink with one hand. The only thing that would alleviate the suffering was medication designed to ease the withdrawal process or more opioids. She was sure there were no withdrawal meds on board, but the opioids . . .

Gillian moved away from the sink, the room slithering colors and shapes at the corners of her vision. She made it to the door and scanned through into the hallway, which seemed even brighter than the lounge.

Now, which way was it? She couldn't quite rememb—

Movement drew her attention to the right, and she had a split-second impression of something hazy and white disappearing around the corner.

She rubbed her eyes, fighting down another bout of nausea. "Seeing things," she mumbled, but nonetheless walked in the direction of the movement. "Visual and auditory hallucinations."

But that was wrong. Even in her current state, she knew the symptoms of opioid withdrawal, and hallucinations were not typically amongst them. Despite that clinical assertion, she was too sick to argue with her senses. Feeling was believing. She rounded the corner, meaning to assess whether this corridor was the correct one, and froze.

Carrie stood halfway down the hallway looking at her.

Gillian wobbled, her left leg failing her as she fell against the nearest wall. She stared at her daughter, willing the image to evaporate, but it didn't.

Carrie wore the long nightshirt she normally slept in. It was her favorite. Even from the distance, Gillian could make out the pattern of small pink boats dotting it.

"C-Carrie?" Gillian said.

The girl's face was expressionless. Giving no sign she'd heard her, Carrie turned away, walking quickly down the hall.

"Carrie!" Gillian yelled, trying to hurry forward. Both legs gave out, and she hit her knees, skidding painfully to her hands. She crawled after her daughter, who had stopped at a doorway.

This was real. How? How had Carrie gotten here?

The door slid open as Gillian regained her feet and stumbled onward. Carrie stepped through out of sight.

The door hissed shut.

"Carrie!" Four more lunging steps and she bounced off the opposite wall and slid to a stop in front of the door Carrie had disappeared through.

It was the airlock leading to the shuttle, and Carrie stood not by the port they'd entered through originally, but by another, larger bay door. Her small white hand stretched out and touched the control panel, and Gillian heard the access before her lock securely.

There were three short beeps, then quiet.

It took Gillian half a second to realize what was happening before she started screaming.

The outer bay doors began to open as Carrie turned to face her. There was a slight visible change in the airlock's atmosphere as the oxygen was sucked out, and Carrie gazed up as Gillian pounded on the window, every molecule in her being willing it not to happen.

Carrie smiled.

An unseen force ripped her small body free of the bay, and she was gone.

"No!" Gillian fumbled with her key card, her hand bloodied from smashing it into the door. She scanned the card across the control panel, mind numbed in complete horror. Awash in the abysmal grief, she realized her mistake too late.

She would be pulled out into the void as well. Not that it mattered now that Carrie was gone. Nothing did.

But the anticipated yank of decompression didn't come.

Gillian blinked, standing on the airlock's threshold.

The bay doors were closed. Sealed tight.

Their space suits were all accounted for, all neatly arranged with their helmets resting above them on a shelf.

She moved into the bay, feet trying to tangle themselves. Struggling not to be sick again, she peered out the small viewing pane beyond the ship.

Stars rotated past.

Silence.

Gillian reached out to the control pad beside the bay doors and touched it. The screen flashed red, and the words KEY CARD AND PASSCODE REQUIRED appeared.

It wasn't real. She'd imagined it.

Hallucinated the whole thing.

It was as if she were crashing back into herself from somewhere far away. She inhaled great whooping breaths, relief washing over her as her mind refastened itself to its moorings.

Of course it wasn't real. Carrie's on Earth.

The reasoning gathered another layer of calm around her like an added blanket. But even as it did, the reality of what had just happened stripped it away. She couldn't trust her eyes anymore.

Couldn't trust herself.

◆　◆　◆

Gillian found the pry bar packed in foam just like all the other tools in the clasped toolbox. The box itself was secured to one wall in a cramped maintenance closet in the hall between Quads Two and Three.

Tools of all shapes and sizes were carefully arranged in the multi-tiered box, most of which she assumed were for spacewalks and repairs to the exterior of the ship; several cable-woven lengths of tethers supported her assumption.

But she had no use for any of the other equipment. She just needed the pry bar.

Its steel shaft was cold in her hand as she walked unsteadily down the corridors, and she studied its broad end of flattened iron as well as the handgrip that terminated in a round ball of steel.

Gillian had to pause several times on the way to control, lightheadedness and her sloshing stomach trying to send her to the floor. Each time she steadied herself, replaying the image of Carrie being sucked out of the airlock, and it was enough to get her moving again.

She scanned in to control and moved to medical, stopping directly before the small panel inset she was sure held the drugs. She raised the flat end of the bar and tried wedging it into the sealed edge of the compartment.

It slipped free as she began to pry, the muscles in her arms betraying her. "Shit," she swore, lining up the bar's edge again, trying to find purchase in the seal.

Resistance torqued against her as she pried.

It was working.

She pushed harder, her breath blasting out of her with the effort.

The bar slipped free again and sent her crashing into the counter. Sweat ran down her forehead, plastering her hair to the sides of her face. Gillian reset herself, ramming the bar into the seal as hard as she could. It bounced away, chipping a piece of texture from the wall. The impotence of the situation overcame her, and she slammed the heavier end of the bar into the center of the panel. It rattled but gave no indication of breaking.

She swung again.

And again.

And again.

Each time the bar shivered in her hands like a rung bell, sending vibrations of pain through her hands and arms. She brought the bar back one more time and stopped, breathing hard.

The panel was scratched and chipped, but there were no buckles, no give when she pushed on it.

"Okay. Okay, you bastard," she said between breaths. She stalked out of medical and scanned in to stasis.

Everything was the same as when she'd last been inside the area. The urge to check each unit's occupation status was strong, but she veered away from them to the lockers across the aisle. If she couldn't get the drugs by force, she'd use finesse.

Leo's locker was located diagonally from his unit, the gap between its door and frame even thinner than the panel in med bay. Nevertheless, she jammed the bar's end at the gap. It slid uselessly down, peeling a curl of paint off as it went.

"Goddammit!" She stabbed the locker twice more before turning the bar around to bash it with the handle. Gillian put her remaining strength as well as the simmering anger behind each swing, an ear-shattering clang making her wince at each connection.

Her frustration hit a boiling point.

In one motion Gillian spun away from the locker, cocked the bar over one shoulder like a bat, took a step, and swung as hard as she could at Tinsel's stasis unit.

The steel bounced off the pod's lid, sending the bar spinning free of her hands and through the nearby doorway.

She stood, panting, shoulders rounded and heaving, tremors running through her like swimming eels.

There wasn't even a mark where she'd hit Tinsel's unit, but as she swayed drunkenly in place, the reality of what she'd done closed in.

If he had been standing there, she would've bashed his brains in.

Gillian spun away, vomiting up a tablespoon of bile and mucus. She coughed, tears mixing with the sweat that dripped from the tip of her nose.

What the hell was she doing? What had she become?

She needed to get out of here, away from what she'd done.

Her legs carried her as far as control, and as she passed the pry bar, she faintly considered taking it, but the effort to retrieve it would've been titanic. Even walking was too much now.

She stumbled and barely caught herself before her face connected with the cold, sterile floor, its whiteness filling her vision.

And she drifted into it like a ghost mingling with fog.

TWENTY-TWO

Gillian came to crawling down the hallway.

The tangled mess of her hair was the first thing she saw, its mass like thick cobwebs distorting everything beyond.

Her hands throbbed each time she put pressure on them. Probably from pounding on the airlock window, maybe from the pry bar's reverberations.

The last few hours came back to her then, and she scooted to the wall, using it to lean against. How she'd got out of control she didn't know. Must've managed to stand and scan her key card. Dizziness assaulted her like a swarm of hovering wasps.

She needed water.

Needed food.

After three tries, she was able to stand and plod to the lounge. Inside she pawed a meal pack from storage but didn't bother heating it. Hunger clawed at her stomach even as the thought of eating sent a shudder of revulsion through her.

Concentration and will.

Spoonful after spoonful she ate the high-caloric mixture and sipped water, stifling her gag reflex the entire time.

When she'd downed half the meal, she pushed away from the table and collapsed on the bench seat, shivering and sweating beneath a blanket.

Consciousness came and went, fever dreams pulling her into melting worlds with capering demons disguised as people she knew, or thought she knew. There were unholy sounds, screams from ravaged throats. There was heat strong enough that she could feel her skin blistering, then cold so deep her veins became December streams.

Gillian woke to more whispering, sure it would fade with the nightmares as she cracked one eye open.

The room yawed hard to the right, but even with the vertigo, she saw the door to the lounge sliding shut.

She bolted upright, an electric current of pain sizzling in her head, heart fluttering out of control.

She'd seen it. Seen the door closing. She wasn't asleep. She was wide-awake.

You also saw your daughter get ripped out of an airlock. You can't trust your eyes.

Over the sound of her pulse, she heard something else.

Footsteps receding down the hallway. Quiet, but there.

Gillian struggled to her feet and listened again. She wavered, all concentration centered on standing and listening.

Nothing.

No. There. Wasn't that another door opening somewhere?

She moved to the lounge's entrance, hesitantly bringing her key up to the scanner. What if there was someone right outside, waiting for her? Waiting to lunge and grab her as soon as the door opened? She imagined she could hear whoever it was, their excited breathing barely audible through the barrier.

She scanned the key card. The door slid open.

Empty.

Gillian stepped into the corridor and stopped as another sound met her.

Definitely a door closing or opening in the next hall.

She felt like a mouse in a field, the shadow of a hawk falling over her. She needed to get out of the hallway, but an idea suddenly struck her, pulling her away from the lounge in the opposite direction of the sounds.

After scanning in to control, she settled in before one of the pedestals and touched the screen, mentally cursing herself for not thinking of this sooner. After stopping several times to ward off bouts of dizziness, she managed to find the camera-option control.

ACCESS SYSTEM MULTI-VIEW

She touched the selection, and the screen split into a dozen different viewpoints of the ship.

There were angles of the lab, the rats scurrying in their cages, various empty hallways in the crew-quarter areas, but the external camera pane was the one that snagged her attention and held it.

Floating in the dark void of space was Mars.

The planet was still small and indistinct, but she could make out its definitive reddish hue and what appeared to be darker patches, which she could only assume were impact craters or crevasses.

The sight transfixed her. Enough so that the vertigo and nausea felt as if they belonged to someone else. Even the unsettling fear of the hallucinations became muted.

Her destination was in sight. She was going to another planet. Awe settled over her, and she wondered faintly if this was what people had felt the first time they'd understood what those distant points of light were in the night sky.

Movement in the lower right corner of the screen brought her attention back to the present.

The view was of the airlock. As she watched, the port leading to the shuttle settled into place.

There was a plunging in the middle of her stomach that had nothing to do with the withdrawals.

Someone had just closed the hatch.

No, you're seeing things again.

Slowly her gaze left the screen and fixed on the door to stasis.

One of them was awake.

Who was it, and what were they doing?

Hesitantly she rose and was about to scan her key card when she stopped. If one of the crew was awake, they could have manipulated their pod's display to make her think they were still in stasis.

That would explain everything.

But the same question hounded her even as the explanation settled into place.

What are they doing?

She shifted to the left, and her foot nudged something that emitted a quiet clink as it rolled away.

The pry bar.

Gillian retrieved it from the floor, hefting its weight.

They had lied to her, drugged her, whisked her away from the only thing she kept breathing for. Whatever they were doing, it wasn't good.

She gripped the bar and headed for the corridor.

February 5, 2030.
Eighteen months after Discovery VI disaster.
Sci-Beat interview with James Conroy, former mission operations
program manager for NASA.

Sci-Beat (SB): *Mr. Conroy, thank you so much for sitting down with us.*
James Conroy (JC): *My pleasure.*
SB: *I know you've had a lot on your schedule over the past year with all of
the controversy surrounding the Discovery VI mission. You're no longer with
NASA, and you've written a book about your tenure there.*
JC: *I have. It's part memoir, but a good portion of it's dedicated to Discovery
VI—I know most people are going to pick it up more because of that than
to hear about my career.*
SB: *Well, that's a good jumping-off point: your career. You were an IT specialist in the navy for seven years. You worked briefly in Silicon Valley before
accepting a position with NASA. You spent seventeen years there heading
up five missions as program manager. My point being, there's been a lot of
criticism of the claims you've made in the last year, many people trying to
disparage your experience or record even though your career has been free of
scandal. What do you make of that?*
JC: *Well, it's like anyone who steps forward with information that goes
against the grain of what an establishment has stated: they're going to get
criticized. Someone's going to yell fraud; the next will say conspiracy theory.
It comes with the territory.*

SB: *In your book you mentioned the involvement of, and I quote, "several nameless contractors hired by the United Nations who were the direct contact points for the Discovery Mission. Everything ran through them. We were just the picket fencing in front of the suburban house—an official facade that concealed their secrets." End quote.*

JC: *That's right. I swear to God, every official I met who was a contact liaison for the mission was named John. They were all very cold and businesslike. Not people you'd hang out with for beers after work.*

SB: *So you're saying these men filtered information for the mission before handing it to you to interpret and present to operations?*

JC: *Yes. That's correct.*

SB: *Why do you think that was?*

JC: *Honestly? Because there was a lot more going on besides what was stated in the mission documents.*

SB: *Such as?*

JC: *I can only postulate on that because so much was restricted, but I did come across several memos mentioning an advanced transportation system. Some kind of revolutionary process that would change the way humankind moved from one place to another.*

SB: *So that was specifically why the UN was involved?*

JC: *I can almost bet on it.*

SB: *Beyond this possible transportation system, can you shed any light on the other, more shadowy aspects of the mission?*

JC: *[Laughs.] You mean the "space sickness" the Russians reported on?*

SB: *Yes, among other things.*

JC: *I can't say what actually caused the disaster, but a disease could've been a prominent factor. As far as space sickness goes, I'm not aware of any medical diagnosis that fits the observations noted by Dr. Ryan.*

SB: *That's another very interesting topic: Dr. Gillian Ryan. Do you believe the official reports released two weeks ago by the investigative committee formed by deputy administrator of NASA Anderson Jones?*

JC: *You mean the insinuations she was partially or directly responsible for the disaster itself?*
SB: *Yes.*
JC: [Long pause.] *I don't know. I was present when her distress call came in. It sure as hell didn't sound like someone who had caused what happened shortly thereafter. She sounded terrified but in control of her mental faculties. But that's the real question about all this, isn't it? Who really knows what a person is capable of?*

TWENTY-THREE

Her footsteps were unbelievably loud in the hall as she approached the airlock.

Over the last two months, she'd become more accustomed to the quiet of the ship, the sound of her breathing, talking to herself. It had become the norm.

But now, trying to stealthily sidle up to the airlock door while keeping her balance despite the urge to vomit, each noise made her wince internally.

Gillian stopped outside the door, risking a glance inside before ducking back out of sight.

Everything seemed to be in its place, and there was no one standing on the other side of the viewing pane.

She took a steadying breath, the iron bar cold and slick in her palms. What the hell was she going to do if she caught whoever it was inside? Brain them with the bar? Of course not. Get some answers as to why they were skulking around the ship and scaring the shit out of her? Yes. Most definitely.

Another look through the window confirmed the airlock was still empty. Whoever it was must still be down in the shuttle. A vague warning bell chimed in the back of her mind. Something was wrong here, beyond the idea that one of the crew was sneaking around when they should be in stasis. When she tried to identify what it was, it slipped away like lyrics to a song heard only once.

It could be the fact that there's no one inside at all. You're sick and you've had a break with reality.

"I saw it," she whispered, and scanned her key card.

The door whisked open.

Silence. Stillness.

Gillian forced herself to move forward, eyes fastened on the port leading to the shuttle. Maybe she could simply wait here for them to come back out and confront them then. If they thought she was still asleep in the lounge, they wouldn't be cautious about their passage throughout the ship.

A tremor coursed through her, stabbing her stomach with cramps. No, there would be no stakeout for her. She needed to confront whoever it was, find out what they were doing, and get to a bathroom.

Unlatching the port, she drew back the cover, revealing the ladder leading down into the shuttle.

It was dark inside. She hadn't anticipated the darkness. Hadn't thought to bring a flashlight. But the more uncomfortable notion rose with the blackness eating the ladder just below the third rung: What were they doing down there alone in the dark?

She licked her cracked lips, readying to call out. Should she say anything? Whoever it was, they were up to something nefarious; that was for certain. But what would their reaction be when they realized they were caught? She couldn't imagine any of the crew becoming violent, but even as the thought crossed her mind, she recalled Tinsel jabbing the needle into her shoulder. If she was honest with herself, she didn't know any of these people well except Birk and Carson, and Carson's actions hadn't exactly elevated her trust.

She peered into the darkness, trying to see if anything was moving within it. Had something shifted down there? Gillian leaned over, clutching the bar close. She opened her mouth, finally deciding to call out, but a sound stopped her.

Her skin prickled with gooseflesh so strong it felt as if she'd stepped into an iron maiden.

Because the noise hadn't come from the space below.

It had come from behind her.

She turned and looked down the row of space suits hanging neatly on their hooks, and all at once the needling sensation from before snapped into utter clarity.

When she'd seen the movement on the screen in control, one of the suit hooks had been empty.

Now they were all full.

The suit two steps down from her came alive.

Even as she screamed and stumbled back, barely missing the open port at her feet, she noticed the helmet attached to its top.

The suit reached toward her, trying to snag the front of her jumpsuit.

She batted the hand away, feeling the bar sliding in her grip.

Then the suit was stepping away from the wall and coming toward her, its animation something out of a nightmare.

But what filled up the helmet's visor was so much worse.

Kent's rotting face stared out at her.

His eyes were gone, sunken into black holes, the skin a leathery parchment over jutting cheekbones. His lips were blackened worms, shriveled away from yellow teeth. And she knew in the split second before he lunged at her that she was seeing what he looked like in the grave. This was his face after eight years underground.

Her scream tore free as his hand closed on her wrist.

Gillian twisted away and fell to the floor, the bar skidding ahead of her as she tried to gain her feet.

Her mind threatened to unhook then. What would her husband's corpse do to her once it pinned her down?

Gloved fingers snagged her ankle.

Her sanity flickered like a lamp during a lightning storm.

She pushed forward, breaking his grip, and scooped up the bar.

With a burst of adrenaline, she turned and swung the steel.

The heavy handle whistled around and caught him high in the chest.

He grunted in pain and staggered to the side. A part of her mind chanted to keep swinging. Crack the helmet open and dash whatever was inside it to pieces, because it was an abomination, something evil and unholy broken free of hell.

But the stronger part forced her to run.

Gillian fell against the airlock door, fumbling her key card in wooden fingers for an excruciating second before scanning it across the sensor.

Something grazed her hair, and she screamed as she barreled free of the airlock and down the hallway.

She was nothing but prey as she ran, panic and terror clouding her senses.

Where could she go? There was nowhere to hide.

Gillian pounded around the corner, air like acid each time she breathed in, the old injury in her leg throbbing. Ahead to the left was the entry to Quad One.

She slid to a stop, fumbling the key card again, and missed the scanner as she looked back the way she'd come.

The hallway was empty.

She tried scanning the key card without looking, unable to wrench her gaze away from the nearest corner.

What if she'd imagined it all? What she'd seen—it wasn't possible. It wasn't—

Kent rounded the corner and ran toward her, arms pumping at his sides, features mercifully lost in the reflection of his visor.

An animalistic cry came from her, and she scanned the key card, turning to slide through the opening door.

She fled past Tinsel's and Birk's rooms.

Around the corner to her own.

She barely slowed as she swiped her key and hurtled through the doorway, almost pausing to try locking her berth, but it required a four-digit code that was blurred now by fear.

Her feet skidded out from her as she crossed the room, her leg flaring with pain as the bar slipped from her grasp, pinwheeling once before disappearing beneath the bed.

No time to retrieve it. She could hear him in the hallway. Hear his footsteps coming closer.

She slung herself up and into the tiny bathroom, slammed the door shut, and scrabbled at the lock. Her fingers were mutinous, unable to turn the mechanism.

She heard the door to her room open.

Turn the lock.

He was right outside.

Turn the lock!

There was a small click as her fingers twisted.

The lock engaged, and half a second later, the door rattled in its frame.

Gillian plastered herself against the opposite wall, a moan of terror escaping her.

The door shook again. Could he get through? Would he find the pry bar and force his way in? And, oh God, what would he do when he got inside?

Oh God, please, please make him go away, please, please, please, please.

Over the sound of her labored breathing and machine-gun pulse, there was a sliding footstep.

A long pause.

At that moment the fear was too much. The urge to reach out and unlock the door and simply end it was so powerful, she found her hand twitching toward the knob.

Gillian laced her fingers and clenched her palms together in supplication.

"Please, please, please," she whispered.

Another sound came from the room, and her breath fishhooked her lungs.

The door had opened and closed.

Was he gone, or just quietly waiting outside?

She swallowed, gathering the nerve to press her ear against the bathroom door. Listened.

Nothing.

No movement.

She waited for nearly five minutes before easing away. It seemed he was gone.

But had he really been there at all?

Yes. She'd seen him, felt the bar connect with his chest. But even now the memory had taken on the melting quality of a dream, the details blurring into one another like paint splattered with turpentine.

All at once she couldn't stand anymore and sunk to the floor, then scooted as far away from the door as she could into the shower. She drew up her legs and became as small as possible, rocking back and forth. Maybe it had been another hallucination, like seeing Carrie. Maybe she wasn't even in the bathroom right now. Maybe she was asleep in stasis like all the others and the last two months had happened solely in her mind.

She whimpered, pressing the heels of her hands to her eyes. Pain thudded softly in her right wrist, and she pulled her hands away, glancing down.

An angry blaze of red encircled her wrist. Kent had grabbed her there in the airlock. It was proof she wasn't imagining things. But did she actually believe what her eyes had told her? Her husband's corpse had attacked her, pursued her to her room, tried to break through the bathroom door?

The room swam around her, and tears slipped from the corners of her eyes as she pulled her knees even tighter to her chest, focusing on the one thing she knew was real.

Sweating and trembling, she pictured Carrie, recalling their last hug, and whispered the final thing she'd said before letting her go.

"It'll be okay. Forever. Forever. Forever . . ."

Audio file transcript—#179088 August 5, 2028.

I think I saw him again.

Kent. In the hallway near control. I don't . . . don't know.

Someone was there. I can't . . . [Heavy breathing.] *can't tell what's real anymore. Ran all the way back to my room and locked the bathroom door again.*

Been in here for a day at least. Only left because I had to get food, had to eat.

Shakes are bad. Can't concentrate. So dizzy. Don't know if this will ever end.

I'm . . . [Inaudible.] *so sorry, honey. I should've never left you. Never left. Miss you so much. I want you to know that if I don't come back . . .*

I did this for you.

[End of recording.]

TWENTY-FOUR

Gillian stepped out of the shower and dried off, running her fingers loosely through her hair.

The square mirror above the sink revealed the trauma of the last two weeks, everything told in the dark bags beneath her eyes, the sallow skin of her face. Shame tugged at her again like a riptide. The feeling was nothing new; she assumed most addicts harbored it more or less all the time, but this was a different animal altogether. How messed up had she been to see and feel the things she had?

Downing a bunch of hydros over a short period of time and not recalling it, that's how messed up you were, sister.

It was the only explanation for everything. At some point she must have lost track of time and binged on more pills than she ever had before. Probably spilled the rest down the sink without realizing it.

And the withdrawals had been the fallout.

God. She didn't even want to think about it right now. It had been only a day since she'd last thrown up, and the weakness was still a constant companion. But as bad as the physical suffering had been, it was nothing compared to the mental side of things.

The hallucinations had been so real.

Gillian recalled the fear and sense of clarity of the visions, but the actual memories were shrouded outlines of a fever dream. None of it made sense now or coalesced into anything resembling reality.

Carrie opening the airlock and being pulled out.

The space suit coming to life, Kent's putrid face filling its visor.

The intermittent thumps and bangs accompanied by phantom footsteps.

Her mind had manufactured all of it.

But now she was free.

She left the bathroom and surveyed the rest of the berth. The floor was littered with half a dozen food-pack casings and two water bottles. Soiled clothes filled up one corner, and the blankets of her bed were a tangled and stained mess. She recalled leaving the room in a terrified scramble at one point, sick but starving, and raiding the lounge before hurrying back here. She'd thought she'd seen something then. Someone in the hall. Just another flicker of her struggling psyche. Afterward, the withdrawals had started loosening their grip. More and more rationality returned with each day. Enough so that she'd quit sleeping in the bathroom behind the locked door and returned to her bed.

Taking a deep breath, she set about getting dressed in the last clean jumpsuit she had, wincing as she gripped the zipper to draw it closed. There was a shallow cut across the meat of her palm she had no recollection of receiving. Just another span of missing time like so many others over the past two weeks. But, of course, it wasn't only the last two weeks. How much time had she given away to the addiction over the years? Too much.

Gillian sighed. It was the truth, but all she could do now was go forward. She'd been given another chance by having survived quitting cold turkey, and her thoughts felt clearer than they had in a long time.

Slowly she began picking up the trash strewn about the room. She nearly gagged at the smell of her clothes and, not knowing what else to do, shoved them onto the floor of the closet. Next she stripped the bed and deposited the sheets and blanket with her clothes. It was actually beginning to look like a normal person's room. She bent to retrieve a water bottle that had rolled beneath the bed and paused.

The pry bar was gone.

For a moment she frowned, wrestling with her memories. She had dropped it here while fleeing a phantasm of her mind, had watched it roll under the bed, and she didn't recall ever retrieving it, not even when she'd left to gather food. But that didn't necessarily mean she hadn't. There were more than enough explanations about where it might have ended up, and she didn't have the energy left to parse all the drug-addled decisions she'd made.

Straightening up the rest of the room, she took account of everything. It wasn't perfect, but if someone were to glance inside, the first emotion they'd feel wouldn't be alarm or disgust. The smell might be another story, but for now it was the best she could do.

Gillian grabbed the lanyard attached to her key card and looped it over her head, then braced one hand against the wall as a bout of vertigo came and went. She wasn't completely out of the withdrawal woods yet.

She left the berth, taking her time as she moved down the hallways. The corridors and quiet solitude of the rooms no longer had the same effect on her as they had before her descent. Now they were just hallways, empty rooms. Nothing frightening or menacing beyond what her mind had created.

As she scanned in to control, trepidation settled over her. Going by the date Leo had written in his notes, the crew would be waking today. Gillian glanced in the direction of medical, picturing the damaged panel she'd tried to pry open. She'd cleaned up the station as well as she could, but there would be a lot of explaining to do. On the bright side, she had the breakthrough with the neural mapping to show for her time spent awake, and that intrinsic value was undeniable.

Gillian settled into one of the seats before a pedestal screen. She hadn't been inside stasis since the day she'd tried to pry open Leo's locker to retrieve his key card. Maybe she should go in and try cleaning up the damage she'd caused. She stood from the seat but made no move toward the next room. Because, really, there was no way she could make the destruction unnoticeable. She would have to own up to it like every other choice she'd made; there was no alternative. At least she hadn't done anything worse than scratch some paint and mar up a panel.

She registered a flare of excitement as she settled back into the chair. Once everyone was out of stasis and she'd explained what had happened, perhaps she could convince Carson to get a message to Carrie and Katrina. He owed her that much at the very least.

She held on to the idea of actually being able to see Carrie's face for the next half hour while she waited, lost in the fantasy of hearing her voice and being able to tell her how much she loved her.

Just as she was considering a trip to the lounge for some water and a snack, she heard the first sounds coming from stasis. Gillian rose from the chair and approached the other room's door. Yes, she could hear the distinctive hiss of the pods opening.

Bracing herself, she scanned her key card, and the door opened.

Inside, the units yawned like giant mouths. She spotted Birk's at once, the man himself stirring within, and a surge of emotion nearly overcame her. She hadn't realized how much she'd missed him. The sensation increased with seeing the others emerging from the pods, their movements sluggish, like houseflies in midwinter. The isolation and fear she'd endured over the last couple of months fled, and despite the lingering anger at seeing him, she found herself tearing up as Carson moved toward her down the center of the room.

Gillian took a step forward, a greeting on the tip of her tongue, but stopped.

There was a look of alarm on his face that she didn't understand until she followed his gaze.

Tinsel's unit was still closed, and it took her several seconds to see why.

Two of the heavy tether straps she'd seen in the maintenance closet were wrapped tightly around the entire pod, preventing the lid from rising more than an inch. But her gaze held on the strange sight only for a moment before it was drawn to something long and shiny on the floor beside the unit.

She took two steps to the right, the area behind the pod coming into view.

The pry bar lay beside a jumble of supply tubes and wires running from the room's wall into the rear of the stasis unit. Halfway down their length, they'd been severed roughly, jagged exposed copper and bent aluminum shining in the light.

Gillian stared, shifting her eyes from the sealed unit to the broken tubes, to the pry bar lying on the floor, and back again before she was shoved aside.

Carson pushed past her and fell to his knees at the base of the pod. His hands worked at the tether straps, shoulders and back flexing with effort beneath his suit. All the while voices began asking questions throughout the room, and more of the crew crowded in around them. Gillian felt a fluttering in the back of her skull: the scene before her wasn't computing.

Didn't make sense.

Her eyes fell from where Carson worked to the pry bar, and she tried to swallow the dryness that was consuming her mouth and throat.

There were dark-red smears on the bar's handle, dried almost black, and more of the stains beneath the separated supply lines.

Blood.

Slowly her gaze slid down to the healing gash on her right hand.

Everything took on the surreal quality of a dream, and she wondered if she was still in the grip of withdrawal, if this was just another heinous delusion.

There was a guttural grunt and a quiet clack of metal releasing. Carson stood, yanking the two tethers free before grasping the unit's lid and lifting it.

The smell was instantaneous, spurring unbidden images in her mind's eye.

Putrefied meat left in the sun.

Crawling maggots.

Death.

Someone gagged and spun away as Gillian made herself step forward.

Tinsel's eyes were open and swollen in their sockets, his jaw gaping wide, something blackened inside it that might've once been a tongue. There were bloody furrows in the skin of his face as if he had scratched himself, and when she was able to tear her eyes away from his features, she saw that his fingers were curled into crimson claws, blunted with the effort of trying to escape the locked confines of his unit.

For a drawn second, it seemed as if they were all in stasis again, transfixed by the horror contained within the pod.

Carson broke free of the moment's grip and reached into the pod to press his fingers below Tinsel's hanging jaw.

He stood that way for a beat, the miniscule hope within Gillian extinguishing as he turned away from what was now a coffin.

His eyes flitted across the rest of them, burning with intensity as they landed on her and held.

"My God, Gillian. What have you done?"

Audio file transcript: Recorded transmission by Dr. Gillian Ryan to unnamed UN official.
August 6, 2028—eleven days prior to rendezvous with UNSS. Fifteen days before Discovery VI disaster.

Dr. Ryan: *Can you hear me?*
UN: *Gillian. I didn't expect you to call again.*
Dr. Ryan: *There's someone here. On the ship.*
UN: *There's several people on the ship. They're called the crew. Gillian, are you okay?*
Dr. Ryan: *They're all supposed to be sleeping. One of them is awake. I know it. Carson lied. Tinsel lied. They're still lying. I can hear them whispering.*
UN: [Long pause.] *Are you all right, Gillian?*
Dr. Ryan: [Inaudible.] *The floors are bleeding. There's blood everywhere. It creeps under my door.* [Inaudible. Laughing.]
UN: *You should probably lie down before you hurt yourself. There's a lot at stake here. Remember what we talked about before?*
Dr. Ryan: *Yes. You wouldn't let me talk to her. Carrie.*
UN: *Gillian, I think you—*
Dr. Ryan: *You took her away from me.*
UN: *Gillian, your daughter's fine.*
Dr. Ryan: *I'll kill you. I'll kill all of you.*
[End of transmission.]

TWENTY-FIVE

She had thought the insomnia was bad coming out from under the hydrocodone shadow.

This was worse.

Her mind wouldn't stop running. It was a set of gears, sometimes meshing to form cohesive lines of thought, then disengaging, freewheeling, churning up disjointed memories.

Kent's breath hot on her neck while they slept inches apart.

Carrie's second birthday when she'd found her cake early in the refrigerator and pushed her entire face into it, taking half a dozen bites from it before Gillian could stop her. She'd had to sit down from laughing so hard, the sight of Carrie's tiny features covered in blue frosting too much to handle.

The rat's neurons firing in wave upon wave, its hippocampus lighting up like condensed fireworks.

Tinsel's dead body, bloated and staring out at her from inside the stasis unit. Eyes accusing, cursing her.

Gillian sat up on the bed and swung her feet to the floor. She breathed in through her nose, out through her mouth, all the while trying to shake the last image. But it wouldn't leave her. It was like an afterimage from staring at something overly bright, except there was no merciful dulling in her mind's eye.

She saw everything. Remembered everything.

With the stasis unit severed from the wall, the chemical compound keeping Tinsel in suspension had stopped. That meant he had woken up in the dark without food, without water, trapped by the tethers as if buried alive, and after an unknown number of days clawing his fingers to bloodied stumps, he'd died of dehydration.

She couldn't imagine a worse death.

Her stomach roiled at the thought of what the man had gone through, what she had done.

No. She hadn't. There was no way she could've done something like that. No way—

Gillian noticed the thumb of her left hand worrying the healing cut in her right palm and closed both hands into fists. She wasn't a murderer. An addict, yes, but that was a far cry from having the capacity to kill another human being. But even as she tried assuring herself, the memory of striking Tinsel's pod with the pry bar came back to her with utter clarity. In that moment she could've killed him; there was no lying to herself about that.

Had she done it? She put aside the automatic self-defenses of her mind and let the notion in, let it take full form. Yes, she'd hated Tinsel, hadn't liked him from the first time they'd met, but to inflict that kind of suffering on another person? Murder him like that?

Everyone saw you punch him right before he went into stasis. You looked like an absolute psychopath. And now they know how fucked up you were on the pills. You could have done anything and not realized it.

She tried clearing her mind, imagining the familiar tempest within slowly calming before retracing every memory she could recall over the last several weeks, looking for an instance she could pin down as reality. Mostly it was blurred images, sickness, and lightning strikes of fear that still brought goose bumps to her skin.

Gillian walked past the bed, turned at the desk, and took the four steps before having to about-face at the bathroom door. It had been three days. Three days locked inside the room. Carson had led her here after opening Tinsel's unit, Easton following quietly behind them as she pled with them both. Carson had been beyond stony, unwilling to speak or acknowledge her. Even the grip on her arm had been like a rock: cold, strong, unmoving. The last thing she'd seen were his eyes as the door slid closed, and there had been no hint of the emotion that was there before he'd gone into stasis, when he'd been trying to tell her . . . tell her . . .

Gillian stopped pacing, listening for the sound she thought she'd heard in the hall. Maybe it was Leo bringing her meals again. The physician had been the only one she'd seen since being incarcerated. Initially he'd simply checked her over, taken a blood sample, asked several questions about her addiction, if she was suffering from any other ailments. When she'd broached the subject of Tinsel's death, he'd stiffened and left the room, abandoning her to her churning thoughts, and the doubt.

"I would remember it," she said, beginning to pace again. But the truth was, she had no idea if she would remember it or not.

And at that moment, alone and terrified of herself—of what she might have done—she'd never missed Carrie or their life as much.

The sound of someone approaching her door slowed her movement, and she waited, watching as it slid open.

Birk stood there, completely filling up the doorway.

"May I come in, Doctor?"

Her held breath whooshed out, and she embraced him as he stepped inside. He patted her back in his usual way. When he released her, she noticed he wasn't alone. Leo entered the room as well, nodding quickly at her.

"I'm sorry I couldn't come sooner. It was . . . forbidden," Birk said.

"Carson needed some time before—" Leo began, gesturing once with his hand before dropping it to his side.

Time to decide what to do with me.

161

Gillian lowered herself to the bed while Birk perched on the desk. Awkwardness filled the air before Birk cleared his throat and said, "I had no idea, Doctor."

She glanced at the floor. This was why she'd gotten clean before completely on her own. The shame had been too much. "No one did," she managed. "Maybe some people wondered, but no one knew."

"How long?"

"For a year and a half after Kent died. Then I quit until Carrie was diagnosed, and I fell off the wagon." She held her palms up and dropped them back to her lap—*and here we are.*

"You're not on the pills now?" Birk asked, shifting his eyes from her to Leo.

"No. I . . . I was done with them weeks ago. Still weak and shaky, but they're gone." When no one spoke or moved, she pushed forward. "I didn't kill him."

Birk licked his lips. "Doctor, they showed me the damage in the medical bay and on the locker."

"I know, I know. I did that, I remember doing it. But . . ." *But what?* "The cameras," she said, the ray of hope flaring inside her again. "Leo, there's surveillance on the ship, right?"

The physician met her gaze but quickly looked at his feet. "Yes." And in the way he said that one word, her hope was extinguished. "The internal cameras' archives were disabled shortly after we went into stasis. Nothing was recorded."

"What? No, that's not possible. I didn't touch any of the controls. I didn't." Her entire body felt as if it had been injected with novocaine. This wasn't happening. "It had to be someone else. I don't even know how to work the cameras." Neither Leo nor Birk would look at her. "Goddammit! I didn't touch the controls!" Her voice rang off the walls, and the desperation in it made it sound alien. Gillian swallowed, trying to keep her voice even. "I saw someone, someone else on the ship. Someone was awake. One of the others, they had to be. I thought I was hallucinating, but now I realize they must have been real. They turned the recordings off, they killed Tinsel."

"Gillian. Who? We were all in stasis," Leo said.

"I don't know. But it's possible, right? What if someone were awake? They could climb in and out of their pod and it would look like they were asleep."

Leo seemed to struggle with something. "Yes, it's possible. But we're talking two months of time spent on and off inside the unit as well as evading you when they were outside."

"I saw the door to control closing. Thought it was somebody waking up early and followed them inside. There was a smell in medical, like someone had just been there."

"Gillian, you're not making any sense," Leo said, grimacing. "The blood on the pry bar, it was yours."

A wave of unreality washed over her. "No. That's—" She was about to say "impossible," but already she was looking down at her hand, at the healing cut, still red and ragged.

"I think you were having visual and auditory hallucinations due to withdrawals. And . . ."

She shook her head, vision swimming with tears. "You don't hallucinate coming off opiates."

"Each person is unique. It may have affected you differently."

So there it was. While she'd been locked away, everyone had decided she was guilty.

An emptiness filled her as if everything vital were draining away.

Leo cleared his throat. "We need to go to control. We'll be docking with the station shortly."

"What will happen to me once we get there?" she asked.

"I don't know." He motioned toward the door, and she rose, half expecting her legs to give out. When they didn't, she glanced at Birk. He looked crestfallen and pale, but what hurt the most was the angry set of his jaw. He was furious at her.

They left the room, Leo leading the way with Birk bringing up the rear. As they walked, her mind ran forward, leapfrogging through the next few months until they returned to Earth. What would happen when they landed? She supposed she would be formally charged.

And Carrie. How would she explain everything to her?

Gillian's throat drew shut, and she had to blink rapidly to keep tears from spilling free of her eyes. Even as despair tried to swallow her, the irony of the situation didn't escape her. She had been brought here to help shed light on a mystery—potentially solve a murder.

And now she was accused of committing one herself.

But the cameras . . . she knew she hadn't shut the recording off. And if she hadn't shut down the cameras, then it had been someone else. One of the others who had feigned stasis. But why? Why kill Tinsel and frame her?

The maelstrom of thoughts was swept aside as they neared control and Leo scanned them through.

The room was alive with movement and sound when they entered. Dozens of screens flickered with data, soft beeps and a robotic voice intoned something from somewhere overhead, and Lien and Carson were seated before two of the nearest pedestals.

Both of them looked over at her as she stepped into the room. She gazed back, feeling like some dangerous virus beneath a microscope.

"Everyone can get settled in," Carson said, bringing his attention back to the screen before him. "We'll be docking in ten minutes."

Leo led her to one of the rearmost seats in the room and told her to buckle the two sets of safety harnesses across her legs and chest as the others did the same. Birk sat to her left, and though she stared at the side of his head, he refused to meet her eyes.

Easton appeared several minutes later, glancing her way briefly before reporting to Carson. "Airlock is go for attachment, and all external apparatus are prechecked."

"Thank you," Carson said, nodding toward the seat beside him. "We're two from docking sequence."

A bank of screens lit up across the command area, and red light coated the room.

Mars filled the entire display with its murky glow.

Despite everything, Gillian was awestruck once more. The planet was so much closer now, vivid and looming in a way that made her feel insignificant, lonely, and mesmerized all at once.

As Carson and Lien spoke back and forth to each other as well as into the headsets they wore, Gillian noticed something on the planet's surface.

No, not on the surface. Above it.

The object was shaped like a pyramid, its base wide and rounded with two more levels stacked one after the other, each progressively smaller. Four square supportive columns extended upward from the base and met at a blunted point above the third level. As they neared it, the station took on more definition, stabilization struts spanning like a steel spiderweb between the different sections, which were coated with dozens of reflective panels. Gillian assumed they were solar shields that also doubled as collection points for power.

The station grew and grew until it blotted out the camera's entire field of view. Carson rattled off a checklist at high speed, which Lien confirmed while the ship began to turn sharply, arcing in gracefully to parallel the station's nearest angled column.

"Docking initiated," Carson said, seeming to be listening to someone through his headset. "Confirmed. Contact in five, four, three, two, one."

A slight vibration traveled through the floor, and the camera's view stuttered once.

"Attachment couplings secure," Lien said.

"Sync airlocks," Carson replied.

"Syncing."

The ship shuddered and then was still.

"Secure," Lien said.

Carson glanced around, his gaze finding Gillian briefly before he unbuckled himself and stood. "Welcome to Mars."

TWENTY-SIX

They transferred to the station via the airlock she'd watched Carrie get sucked out of.

Hallucinated, she reminded herself. Gillian glanced at the row of space suits as they passed, an unconscious shiver running through her when her eyes fell on the one that she'd seen Kent's face in.

The airlock led to another chamber much like the one they'd left, except larger and with hinged storage cabinets and benches below them lining each wall. The door thunked shut with finality behind them, and after several seconds, the one ahead slid open.

A wide, curving hallway met them along with two tall men in dark-gray jumpsuits, their hair military short, faces slack as they stood to one side of the entry.

"Commander LeCroix?" one asked, nodding to Carson.

"That's right," Carson said, shaking the man's hand.

"Stephen Vasquez." Vasquez's gaze found Gillian, pinned her to where she stood. "This her?"

"Yes," Carson said, stepping aside as Vasquez and the other man approached.

"Come with us, ma'am," Vasquez said, gesturing to the left of the airlock.

"Where are you taking me?" she asked.

"Someplace secure for now," Carson answered as she passed him. His stony expression was gone, replaced by one of blankness. She could've been a piece of furniture being hauled away.

"Doctor?" Birk asked, taking a step in her direction.

"It's okay," she said as Vasquez placed a hand on his belt where a compact Taser hung. "I'll be fine."

They set off down the hallway, Vasquez on her left and the other man on her right. Neither touched her, but she could almost feel their hands on her arms and knew if she made any sudden moves, the sensation would become real.

The hallway continued to curve to the right, and she took in its paneled walls, their sections glinting a sterile white. Every so often a window would appear, giving the briefest impression of the void beyond. Her footsteps were light, airy in a way that made her feel like she could fly, and she guessed the gravity on the station was much like that of the ship. When she glanced over her shoulder for a last look at the group, they were already gone.

Ahead, a solid partition blocked their path, and Vasquez scanned a key card very much like the ones they used on the ship across a reader.

Part of the barrier slid aside, and they continued another dozen paces before slowing to a stop beside a door set in the left-hand wall. Again Vasquez scanned his key card and opened the door.

The room inside was narrow—she was sure she couldn't raise her arms without brushing her fingertips against the walls—with a low bed set below an expansive window looking out into the depths of space. Below, the red rim of Mars sliced the darkness, a vague aura drifting from its surface like blood diffusing in water, staining the room with its presence.

"There's a bathroom in the corner. Knock if you need anything," Vasquez said as she stepped inside.

"When will I—" But he was already gone, the door whisking shut like a horizontal guillotine.

Silence.

Gillian moved to the bathroom, turned the light on. Off. She stepped to the window and looked down.

This close, she could see the serrated definition of the canyons and dark yawning holes of impact craters on Mars's surface. Everything tinged in that blood glow.

It was hypnotic and unpleasant at the same time.

With another half turn, she gazed around the room. It was featureless. A prison cell if there ever was one. Maybe this was where she belonged. Tucked safe away where she couldn't hurt herself or anyone else.

She slumped to the bed, fatigue drawing her downward. It would've pulled her through the bed, the floor, right down to the red planet if it could've. But she knew sleep wouldn't come. That was the cruel reality. What she wanted, needed most, was miles away.

Instead, her mind spooled out, latching on to and discarding everything that had taken place over the recent months.

Aside from the lingering cravings for a hydro, the one thought that kept coming back was the cameras.

Their recording had been turned off. She hadn't done it. She was sure of that. Everything else, not so much. But it did mean one thing.

"There was someone else awake," she whispered to the room, and closed her eyes to the redness of Mars.

◆ ◆ ◆

The sound of the door shushing open brought Gillian up from sleep, utterly surprised at having drifted off.

Carson stood in the hallway, Vasquez's face hanging over his left shoulder. Carson watched her for a moment before saying, "I'll be out in a minute."

He stepped inside, and the door shut behind him.

Gillian blinked away the vestiges of sleep, orienting herself as quickly as possible.

"How are you feeling?" Carson asked, leaning against the wall beside the door.

"Cramped," she said, waving a hand at the tiny room. "But at least the ambience is nice."

They were quiet for a time. She waited, not wanting to be the first to speak.

"You didn't have to do it," Carson finally said, his voice barely audible.

"Carson, I—"

"I know we misled you, but this . . ."

"I didn't kill him."

"Your blood was on the bar, Gillian. Come on."

She held out her hand. "I have no recollection of this cut."

"From what Leo tells me, you don't remember much of anything."

"I remember, it's just . . . hazy. Indistinct." She took a breath. "I hallucinated, I know that, but I remember most of it—the luciferin test, trying to get into the medication panel and Leo's locker. But Tinsel . . ." She shook her head.

"This is my fault, I know that. I should've never brought you here."

"You should've told me the truth."

"And then what? You would have refused and gone back to your lab to run out of money. Then Carrie would've died."

"You don't know that," she said, stomach churning with his words. "And you sure as hell didn't have the right to bring me here."

"It's my fault," he repeated. "But that doesn't change the fact that a man is dead."

"I didn't kill him!"

"Then who did, Gillian? Who?"

"One of the crew. Someone else was awake. I saw them."

"Who?" Carson pushed away from the wall, not looking at her. "Who did you see?"

"I don't know, but there was someone else awake on that ship."

"Well, it wasn't Tinsel because he's dead," Carson said, ticking off a finger. "Your giant isn't a suspect, I'm sure, and I'm guessing you don't think it's Leo. So who's that leave? Lien, Easton, and me." He faced her. "You think I killed him?"

"Since I don't even know why you brought me here, I'd say anything is possible." She stood from the bed, anger forcing its way into her veins. "What are you getting out of all this?"

He stared at her. "I was promoted to commanding officer on the station."

"Then you probably didn't want Tinsel shutting this place down."

He shook his head. "You haven't changed, you know that?"

"Neither have you."

They gauged each other, and she held his gaze until he finally looked away.

"Shit, Gill. Seriously, what the hell?"

Some of her rancor drained at the defeat in his voice. He sounded exhausted.

"Look," she said after a moment. "I don't know exactly what happened on the ship, but Leo told me the cameras were messed with, and I know I didn't stop the recording. I don't even know how."

"There's a half dozen witnesses who saw you hit him."

"I know that. I despised the guy, but I didn't kill him." She watched him take a step toward the window and look out. "This is all so . . . wrong. Everything is wrong."

A beat.

"What happens now?" she asked.

"I don't know. I don't have any choice but to keep you here."

"What about the mission?"

He half laughed. "What about it?"

"We came here to solve a problem. I can help."

Carson eyed her before returning to the door. "No. That won't work."

"You can have a guard with me at all times. I'm unarmed."

"Gillian—"

"Let me help," she said. "Please. Lock me up, put me on trial when we get home, whatever, but let me try. Then at least Carrie . . ." Her throat tried to close, but she pushed on. "At least I can help her."

Carson stopped at the entryway, his fist hovering in front of the door before he pressed it flat, knuckles whitening. "I'm sorry," he said, and knocked. The door slid aside, and he stepped out, leaving her alone in the cell.

◆ ◆ ◆

The hours passed. Each one stretching longer than the last.

She watched Mars, part of her registering they weren't orbiting but seemed to be anchored in place, impossibly unmoving above the planet's surface. The fact tried to ignite the scientific portion of her mind: Was it some new technology, like the one that had brought them here in the first place? But her thoughts came back to why. Why had all this happened?

She lowered herself to the bed, twining her fingers, one thumb rubbing against the gash in her palm. Tinsel had been coming here for what? To assess the situation, reexamine the mission and the promise of Ander's technology. What had his exact words been?

It's my job to evaluate whether this whole thing continues to move forward or is shut down and brought back to Earth for further study.

So there it was. Why?

Someone didn't want Tinsel to do his job. She reconsidered every-one on the ship. Who would want him to fail? Who would want the program to continue at all costs?

Think. Think. Think.

She didn't know any of the others enough to make a conclusion. Didn't know their motivations or standings.

But she would. She'd learn.

Hours or minutes later, her thoughts scattered as a sound came from the hallway.

The door slid away, revealing Carson. He stayed outside, one hand resting on the doorframe. He gazed around the room, then finally focused on her.

"Come with me. I'll show you why we're here."

TWENTY-SEVEN

"Elevators. Whole damn place is full of them," Carson said as he glared at the ceiling of the car they rode in, Vasquez standing in the left corner behind them, a watchful specter.

"Isn't that an unneeded risk? More moving parts?" Gillian asked, rubbing her wrist with one hand. Vasquez had snapped on a set of biting handcuffs before Carson could object, and by the time they'd removed them, grooves had already been dug in her flesh.

"Yeah. But the design of the station required it. Stairs weren't an option."

They rode in silence the rest of the way, the upward thrust of the elevator unlike those of Earth with the reduced gravity. It was more like she was floating skyward.

The car came to a stop without a sound, doors opening onto a corridor with dead ends in either direction. Ahead was an archway, a vestibule occupied by a dark-haired woman behind a utilitarian desk, a touchscreen before her.

"Commander LeCroix, nice to see you." Her smile faltered as she glanced at Gillian. "And your guest."

"I think Dr. Ander is expecting us," Carson said.

"He is. Go right in," she said, touching her screen. A ping issued from the door, and they went through.

They were halted almost immediately by the sectional couches.

There were three of them, cobbled together to make one large lounge that sprawled across the wide space before them. On the farthest wall was an immense flat screen that stretched from floor to ceiling and at least twenty feet across. At the moment, a scrawl of French was displayed there, the phrase somewhat familiar but escaping her at the moment. To the right was a featureless wall, double doors set in the middle, and to the left was an "L" of counter space cluttered with haphazardly stacked papers, a bank of touchscreens, and what appeared to be model airplanes set upon a small dais in neat rows.

A gray-haired man sat upon a rolling stool facing the closest touchscreen, his back to them. As the door slid closed, he turned, a smile breaking over his long face.

"Carson! My God, it's good to see you, son!" Eric Ander rose from the stool quickly, belying the movements of a man his age. He shook Carson's hand and grasped his forearm. "Apologies for not meeting with you until now."

"It's fine, Doctor, I know how busy you are. This is Dr. Gillian Ryan," Carson said.

"Nice to meet you," Gillian said, holding out her hand.

Ander gazed down, hesitating before shaking it. He gave her a fleeting look she couldn't read before he said to Carson, "You're sure about this?"

"No. But we need to try every option."

"Very well," Ander said.

Gillian's indignation at being discussed while standing right before them drained as Ander motioned to one of the couches. "I'll bring up the necessary information," he said.

Carson followed Gillian to the nearest seat as the doors in the right side of the room opened.

A man near their age emerged. He wore a pair of black slacks and a dress shirt, the sleeves unbuttoned and rolled up, exposing muscular forearms. He was clean-cut with dark hair trimmed close, a razor-line jaw, and eyes that were blue, sharpened points. Ander turned from the touchscreen he was working on, noticing the man moving toward them.

"Orrin, meet Commander Carson LeCroix and Dr. Gillian Ryan. This is my son, Orrin."

Orrin stopped before them, shaking Carson's hand first before gripping hers. A white threaded scar ran in front of his ear, disappearing into his hairline. Gillian recalled reading he had served overseas and seen direct action, receiving some kind of medal after coming home. She caught herself staring as he let go of her hand. "Good to meet you both, I—" Orrin said, something changing in his eyes as he looked at her. "Oh. You're . . ."

"She's here to be briefed on the situation," Carson said before clearing his throat.

Orrin glanced from him back to her before nodding. "Of course."

The huge flat screen lit up, a colorful line graph gracing its surface as they settled into their seats. "I won't bore you with pretense, Doctor. Instead, I'll get to the meat of it," Ander said, moving to stand before them. "Every human being alive at this point is aware of the effects of rising pollution rates. Major cities that never dealt with smog before now have air-quality issues. Declining water conditions are on the rise, catastrophic storms are becoming more and more common, and the recorded species extinction has nearly tripled in the last decade alone." He motioned at the screen. "These are the latest greenhouse-gas readouts released to the public from the Environmental Defense Organization, who did a two-year study in conjunction with NASA scientists. And these are the actual results."

Ander touched the screen in its center. The chart changed, the central column doubling from its prior position.

"In a word, their findings are devastating. The Earth's temperature increased one degree Fahrenheit in the twentieth century, which has caused monumental environmental problems, but I'm afraid it is nothing compared to what's coming. The study projects that within the next one hundred twenty years, the global temperature will rise another three degrees. To put it into context, the last ice age was only five degrees cooler than Earth's current temperature."

Gillian felt her brow crease. "What about the advancements in clean energy production? The last reports I heard—"

"Were purposefully inflated," Orrin broke in. He smiled sadly. "Too little too late, I'm afraid."

"But it has to have made a difference."

"Not nearly enough," Ander said, tapping the screen again. It changed to a time-plot line graph. "By the year 2135, the polar ice caps will not only be gone, but the sea will have begun to evaporate faster than the normal water cycle, causing increase in droughts, disease, disruptions in the food supply chains." He paused. "It will be the beginning of the end of life on Earth as we know it."

Gillian blinked, trying to absorb the information, but it was too large for her to fathom. "What are you saying? There's no hope?" She looked to Carson, whose mouth was a bloodless line.

Ander frowned. "There's always a chance that some other type of technology will be developed to battle the catastrophe but so far every advancement has been a failure. Partially this is due to the fact that the pollution accruement is still picking up speed from past years. Imagine a person trying to stop a semitruck that's rolling downhill by grabbing the rear bumper and digging their heels in. That's what the attempts have been like so far."

"I don't understand," she said. "What does all this have to do with your breakthrough? Why are we here?"

"Terraforming."

"Terraforming? You mean Mars? What—"

But the pieces were already connecting, forming a picture she could barely conceive, let alone put words to. "We're abandoning Earth," she managed finally, looking at Carson, who blinked once before training his eyes at the floor. "The teleportation is for when the terraforming is finished, isn't it? To mass transit the human population to Mars."

"You're headed in the right direction," Ander said, touching the screen again, and red light flooded the room. A single orb of bright crimson shone on the screen, its molten surface undulating. "This is Proxima Centauri, a red dwarf star, part of the Alpha Centauri system 4.2 light-years away from Earth. In early 2016, astronomers in South America confirmed the existence of an Earth-like exoplanet orbiting Proxima Centauri. The distance of orbit and all recorded conditions surrounding the discovery pointed to the possibility that this planet, Proxima b, could harbor liquid water, and potentially life." Ander ran a hand through his unruly hair. "Mars is an inhospitable planet. There are traces of liquid water, but it is briny. The temperature swings between day and night are extreme. In other words, Mars is not our destination. It is our testing grounds."

"There are three biospheres operating right now on the surface of Mars," Orrin said from beside her. His voice was quiet, almost airy. "The experiments in terraforming have gone well. That was the purpose for the station's positioning: to see if we could establish atmosphere and life in the harshest conditions away from available resources."

Anders nodded.

"So we're not moving to Mars when we leave Earth," she said slowly.

"No. We're going there," Carson said, gazing at the screen. "Proxima b. There's a very good possibility that there's water, breathable air, maybe even consumable flora and fauna. It's our first option, and Mars is our second. Maybe we will live on both, but Mars is not ideal."

Dead silence settled over the room while Gillian tried to absorb everything, but the knowledge was overwhelming. She swallowed, wondering if she was going to be sick.

"It's a lot to take in," Carson said. "The crew on the station as well as the ship was handpicked and is under strict confidential parameters agreed upon by the UN. This is a global initiative. Every major nation is on board."

"Self-assembling equipment and some of the most cutting-edge biotech is on its way to Proxima b now, traveling on solar sails at seventy percent the speed of light," Ander said. "Any ship that was already assembled would take three to four times as long to reach the destination."

"And one of your machines will be created along with it," Gillian said. "You're going to teleport people from Earth to the ship."

"Yes. All in due course. When the ship and machine have successfully assembled, a brave explorer will be sent via shifting. They will collect data and send a message home to be analyzed. This will take quite some time because even light, which is how we transmit and shift, takes over four years to travel the distance to Proxima b."

"When was the equipment launched?"

Ander smiled. "Over two years ago."

"And people know nothing about this?" Gillian said.

"No one outside the mission was told because of the emotions you're feeling right now," Ander said, coming closer. "Devastation, panic, depression. We needed an answer to the problem before we laid waste to people's hope." His gaze fell to the floor. "That is what we're working for now. Hope."

"But you're concerned there's something wrong with the shifting."

Ander and Orrin both stiffened, and Carson gave her a sharp glance. "We're not completely sure this affliction is being caused by shifting," Ander said. "But admittedly the correlation is troubling. Nearly thirty percent of the crew who've shifted have reported symptoms, though all CAT scans and MRIs have come back without anomalies."

"Do you think it could be Losian's, Doctor?" Orrin asked quietly.

"It's possible, but group onset has never been recorded before. Only neural testing could determine what's happening to them," Gillian said.

"Yes, well," Ander said, "regardless of what it is, you're right, Dr. Ryan, we can't proceed with trials any further until we've found the cause and addressed it." He appraised her. "Are you still up to the task given the . . . situation?"

She met his gaze. Held it. "Yes. I'll have to be."

TWENTY-EIGHT

"I'll get release forms signed by all the crew who are willing to undergo the tests," Carson said as they left Ander's quarters and passed the desk outside.

"Good. I'll need a dedicated lab and Birk." Gillian frowned. "If he's willing."

"Maybe Leo should stop by and give you another exam. Make sure—"

"He checked me after the withdrawals. I'm okay."

He was quiet for a moment. "You'll need to be under lockdown whenever you're not in the lab."

"Didn't expect anything less." She noticed him glancing at her as the elevator traveled quickly downward to the floor where her room was located.

As they stepped into the hall, Carson motioned to Vasquez. "Go ahead and get yourself a coffee."

Vasquez's eyebrows rose in a question, and Carson nodded.

"Yes, sir," Vasquez said, giving Gillian a last look before striding away.

They walked in the opposite direction toward her room, her cell.

"You know I don't have a choice," he said after a long silence. "Can't jeopardize your new command."

His jaw tightened, and he said nothing more as they stopped at her door. He scanned the room open, and she stepped inside.

"I'll let you know when everything's ready," he said, beginning to turn away.

"Carson?"

He stopped, his hand on the doorframe, not looking at her.

"Thank you."

The barest of nods and he was gone, the door sliding shut.

And she was alone again.

♦ ♦ ♦

The need for a hydro came as she rose from sleep. Deeper than lust. The thought of swallowing a pill was like the slow lead-up to an orgasm, sensuous and hypnotizing.

As she sat up on the bed, the craving lessened. She was free of the drug. It was over, and the thought of descending into the vicious addictive circle again was chilling. Not because she feared the drug and what it would do to her, but because of how much she wanted it.

Gillian showered, washing the thoughts away along with the sweat and grime. She had no idea what hour it was, what day. Time was an alien thing in the red light of Mars. Something belonging to work and school schedules, bedtimes, and alarms.

Here there was only the pull of sleep, exhaustion the hands of a clock she couldn't see.

When she was finished, she left the bathroom and dressed in a clean jumpsuit. As she was combing her hair with her fingers, a knock came from the door, and a second later it slid aside, revealing Orrin Ander.

"Oh, I'm sorry," Orrin said as she zipped the jumpsuit the rest of the way up to her throat. "Commander LeCroix was indisposed, so he asked me to escort you to the lab. I'll . . . I'll wait outside."

The door hissed shut, and she stared at it for a moment before tying her hair in a tight knot atop her head. When she was ready, she knocked on the door, and it moved aside. Only Orrin waited in the hallway.

"I apologize. I should've waited longer before walking in," he said. His voice had the same airy quality she'd noticed before. "They told me you'd be ready."

"It's okay. Surprised me, that's all."

They walked down the hall, passing several people heading in the opposite direction. They greeted Orrin, and Gillian could feel their eyes linger on her. As they neared the first checkpoint and Orrin scanned through, he tilted his head back the way they'd come. "They looked at me the same way for the first month. Not an astronaut, so I'm an outsider."

"Guessing you weren't accused of murder."

Orrin grimaced and began walking again.

After they'd entered an elevator, her eyes stole to the scarring on the side of his head again. It was deeply ingrained in the skin, a lightning bolt of puckered flesh. He glanced at her, and she looked away.

"So if you're not an astronaut, then what are you?" she asked, trying to break the awkwardness.

"I'm the great Eric Ander's son," he said, half a smile pulling at his lips.

"Just along for the ride?"

"Robotics, actually. Operation mostly, but I've done some design too."

"You've worked down on the surface, I take it?"

"Not extensively. Ran some sample-collection studies when we first got here."

"So I assume you've shifted?"

He nodded. "A few times."

"What's it like?"

"Honestly? Scary as hell. Not my favorite thing to do. Don't tell Dad, though." He gave her another smile. "I used the transport ships whenever I could instead. Of course, that was before everything . . ." His voice trailed off, and she was about to ask him another question when the elevator door slid open.

Orrin led her down a short corridor lined with windows gazing out onto the staggering drop below, the planet there in livid glory. The view told her they were on the level below Ander's office.

Through another doorway, and then they stood in an alcove outside a glassed-in area with banks of touchscreens as well as two reclining chairs that reminded her of the last time she'd taken Carrie to the dentist. Birk stood in the middle of the room near a counter filled with their equipment from the ship. He looked up at the sound of them entering the room.

"Doctor." There was nothing in Birk's voice she could identify. No relief, no disdain.

"Hi." She glanced at Orrin, who remained slightly to one side of the door. Birk resumed setting up their work space as she neared.

"Quite the leap. From rats to human beings inside two months."

"Birk, I . . ." She struggled. "Thank you for helping."

The big man paused and jerked his head once. "It is why I'm here."

"You know what I mean." She placed her hand over his as he reached for a length of rubber tubing.

He stared at their hands. "You could have been honest with me from the beginning. You should have. I am owed that much respect."

"You're right. I'm sorry. It's so . . ." She sighed. "So hard to ask for help. And when you decide to, sometimes it feels like it's already too late."

"I can understand that," he said after a pause. When he brought his eyes up to hers, his gaze had changed. "I believe you, Doctor," he said in such a low voice she barely heard him. "I don't know what is happening, but it is not what it appears."

A feeling equal parts elation and unease passed through her. She was about to respond when the door to the lab opened.

Carson strode inside with Ander close behind him. Carson looked as if he hadn't slept, and Ander appeared to be wearing the same clothes as the last time she'd seen him.

"Everything ready?" Carson asked.

Gillian cleared her throat. "Yeah. We're good."

"Okay. Let's get started."

♦ ♦ ♦

The biologist's name was Dennis Kenison. He was short and thin with a drastically receding hairline. A cord hung around his neck with a pair of glasses attached to the end he couldn't stop fidgeting with. He lingered in the doorway of the lab, looking at them each in turn before smiling at Orrin, who shook his hand warmly. After they'd greeted each other, Kenison's attention came back to the pedestal seat Gillian had arranged beside their equipment.

"Go ahead, Dennis," Ander said, patting the man on the shoulder.

Kenison hesitated, throwing another look at her. She didn't blame him for faltering; everyone on the station was aware of the accusations surrounding her.

She smiled as warmly as she could as he approached. "Hello, Doctor. Thank you for agreeing to see us."

He nodded, sitting quickly in the chair as she took a seat beside him. This close, she could see his eyes were watery, and there was something swimming in their depths as he continued to glance around. Fear. He was terrified.

"So what exactly does this all entail?" Kenison said, his voice a reedy reflection of his appearance. "Some kind of brain scan, but what else?"

"First I'd like to ask you some questions. Then we'll be inserting a small cranial port before proceeding with the neurological analysis," Gillian said, pressing the "Audio Record" button on the nearest tablet. "What's your job here, Doctor?"

"Anatomic botany mostly. I study the plants' structure from the biospheres, make sure there's no mutations. No growth inhibitors or nutrient deficiencies."

"And you came here on the first flight?"

"Yes. Before the station was even fully assembled," he said, gesturing at the room around them.

"When was the first time you shifted?"

Kenison squirmed in the chair. "Two months after the initial biosphere was sealed. I . . . ." He looked at Ander before continuing. "I went from here down to the surface."

Gillian watched him. "How did it feel?"

"Like . . . like being born."

"Born? What do you mean?"

He cleared his throat. "You ever get a great night's sleep, like beyond restful, and you feel almost like a different person than you did when you went to bed? It's like that but tenfold. Pure elation."

"And how many times did you shift overall?"

"Six."

"When did you start noticing something was wrong?"

"The second or third time." He was silent for a moment, the only sound the clicking of his glasses as his hands worked. "Had a nagging sensation in the back of my mind. Like when you leave the grocery store and just know you've forgotten something."

Gillian shared a look with Birk, whose eyebrows rose slightly. "Can you tell us how you've been feeling lately?" she asked.

The glasses folded.

Unfolded.

"Anxious and tired. Haven't been able to concentrate on work as much as I should. Sometimes I think I fall asleep sitting up or even standing because I come awake all of a sudden and there's a little break from where I was a second before." A nervous laugh emerged, and he wiped his lip again. "Does that make any sense?"

She smiled again. "I'm sure it will soon. Are there any other symptoms?"

Kenison blinked rapidly. "Things are missing."

"What things?"

"Things I should remember. They're small, mostly inconsequential. Like what color my house is back home. I know my address, and I know how many rooms there are and what they look like, but the color." He shook his head. "It's not there. I don't know if it's blue or yellow or red." All at once the shimmering in his eyes spilled over, and he was crying, had been trying to keep from doing so since they'd first started talking, Gillian realized. "It shouldn't bother me, right? But that's not everything. My mother passed away five years ago. I lived with her, took care of her up until the end." Kenison spoke through his teeth as if it was painful to utter the words. "I can't picture her face. I'm not sure I could tell you if it was her if you showed me a picture." His voice broke on the last word, and he wept openly.

Gillian stood, crossed to the nearest wall, and grasped several handfuls of paper towels from a dispenser there. On her way back, she glanced at Carson and Ander, their expressions unreadable. Orrin's face was creased as if he was deep in thought. Gillian handed Kenison the towels, and he blotted his face with them.

"I'm sorry," he said. "It's terrifying. To not remember."

In that instant he could've been a little boy, not a middle-aged man. Could have been someone's scared child.

"It's okay to be frightened, but we're going to figure out what the problem is. Okay?"

He blew his nose quietly and nodded. "I get angry sometimes too."

"Angry?"

"When the memories aren't there. It's like looking for your glasses when they should be in their case where you put them and they aren't. That's why I carry them like this. Used to lose them all the time. I try to remember something that won't come, and sometimes the anger shows up in its place. It's like someone else is mad, not me, someone outside."

Gillian felt her scalp prickle. "Anger is a common reaction when a person isn't able to recall something. That seems normal to me."

He dabbed at his eyes again, nodding slightly.

"If you're ready, we'll begin the procedure now," she said, moving to the table near the equipment, the instruments laid out in neat rows. She grasped a small syringe filled with a numbing agent.

"You won't be putting me under, right?" Kenison looked from her to Ander and back again. "They told me I'd be awake."

"No, there won't be any anesthesia. Do you have a problem with going under?"

Kenison swallowed and repositioned himself in the chair. "I've been having dreams," he said. "Nightmares. Haven't been sleeping a lot."

"Do you mind telling us what they're about?"

He shook his head. "Something . . . something like a hole, but it isn't a hole. It's a gap that I'm at the edge of, and I . . ." His voice trailed off.

"It's okay."

"I look down and it's endless. There's nothing there. It goes on forever. And I wake up as I fall in." A glimmer of sweat shone on his upper lip, and he wiped it away.

Gillian rolled the syringe around in her fingers, trying to steady her hands. "We won't put you out. Just a small shot to numb the area where we have to insert the port."

Kenison relaxed slightly and leaned back in the chair, exposing the crown of his balding skull to her. Birk handed her a lidocaine swab. She sterilized a small area on the top of Kenison's scalp before applying the swab. After waiting a few seconds, she slid the syringe at an angle into the numbed skin and depressed the plunger.

"Will this hurt?" Kenison asked as she turned back to the table and grasped the small surgical drill prefitted with the cranial port.

"You shouldn't feel a thing. If you think you need a sedative, just say—"

"No. No, I'll be fine."

Taking a deep breath, Gillian placed the drill against Kenison's skull. She shared a fleeting look with Birk before pressing the trigger.

The drill whined, its shrillness filling the room, and she caught a whiff of heated bone. The bit sunk eagerly into his head, and the port spun once before releasing from the drill.

It was done.

"There," she said, ignoring the two steps Carson had taken toward her when she began drilling. She nodded to Birk, who attached a tube and neural monitor line to the port before injecting a dose of luciferin into Kenison's skull. He readjusted himself in the seat. "Feeling okay?" Gillian asked.

"Yeah. My head got cold. Tingly."

"That's the luciferin compound. Tell me if the sensation becomes too much. We have to wait a few minutes, so just try to relax."

She glanced at Carson, who had turned and was discussing something with Ander and Orrin near the door.

Birk settled onto a stool before the multitude of screens and began recording Kenison's vitals. "Everything appears normal so far, Doctor. Blood pressure and heart rate are slightly elevated." He shot her a look and said in a near whisper, "Though mine would be too if I were the first human trial."

"All the compounds are organic," she replied, skirting him to get a better view of the displays. "The worst we're risking is infection at the injection site."

"But how do we know it will work?" he continued in a hushed voice. "What if this is just a shot at night?"

"Shot in the dark," she corrected automatically. Carson looked at her before Ander said something, drawing his attention away. "Because we all remember."

Several minutes later, they loaded the dosage of luciferase, and Gillian took her seat once again beside Kenison. "Still doing okay?"

"Sure."

"Good. All right, Dr. Kenison. In a few seconds, I'm going to ask you something, and I don't want it to upset you. I'm going to ask you to think of the happiest memory you can." The biologist blinked rapidly before squeezing his eyes shut. "When I tell you, I want you to focus on it and imagine that you're there again. Can you do that?" Kenison nodded but didn't open his eyes.

She pointed at Birk, who touched one of the screens.

The luciferase slid through the tube, disappearing into the port. She could see Kenison's neurons lighting up already on the display tilted in her direction. An incredible urge to simply watch the reaction overcame her, to see the intimate lightning of another human being's essence. The awe of it nearly matched that of seeing Mars up close for the first time. And now she was witnessing not just millions of cells firing, but billions.

She tore her gaze away from the screen and focused again on Kenison. "Doctor, do you have your memory?"

"Yes," he whispered. A tear leaked from the corner of his right eye.

"Good. Hold on to it."

The compound flooded Kenison's hippocampal region, the entire area erupting in daggers of light.

It was working.

The neural flashes intensified. The movements became faster than she could track, coalescing into a supernova that consumed the rest of his brain.

Gillian tried to breathe, but her lungs were paralyzed. She stared at Kenison, but he gave no indication of the firestorm rolling through his mind.

Gradually the neurons darkened, flares caused by the compounds coming less and less.

She looked to Birk. His jaw hung slightly open, and when he met her gaze, his eyes were wet.

He nodded. "It worked."

Gillian nearly leaped from her seat, pure elation flowing through her. There had been some doubt, a lot if she was honest with herself, concerning the transition between animal trials and human testing. But now they had proof, concrete evidence that the theories and research were sound. And if it worked on Kenison, it would work on Carrie.

She touched Kenison's hand, and he looked around, swiping one palm across his cheek. "Did I pass out?" he asked.

"No. You did great. We're done."

"Everything was so vibrant. Like a dream but . . ." He shook his head. "It was beyond real, like reliving it all over again." A small smile crept onto his face. "It was beautiful."

"I'm glad."

"How long will it take for the results?"

Gillian moved behind him and began unhooking the monitor wire and tubing from the port. "Not more than a day. We'll let you know as soon as we're finished." She used a pair of forceps to twist the port gently from his head and placed a suture pad over the small hole. "That should heal pretty quickly," she said, helping Kenison to his feet. "Keep the bandage on for twelve hours, and don't let your head get wet for two days."

"Won't be a problem, doesn't rain here much."

Gillian laughed, and Kenison smiled again.

"Thank you, Doctor." Kenison nodded, sobering. He lingered before her, hands holding his glasses shaking slightly.

"Are you sure you feel okay?" Gillian asked. His color had drained in the last few seconds.

Kenison licked his lips, tilting his head as if he'd heard a sound he couldn't identify, and she wondered if he might be on the verge of passing out. "There's something wrong with them," he said quietly.

Gillian threw a glance over his shoulder at the three men by the door. They were in conversation again, not looking their way. "Who?" she asked, matching the biologist's volume.

Kenison leaned forward so suddenly, she nearly shrank back. His lips moved, and she read the word more than heard it.

"Everyone."

TWENTY-NINE

Gillian watched Kenison move toward the exit.

Her mind freewheeled, trying to make sense of what had just happened.

Ander shook hands with Kenison as he neared the door, murmuring something the biologist frowned at. Gillian strained to hear what he was saying but was distracted as Carson approached the work space with Orrin close behind.

"It worked," Carson said.

"It did," she said, trying to gather her wits.

"You weren't sure it would, were you?"

"No. There aren't any sureties when dealing with the human mind."

"Isn't that the truth."

Orrin made his way around the table to stand behind Birk. "So you mapped every neuron?" he asked, not taking his eyes off the screen.

"Looks that way," she replied, watching Ander pat Kenison on the shoulder before the biologist left the room.

"And this will tell you if shifting is the cause?"

"The scan will tell us if any of the neurons are damaged in any way and where they're located in the brain."

"I didn't mention it before, but this is an amazing breakthrough," Ander said as he stepped up beside Carson and began studying the screen's readouts.

"Coming from the man who invented teleportation, I'll take that as a compliment," Gillian said.

A flicker of amusement passed over the old man's face. "I didn't invent it. Only perfected the concept."

"I don't know if I'd call it perfect," Orrin said. Ander gazed at his son, his expression darkening.

Carson coughed into his hand. "You said the results will take twenty-four hours?"

"Somewhere around there, I'm guessing. At least that's what our estimate was initially," Gillian said.

"Nonsense," Ander said. "Upload your program into the station's mainframe. It's a quantum model. We should have the results back much sooner than a day."

"How soon?" Birk asked, beginning to type on the keyboard before him.

"A few minutes. Maybe less."

Birk paused, shaking his head as if he'd been struck before resuming typing. "Okaaaaaay."

Gillian coiled the monitor cable and tubing into two overlapping circles on the table, Kenison's last word echoing in her head. "Is there a way to get down to the surface? Without shifting, of course," she added, seeing the looks Ander and Carson were giving her.

"Why?" Ander asked.

"I'd like to visit the biospheres. Try to rule out any foreign agent that might be causing this. Also, seeing the environment they're working in might indicate if there's a psychological aspect we're missing here."

"We've already run extensive screenings on everyone who's been to the surface and back," Ander said. "Physically they're fine."

"Psychological screenings too?"

"Dr. Pendrake handled the evaluations until . . . the incident." Ander paused, a current of anguish running beneath his features. "Other than the symptoms, the crew is mentally sound," he finished.

"That might be true, but there's only two things the people who are afflicted have in common: one, they've all shifted multiple times, and two, they've been to the surface."

"I've done both of those, and I am fine," Ander said. "Orrin is fine."

"But the majority isn't."

"She's got a point," Orrin said. "Besides, two of the crew down there are due for a shift change tomorrow anyway. Right?"

"Yes." He grimaced. "Carson, what's your take on this?"

Carson stared at the floor. "I think it's necessary to explore every option. We've come too far, and there's too much at stake."

"All right, I'm in the minority here. The lander leaves in the morning. I'll notify the pilot that you'll be accompanying the crew down for the change."

Gillian turned to the closest screen, letting her thoughts spool out as she watched the data compile.

There's something wrong with them.

What had Ander said to Kenison as he left?

She glanced at the old man and found him studying her as well.

"Wow. That was beyond fast," Birk said, drawing everyone's attention. He tapped his keyboard several times and turned the screen for them to see.

The neural topography of Kenison's brain played in a looping video of bioluminescence at the top right corner. The rest of the display held categories of compiled information in separate rows. Gillian stepped past Carson, squinting at the screen. Her eyes ran down the data in quick ladder steps.

"And?" Orrin asked after a span of thick silence had elapsed.

"Normal," she said, turning back to the group. "Completely normal. No signs of trauma or neurofibrillary tangles."

Carson blinked, his gaze turning inward while Ander stepped closer to study the screen himself.

"So that means?" Orrin asked.

"There's been no physical damage to his neurons," Birk said. The words sent a spider made of ice skittering down Gillian's spine.

"None," Ander said, and it sounded like he was saying "victory."

Carson crossed his arms, uncrossed them, like Kenison folding his glasses over and over. "And it's conclusive?"

"This makes an MRI look like an Etch A Sketch," Gillian said absently. She bit her lip. "It rules out Losian's for sure."

"And shifting?"

"Not necessarily."

"What do you mean?"

She frowned. "There still could be an issue with teleportation we're not seeing."

"But there's no neurological trauma," Ander broke in. "You said so yourself."

"I know that. It's just . . ."

"Just what?" Carson asked gently.

She squinted at the readout again but finally shook her head.

Carson watched her for another second before saying, "Since we have some findings on this front, we need to explore other possible causes. Where does that leave us?"

"Perhaps a toxin or foreign agent of some kind like Dr. Ryan mentioned," Ander said, stepping back from the display. "Something that was missed in the testing."

Gillian looked down at the coiled, interlocking loops of the monitor lead and tubing. Something in the recesses of her mind turned over in its sleep, the idea not awake yet, not distinct enough to even call an idea. And for some reason she could hear a train, see it passing by on clattering wheels.

"I'd like to test them," she said, tracing the curve of the monitor wire before looking at Carson.

"Who?" Ander asked.

"The two people most afflicted. I want to meet the man who killed your partner."

THIRTY

While Ander and Carson conferred at the next table over in low voices, Gillian and Birk reset the equipment.

Every so often she would hear Carson's voice rise slightly and knew from their past arguments that he was drilling home a point he wouldn't let go.

"I'm not sure I like the way that man is looking at you, Doctor," Birk said beside her.

She glanced up and found Orrin gazing at her from the seat he'd taken across the room. There was a languid quality to his eyes, the soft thoughtfulness of an astronomer considering a new light in the sky.

"He's okay," she murmured. "Think it's mostly seeing new people after such a long time."

Birk grunted.

She watched his hands work with a vial of luciferin. Steady as stone. "I didn't get a chance to ask, How're you feeling since waking up?"

He stopped moving as if to take inventory of himself. "Very well, actually. I had a few bouts of vertigo at first but nothing like before."

"No more sounds or . . . seeing anything?"

Birk blushed. "No. I believe you were right, Doctor. I was sleep deprived, stressed, and most likely dehydrated."

"I'm glad." She smiled, feeling like this could almost be a normal day in their lab. Like she wasn't accused of a man's murder or over thirty million miles from home.

Thirty million miles from Carrie.

She'd tried keeping thoughts of her at arm's length for the past few hours, moving by them quickly as soon as they came so she could continue working, but they were always there, half a heartbeat away. And now, without the rush and exhilaration of the testing, the absence of her daughter was an ulcerous ache inside her.

Find the teleportation unit, and shift back to Earth.

The thought was a sucker punch sending her mentally reeling.

The units were functional as far as she knew, one of the originals still on the NASA campus in Florida waiting for a signal. She could be home in a matter of minutes.

But she had no idea what it would do to her.

It might not be shifting that's causing this at all. It could be a foreign agent, some virus or chemical unfamiliar to known science, something that wouldn't register on any of the tests.

The temptation was intoxicating. She muscled away from it. Until they knew exactly what was happening, she couldn't take the risk for herself or Carrie if there was a contagion involved.

God, she needed a hydro.

"Okay, Doctor?" Birk asked.

"Fine." She resumed resetting the program on the display.

"All right, here's the deal," Carson said, walking toward them. "We'll bring in Mary Cranston, the other severely afflicted crew member first. If all goes well, we'll test Diver."

"Why wouldn't it go well with her?" Gillian asked.

"It wasn't in the report you were issued, but Cranston attacked a coworker as well. Didn't do any real harm—couple of shallow cuts—but she's considered dangerous."

"Anything else that wasn't in the reports we should know?"

Carson shot her a look.

"Why did she do it?"

"No idea," Carson said. "There were no witnesses, but the crew member she attacked said he found her in a hall in the lower part of the station turning in circles like she was lost. When he asked if she was okay, she cut him with some glass from a window she'd smashed out earlier."

"Lovely," Birk said.

"Don't let her appearance throw you off. She could be dangerous." Carson started to say something else but stopped and moved back to Ander, who stood rigid, arms crossed over his narrow chest.

Less than ten minutes later, Mary Cranston arrived.

Vasquez and the other man who had escorted Gillian to her quarters upon their arrival at the station walked Mary into the room, their hands on her upper arms. She was waifish, with hair so blonde it looked like a white fog around her head. If Gillian had to guess, she would've put the other woman in her midforties, but she could've been younger given her smooth complexion. A solid set of manacles enclosed her kindling-like wrists, their brutish thickness a startling contrast to the woman herself.

The guards settled her into the exam chair and stepped back. Mary took in the room, eyes half-lidded as if she were on the brink of drowsing off. Gillian sat beside her, clicking on the audio recorder.

"Hello, Mrs. Cranston. I'm Dr. Ryan. Should I call you Mrs. Cranston or Mary?"

Mary's mouth tilted in half a smile. "Just don't call me late for supper."

"Okay. We'll stick with Mrs. Cr—"

"'Supper.' Maybe its origin is from the word 'sup.' To drink. Some think it came from the French. 'Souper' or 'soup.' No one knows for sure." Cranston looked away from her and focused on Orrin. Her head cocked to one side. "You're very handsome. If it weren't for those scars, you'd be gorgeous. 'Fuckable' is the word."

Orrin shifted in his seat uncomfortably. Cranston winked at him.

"Mrs. Cranston, we'd like to ask you some questions," Gillian continued.

"Answers. Opposite of questions."

"Yes. I understand you're a communications specialist. Is that right?"

"Maybe. Maybe something else."

"Do you not remember?" Cranston sat motionless, and after nearly a minute of silence, Gillian leaned closer to her. "Where are you from? What state?"

"So many states. Limbo. That's appropriate. In between."

"In between what?"

"Everything."

Gillian sat back. "It says in your file your husband's name is Jacob. Is that right?"

Cranston nodded.

"Can you tell me a little about him?"

"I'd like to go now."

"We have a few more questions for you."

"In the tunnel. That's a good place. The tunnel forever. Forever and ever."

"What tunnel, Mary? Which one?"

"The only one. The one. The one I want. I'd like to go there now."

Gillian glanced at Carson, who shrugged slightly. Ander glowered, eyebrows drawn together. "Do you recall going down to the surface? Down to Mars? You helped establish communications in the biospheres, right?"

Cranston had begun rocking from left to right. In a quiet, tremulous voice, she began singing. "Down, down, down in the dark. Winter came early inside my heart. You went away and left me here. Why don't you ever call me, dear? Your love went and took me apart. Down, down, down in the dark."

The words ended on a raspy note that turned the skin on Gillian's arms into braille. Cranston quit rocking, and her chin drooped to her chest.

Gillian tried wetting her lips, but her tongue was covered in sand. "Mary?"

No response.

"Can you hear me?" Gillian leaned in. "Mary?"

Cranston's head snapped up and to the right. Her teeth came together with an audible clack an inch from Gillian's face.

Gillian flinched away and fell from her chair, a scream lodging itself in her throat as the two guards leaped in and pressed the woman back into her seat. Birk stood and pushed one massive hand against Cranston's forehead.

"The tunnel!" she yelled, her face a twisted mass of fury.

Gillian rose, limbs full of electric current, muscles shaking. With two quick steps, she rounded the table and grasped a syringe lying beside the vials of luciferin and luciferase. Without hesitating, she moved to the thrashing woman's side and plunged the needle into her shoulder, depressing the liquid with her thumb.

Cranston slid down in the chair, still struggling, teeth bared and snapping at the nearest guard's arm. Carson appeared at her feet, grasping her thin ankles and pinning them down.

"Hold her!" Ander yelled from the other side of the room.

She surged against them all one last time. Then, like a windstorm losing its fury, Cranston's convulsions slowed, gradually lessening until she slumped to her side, fists unclenching.

"She's out," one of the guards said, hoisting her upright in the seat.

"Christ! I knew this was a bad idea. Didn't I tell you?" Ander said, pointing at Carson.

But Carson wasn't listening. He was standing beside Gillian, one of his hands on her shoulder. "Everyone okay? Did she get you?"

"No, I'm fine," Gillian said. But all at once she felt sick. She swallowed bile and put a hand on the table.

"You're not fine."

"I will be. Let me breathe."

Carson gauged her for another beat before moving toward Ander, who looked as if he was going to erupt again at any second. Orrin stood on the other side of Cranston's chair and nodded to Gillian. "Okay?"

"Yeah. I'm good." It wasn't a complete lie. Some of the strength was returning to her legs and arms, heart calming to a jog from a sprint. She found her hand straying to her jumpsuit pocket, fingers searching for a pill bottle that wasn't there.

"Back to her room?" one of the guards said to Carson.

"Let's run the test since she's sedated," Gillian said, pleased her voice didn't shake. "I didn't give her a lot. She should be conscious enough in a few minutes."

Carson threw a look at Ander, who tipped his head back, closing his eyes before letting out a long exhale.

"All right," Ander said. "But keep your hands clear of her mouth. I don't want anyone losing a finger."

◆ ◆ ◆

"Normal," Gillian said, pivoting away from the screens so the others could see. The results had come back from the quantum processor only minutes after the guards left the room, Cranston half walking, half carried between the two men. She'd been groggily repeating what Gillian had said to her in the midst of the test to trigger a memory.

The tunnel. The tunnel.

"I don't understand it," Gillian said, looking down at her hands.

"You expected to find something?" Orrin said.

"With the way she acted? Absolutely. She has classic signs of dementia, memory loss, decoherence with reality." Gillian thought for a moment. "Maybe it's like ciguatera."

"Think one of my buddies got that when he was deployed in the Pacific," Orrin said.

She nodded. "People get it from eating certain fish that feed on eukaryotes, which produce a toxin. The toxin causes all kinds of physical ailments but also neurological issues like short-term memory loss. But Mary's symptoms go beyond that. She either couldn't comprehend the questions, or she doesn't remember the answers."

"So you're saying she might've ingested a toxin?" Carson asked.

"I don't know. There aren't any signs of neurological damage, so a neurotoxin doesn't really make sense. But if there's something we're dealing with here that's beyond our experience, then my guess is it came from the surface."

The implication of what she was saying settled over the room.

"You mean alien life? Something biological?" Ander said. She shrugged, and he huffed a laugh. "I'm sorry, Doctor, but that's hard to swallow."

"No offense, but a few months ago, as far as I was concerned, teleportation was science fiction."

Ander studied her before looking away.

"And I'm not necessarily saying life. It could be a mineral we're not familiar with. Look at the effects of mercury poisoning."

"For the sake of argument, say it is biological," Carson said. "Only eighteen of the fifty-five crew members have complained of symptoms. Forty-eight out of the fifty-five have shifted and been to the surface. If it's contagious, it's not very effective."

"Speaking of numbers, Mary Cranston has only shifted four times," Ander said. "Less than Dennis, and yet she is profoundly worse than he is."

"How about Diver?" Gillian asked.

"Only nine. We have several crew members who have done twice that and are exhibiting no symptoms. I see no real correlation."

Gillian tried to work her way around a response, but each argument fell apart under Ander's reasoning. "What about the tunnel she kept mentioning? Is there anything on the station like that?"

Orrin and Ander looked at each other before shaking their heads.

"Not that I know of," Orrin said.

"How about on the surface? Any drilling or excavation?"

"No," Ander said, "but there is an umbilicus hall from the main biosphere to the second largest. It somewhat resembles a tunnel."

Gillian nodded. "Okay. That's something."

Ander glanced at the nearest display. "I'm sorry, but I have something I need to attend to."

"I think that's all we can do for today anyhow," Carson said. "Easton and Lien can accompany us to the surface tomorrow to help investigate. Afterward we'll finish testing the rest of the crew who have symptoms."

A part of Gillian wanted to protest, tell them they should continue examining the crew now, but a larger part was glad to be leaving the lab, even if the confines of her tiny room were all she was trading it for.

After squeezing Birk's hand once in good-bye, her mind returned to what Kenison had said, like a tongue probing the crater of a missing tooth. And beyond that, something else Birk had mentioned about the biologist's test results, a needling she didn't understand. *There's been no physical damage to his neurons.*

No physical damage.

"That was impressive in there today," Carson said, pulling her back to reality as they came to a juncture in the hall.

"Thanks."

"If we can figure this thing out, I want you to know I'll do everything I can to help once you get back to Earth."

"And if we can't?"

"You weren't yourself. I'll testify to that."

"I didn't touch those cameras, Carson. I didn't kill him."

They walked the last hundred yards without speaking. The station hummed like some artificial womb. When they stopped at her door and Carson scanned it open, she turned to him.

"I'm not worried about me. Help my daughter."

She stepped inside and waited for his reply, but heard only the sound of the door sliding shut behind her.

Tears welled in her eyes, and she blinked them back, going to the sink in the bathroom to douse her face in cold water until it burned. She was about to undress and lie down to hunt sleep she knew wouldn't be found when she saw that one corner of her thin blanket was turned up. There was a small lump lying beneath it in the center of the bed.

Gillian grasped the covers and tossed them back, heart missing a beat then double-timing.

The pill bottle was dark amber, but even through its tint, she recognized the shape of the hydros within.

THIRTY-ONE

Gillian stared at the bottle in Carson's hand.

She realized too late he had asked her something, and before she could rewind the moment, he said, "Are you listening to me?"

"Yes."

"Where did you get them?"

"I told you, they were in my room when I came back."

"Someone put them in your bed?"

She nodded.

"Why?"

"Because whoever it is knows I'm an addict. They're pushing me."

"To do what?"

"Start using again." She hesitated. "Overdose."

"That doesn't make any sense."

"It wouldn't make any sense if I smuggled them in here then told you about them."

"So someone's trying to get you to kill yourself?"

"I don't know what they want." She stood from where she sat on the bed and pointed at the bottle. "But that proves I wasn't the only one awake on the ship."

"It doesn't prove anything except you somehow managed to get access to them in the lab."

"When did I have a chance to do that?" Her voice tightened with indignation.

"Before Dr. Ander and I got there. Maybe Birk slipped them to you."

She wanted to pull her hair out. "Are you serious?" He stared at her. "With all due respect, you're being unbelievably fucking obtuse."

Carson's gaze hardened. "No one was awake on that ship. Besides, I trust them with my life."

"You really can't ever know someone, Carson. Not really."

"Finally something we agree on." He gave her a last look. "Get some sleep. We leave in ten hours."

Gillian watched the door lock behind him. A cry of frustration perched on her tongue. She bit it back and turned, looking out at Mars, a red swath against the darkness of space.

Gillian moved away from the bed and into the bathroom, then gripped the sink before kneeling. On the wall beneath the stainless-steel basin, she pinched the head of a small exposed screw and turned it a half dozen times before it came loose.

The corner of the panel it held in place popped free of the wall. She pried it open and reached inside, then slid the dozen hydros off the narrow support strut into her hand.

Gillian scooted away from the sink and sat with her back pressed against the toilet, the pills stark pink in her palm. She'd stashed the opiates without thinking, a familiar autopilot taking over after she'd shaken the drugs free of the bottle, all the while a voice inside screaming, *What are you doing?*

Keeping some evidence. Something to prove she wasn't crazy, hadn't imagined everything that happened on the ship.

And what else?

Trying to deny the addict inside her hadn't had something to do with stashing them was like pretending the sun didn't exist. But she wasn't going to take any. She was past that now, clean and thinking clearly.

"If you were thinking clearly, you wouldn't have kept them," she murmured. Willing herself to move, she slid forward and placed the pills back in the hidden nook. Tightened the screw and returned to the bed, where she sat with her elbows on her knees, chin in her hands.

Which one of the crew had done it? Leo had access to the drugs, but no matter how hard she tried imagining him locking Tinsel's stasis unit shut and severing its lifelines, she couldn't do it. That left Easton and Lien since Carson had been with her all day during testing.

No. That wasn't right either. He'd shown up after having Orrin bring her to the lab. He could've easily brought the pills to her room. Then there was Ander. The scientist knew the details of what had happened on the ship. What had he said to Kenison before the other man left the lab? The biologist hadn't liked it; that was apparent. She needed to speak with Kenison, without anyone else listening.

Her mind felt as if it were being drawn and quartered, none of the pieces able to reckon anything from what she knew.

Gillian blew out a long breath and lay back on the bed. She stared up at the low ceiling bloodied with the planet's light.

"Gotta stay sharp. Concentration and will. Concentration and will." She repeated the old mantra until it bore her away on wings of restless sleep.

♦ ♦ ♦

"The lander probably isn't what you're thinking," Orrin said, walking ahead of their group as they stepped out of the elevator on the station's lowest level. "It's way more versatile. A ship rather than a jumper from the station to the surface."

Gillian listened to Orrin talk about various aspects of the lander and how long the trip would take, but it was background noise. While they walked, she studied the others in the group.

Carson walked directly behind Orrin, and she followed, Easton and Lien on either side of her. Carson had barely acknowledged her that morning. His stoicism was overshadowed by Lien's, a single inclination of her head the only greeting when they'd met in an adjacent hallway in the level above. Easton was the exception. He asked Orrin constant questions about the station and cracked several jokes he laughed loudly at, even when no one else did. Gillian imagined each of them depositing the bottle of pills in her room, trying to catch a look of guilt in their expressions.

"So the lander's an Exo Mark 3?" Easton asked as they turned a corner, coming even with an intersecting hallway to the right.

"That's right," Orrin said over his shoulder.

"We did some simulation training on those back home. Got some get-up-and-go."

"That's for sure." Orrin slowed at the mouth of the branching hallway and pointed to a set of sealed doors. "This is elevation control. Inside is the technology that keeps us tethered above the planet."

"I was wondering about that," Gillian said, and all eyes turned to her. "I noticed we weren't orbiting."

"It's all in there," Orrin replied. "In essence, the most powerful magnet in creation is behind those doors. It works against the planet's magnetic fields and the sun's solar winds carrying magnetic field lines. There's also a reverse field around the whole area to keep the integrity of the station in place. My dad explained the whole thing to me once, but you'll have to ask him if you need more details. All I know is, steer clear of that area if you've got any metal on you. You'll end up flipped on your head or worse."

They started moving again, and Gillian eyed the double doors, seeing a key card reader beside them and a sign in bold letters listing a dozen or more warnings about proceeding beyond this point.

Past the juncture, they stopped at an unremarkable door, which Orrin scanned them through. Inside was a waist-high bank of windows. Beyond the glass was something that made her slow and stop, one hand pressing against the barrier.

The teleportation unit was exactly like the one she'd seen in Ander's test videos; only it seemed much larger. The tube was nearly four feet across, and the quantum computer umbilicalled to it towered over every other piece of equipment in the room.

"Through here, Dr. Ryan," Orrin said, holding the next set of doors open down the hall the others had already filed through.

"Sorry," she said, stepping past him.

"It's okay. Guessing it's the first time you've seen one in real life."

"Yeah."

"Kind of unreal knowing what it does, right?"

"Very."

The next chamber was a narrow waiting room with several chairs and benches placed along the walls. A tall man with a crew cut stood beside an archway leading to what looked like towering cubicle walls set in rows.

"This is our pilot, Byron Guthrie," Orrin said. "He'll take it from here."

Orrin passed by them, shooting her a quick smile as he left the room. Guthrie gave a small wave and placed his hands on his hips.

"Don't normally have so much company on the trek. Usually just the two people rotating every few weeks. Be a nice change of pace."

Something hissed in the next room, and a plume of what looked like steam rose over the sections of walls, pooling foglike at the ceiling.

"So here's protocol: There's two decontamination stations in there, left and right. Go in one at a time, no hanky-panky, guys." When no one laughed, he cleared his throat, face sobering. "So once you're through decon, put the clean jumpsuit on, then your space suit. Once you're suited up, I'll . . ."

Guthrie's voice became blunted, something unintelligible. Gillian breathed in deeply for a second time through her nose, senses blistering.

Couldn't be.

She took a step back, watching the others, their attention glued to Guthrie, who was droning on about an airlock.

But she wasn't listening. Couldn't hear anything over the slamming of her pulse.

The smell. She knew that smell. How could she not have recognized it before?

She sucked in a quick breath, and Easton glanced at her, expression going from surprise to concern like a flipped switch.

"Doc, you all right?" he asked. When she didn't answer, couldn't gather the air, he grasped her forearm. "Hey, Commander, something's wrong here."

Gillian searched past the group as they gathered around her, looking for the source of the smell, but it was obvious. The clouds of steam. Had to be.

"Gillian, what's the matter?" Carson said, coming close.

She swallowed once, twice, trying to gather saliva that wasn't there. "The smell on the ship I told you about. Now I remember. I remember where it's from."

THIRTY-TWO

Gillian drank the water from the plastic cup in several gulps, its taste metallic with a hint of chlorine.

She and Carson sat across from each other, the smell still drifting out of the decontamination area's entrance at the far end of the room making her stomach roll on itself. The others stood talking quietly near the door leading to the teleportation unit.

Carson waited, watching her finish the water. "Want more?" he asked when she set the cup down.

"No." Her mouth was already drying out again, the fear she'd felt earlier lingering in the form of a tang the water hadn't washed away. When Carson continued to stare at her, she leaned back, settling her shoulders against the wall. "Before Kent died, he stabbed me with a pair of scissors in the hospital when I went to see him. It was near the end. He had no idea where he was or who he was. He lashed out since he didn't recognize me either."

"Jesus, Gill," Carson said. "I didn't know."

"No one did other than the nurses and doctor who stitched me up." She glanced at the decontamination area. "Kent used to smell like that. It was some antibacterial compound they coated him with so his bedsores wouldn't get infections. I hated that smell. It was like they tried to make it nice, something like vanilla and lavender, but fell short. It stunk." She brought her gaze back to him. "I smelled it on the ship while you were all in stasis."

"Maybe you shouldn't go to the surface."

"I'm not crazy." She leaned forward and lowered her voice. "Carson, someone else was awake. I didn't kill Tinsel."

His jaw worked side to side. He was quiet for nearly a minute, motionless except for his eyes tracking back and forth on the floor between them. Finally he said, "You think you can make it?"

"Yes."

"Even with going through decon?"

She hesitated. "Yes."

"Then let's get moving."

◆ ◆ ◆

Gillian tried breathing through her mouth, but she could still smell the decon compound, cloying funeral flowers rotting in a vase. She'd hurried through the sprays of fog in the labyrinth-like area and toweled as much of it off as she could before donning the fresh jumpsuit. But now, strapped into the lander's seat with her space suit and helmet on, the scent was building, coalescing into something alive on her skin and intent on flowing into her lungs with every breath.

The small ship shook once, everyone in the seats across from her jerking with the movement. The two crew members being taken to the surface to relieve their counterparts appeared almost bored through their visors. She tried recalling both of the men's names, but they escaped her.

"Okay, people. Here we go. Little drop as we clear the station, then a bit of turbulence when we enter the atmosphere. After that, smooth sailing," Guthrie said through the earpiece in her helmet.

The sensation of falling was overwhelming, much stronger than any roller coaster she'd ever been on and eclipsing the parabolic flights during training. She gritted her teeth, every nerve in her body humming as they plummeted away from the station. Someone swore, and she could feel a moan trying to break free as gravity returned full force, sinking her into her seat.

The ship turned halfway over before righting, and then they were falling again.

Outside the viewports, the wide bottom of the station slid away, leaving only empty space behind.

The ship rattled, tossing them all forward against their restraints.

"Whoa now," Guthrie muttered.

"Pardon me, everyone, but woo-hoo!" Easton exclaimed.

"Easton," Carson said.

"Sorry, Commander."

"You're not sorry," Lien said, a smile in her voice.

"Sorry, not sorry," Easton replied.

The ship bucked again, and the atmosphere outside became a white gauze as it passed the ports.

"Ander arranged for two of the botanists to show us around. We'll split into two groups when we land," Carson said. "We'll cover more ground that way."

There was another free fall followed by the hardest shudder yet, then silence and steady gravity as the ship leveled out.

"Apologies," Guthrie said. "Some drops are smoother than others."

"Fucking say that again," one of the station members muttered.

"I thought it was butter," Easton said.

"You're a sick man, you know that?" Lien said.

"Just enjoying the thrills when they come along, that's all. It's invigorating. This thing I call 'life.' You should try it some time."

Icy silence from Lien. Despite her suspicion, Gillian had to smile as Easton caught her eye and winked.

The lander descended quickly, and less than five minutes later, they pivoted hard to the right, and she felt the craft slow almost to a stop. A moment later, there were two bumps as its gear set down. They'd landed.

Everyone unbuckled, and a minute later, the entry port near the front of the ship corkscrewed outward and slid to one side, revealing a wide airlock they moved through.

"We're pressurized now, so we can get rid of these suits," Guthrie said, unlatching his helmet. "You guys are going to be touring the main and secondary spheres before heading over to number three. Put your gear on the cart outside the door, and I'll run it down to the next lock for your walk outside."

Gillian unhooked her helmet and twisted it free. Easton did the same beside her as she began unzipping her suit.

"We're going outside?" she asked him.

Easton tilted his head. "Didn't you hear Orrin say that up top?"

"No. Guess I missed it."

"Technical briefings can be some real boring shit, that's for sure."

She tugged off the last of her suit and folded it over one arm. "You seemed to be enjoying yourself back there."

Easton grinned. "Whole reason I'm here, Doc. Love the rides. Always flew a little faster than I should have back in the military. Dreamed of coming out this far someday. Would go farther if they let me."

"You two ready?" Carson asked from the airlock's door.

"Lead the way, Commander," Easton said.

Carson opened the door and stepped inside.

A thick blanket of wet air laced with the pungent smell of fresh dirt washed over her. Beyond the airlock, the biosphere opened up, and she blinked, taking in her surroundings.

Green was everywhere. Plants of all varieties grew in raised beds above a white, plastic-sheeted floor, some only a few inches tall while others towered six feet or more in luscious canopies. The walls of the dome were at least a hundred yards apart, crowning up to meet over-head in a high arch crisscrossed with pipes fitted with sprinklers. Ahead between the rows of plants, a rectangular pond stretched all the way to the farthest wall, where a stand of young trees grew in the illusion of a forested edge.

Carson nudged her shoulder, pulling her attention away from the spectacle. He motioned at the nearby cart holding the rest of the crew's suits and helmets. She placed hers alongside the others, and Guthrie pushed the cart away, moving toward the opposite side of the pond.

"Alien invaders," a voice said from the nearest row of bushes, and a middle-aged man appeared carrying a long plastic bag. He was short and thick through the shoulders with a bullish walk. He smiled, reveal-ing very even teeth.

"Same damn thing every time we rotate out," one of the station crew said in a dour tone, passing by Gillian. "Get some new material, Vern."

Vern's smile didn't dim. "Hello, everyone. Vernon Figg," he said, shaking hands with them all. "I'm the ranking botanist on staff and your tour guide for the day. Everyone calls me Vern." He glanced at the rotating station members, who were heading off through the rows of plant life. "The itinerary's been updated, guys. Make sure to take care of your checklists before you—"

"Yeah, yeah, Vern. This isn't our first rodeo," one replied over his shoulder as they continued away.

Vern watched them go, frowning slightly before clapping his hands together. "Okay. I'm told you all need a look around. I'll give you a little tour."

"Dr. Figg?" Carson said. "I was told another member of your team would be able to brief my other crew members for efficiency's sake while we're here. Is he available?"

"Oh. Guess I didn't get the memo. Not at the moment, he's in number three."

"That's fine. They'll suit up and make the walk over." Carson turned to Lien and Easton. "Take a look at all the sample data. Make sure it corresponds with what we've seen at the station. We'll meet you there if you're not back by the time we're done."

Easton and Lien headed off through the plants in the same direction Guthrie had gone, their footsteps squeaking on the synthetic flooring.

"I was under the impression we'd all stay together," Vern said. "But never mind. I'm sure Ben will take care of them. Right this way."

Vern led them to the left, the same direction the station members had gone. As they walked, one of the sprinkler heads opened up and rained on several rows in a gentle drizzle.

"Starting with the sphere itself," Vern said, turning partially toward them as he walked, "it looks opaque, but the solar panels on the outer shell actually allow the correct amount of the sun's rays to penetrate and reach the plants while also collecting enough energy to run the facilities."

They came upon a door set into the left wall, a keypad and scanner beside it.

"What's in there?" Gillian asked as Vern moved past it.

"Oh, that's the teleroom. What I call it anyway. Teleportation unit's inside. Been sealed up since the issues began."

"Have you shifted before, Doctor?"

"Please, call me Vern. Yes, about a dozen times or so."

"I noticed you haven't complained of any of the issues the other crew are experiencing."

Vern laughed, a loud booming that died against the foliage and rounded walls. "No, no. My memory's sharp as a tack. Haven't had a problem. Actually, it's pretty exhilarating. Have you had the honor yet?"

"No. I haven't."

"Pity. It's really something."

They continued on, meeting an archway that led to a small work area with two folding tables cluttered with computers and several trays of sprouting plants. Beyond the tables was a kitchenette where the two station crew members leaned, both sipping on cups of coffee.

"This is our main workstation. Pigsty, I know, but it does its job. I collected all of the physical printouts like you asked, Commander," Vern said, grabbing a large binder off the nearest table. "It will match all of the digital readouts logged on the station."

"Have you taken any other samples from the surface since your initial explorations?" Carson asked, taking the binder.

"No. Not since Orrin Ander was down with his rover. Not really our specialty. We're solely here to see if we can create a habitable biosphere in the most inhospitable environment." Vern grinned again, gesturing to the walls. "And we've succeeded. We're no longer using the CO_2 scrubbers. This sphere would support fifteen people full-time with the amount of plants we have here producing oxygen. Major accomplishment."

Gillian listened as she moved past the men into the room, ignoring the station members' eyes on her as she studied the walls and work surfaces. The smell of coffee nearly overpowered the greenhouse scent in this closed space, and she realized, thankfully, she could no longer smell the decon on her skin.

"Both of you have shifted?" she asked without taking her eyes off a whiteboard with a sloppily drawn bar graph in its center.

"Yeah," one of the men answered. "Twelve, fourteen times."

"Any problems with memory? Lapses in consciousness, anger issues?"

"Only when Vern eats all the best freeze-dried meals." The other man snickered into his coffee.

"Have either of you come into contact with anything strange? Seen or heard anything out of the ordinary?"

"Lady, this is Mars. There is no ordinary."

She turned to face him. "What do you mean?"

"We work in isolated conditions where a minute mistake could kill you instantly. Tension is a constant. That's all. Some are better suited to it than others."

"You're saying the people who have symptoms are unbalanced? Weak?"

He shrugged, a lopsided grin on his face. "I'm saying this place can get to you."

Gillian looked at him for a moment before nodding. "I can see that."

Vern clapped his hands together. "Let's move on, shall we?"

The station member smiled and held Gillian's gaze. She turned and followed Carson and Vern from the room, feeling the heavy weight of the man's eyes on her as she left.

"I'm sorry for those two. They're both very good at botany, not so good with people," Vern said, leading them through a row of blooming orchids beside a planter of cornstalks heavy with tasseled cobs.

They moved farther and farther into the maze of greenery, a sense of claustrophobia enveloping Gillian. She imagined this was what someone might experience wading through a wild rainforest with nature outnumbering humanity a hundred thousand to one. All that was missing were the whoops of monkeys and the chirps of hidden birds overhead.

Instead, the air was sterilized of sound, save for their footsteps.

"These silver aspen really took off in the last six months," Vern said, patting one of the narrow trees lining the end of the pond as they passed. "Some of these were transplanted instead of sprouting from seeds. That's why they're so tall."

Beyond the trees was an opening in the sphere's sloping wall, a low-domed hallway leading away and turning out of sight.

Gillian nudged Carson as they neared it. "The tunnel," she said quietly, and he nodded.

She inspected the walls and ceiling of the hall as they moved through it, but there was nothing damning or even interesting about its structure. It was made from the same material as the sphere, with thin light strips equidistant from one another overhead. If Mary Cranston had been referring to this tunnel, Gillian couldn't see anything unique about it.

They emerged into another biosphere, a miniature version of the main area they'd left. Many of the same plants were represented as well as several potted ferns so thick and healthy she wondered if she would cut her finger by touching one of their sturdy fronds. A small, rounded pond sat in the very center of the rows.

"So same setup here in number two, just less life and maintenance," Vern said. "Really, beyond keeping the proper mineral levels in the soil, there isn't a whole lot to do besides record data while we're here. Sometimes we watch reruns of old sitcoms to pass the time. Have you guys seen *Seinfeld*?"

Carson ignored the botanist and glanced at Gillian as he moved toward the pond, the look he gave her asking, *Seen enough yet?*

She had and hadn't. The biospheres were impressive. Awe-inspiring almost, when considering what was outside of them: miles upon miles of nothing, no life, no real atmosphere. Just emptiness and the wax and wane of light from a distant sun. There wasn't anything suggesting a threat she could see, something that might cause the symptoms the crew was suffering from. If they had made a discovery on the surface that put everyone at risk of infection, they were conspiring to keep it a complete secret.

There's something wrong with them.

"Gillian. Ready to move on?" Carson asked, breaking into her thoughts.

"Yeah, I'm ready."

As they walked through the remaining space of the sphere, a droplet of water fell from the irrigation system into the pool, rippling its surface outward in ever-expanding rings.

She followed the two men to an airlock much like the one they'd entered through from the lander. The cart with their gear was to one side, and a viewing pane of reinforced glass looked out through the door at the far end. Gillian went to it and peered outside, getting her first real glimpse of the surface up close.

It was red, but not the bleeding color she'd seen from space. Up close it was muted, an orange-and-tan composite dotted with rocks. Past a house-size boulder twenty yards away was another biosphere half the dimensions of the one they stood in now, its rounded skin alabaster against the Martian landscape.

"Why don't you have another tunnel linking the third biosphere?" Gillian asked, turning to face Carson and Vern.

The botanist rubbed the back of his neck and winced. "Technical error on our part when we began assembly. Construction placed both umbilicals together between numbers one and two. By the time we realized the mistake, setup was complete. So instead, we've been making the walk over to three via suits. It's actually not as uncomfortable as you'd think, especially this time of day. The temp's around zero Fahrenheit. Wait a few hours and it'll be fifty below."

Gillian looked out again at the panorama's stark beauty, the thought of how quickly it could kill a person hovering at the back of her mind. And for the first time, she truly hoped the distant planet Ander's spaceship was traveling toward would be the answer to humankind's plight. She couldn't imagine people surviving here, let alone thriving.

Vern snapped his fingers loudly. "Damn, just remembered I need to bring a couple trays of anthuriums over to three. Would you two be kind enough to carry them for me?"

Carson glanced at Gillian, who shrugged.

"Sure. We're going anyway," Carson said.

"Thank you. It'll save me digging my suit out of storage. I'll just run back to the station room and grab the trays."

"Need help?" Carson asked.

"That would be great, the trays are a little bulky."

"You wanna get suited up while you wait?" Carson asked Gillian, a hint of impatience in his eyes.

"Sure," she said.

"Be back in a jiff," Vern said as he and Carson moved into the biosphere and disappeared amongst the rows of plants.

Gillian walked to the cart against the wall and found her suit, pulling it free from beneath Carson's. She moved to a bench farther down the wall, sat, and began drawing on the heavy material. As she was closing the first pressure seals over the suit's main zipper, she heard the soft squeak of footfalls on the plastic flooring approaching the airlock entry.

"That was fast," she said, standing up and bringing the zipper all the way to her neck. Glancing at the doorway, she expected to see Carson and Vern there holding the trays of flowers, but the area before the lock was empty.

Stillness.

She waited. Listening.

Another squeak. And something else.

The smell of the decon compound.

Her heart seized before double-timing.

"Carson?" she said.

There was a series of quiet beeps, and the overhead door descended quickly into place, cutting her off from the biosphere.

Gillian rushed forward. Her feet slipped and she fell hard against the barrier. She looked out through the small viewing pane, straining to see to either side of the door.

Nothing. No one.

A coolly mechanical female voice spoke from above.

Airlock decompression in ten seconds.

"No! No! Stop! I'm in here!" Gillian yelled, hammering her fist on the glass.

Nine. Eight. Seven.

Panic swallowed her whole. She spun, vision blurring as she looked at the opposite door leading outside. A green light blinked on a control panel beside it.

Six. Five.

She sprinted to the panel and began hitting buttons at random. Then, spotting the "Emergency Shutdown" option, she stabbed it with a finger.

Four. Three.

She hit the button again and again. No response.

Gillian turned, knowing there was only one option now: get her helmet on before decompression. She ran toward the cart but froze after three steps.

Her and Carson's helmets were gone.

Two. One.

There was a hiss and pop as the outer door released its seal.

She sucked in two breaths and held the air as the door rose, Martian dust flitting inside on the floor. Frantically she searched the room and in one glance could see the helmets were nowhere inside.

Gillian hurried to the control panel and punched the "Seal" option again and again.

The door continued to rise.

Frigid cold consumed the airlock, trying to rip her breath away.

She turned, searching the biosphere's entrance window for some sign of Carson or Vern, but it was empty.

Already her lungs were beginning to smolder.

The door clanged fully open, and she could hear a hollow hum of alien wind on the landscape outside.

She hammered the "Door Close" option three times.

Nothing.

Her vision shimmered, a strange prickling enveloping her eyes. She tried blinking it away, but it only worsened the sensation. The last thing she saw before she had to close her eyes completely was the third biosphere's entrance door across the red plain.

Gillian ran.

The cold was like January in Minnesota: relentless, unforgiving. The planet's gravity difference made her feel as if she were running on a trampoline, and she stumbled on a loose rock, barely keeping her balance. The ground tried to trip her, make her fall. Was she still going in the right direction?

The air in her chest burned, lungs igniting as they hitched, crying out for oxygen.

But there was none.

Something slammed into her left arm, and she staggered away from it. The boulder she'd seen from the airlock, had to be. She was halfway to the biosphere. Nausea flooded her stomach, and she felt her consciousness flutter, the need for oxygen undeniable now.

Stale air blasted from her lungs, and she inhaled a shrieking breath, opening her eyes at the same time.

The biosphere was a dozen yards away, its door there and gone as her vision blurred, a rising heat in her eyes even as they became gritty and arid. It felt like she was swimming through sand. She coughed, the breath she'd taken doing almost nothing to ease the aching need for air.

Gillian tripped, her bad leg a tuning fork of pain. She sprawled into the dirt, a racking sob breaking free. She crawled forward, the edge of the biosphere appearing at the top of her vision that was darkening by the second. Her tongue was parchment, cracking as she drew in another worthless breath.

An image of Carrie at the beach in the sunlight flooded her mind as she lunged forward, the last of her strength evaporating like the moisture of her body.

Her hand thudded hard against something solid. She was cold. So cold.

Someone was yelling, screaming her name. But she couldn't hold on anymore.

Forever. She thought the last word and held on to the picture of Carrie even as wings of darkness folded over her and she let them carry her away.

Transcript of recorded conversation between former NASA mission communications manager Duane Freeman and former UN operations support specialist Olivia LePit, eleven hours after Discovery VI disaster. Logged evidence for federal investigation 100987, case 32. Also used as exhibit A12 by plaintiffs in class-action wrongful-death suit filed against NASA concerning Discovery VI disaster.

LePit: *Hello?*
Freeman: *Have you been briefed yet?*
LePit: *Partially. What the hell happened?*
Freeman: *We're not sure exactly, but from what we can tell, it's catastrophic.*
LePit: *Catastrophic. Define that, please.*
Freeman: *Complete loss. Something to do with magnetic operations.*
LePit: *Fuck. What do we know so far?*
Freeman: *Several emergency transmissions that don't make any sense. We're combing through them now to try and narrow down what caused it.*
LePit: *Mechanical or human error?*
Freeman: [Inaudible.]
LePit: *What did you say?*
Freeman: *I don't see how it can be mechanical. Not on this level.*
LePit: *We need someone on damage control. Find out who knows what, and keep this thing contained until we have a plan of action. If this gets to*

the press before we can come up with a briefing, we're done, all of us. The entire project is probably going to be scrapped in any case.

Freeman: *I think it's over. There's no coming back from this. Just remains to be seen if it was an accident or not.*

THIRTY-THREE

Gillian could hear waves rushing onto the shore, their cascading sound triggering a deep calm that spread from her center outward.

She was home, back on the beach out in front of Katrina's. She must've fallen asleep in the sun while Carrie was playing in the sand.

Something tightened around her arm, cinching to the point of pain.

Gillian cracked open her eyes.

What she thought was the sun at first dissolved into an overhead light. Sterile ceiling and walls. The blood-pressure cuff eased its grip on her arm as it deflated, and the ocean's waves became the static hiss of oxygen flowing from the tubes inserted in her nostrils. And something else. A low voice speaking quietly.

Orrin sat in a chair to her left. He was reading from a book, the title on the cover blocked by one of his hands. He stopped, noticing the turn of her head, and set the book aside as he stood.

"Welcome back. How you feeling?"

She took an assessment of herself, licked her cracked lips. "Eyes and mouth are sore. Chest hurts a little too." She winced, trying to move an arm. It felt like her joints were full of broken glass. "What happened?"

Her voice was thick, and she felt the faint pull of painkillers, deliciously familiar.

"You took a walk outside without a suit on."

Slowly the memory came back, easing into clarity like a sunrise. "Someone opened the airlock."

Orrin frowned. "Who?"

"I . . . I don't know. I . . ." She had to stop, the dryness of her mouth and throat killing the words.

"Here." Orrin held out a container with a straw poking from its top.

She sipped, the water cold and heavenly. "Thank you."

"You weren't able to see who did it?"

"No. There was no one there. And . . . they took the helmets so I'd . . ." Her voice broke, and she shook her head.

"It's okay now. Just rest. I volunteered to sit with you while Carson took a break. He's been here almost constantly since you were brought back up."

"How long?"

"About eighteen hours. But you were lucky. Easton saw you coming and was able to get you inside number three's airlock right after you passed out. The doctor said there weren't any signs of permanent damage. Your eyes and tongue hurt because the moisture in your body was boiling away without the atmospheric pressure. You also got a slight case of the bends. Joints hurt?"

"Yeah. Feel hungover."

"I bet. I'll let Carson know you're awake."

Orrin was almost to the door when she cleared her throat and said, "Thank you."

He nodded. "No problem. Feel better."

Then she was alone, listening to the faint sounds of people moving and speaking outside the infirmary room, the whir of a monitor fan beside the bed, the sluggish chug of her heart below it all. The lingering drug in her system tried pulling her back down into sleep, but she fought it, the knowledge that someone had tried to kill her and might not be far away even now keeping her awake.

It was only a few minutes before the door opened and Carson appeared with Leo close behind. She could see relief on Carson's face as he approached, and something else indefinable.

"Hey, good to see you awake," he said, stopping beside her bed. Leo gave her a warm smile and began studying her vitals on the digital readout.

"Good to be awake," she replied, her voice smoother than before.

"Gave us quite a scare," Leo said. "You remember who I am?"

She nodded. "You're a King fan, like me."

He smiled again. "I don't think there's been any permanent damage. You'll be sore, and your mouth and eyes will be irritated for a few days, but you'll heal up just fine."

"Good to hear."

"I'm sorry, they issued you a dose of morphine. They gave it to you before I could explain your situation. You can have ibuprofen from now on."

She nodded and gave Carson a look.

"Leo, could you give us a few minutes?" Carson asked.

"Sure thing." To her he said, "You hit that 'Call' button and I'll come running."

"Thanks, Leo."

As the door closed behind the doctor, Carson drew the chair Orrin had been sitting in closer to the bed and settled onto its edge. What she'd seen in his expression before was clearer now. Unease, a nervous tension extending from his features down into his shoulders and posture.

"Believe me now?" she asked quietly.

He let a long breath out. "What happened?"

She relayed everything she could remember, fear coursing along her skin like a cold draft as she told him what it was like fleeing the open airlock and running blind to the third biosphere. "Thought I was going to die," she finished. "And I gave up right at the end. Thought I had more fight in me than that." A teardrop welled in her right eye, and she wiped it away.

"It's a miracle you're all right," Carson said. "Most people wouldn't have made it half as far as you did. I'm glad Easton was where he was, when he was."

"Ditto." She took a deep breath, siphoning off the anxiety as she cleared her mind of the memories. "Who was it? One of the botanists or Guthrie?"

He took his time answering. "None of them."

"What?"

"When Vern and I got to the office, Guthrie was there chatting with the other two. We grabbed the trays of plants, and when we came back, the door was shut and you were gone, already inside the next biosphere."

"That's not possible. Someone closed the airlock and opened the outer door. Someone tried to kill me, Carson." She could feel hysteria returning, the blip of her pulse revving on the monitor beside the bed.

"I know."

She'd expected him to try rebuffing her, explaining to her or accusing her of what had happened. "You believe me?"

"Yes. We found the helmets hidden behind a stack of fertilizer halfway across the second sphere."

She let the gravity of it all sink in as another memory returned to her, solidifying out of the darkness of her mind. "I smelled it again. The decon compound. Right before the door closed."

He stiffened. "I think I know why." When she said nothing and waited, he wet his lips and leaned forward. "The decontamination chamber isn't the only place the compound is used. The insides of the teleportation units are coated in it too. It kills any bacteria or virus in the tube so there's no chance of contamination when someone shifts. You're covered in the stuff when you re-atomize."

"Carson—"

"I'm sorry I didn't believe you, but you have to understand, you were the only one awake, and your blood was on the pry bar. Nothing else made sense. And the way Tinsel died . . ."

It was several seconds before all the pieces fell into place. "There's a shifting unit on the ship," she said.

He put a hand over his mouth and sat back in the chair, watching her.

"Where?" she asked.

"There was a hidden door in medical. Dr. Ander asked that we keep it a secret from the crew. Only Tinsel and I knew."

She saw the outline of the entrance, recalled studying it, wondering what was behind it. "Why?" she asked after a moment.

"I don't know. Ander said something about more trials, but the possibility didn't occur to me until you mentioned the smell of the decon."

"Someone was shifting onto the ship," she said, a prickling sensation creeping across the back of her neck.

Carson was like a statue, only his jaw moving slightly side to side.

She lowered her voice to a whisper. "Someone from the station."

He tipped his head slightly.

"That's who I saw on the ship. Someone killed Tinsel. They didn't want him getting here, and they shifted down to the surface to try and kill me too. I wasn't hallucinating."

Carson looked away. "That's partially true."

"What do you mean?"

He hesitated before rushing through the words. "Birk's food was laced with a drug called salvenin. It's a derivative of a plant called salvia. The drug induces nausea, disorientation, and mild hallucinations."

White-hot anger rose within her. "Why was it in his food?"

"Tinsel suggested it when he found out you were bringing an assistant. And after he saw Birk, he insisted on it. Tinsel thought without the drug Birk could force us to abort the mission, possibly on your behalf, when you both found out we were coming here."

"Are you fucking kidding me?" Gillian tried to go on, but her throat spasmed painfully, and she coughed. Carson handed her the cup of water, and she restrained herself from batting it out of his hand. She drank, trying to let the cool liquid quench her rage. "So you drugged us to keep us in line."

"Not you, only Birk. Neither of you were supposed to stay awake. I assume you ended up eating some of his food during the trip?"

She recalled bumping Birk's food containers onto the floor, their number mixing in with her own. She'd known all along what she'd seen wasn't typical opioid withdrawal.

"That was low even for you, Carson."

"Look, I was completely against it, but Tinsel had authority over the mission. Without agreeing with him, nothing could move forward."

"You mean you couldn't have kidnapped us."

Carson sat back, features darkening. "The drug is harmless and temporary."

"That makes everything better."

"Gillian, please—"

"No, listen to me," she said, ignoring the pain in her throat. "I need to know you're on my side, that I can count on you. No more lies. So if there's anything else you need to tell me, do it now."

She watched him, searching for a sign he was hiding something more, but didn't see it.

"That's it," he said.

They sat quietly, not looking at each other for several minutes, letting the moment of tension pass. "Knowing we were drugged does clear up the possibility space travel has anything to do with the symptoms here. I was worried that might be another factor."

"A silver lining to this shit-show," Carson said.

"Yes, thank you so much for your help."

"I'm sorry. Like I said, I was against it the whole time."

"So where do we go from here?" she asked, stepping past her anger.

"I'm not sure. I'm not a cop."

"I had some thoughts about why someone would want Tinsel dead."

"He might've stopped the mission."

"Right." She gestured to the room. "Everything going on here, especially the teleportation."

"You think it was Ander?"

"He has the most motivation if something critical is wrong with his breakthrough."

"He's brilliant and driven, but I couldn't imagine him doing something like that."

"But I fit the part?"

He let the barb sail by. "It would have to be someone familiar with the technology and ballsy as hell to try shifting that distance." Carson glanced at her. "That's the main reason I suspected you and not someone from the station. I didn't think anyone would try something like that. No one's ever traveled that far before."

"Whoever it was must've known Tinsel would be a problem. And now I'm next in line because I've been testing the crew." She paused. "Getting closer to the truth."

"Doesn't make any sense," he murmured.

"What?"

He was a long time answering, and she was about to prompt him again when he said, "After what happened on the surface, I checked the security-log key scans for your room on the station."

Gillian could feel something coming, some unseen force bent on knocking her off her axis. She didn't want to know, didn't want to say the words even as she spoke them. "Who was it? Who was in my room?"

Carson took a breath. "Dr. Ivan Pendrake."

THIRTY-FOUR

"Pendrake? Carson, he's dead."

"I know. I've seen the autopsy report, pictures of the body, everything. But his key card was used to enter your room. I checked the video feed, but the camera system had been reset. And that's not all." He brought his voice to an even lower volume, and she shifted toward him, aware that not all but most of the anger had dissipated from her. "Pendrake's body is missing."

"What?"

"I went down to the storage level where they were keeping it a few hours ago after looking at the security logs. The station manager on duty let me in, but there was nothing inside the remains container."

"Someone took the body?"

"Either that or Pendrake's not really dead."

"Why would everyone help fake his death? Make up a murder?"

"No idea. But . . ."

"But what?"

"Before he was killed, we received transmission notations from him on certain crew files concerning psychological assessments. That's what started this whole mission and put a halt to shifting. Pendrake hadn't come right out and said he had concerns with the project, but it was between the lines. Enough so the order was given to put a freeze on using the technology."

Gillian tilted her head back, resting it on a pillow. "So Pendrake starts making waves and Diver kills him shortly after."

"Maybe."

"What the hell's going on?" she whispered, a thought striking her quiet for a moment. "The other day right after we tested Dennis Kenison, he said something to me. He said there's something wrong with everyone."

Carson frowned. "What did he mean?"

"I don't know. He said it so only I'd hear and walked away. Could be something to do with Pendrake's death."

"We should talk to him."

"Definitely."

"And there's something else. The crew who complained of symptoms prior to our arrival refused to sign the permission forms for your examination."

"What?"

"Said they weren't comfortable with the procedure. Now that could be true, but why turn down a test that could help?"

"They might've been leery of me with the accusations, but you're right, if I was sick I would want to get help." They stared at each other, the questions hanging thick in the air. "Let me get dressed," she finally said, swinging her legs to the side of the bed.

"Whoa. You need rest."

"Carson, I'm pretty much done with taking orders from you. You can help me or stay out of my way."

He stood gazing at her for a moment before crossing to the door. "I'll be outside."

She watched him go and listened to the door click shut before drawing out the IV from her arm and climbing from the bed to find her clothes.

◆ ◆ ◆

There were a few seconds while drawing on a fresh jumpsuit Gillian was sure she was going to pass out, but after several deep breaths while holding on to the bed's frame, the dizziness passed. The painkiller was completely gone from her system, and its absence was so achingly familiar, the hydros she'd hidden in her room came to mind. She shook off the temptation, the irritating hitch of her lungs each time she breathed gaining her full attention. Her tongue felt like she'd held it to a belt sander, and her eyes had grit in them whenever she blinked.

But it felt good to get up and move around. Except for the dull twinging in her leg, her body felt stronger than she'd anticipated. Maybe some of the strength she'd had prior to withdrawing from the hydros was returning.

Outside the room, Carson fell into step beside her, and as they passed a compact station desk at the center of the ward, a medical technician with a flat-eyed stare watched them, her graying hair pulled back in a bun so tight it seemed to stretch her forehead taut.

"I let them know you were discharging yourself," he said as they turned a corner and headed toward the central elevator system.

"She seemed broken up to see me go."

"No one's been really cordial. Here, you'll need this now," he said, handing her a key card. "It'll open pretty much any door in the station. And this too, forgot to put it in your personal effects before." He held out her mother's rosary, and she took it from him faster than she meant to.

She tucked the rosary away and turned the key over. "Thank you."

They walked in silence for several steps before he said, "I wish you would take it easy. You don't know how close you were."

"Someone in this place tried to kill me, more than once. I want nothing more than to leave right now and head back to Earth to see my little girl, but we still haven't figured out what's causing the symptoms. Right now I don't have a choice."

They stopped by the elevators, and Carson called one of them. "You think it's the shifting?"

"There's nothing else that makes sense."

"That would mean most of the crew is lying about not having any symptoms."

The elevator door opened, and they stepped inside. "Maybe that's what Kenison meant. But diseases progress differently in people. Maybe it's not affecting them all yet."

They rode upward, getting off on a level she hadn't visited before. Several crew members were playing a game of pool in a room to the right; a long, fully stocked bar stretched behind them. Carson led her past what appeared to be a large kitchen and group dining area before scanning in through a set of doors on the left. The room inside was spacious, with a rounded bank of windows on its far side opening up to endless space and a trillion stars dotting the curtain of darkness. A conference table was centered in the room, and Easton, Lien, and Birk were seated at one end.

Birk rose and hurried to her as soon as she stepped inside, grasping her shoulders tightly to hold her at arm's length. "Are you all right, Doctor?"

"Better now."

He hugged her gently. "I'm beginning to think coming here was a mistake."

She had to laugh. "You might be right."

He studied her again as if making sure she was real before finally releasing her. When she moved to take a seat at the table, she was surprised to see Lien standing, facing her.

"I owe you an apology, Doctor," Lien said. "Both for being complicit in your deceit and for doubting your innocence." She bowed slightly before bringing her gaze back to Gillian's.

"Thank you, Lien."

"I for one never believed any of that bullshit about you," Easton said loudly. "Everybody has their vices. I love vodka like a fish loves water. And Commander, no offense, I've seen you chow those little cream cake things like there's no tomorrow."

"Easton . . ." Carson sighed.

"All I'm saying is, you being a murderer because you were fucked up on some pills didn't make sense to me." He held up his hands. "Glad we're all on the same page now."

"Thank you," Gillian said, smiling. "And thank you for saving me. I wouldn't be here otherwise."

"No problem, Doc. Right place right time is all. You feeling better?"

"On the mend."

"Good. Now we can get down to this thing," Easton said.

They all settled around the end of the table as Birk placed a steaming cup of coffee before each of them that completely surprised Gillian with the richness of its taste.

Carson began talking, telling the others what he'd discovered concerning Pendrake. When he finished, they all glanced at one another before Lien broke the silence. "So does that mean he's alive? He's the one doing this?"

"It just means someone's using his key card," Carson said. "I find it pretty unlikely everything surrounding the murder was staged. And why would they do that?"

"So he's still dead and someone got rid of the body," Easton said, reclining in the chair before putting his feet up on the table.

"That's my guess," Gillian said.

"Then there's something up with the corpse they didn't want us to see."

"Might be. If there was something incriminating Leo could've picked up on, they didn't want to take a chance."

"Like what?" Birk asked.

"I don't know," Gillian said.

"Listen, I have to ask this just so we're clear," Easton said, sliding his boots from the tabletop and sitting forward. "We came here to iron out the kinks in Ander's voodoo units, right? Now we're dealing with a psychopath. Which are we focusing on?"

"I think they're intertwined," Gillian said slowly. She gazed around at the group, the image of the interconnected rings of her glass's condensation on the table in Florida surfacing in her mind. "Whoever's doing this doesn't want us here, doesn't want us finding out what's wrong with shifting. That's why they killed Tinsel. He had the authority to shut this all down."

"Because whoever it is knows the truth," Lien said.

"Exactly. And I have an idea where we should start looking."

THIRTY-FIVE

"So you haven't told Ander anything about what happened on the surface?" Gillian said.

"I briefed him but didn't broach the subject of someone using teleportation to get back and forth from the station to the surface," Carson said.

She, Carson, and Easton rode upward on the elevator, the levels ticking by in red numbers. They had left Birk and Lien in the hallway of the crew-quarters level, Carson instructing them to find Leo and fill him in on their conversation.

"He's gonna take that well," Easton said, staring at the car's ceiling.

"After this, I'd like to see Kenison," Gillian said, all of their feet lifting slightly off the floor as the car came to a stop. "Maybe he'd be willing to tell us what he meant the other day."

The doors opened to Ander's level, the vestibule empty of the receptionist. Ahead the door to the doctor's quarters was open, faint classical music drifting out. Inside the lights were low, the large sectional couches slabs of shadow. The same phrase in French she'd seen the first time floated on the main display. Ander himself reclined in one of the rolling chairs before a touchscreen, fingers rubbing in slow circles at his temples.

"Doctor?" Carson said.

The old man bolted upright.

"Sorry to startle you."

"No, no. It's all right. I was miles away," Ander said, standing. "Dr. Ryan, glad to see you up and about. Quite the ordeal you went through."

"Yes, it was. That's actually why we're here," she said, studying Ander's eyes. There was no alarm or panic in them, just steady scrutiny. "Someone tried to kill me."

Ander sighed. "Carson explained this to me, but he also said everyone who was in the biospheres was accounted for at the time in question."

"They were. It was someone else, someone from the station."

A soft laugh escaped him as he looked between her and Carson. "There's only one lander, and it was on the surface. There's simply . . ." His voice died away, and he squinted at her. "You're not suggesting—"

"Yes, we are," Carson said. "Gillian smelled the decontamination compound before she was forced out of the airlock, and she also smelled it on the ship before Tinsel's death."

"That's preposterous. We are under strict protocol. No one has shifted in over four months."

"Someone left opioids in my room," Gillian said. "We checked the security key scans."

"And?"

"Ivan Pendrake's key card was used," Carson said.

Ander looked from one of them to the next, a gradual smile breaking out on his face. "This is some kind of joke." When no one said anything, he sobered instantly. "Ivan was my friend for over twenty years. A partner in the development of my life's work. He is dead, murdered by an unhinged individual, and I don't appreciate you sullying his name."

"His body's missing," Easton said, settling onto the back of a sectional.

"What? Nonsense. It's in—"

"The remains container is empty," Carson said. "I looked myself. We're not saying Dr. Pendrake is still alive, but someone has his key card and is using it to access rooms."

Ander looked like a boat's sail without wind. He lowered himself into his chair, his face slowly draining of color.

"Do you have any idea who could be doing this?" Carson asked.

The old man shook his head, seeming to barely hear him.

"Doctor?" Gillian said, stepping closer. She waited until he raised his gaze to her. "We'd like you to access the teleportation log for us."

For a moment Ander didn't move. Then he swiveled, drew his chair close to the nearest touchscreen, and entered a code before punching in a series of commands. Gillian shared a look with Carson and Easton.

Ander pressed the screen a last time, and a new window opened. He stared at the line of text in its center before sinking back in his chair.

"What's it say?" Gillian asked, her heart punching at her ribs.

Carson stepped close to the doctor, reading over his shoulder before turning back to her. "There's one access listed for a shift down to the surface fifteen minutes after we left in the lander."

"Who?"

"Dennis Kenison."

◆　◆　◆

"I want stun guns out and ready when we go through the door, clear?" Carson said as they hurried down the main corridor in the crew quarters. The two men striding beside him both nodded, hands going to the Tasers on their belts as Gillian followed behind. Her heart was pounding, had been ever since Carson said Kenison's name out loud ten minutes before. But something felt off. Kenison hadn't seemed like someone capable of any of this. He'd been terrified before they'd tested him, a man waiting for a death sentence. He was either an unbelievable actor, or . . .

"You sure you want to be here for this?" Easton asked from beside her.

"Yeah. Definitely."

"Good thing there's no guns up here, or shit could get messy."

"This is it," Carson said, slowing to a stop before a door exactly the same as the dozens they'd already passed. Before they'd left the upper level, Carson had had Ander check Kenison's key scans. He'd entered his room two hours ago and hadn't keyed through any other checkpoints since.

And that was something else that bothered her. Why had he used Pendrake's key to leave the hydros in her room but his own when shifting to the surface?

Gillian brushed the thought away as Carson glanced at the two security personnel before swiping a card across the door's reader.

There was a click, and Carson pushed forward, moving fast inside the room. The men behind him followed, and Gillian hesitated before going after them.

Kenison's room was much larger than her own, with two windows facing into space and what must've been a queen-size bed beside a large desk. There was artwork on the wall, several small pieces of abstract done in black and white.

She saw everything but registered none of it.

At first she couldn't make sense of the shoes hanging five feet off the floor, her mind trying to relate it to some type of zero-gravity interference. But then her eyes traveled up Kenison's form to the purple hue of his face, the ashen stub of tongue protruding from between his teeth, and the belt cutting deep into his throat as he dangled from a support in the ceiling.

THIRTY-SIX

Gillian stared at the screen before her, not seeing the data she clicked through with absent strokes of her finger.

The lab was quiet, the hum of the station itself an undertone broken only by an occasional whisper of the oxygen-exchange system. She had come here directly after leaving Kenison's room, knowing the lab would be the only place anything would make sense, the only place things had ever made sense after Kent had been diagnosed. The image of Kenison's twisted features continued to flash through her mind, taking up position alongside Tinsel's. She'd passed a crew member on the way here carrying a compact ladder in the opposite direction, realizing later it was for climbing onto to cut Kenison's body from the ceiling.

She jolted as the door swished open and Birk entered, two steaming cups of coffee held before him.

"The finest space roast I could summon, Doctor," he said, placing her cup on the table.

"Thanks. It's really not that bad, considering," she said, taking a sip of the dark brew.

Birk made a face. "It is, for lack of a better word, shit."

She laughed. "I guess we can't be too choosy. Can't zip over to Starbucks. Although that name would make a lot more sense out here." Birk gave her a blank look. "Never mind. It was a joke."

"Thank you for informing me."

"Watch it or I'll fire your ass, kid."

He sighed, glancing at his cup. "If we were at home, I would make it with egg, like my mother."

"Egg? In the coffee?"

"Of course. It is the best. An old Swedish tradition."

She shivered. "Sounds disgusting."

Birk smiled evilly. "Really? You've drunk it dozens of times, Doctor."

"What?"

"Whenever it is my turn to bring coffee to the lab, I always make it with egg."

"You monster."

He bowed slightly. "You're welcome."

The levity felt good after the last twenty-four hours. Her eyes and tongue were still sore, but her lungs no longer ached when she breathed in deeply. Gillian returned her attention to the screen, scrolling through Kenison's test results before continuing on to Mary Cranston's.

"Do you think it is over, Doctor?" Birk asked.

"You mean what's happening here?" She sat silently for a long time. "No."

"Then we cannot go home."

"There's nothing I'd like more. But if we leave now without knowing if there's something wrong with shifting, I wouldn't be able to help Carrie." Her voice tried to close off before saying her name.

"Maybe there is another way now that you have perfected our work. Perhaps the surgeons at—"

"There's no surgery that can fix all of the tangles. Not yet anyway. And I can't risk her life when there's an answer right here." She pointed at the screen. "I can feel it."

"But what was this Kenison trying to hide by killing Tinsel?"

"I don't know. I don't—" But she stopped herself before she could say the rest of the thought. The inkling that had been gnawing at her from the second after seeing Kenison dangling from his own belt. "There's something we're missing," she said.

Birk stifled an enormous yawn before staring down at his coffee with a look bordering on loathing.

"You should go to bed, it's really late," she said.

"You as well, Doctor?"

"I'll stay here for a bit. Don't think I could sleep if I tried. Plus, now I've got the run of the place since I'm no longer a murder suspect," she said, holding out her key card.

"That reminds me, Carson told me earlier your new room is ready. It is directly beside my own."

"And here I was just getting used to that Shangri-la they had me in."

"It is most certainly a leap up."

"Step up."

"Yes, yes." He waved his hand at her. "You're sure you want to stay? I can wait until you're ready."

"Get out of here, Birk. Before I fire your ass."

"You know what would make you feel better?" he said, standing from his chair.

"What?"

"Egg coffee."

She picked up a pen and hurled it at him, and he dodged to the side and headed for the door. When he was gone, the silence closed in once again.

Gillian scanned back through the pages of test results.

Normal.

Normal.

Normal.

Nothing physically wrong with their neurons. Why did she keep coming back to that? And why each time did she hear a train, the steady clack of its Johnny Cash rhythm playing in her head even now?

Nearly an hour later, the door to the lab opened, and she turned, expecting to see Birk again, feigning an inability to sleep just so he could mother-hen her.

Instead, Eric Ander stood in the lab's entrance.

For a beat he said nothing, then gestured at the room. "I hope I'm not interrupting. I know I get very aggravated whenever someone barges in while I'm working."

Gillian gathered herself, the surprise at seeing the old man giving way to a trickle of disquiet. "No, not at all. Come in."

Ander moved to the table and placed his hands on the back of the reclining medical chair Kenison had sat in only days ago. As if reading her thoughts, he turned the chair back and forth and said, "Doesn't seem real, does it?"

"No. It doesn't."

"You were there, I'm told."

She nodded.

"I never figured—" He stopped himself, clearing his throat. "I knew Dennis well. Worked together for several years prior to the launch. Stout mind, great scientist. This is so terribly out of character."

"Everyone's a mystery. Even to themselves."

"Perhaps you're right. This will be hard on Orrin," he added after a moment.

"They were friends?"

"Yes. Became fairly close after Orrin received his clearance to join the mission. They both had an affinity for old movies. Watched them together sometimes up on the screens near our quarters like a couple of kids."

"I'm sorry."

He glanced at her. "Thank you. When something like this happens, it always makes you reflect on yourself, your actions. Could you have done something different? Did you miss a warning sign? And to think he was the one responsible for Mr. Tinsel and for nearly . . ." He motioned to her before gazing around the lab. "Those who attempt great and wonderful things always say there are setbacks and hardships on the road to success, but it doesn't really do anything like this justice. The loss of life in vain is the greatest loss of all."

Gillian noticed something she hadn't spotted before beneath the brilliant arrogance and defensive bluster: compassion.

"Why did you choose this?" she asked. "You could have done anything with your talent. Why interstellar travel?"

A sad smile creased his face. "Why did you become a neural radiologist?"

"I'll trade you."

"What?"

"My story for yours."

Ander smiled again and settled into the chair. "Seems fair."

"I was a radiology technician years ago. My husband was diagnosed with Losian's, and I thought I could save him. Went back to school, got my doctorate, started my research on the side."

"He passed, didn't he?" Ander said quietly.

"Yes. He did. And now my daughter is dying too." Her eyes began to burn, but she went on. "That's why I'm here."

Ander gazed down at his hands, the wrinkles and lines seeming to entrance him. "Losian's. Yet another horrid side effect of the larger disease that's killing the Earth. I've read dozens of articles linking the rise in pollution to the condition. If we don't succeed in this endeavor, maybe that's how we'll all go: without memory into the void. And there will be no one to remember us." He shook his head. "I'm sorry."

"It's all right."

"My mother. That's why I'm sitting in this chair right now," he said after a pause. "She was from Syria. She and my father met during the last years of the uprisings there. He was a doctor volunteering abroad to help in war-torn nations. She had been caught in a firefight and wounded. She lost several fingers on her right hand, and the injury was infected by the time my father was able to treat her. It was love, just like that." He snapped his fingers and smiled. "At least that's what my father always said. I was born a year later." Ander blinked, his vision turning inward. "I can barely remember her, mostly her outline when she would tuck me into bed. We lived with her sister and mother in a part of the city that was beginning to be rebuilt. My father continued to work both in the country and abroad. Then the fighting started again."

Gillian watched him reach up and rub his face, noticing for the first time he had a fine growth of white whiskers on his cheeks.

"I was six then. My father had applied a year before for our US citizenship. I had been approved, but we were still waiting for my mother's papers. When the fighting got worse, she made him take me away. He told me it wouldn't be more than a few months and she would join us in our new home. But she never came."

The old man grew quiet, eyes glazing. "What happened?" Gillian asked gently.

"Two days after we left for America, a bomb hit our building. I learned later no one could say what side it belonged to, such is the folly of war. My father received the news weeks after it happened and couldn't bring himself to tell me. Every day I would ask him when Mother would be here, and he always said, 'Soon.'" Ander smiled sadly. "So while I waited, I dreamed first of boats that could speed across the sea to retrieve her and the rest of my family. Then of planes that could fly straight there and back in less than a minute. I dreamed."

Gillian saw Ander's eyes shimmer as he looked away across the lab. "I'm so sorry," she said.

"It was a very long time ago. But I never forgot my dreams of traveling, even after my father finally told me Mother would never be coming home." He slumped lower in the chair as if the story had drained him.

Gillian tried to think of something to say, but everything seemed a paltry shadow of comfort.

"I'd like you to test me," Ander said, straightening.

"Test you? Why?"

"Because I believe you might be right." His jaw worked, and it seemed to take a titanic effort for him to speak. "There may be something wrong with my machines."

Gillian sat forward. "Why do you say that?"

"I . . . I have forgotten certain things." Ander grimaced. "And at first I didn't know if it was old age or something more. My mind isn't what it used to be."

"What have you forgotten?"

"The house I grew up in with my father, my best friend's name from high school and what he looked like, the sound of my wife's voice." His words broke at the end, and she saw the moisture return to his eyes. "First they were indistinct, so I didn't pay attention to them, and now they are gone completely. I worried it might have something to do with shifting when several of the crew complained of the same thing, but I couldn't get myself to accept it." Now he was crying, tears leaking down through the wrinkles of his face like rain through drought-ridden hills. "I needed to continue testing. That's why I wanted Carson to bring me one of the two originals from Earth: to reevaluate the design."

Gillian felt a cold crumbling inside her, something collapsing in on itself. And all at once she was furious with the old man, full of rage that his pride had kept so much hidden.

Some of her anger must have bled into her expression because he continued. "You have to realize I thought everything was fine. I found no substantial correlation between teleportation and the symptoms. And I wanted to help, I've spent my whole life wanting to help when others couldn't. This was my chance."

His shoulders shook as he wept, and despite herself, Gillian reached out and placed a hand on his shoulder. "Thank you for telling me."

Ander wiped at his face and sat back fully in the chair.

She went through the preparations for the test automatically, mind on a sidetrack fully consumed with the implications of what Ander had told her. If he hadn't been truthful, who else hadn't?

After she had drilled the hole in his skull, inserted the port, and injected the luciferin, she stood before him. He looked frail, nearly skeletal, reclining in the chair beneath the harsh overhead lights.

"Find your happiest memory, Doctor. Tell me when you have it."

He closed his eyes. She waited.

"All right," he finally said.

Gillian moved to the table and touched the control screen, tapping the injection command.

The luciferase flowed through the tube.

She watched in awe again as the compounds did their work. Ander's mind was revealed to her, there in flashing brilliance all that made him who he was.

Gillian froze, the last of the synapses firing on the screen. An idea, amorphous and huge, loomed over her, too indistinct to grasp, but there nonetheless. It was like the passing shadow of a low-flying plane, darkening all around her and then gone, leaving only an impression of its presence behind.

Ander grunted, his eyelids fluttering. She moved to his side. "Can you hear me, Doctor?"

"Yes, yes, I'm fine," he said, but fresh tears had sprung to his eyes. He started to sit up out of the chair, but she pushed him back.

"Let me unhook you." She went to work on detaching the port, then bandaged the miniscule hole in his skull. She fed the scan into the mainframe computer and turned back to him. "I'm not trying to pry, but do all your happiest memories make you cry?"

Ander laughed quietly. "Just that one. I thought about the day Orrin came home from his deployment."

"Is that where he got his injuries?"

"Yes. He was the leader of his explosive ordnance disposal team. When the military called, I thought it was the one all parents of soldiers dread. They would only tell me he had been injured in a roadside attack. Later I found out he was the sole survivor of his squadron."

She recalled Orrin's quiet way of speaking, his thoughtful stares. "That must've been horrible for him."

"It was. He had . . . many struggles. It's another reason I'm worried about him after Dennis. First Ivan, now this."

"Dr. Pendrake and Orrin were close?"

Ander glanced at her, and for a second she expected him to get up and leave without replying.

"Ivan was Orrin's therapist," he said. "He helped him through dozens of ordeals on Earth. It was good Orrin wasn't the one who found Diver in Ivan's room that morning. I'm afraid he would have killed him with his bare hands."

Gillian let the silence spool out, a barrage of thoughts assaulting her.

A soft bleep issued from the touchscreen, bringing her back to the present. She studied the results returned from the quantum computer for several minutes before turning the display toward Ander. "Completely normal. No neurological tangles or any other evidence of damage."

He frowned, gazing at the readouts. "I don't understand," he said almost to himself.

"Neither do I," she said. "Neither do I."

◆ ◆ ◆

Gillian stepped off the elevator onto the crew-quarters level, her footfalls echoing back to her throughout the empty hall. She and Ander had discussed other possibilities for another half hour before the physicist bid her good night, saying he was too exhausted to think clearly and perhaps they could continue working in the morning. As they'd parted ways, she realized something had changed in her assessment of the old man. There was an open, genuine quality about him she hadn't noticed before, possibly stemming from his scientific straightforwardness. In any case, she found herself warming to him despite his prior dishonesty.

She put a hand to her temple, feeling a bout of exhaustion roll through her. It was extremely late, or really early, depending on how one looked at it.

"Last call," a voice said, stopping her in her tracks. She bit back the startled cry that tried to escape her and looked to the left.

Orrin sat behind the bar in the rec room. He was tipped back on his stool, a glass of amber liquid in one hand, and even from a distance, she could see how utterly wrecked he was.

She moved to the bar and took a seat across from him as he finished his glass and refilled it from an open decanter. "How are you doing?" she asked as he settled back into his seat.

"Me? Just fine. Drinking with all my friends," he said, spreading his arms out to the empty room. "Anything?"

"Um, no. I was just heading to bed."

"Come on. One won't kill you." He slopped some of the whiskey into a tumbler and slid it to her. Gillian placed her hand on the glass but didn't drink. "You're up late," he said after taking another sip.

"So are you. I'm very sorry about Dennis. Your father told me you were friends."

Orrin stilled before shrugging. "Didn't know him as well as I thought, I guess."

She hesitated, turning the glass around in circles on the bar. "Did he seem strange to you lately?"

"You mean like he was acting before you tested him the other day?" She nodded.

"Not really. I could tell something was bothering him, but Dennis was a private guy. Took us a while to get to know each other. We both had trouble sleeping. Sometimes we'd watch movies in the rec room.

Both of us liked Cary Grant flicks, *North by Northwest*, *Suspicion*, stuff like that. He was quiet, but he had a real sharp sense of humor. Never would've guessed . . ." His words fell off in a slurred tangle.

Gillian picked up her glass, at first not intending to drink, but the liquor's aroma was so enticing after the stresses of the last few days, she tipped some into her mouth.

Her tongue caught fire but just as quickly became numb as the booze flowed down and bloomed like a depth charge in her stomach. She coughed, eyes watering as Orrin grinned.

"Smooth," he said.

"Smooth," she rasped, coughing again as he laughed. "Maybe not the best choice after being exposed to Mars's atmosphere, or lack thereof."

"We got beer. And wine. And . . . what's your poison?"

Opioids, she thought absently, picturing the stashed pills beneath the sink in her old room. "I'm good."

He stared at her in his unflinching way. "You getting anywhere with all this?"

"I'm not sure."

"Word was you were leaving."

"Not yet, I'm afraid."

"Figured you'd be going home to your daughter."

She stiffened. "Who told you about my daughter?"

"This place, everyone talks. Doesn't matter who they are. Gossip is currency around here. I'm sorry, overstepped my bounds. Just heard she was sick, that's all."

"It's okay," she said. "Yes, she is."

"Can't imagine being that far away. Don't have kids, but my dad's the only person I had growing up. Part of the reason I wanted to come here."

"And what're the other reasons?" she asked, surprising herself by taking another sip of whiskey.

Orrin tilted his glass again until it was empty. He set it down. "Guess I was running away. Why else would someone come way the hell out here?"

"Spirit of adventure."

"Bullshit."

Gillian laughed a little.

Orrin sat quietly for a few minutes, and when he spoke, he sounded completely sober. "I wasn't right for a while. Up here," he said, tapping his skull. "I was deployed. And it was . . . bad."

"Your father told me a little."

His eyes snapped up to hers.

"He didn't go into detail," she said.

"What did he tell you?"

"That you were the only person in your squad who survived."

Orrin poured another dose into his glass and stared at it. "He tell you it was my fault?"

She managed to keep the surprise from surfacing on her features. "No."

Orrin drank his glass dry and held it loosely in one hand. When he spoke, the soft airiness of his voice she'd grown accustomed to was gone. Instead, he sounded flat and hollowed out, like the words were echoes from someone else. "We were clearing a side street in this devastated neighborhood in a town I couldn't pronounce if you paid me. There was a Stryker on point carrying half a dozen guys. Me and my team were next, followed up by two jeeps and twenty or so on foot. Thirty-nine in all. Good guys. The best. From all over, every last one of them there to do their job, nothing more." Orrin grimaced, and she could see his teeth clenched tight.

"You don't have to—"

"We were coming up on an intersection, and something set me off. Half the time I had these—I don't know what you call them—omens? Premonitions? I learned to trust them. We roll up on this intersection, and I call a halt. My team and I move up, and there's this hubcap lying in the dirt beside a street sign that's bent over flat. See, normally there's all kinds of junk in the dirt, everything from old batteries to rusted spoons, but this hubcap is shiny in places, like someone's been handling it." He paused, pouring the last dregs of the bottle into his glass. "I run one of the bots up and start digging. Sure as shit, there's a pressure trigger in the road. I do my thing and call the all clear."

Gillian felt herself sitting forward, a sick anticipation growing in her stomach. Orrin sipped, eyes unfocused.

"What I didn't see was the secondary trip. Concealed infrared projector. It armed the other fifteen bombs hidden next to and behind us like dominoes falling over."

"God."

"Thought I was dead," he said tonelessly. "It was the loudest thing I ever heard. Then the shooting started. They came out of one of the buildings on the north side. Just mopping up since almost everyone was already gone. One of the jeeps' doors landed on me after the blast. That's why I'm alive. Came down like a shroud covering me up, and I couldn't move, couldn't reach my rifle, and I had to listen to the last of my friends die until it was all quiet except for the ringing in my ears."

Orrin finished his glass and tried to set it on the bar, but it slid from his fingers and thumped to the floor, then rolled away until it clinked against the wall.

"I'm sorry," she managed to say after a moment.

He looked at her finally, returning from the past. "Not as sorry as I am."

◆　◆　◆

She held his arm lightly on the way down the hall, not unlike a nurse helping a bedbound patient walk for the first time after a long illness.

Orrin's shoulder brushed the wall every few paces, and she kept him from stumbling too far away from it.

"Me," he mumbled, half pointing at the next door on the left. Gillian guided him to it, and he brought his card out, having to swipe it twice past the reader before the lock disengaged.

"Are you going to be all right?" she asked as he pushed the door open and stepped inside the room.

"Be fine. Been in worse shape before." He glanced at her, the fog of liquor clearing from him for a second. "I knew you weren't what everyone was saying you were. I could tell."

"Thank you."

"Overheard people talking about me too. We've got that in common, I guess."

He looked so vulnerable, so sad, she felt the urge to reach out to him, but stopped herself. "Always another side, isn't there?" she asked.

He smiled in a way that broke her heart a little. "That's right."

"Sleep well, Orrin," she said, starting down the hall.

"Doctor?"

She paused and looked back.

"Thanks for listening."

"You're welcome."

She waited to hear his door click shut before continuing on to her own room. The hall was still void of anyone else, and there wasn't another sound besides the soft squeak of her shoes. It reminded her of the months alone on the ship, the quiet so palpable it was like a presence. At that second, she could've been the only person on the station, the only person for hundreds of millions of miles.

The notion sent tendrils of ice through her. She moved faster, located her room, and threw a last look down the deserted hallway before scanning inside. With something like relief, she locked the door, leaving the thoughts outside.

THIRTY-SEVEN

A soft knock woke Gillian.

The bleariness of hard sleep followed her across the room to the door she opened a crack. Carson was there, hands clasped behind his back.

"Breakfast?" he asked.

When they entered the communal dining room, half the seats were already filled with crew members eating quietly. A few sets of eyes found them as they gathered an assortment of food from a dozen stainless-steel bins and moved to a corner table where Easton and Lien were already waiting.

"How's your new digs, Doc?" Easton asked as they sat down.

"Roomy."

"You look a hell of a lot better than you did yesterday."

"Such charm. Wherever did you pick it up?" she said.

"Born with it."

He chuckled and winked, sipping his coffee. Carson drained nearly his entire cup in a few gulps, took a breath, and drank the rest.

"Guessing you were up almost as late as I was," she said.

"Took a long time to get things in order."

"I can imagine."

"Pendrake's key was in Kenison's room," Carson said quietly.

"Really?"

"Under his bed frame."

"Did Leo do an autopsy?"

"He did. I had to get fairly firm with the ranking physician before he stepped aside. I think Leo finished up late last night. You can ask him about it yourself," Carson said, inclining his head to her left as Leo sat down beside her.

"Morning, all," Leo said.

They rumbled their greetings as Leo dug into a pile of powdered eggs.

"Carson said you finished Kenison's autopsy?" Gillian asked.

"I did."

"And?"

"Asphyxiation. But, of course, we already gathered that much."

"Anything else unusual?"

He sat back from his plate. "Not really. Gouges from his fingernails on his neck where he clawed himself."

"Is that . . . common?"

He nodded before beginning to eat again. "Automatic reaction to strangling. Why do you ask?"

Gillian pushed the contents of a protein pack around her plate. "He didn't seem suicidal."

"People hide things, the worst of themselves, from everyone," Lien said. "My father killed himself, and up until the day my mother found him, we thought he was happy."

"I'm sorry, that's—"

"It's okay. It was a long time ago. I was only a child. My point is, there is no way to truly know someone."

Gillian and Carson shared a glance.

"You saying you don't think Kenison killed himself?" Easton asked.

"He was afraid," Gillian said after a moment. "When I tested him, I think he was expecting terrible news, like he had a tumor or something."

"So someone else killed him? Used his key to shift down to the surface and planted Pendrake's key in his room?"

"I don't know. But something did happen last night."

The others leaned closer as she told them about Ander's visit.

When she was finished, Carson frowned and shook his head. "So do you think Ander's affected, or is it just old age like he said?"

"It didn't sound like typical forgetting. This phenomenon, whatever you want to call it, it takes certain things but leaves others. It's not a natural fading of memory, it's a deletion." When she finished speaking, she felt an incremental movement in her mind as if she'd just cleared some kind of barrier, had taken another step in the right direction. But the overall pall of mystery remained. The answer was somewhere in their midst, an evanescent shadow in the corner of her mind's eye.

And it was close.

"Uh, you guys feel like the air just got a little heavier in here?" Easton said in a low tone.

When Gillian looked at him, he was calmly surveying the room behind her. The crew members were staring at them.

"Let's adjourn for now," Leo suggested, tossing his fork on his plate. "Food sucks anyways."

They left the dining room with the weight of steady stares on them. Once in the hall, Easton said, "That was some *Village of the Damned* shit in there."

"They're leery of us," Gillian said.

"They have no reason to be," Carson said, a militaristic edge to his voice. "We're all here for the same purpose. There's billions of people depending on what we're able to accomplish."

"So what's next?" Easton asked. "Far as everyone else is concerned, the bad guy's dead, right?"

"I sent a message to control last night bringing them up to speed. Should hear back within the next twenty-four hours."

Gillian chewed on her lip, a sudden craving for a hydro almost overwhelming. "There is one person we haven't talked to yet," she said, forcing away the need.

"Who?" Carson asked.

"Someone who's actually the most affected of all. Henry Diver."

♦ ♦ ♦

Diver's cell was located on the lowest level, several doors from elevation control. Carson explained to her as they rode down the elevator that security had needed to retrofit one of the few vacant storage rooms on the level to hold Diver since no one could get close to him while he was awake.

"He injured the person who found him in Pendrake's room pretty badly. Luckily the guy knew some self-defense and was able to choke him unconscious."

They stopped before an unmarked door where Vasquez, the guard who had accompanied her several times while she was under suspicion, stood outside.

"We need to see him," Carson said.

Vasquez eyed her before turning to scan his key card. The door unlatched, and he held it open for them.

The room was square, perhaps a dozen feet long and wide. A clear plastic wall bisected the space, fastened on all four sides by large steel anchors. In its center several holes were drilled, and a small makeshift sliding door was cut near its bottom, a lock securing one end.

The smell was the first thing that hit her.

It was fecal matter and unwashed flesh melded together into the scent of despair. It permeated the room so thickly, her gag reflex stopped her in her tracks.

Henry Diver sat rocking in the right corner of the room behind the clear barrier. She had never seen a picture of him, but his file had said he weighed 165 pounds and was six feet two inches tall.

The man before her now might have weighed 110.

He was a scarecrow dressed in sagging skin and a stained pair of briefs. Bones protruded from him at every angle, and his dark eyes watched her out of carven tunnels beneath a jutting brow.

She heard herself make a sound in her throat, a moan of disgust that became a gag as she inhaled more of Diver's stench.

"What the hell happened to him?" she whispered.

"He's been like this for months from the reports I've read," Carson said quietly. "Barely eats and drinks. Doesn't sleep. Moves constantly. They have to sedate him to clean the cell every week."

While Carson spoke, Diver rose from where he sat, unfolding to his full height. His arms looked too long for his body, and Gillian could see the thrust of each hip bone like angled blades beneath the skin. But his hands held her gaze the longest.

They were masses of scars upon scars. Hundreds if not thousands of furrows had been torn in his flesh from the wrists down. Several places wept blood, and dozens were scabbed over, crusted and flaking.

"What the hell happened to his hands?" she heard herself ask as Diver approached the glass.

"He did that to himself," Carson said.

And now she could see the dark crescents of dried blood beneath his blunted nails.

Diver pressed his palm against the barricade below the drilled holes.

Gillian gathered herself, finding that she'd taken half a step back toward the hallway. She moved forward, trying to ignore the smell. She stopped a foot from the glass and watched Diver place his other palm beside the first.

"I'm Dr. Ryan," she said, clearing her throat. "I was hoping you wouldn't mind talking to me today, Henry. Is it all right if I call you Henry?"

Diver tilted his head to the side at the sound of his name like a dog might do.

No, she thought. *Not a dog. A wolf.*

"I've been told you haven't been feeling well," she said, beginning to look for signs or symptoms of brain damage. Several had already been checked off the list. Aggression; change in appetite; change in sleep patterns; loss of speech; loss of bowel control; and Christ, his hands. They'd been flayed and healed hundreds of times.

As she watched, his fingers went to the scars and began to work. Fingernails dug in, penetrating the damaged skin.

"Henry, please don't do that," she heard herself say. "Please. It's okay. I just want to talk. Can you tell me about where you're from?"

The fingers worked. Blood oozed and began dripping to the floor.

"Henry, what was your job here on the station?"

The blood flowed faster.

"Gillian . . ." Carson said from somewhere behind her.

She looked down at the damage Diver was inflicting on himself, the manic movements jerky and erratic.

And something connected in her mind like two copper wires fusing together.

She wet her lips, tearing her gaze from the carnage of his hands, and said, "Henry, tell me about the tunnel."

Diver froze.

His right hand, which had been attacking his left, loosened. The tension in his shoulders slackened. He looked at her, and his mouth opened slightly like his jaw muscles had forgotten their function. She waited for him to speak.

His mouth opened wider, and something gurgled in his throat.

Gillian blinked, leaning forward. Listening.

He screamed.

It was so loud and sudden, she took an involuntary step back as the sound rang through the room. It was inhuman and guttural, an animal mimicking human grief, or anger.

She found her hands halfway to her ears, trying to block the sound out. Carson grasped her by the shoulder.

"That's enough," he said, and she nodded.

And still Diver screamed. It was as if his lungs' volume was eternal. As she watched, he threaded a bloodied finger through one of the holes drilled in the glass and turned his hand flat. A second before he did it, she realized what was coming and tried to look away but was too slow.

Diver yanked his hand to the right, snapping his finger sideways at the second joint.

Carson pulled her from the room as Vasquez and another guard who had appeared out of nowhere shouldered past her.

The hallway air was clean and the most beautiful thing she had ever tasted, but the sound of Diver's finger bone cracking replayed on a sickening loop in her mind.

She doubled over and vomited her breakfast on the nearest wall.

Diver still screamed, the alien noise flowing out of the cell like rancid water.

But above it was another sound, the steady clacking of train wheels on pitted rails.

And she remembered.

After another convulsion, she straightened, wiping weakly at her mouth.

"We shouldn't have come down here. You're pushing yourself," Carson said, holding her arm.

She took two cleansing breaths in and swallowed acid. "I think I know what's wrong with them."

THIRTY-EIGHT

"I'm not sure I'm following you. What do you mean, addicted?"

Gillian glanced at Carson as they walked down the hallway of the crew-quarters level. The dining area had emptied since they'd left, a solitary man in a jumpsuit hunched over a bowl the only occupant. They'd passed two women leaving the elevator, the pair's conversation ending the moment they had spotted Gillian and Carson.

Gillian looked behind them for a second time, ensuring they were alone, and said, "Diver looks like he has brain damage, right? Uncontrolled impulses, aggression, loss of language, but all of those could be extreme withdrawal from an addiction."

"Addiction. You're talking about shifting."

"Exactly. You heard what Kenison said, and your buddy Vern down on the surface echoed him. Shifting is like being reborn. Beyond euphoric. You don't think that could become addicting? And did you see how Diver reacted when I mentioned the tunnel?"

"Yeah, Mary Cranston said the same thing."

"I think the tunnel is actually the teleportation chamber. It would look like a tunnel when you're inside it."

"We have the teleportation logs, though. Diver only shifted nine times. Cranston less than that. How would they become addicted with only a handful of shifts?"

"I have a theory, but I won't know for sure until we go through his room."

"This is it," Carson said, slowing before a doorway near the very end of the hall. "Like I said, it's been swept already. Everything they found was in the report." He scanned his key card, and the door opened.

Inside was a room mirroring her own, except it had been stripped bare. The bed frame was a hollow skeleton, the closet doors open, revealing empty shelves. Even the air was devoid of any smell. She'd actually been expecting a degree of Diver's pungency to be here as well.

They moved into the space, Carson staying closer to the door with his arms crossed, a contemplative expression on his face while she went to the bed frame and knelt beside it. Gillian ran her fingers along the exposed edges, tracing the smooth design of its angles. She lay flat on the floor, eyeing the area beneath the bed. No humps or gaps in the floor or the wall near the frame.

She stood, moved to the closet, and brushed her hands across the top of the door and down its juncture at the jamb.

"Gill, what the hell are you doing?"

"Looking." She turned in a slow circle before stepping into the bathroom.

"Listen, I'm sorry about everything, I truly am. I want to make things right. Maybe you should rest and we can talk afterward."

"I'm not losing it," she said, looking first at the compact toilet before kneeling beside the sink. The screw in the panel slipped twice in her fingers, and she had to dry them of sweat before spinning it free.

"I didn't say that," Carson continued, coming closer. "But I don't know what you're looking for."

The panel's corner sprung free, and she pried the gap wider, seeing a glint of something white within. Her fingertips brushed it, and she yanked harder on the panel, a sharp cracking as it broke, letting her hand slide in farther. Then she drew it out, holding the key card up in front of Carson's face.

"This. I was looking for this."

♦ ♦ ♦

They stood in a half circle around Ander's desk looking down at the key. Gillian watched them from the corner of her eye. Carson was stoic, arms crossed, studying the key like it was a cell phone found deep in the ground in an archeological dig. Ander leaned heavily on the desk, his palms white from the pressure.

"It's impossible," Ander said for a second time since they'd showed him the key card.

"I'd say it's anything but since it's sitting there in front of us," Gillian said.

"One key card and one key card only is distributed and coded to each person. Diver was carrying his when he was found in Ivan's room."

"And if someone loses their key card?"

"It's electronically disabled and they're issued another. And no one's lost their key card."

"But you have spares. Where are they?"

Ander eyed her, any of the connection they'd shared the night before seemingly forgotten, the hard-edged scientist back in full view. "In a safe place."

"Show us."

"Why?"

"Dr. Ander," Carson said, finally looking up. "Please."

Ander squinted and sighed resignedly. "This way," he said, leading them out to the atrium in the hallway. Behind the desk was a doorway Ander scanned through, revealing three of the massive quantum computers, their black hides humming with reckoning melodies. Ander moved past them to a shelf holding an opaque box. He scanned his key across its face, and it opened.

The old man stared into the box for a drawn moment before shaking his head and holding it out as if it were a piece of rancid meat.

"There are three duplicates for each person on board the station," he said, his voice diminished.

Carson took the box from him and tilted it so Gillian could see as well.

It was empty.

THIRTY-NINE

Gillian sat in one of the chairs around the conference table and chewed on her fingernail.

She had to consciously think the word "stop" before her mouth would obey. Her nails were fairly ragged where she'd gnawed at them coming off the hydros weeks before, but they were starting to grow back. All except the one she'd just been working on. It was almost down to the quick, the soft underskin beneath the nail exposed to the biting air.

And in that second, she wondered if she could make it to her room, dig out a pill from behind the sink panel, and get back here before the others arrived. Carson had gone to gather them from their various locations after asking her how she'd known to find Diver's extra key card where she had.

Intuition, she'd said, and he had given her a look that was so frankly disbelieving she'd almost told him the truth.

Instead, she'd sat in the silent conference room chewing on her fingernail while her mind whirred through the notion that had grown from an inkling's shadow. The graffiti she'd seen on the train the day Carson had appeared at her home with his offer came back to her again.

She had thought it said, *Saul Gone*, but she'd misread it. The "a" in "Saul" hadn't been an "a" at all. No, not an "a" . . . the idea was so strange, it was hard to shape into any semblance of reality. But there was no other possibility that made sense. She knew she was right.

And that's what scared her the most.

The door opened, and she jumped. Easton grinned as he strode inside.

"Just me, Doc."

"Sorry. Running on caffeine and nerves."

He took a seat across from her. "No need to apologize. Beneath this calm exterior, I'm getting a little jumpy myself. Place is starting to feel off."

"Starting?"

"Okay, it's been giving me the heebs since we left the ship."

She had to laugh.

"In fact," he continued, "it would feel real good right now to get back on the ship, spin it around, and get the hell out of here."

She opened her mouth to reply, when the door opened again and Carson appeared with Lien and Birk in tow. They greeted one another and found seats around the table as Leo entered the room.

"Lock that, will you, Leo?" Carson asked, and the physician twisted the manual lock. When they were all settled, he said, "There have been some developments. Gillian and I went to see Diver."

While he relayed the events in the holding cell, Gillian found the rosary in her pocket and drew it out. After a brief hesitation, she looped it over her head and tucked it into the neck of her jumpsuit.

"So he's nuttier than squirrel shit," Easton said. "Thought we knew that."

"There's more," Carson said, glancing at her. "Gill, want to take it from here?"

She stood, unable to keep herself still in the chair for another second, and paced partway across the room before turning around. "We found a key card that wasn't issued to anyone hidden in Diver's room. When we brought it to Ander, he said there are three backup keys for everyone on board the station in case they lose theirs. When we asked to see the backups, they were gone."

"Gone?" Leo asked, sitting forward. "As in stolen?"

"Yeah."

"What does this mean?" Lien asked.

"The key card we found in Diver's room wasn't registered to anyone, but it was activated. You could access nearly any door or checkpoint in the station with it." She paused, wetting her lips. "And you could use it to teleport."

There was a stunned silence as the others gazed at her.

"How many times had he shifted?" Easton asked.

"Two hundred and fifty-six." She watched their reactions.

Shock.

Disbelief.

Horror.

"How could this have happened?" Lien asked.

"Someone took the keys and made them active. None of them were tied to crew profiles, and since that's how any activity is tracked, they didn't show up on the security or shifting logs," Carson said.

"But why?" Birk said, speaking for the first time. "What purpose do these extra keys serve?"

"Shifting addiction. Multiple people have told us it's like being reborn. And why wouldn't it? In essence, you are. All of your atoms are freshly remade and reassembled from basic elements. You're a brand-new person. It's the ultimate high." She continued to pace. "Whoever took the keys acted like a dealer, doling them out to crew members who wanted to shift recreationally. Who knows what they got in return. And everything was fine until Ivan Pendrake started sending concerning messages to control. He threatened the scheme and paid the price."

"You're saying Diver was sent by someone?" Leo asked.

"I don't think Diver killed him at all."

"What?" Even Carson was watching her now, head tilted to the side.

"I think Diver was the fall guy. Whoever the dealer is killed Pendrake and then locked Diver in the room with his body. Diver was so far beyond gone, he couldn't explain what happened. And that's why Pendrake's body is missing—they figured Leo might eventually want to do his own autopsy and something would come to light. That's also why Tinsel was killed."

"They didn't want to risk him catching wind of anything," Easton said. "He would've shut this place down."

"Exactly."

"And they tried to frame you for his murder."

She nodded. "Not to mention trying to kill me. Twice."

"So who could it be?" Birk asked. "Who has the motivation to do this?"

"Kenison, right?" Leo asked. "He had Pendrake's key. He took a quick exit when he realized you were still alive."

"But if he had the anonymous key cards, why use his own, or Pendrake's, for that matter?" Gillian said.

"I don't think he killed himself anymore," Carson said.

"Agreed. I think he was murdered. Kenison knew something was wrong here, and he might've been about to tell us. That's why he's dead."

"So who else could it be?" Lien asked.

"Ander. It's gotta be," Easton said.

"I would've said that too a few days ago," Gillian replied. "But I'm not so sure now. He has everything resting on this mission, and what he told me the other night . . . I have a hard time believing he'd do this."

"Who had access to the keys?"

"Almost everyone. The security concerns weren't aimed at personnel since the station crew went through a tough selection process and had rigorous training. Most of the checkpoints are for atmospheric precautions in case of an emergency breach. No one thought one of their own would turn on them."

Everyone around the table seemed to recede inside themselves for a moment.

Lien glanced from face to face. "If this is true, what are the symptoms the crew are experiencing?"

And now to lay out her true theory. The moment of truth where everyone would absorb and accept it or reject it as insanity. She could hardly believe it herself, but there was nothing else that made sense. She stopped pacing and placed her hands on her chair back.

"The last decade of my life has been devoted to seeing what makes a person who they truly are," she said, feeling the weight of her words, the flow of them siphoning from her innermost depths. "I've asked that question of myself a thousand times. What defines us? Our experiences. How we perceive and interact with the world." She paused. "Our memories. Without those, the experiences mean nothing." In her mind, she saw Kent smiling as they carried in boxes to their new home. Felt the excruciating sensation of birth, then the warmth of a new life in her arms. The rise and last fall of Kent's chest beneath her palm. "We remember what makes us who we are."

"What are you saying, Gill?" Carson asked gently.

She gathered herself, letting the past sink away. "Ander's system is based on reaching absolute zero, the stopping of atoms' movement so there's no energy loss. Right?" Nods all around the table. "And from all our tests, there's no physical damage to any of the people who have shifted. It's something you said, Birk, no *physical* damage to the neurons. But what about metaphysical?"

Leo huffed a nervous laugh. "What are you talking about?"

"Can you measure emotion? Graph a memory?"

"Brain waves show a—" Lien began, but Gillian cut her off.

"A correlation with memory and emotion, but there's no measuring the things that make us who we are. In my field, we know memory is located in the hippocampus or certain neurons fire when we feel love for someone, but we've never been able to gauge or count their essence, their energy. It was only on the way here I discovered a person needs to be engaged in the act of remembering to map the neurons associated with memory." She looked at them all. "What I'm saying is, what if the energy loss isn't physical from shifting? What if it's being taken from who the people are? What if the loss of energy is their memories?"

The hum of the station was the only sound, its electronic blood flowing all around them.

"You're talking about a soul," Easton said.

Gillian frowned. "I don't know, call it what you want. It explains the crew's symptoms."

"That's . . . really far-fetched," Carson said.

She shrugged. "You have another explanation?"

"That would mean a greater portion of the crew is lying to us about what they're experiencing. And for what? Addiction? A high?" Carson acknowledged her with a tip of his head as she raised her eyebrows. "Okay, okay, point taken. But why didn't this show up in the early trials on Earth?"

She shrugged. "Maybe the symptoms didn't appear until much later. Maybe it's the accumulation of shifting or the distance between the units that has something to do with it. I'm not sure."

"So what if you're right?" Lien asked. "How do we fix it?"

"We don't."

"We don't?"

"How would you suggest fixing it? If I'm right, we're dealing with something beyond our current scope of science, beyond what we understand. I can't fix something I don't understand. And besides, the people who are affected aren't going to cooperate now. They're not afraid like Kenison was. They're addicted. Who knows what they're capable of."

"What are you suggesting we do, then?" Leo asked quietly.

Gillian looked at the floor before bringing her gaze back up to them all. "I think we should leave as soon as possible."

"You want to leave?" Carson asked. "We're closer to the truth now more than ever."

"Which is why we need to go," Gillian said. "You said it yourself, this would mean a majority of the crew is affected and lying about it. I'm guessing those missing key cards are stashed all over the station. And if they're covering up two murders, what makes you think they'd have a problem covering up a few more?"

Carson watched her, and she saw the clockwork going on in his head. He sat forward, not looking at any of them, and said, "Put it to a vote. In favor of leaving?"

Gillian raised her hand along with Birk, Easton, and Leo. Lien hesitated before slowly joining them.

"Okay," Carson said. "Lien, I'm promoting you to commander, Easton to command pilot. Prep the ship immediately for departure. I think you can be ready to leave in less than ten hours if we hurry."

"What are you doing?" Gillian asked.

"Staying," he said, and returned his attention to the others. "What are you waiting for? You have your orders."

They rose from their seats and filed out of the room, all except Birk, who hovered uncertainly near the door until Gillian nodded, dismissing him. She and Carson had remained, mutually unwilling to leave before the other. She waited silently, looking at him, at the person he'd become.

"You don't have to do this," she said finally.

"You know I do. There's too much at stake. I'm responsible for the mission and everyone on this station. I can't run away now." He smiled sadly. "I knew the risks when I left the ground the very first time. When I looked through my dad's telescope, that was it for me. This is where I belong." He came nearer, and surprised her by taking one of her hands. "Thank you for everything you've done. I don't know if you're right about what's happening here, but you did all I asked of you and more. I know you can never forgive me, but I do wish things would've been different."

"That you wouldn't have kidnapped me?" she asked without malice.

"That I never would've let you go in the first place."

She tried finding something to say, but the words wouldn't come.

The room suddenly lurched around them, the floor canting to the right.

Carson latched on to her arm and braced himself against the table. "What—" he started to say.

But a piercing alarm began wailing, drowning out his voice.

September 17, 2028, approximately one month after Discovery VI disaster.
South Daytona City Police Department.
Incident Report #5547798,
Receiving Officer: Det. Roberto Gonzaga.
Complainant: Katrina Nichols.

Det. Gonzaga: *Mrs. Nichols, we're on the record now. Please state your name and the reason for your visit to the department today.*
Nichols: *My name is Katrina Margaret Nichols, and I'm here in regards to my niece, Carrie Marie Ryan.*
Det. Gonzaga: *And what's the issue with your niece?*
Nichols: *I don't really know where to start. It's . . . it's all jumbled up. Okay, my sister is . . . was Gillian Ryan, she was on the Discovery Mission.*
Det. Gonzaga: *The one—*
Nichols: *Yes, that one. The whole reason she was there was because Carrie was sick. She has Losian's disease. Gillian was a medical liaison for the mission, and I was taking care of Carrie for her while she was gone.*
Det. Gonzaga: *Would you like a tissue?*
Nichols: *No, no, I'm fine. You think you've cried everything out, and then there's just more. There's always more.*
Det. Gonzaga: *You were saying about Carrie?*
Nichols: *She got worse after Gillian left. She has these lapses, she called them the fuzzies. They were coming more and more, sometimes daily, and it was really hard. My husband had to start taking time off work to help, and*

with my pregnancy it was becoming really stressful. Then last month . . . the
disaster. I . . . I loved my sister so much, it was . . .

Det. Gonzaga: *I'm very sorry for your loss.*

Nichols: *Thank you. God was supposed to take care of her, take care of both*
of them. I prayed every night after she left. But . . . I didn't know what to
do afterward. I couldn't bring myself to tell Carrie, and it was terrible try-
ing to keep it from her with it all over the news. She kept asking when her
mom was coming home, and I always told her "soon." So when the men
from NASA showed up at our door, I thought I finally had to come clean.

Det. Gonzaga: *Representatives from NASA visited you? When was this?*

Nichols: *Three weeks ago. They came to the house and offered their condo-*
lences. Thank God Carrie was sleeping then. So after they answered a few
of my questions about the mission and why we hadn't been able to speak to
Gillian before everything happened, they said Gillian had sent all of her
research findings back to Earth prior to the disaster. They said she'd made
several breakthroughs that could possibly help Carrie. They asked us to bring
her to this medical installation on the edge of the NASA campuses and leave
her with the staff who would begin her treatment.

Det. Gonzaga: *And you brought her there?*

Nichols: *Yes. We brought her. I can still remember her being led away. She*
looked back at me like I was the last person she knew and . . . and . . .

Det. Gonzaga: *It's okay.*

Nichols: *And that I was abandoning her.*

Det. Gonzaga: *Would you like to take a break?*

Nichols: *No. No, I need to tell you this. They said the treatment might take*
up to six weeks, and as acting guardians, we would be kept informed of her
status and would be notified within the next week when we could visit her.

Det. Gonzaga: *And did they?*

Nichols: *They called early one morning before my husband was about to*
go to work. They said there'd been a complication with the treatment. And
they wouldn't let us see her. I asked over and over again to see her, and they
said no, it was too dangerous since the procedures they were using were

biohazardous . . . they wouldn't let us see her. That's why I'm here, you have to make them show her to us.

Det. Gonzaga: *Okay, I'm sure we can clear this up with some phone calls. Regardless of treatment, you have a right to visit her.*

Nichols: *No, you don't understand. When they called she was already gone. She died from the treatment, and they won't even let me see her body.*

FORTY

The control room was chaos when they stepped inside.

Six crew members sat or stood at their consoles, all positioned with a clear view outside the station, where the bulk of the area was taken up by the ship they'd arrived on. The station jerked again beneath their feet, this time less vigorously, but now Gillian could see what was causing the disturbance.

The shuttle they'd left Earth on, which was docked to the EXPX, was moving. Or at least attempting to move. A faint glow came from the engines, and the powerfully built attachment struts linking the ship to the station torqued violently side to side.

"What the hell's going on?" Carson asked the nearest crew member.

The man's bloodshot eyes found him before turning back to his screen. "The shuttle's main engines are online."

"What? That's not possible. Someone would have to be on board."

"Then someone is. We need to undock the EXPX now, or the air-lock could be compromised."

"Undock? No, there's got to be another way."

"I'm telling you, Commander, there isn't. And we don't have time for manual shutdown. Either we release and re-attain, or we risk depressurization of the entire station."

The floor vibrated again, violently this time, and the shuttle's engines flared brighter.

Gillian stepped closer to the window. The struts flexed like arms succumbing to a great burden. She turned and locked eyes with Carson, knowing the implications of what was about to happen.

"Do it," Carson said.

The crewman at his elbow typed furiously on the screen, then swiped first left then right before jabbing his finger a last time.

Strobes erupted along the length of the docking struts, and they shook again, sending a quake through the floor. One by one, the attachments holding the EXPX in place loosened, and far below, the airlock twisted before retreating to the safety of the station.

"Carson—" Gillian said.

"It's okay. We have to let it go. Once it's clear of the station, we'll send the lander out and retrieve it."

She watched the huge ship slip free of the attachments and slide away, beginning to rotate beneath the attached shuttle's insistence. The whole thing took on the image of a toy in an invisible child's hand, drawing their only hope of escape away into the darkness of space.

"Airlock stability a hundred percent," the crew member said, studying the screen. "No apparent damage to the station's docking apparatus either. Trajectory puts the EXPX outside of the planet's gravitational pull. So far so good."

"I want one of the landers readied for my crew's use. They'll board and shut down the shuttle."

"Yes, sir."

The fire from the engines lengthened, taking on a white-orange hue as the rotations increased in speed. Gillian stared as the distance grew between the ship and the station. There was a chorus of steps behind her, and she turned and saw Lien, Easton, and Birk entering the room.

"The hell's the ruckus about?" Easton asked, his eyes widening at the sight beyond the glass. "Uh, Commander, is that not our ride swiftly floating away?"

"There was a malfunction with the engines. I'm arranging a retrieval, and you two are going to head it up."

Birk moved past them and stopped beside Gillian. "This is not good, Doctor."

"Did I ever tell you you're a master of the understatement?"

"I believe so. Yes."

The door opened again, and Orrin appeared, the sharpness of his gaze taking them all in before scanning the spiraling ship. As he approached them, Gillian saw his hair was wet, actually dripping onto the collar of his jumpsuit.

"What is going on?" he asked.

"Shuttle malfunction," she said.

"Shit. Anyone on board?"

"Supposedly."

"About broke my neck in the shower a minute ago when the shaking started."

"Gillian, can I speak to you outside?" Carson asked, motioning to her.

"Sure." She started to turn away, but Orrin placed a hand lightly on her arm.

"Thanks again for listening last night. I had way too much too fast. Spent most of the day sleeping it off."

"It's okay. Glad I came along at the right time."

"You really did."

She gave him a smile and started to follow Easton and Lien out of control.

A flash of light filled the room, throwing her shadow forward in a monstrous representation that just as quickly slid sideways and disappeared.

Gillian spun, hearing Orrin draw a quick breath in before he swore loudly.

The EXPX was on fire, and the shuttle was gone.

A corona of flaming debris flew outward from the massive ship, a gaseous cloud obscuring the rear half of the wheel that suddenly ignited in a dazzling ball of light. There was a half-second pause as the scattered fuel burned away before the ship vanished in an incandescent flash.

Her legs weakened, and her stomach heaved. Lien said something in her native tongue, and someone's hand found Gillian's shoulder. Squeezed it.

Pieces of the ship erupted from the explosion, their trailing afterimages like giant meteors compared to the shuttle's wreckage. Orrin turned his head to the side and covered his face with one hand. She knew she should be doing the same, that the brightness of the explosion was probably damaging her retinas, but she couldn't look away, couldn't stop seeing the flames lick outward into space and collapse as the fuel burned itself in almost beautiful halos. Couldn't drag her gaze from their only way home disintegrating into jagged and useless shards that could never bring her back to her daughter.

Then she was being led away, dragged from control as she tried to stay because she had to watch, had to see the last of the fire disappear along with her hope.

FORTY-ONE

Carson was shaking Gillian, looking her full in the face, his nose nearly touching her own.

"Gillian, snap out of it."

She looked to the left, but the door to control was closing, shutting out the vestiges of the fiery blast, the crew members still standing at their stations like carved monoliths.

"Gillian?"

"I'm okay," she said, unsure if she was.

"None of them moved," Birk said.

"What?" Carson asked, letting go of her shoulders.

"The crew. None of them even flinched when the ship blew." Birk looked around at the group. "Like they were expecting it."

Easton rubbed the side of his jaw and nodded. "Goddamn. He's right, Commander."

Birk stared at the closed door as if he could see through it. "What do we do now?"

Gillian thought about it, tried to bring her jostled thoughts to order. There had to be something, some way to still get off the station. "They'll be coming for us," she said quietly.

"What?" Carson asked.

"Now that we're trapped, they'll try to get rid of us. The ship blowing up is the perfect cover. They'll say it was an accident while we were undocking." She was shaking, and her heart was a wounded bird in her chest.

All eyes turned to Carson, who glanced past them down the hallway as a pair of men exited the elevator and stepped into a room out of sight. "Listen, we don't know for sure—"

"Carson," Gillian said. And there was something in her voice that made him look at her. Really look at her and listen. "There's no fixing this. How do we get out of here?"

He was quiet for a moment before saying, "We'll take one of the landers. Easton, make sure it's prepped. Lien, find Leo, he was in medical last time I checked. Bring him to storage on level two, and gather all the supplies you can find. Gillian, you and Birk can help them. I need to go to my quarters, then I'll meet you and we'll load everything on board. We'll especially need water and hydrocleanse units. At least two. Nobody stop for anyone. Keep moving, and do what you need to do."

"Sir, the lander doesn't have that kind of distance capability," Easton said. "We'll run out of fuel a quarter of the way back."

"I know. We'll have to send out a distress call to control."

"And wait for rescue? No, screw that, Commander. That could take six months. Maybe a year."

"I don't think we have a choice," Gillian said.

"They'll come get us. Especially when we tell them what's happening here." Carson glanced around at them. "Is everybody ready?"

"Absolutely not," Birk said.

"Good. Let's move."

They set off down the hall, ignoring the sound of the door to control opening behind them as they entered the elevator.

Several crew members stepped into the hallway and watched them as the doors slid closed and they ascended. The quiet was unnerving, knowing what might be waiting for them on each level. But an ember of hope had flared in Gillian with the plan.

They were going home.

Or would die trying.

The doors opened to the crew-quarters level, and as Carson stepped off, a thought struck Gillian.

The research. All their findings. It was still in the lab and stored on the station's mainframe computers.

"Shit!" Her exclamation drew everyone's attention. "All our findings, the tests and research. It's all in the lab."

Carson grimaced. "How fast can you get it?"

"Five minutes. Tops."

"You and Birk go, I'll meet you at the lab." He looked at Lien and Easton. "Both of you stick with the plan. We'll rendezvous on base level." Without a look back, he turned and hurried down the hallway as the rest of them stepped back inside the elevator.

When they reached the research level, Easton and Birk took position beside the doors, their fists clenched at waist level.

"Swing for the fences if there's anyone there, big guy," Easton said.

Birk quirked an eyebrow at Gillian.

"If there's someone outside, punch them," Gillian translated.

Birk nodded.

The doors opened.

The hall was empty. Easton eased out and glanced both ways before nodding. "Don't be late now," he said as she and Birk moved past him. "It isn't Uber waiting downstairs, you know."

The last thing she saw before the doors closed was his smile.

She led the way, constantly checking behind them as they went. The hall was deathly quiet, no movement anywhere.

They reached the lab, the lights igniting as they crossed the room.

"What should I do, Doctor?" Birk asked.

"Stand by the door and keep watch."

While Birk peered out into the hallway, she opened their research files, verifying each one as she added them all to a single folder. She brushed aside two stacks of paper before finding a microdrive she inserted in the computer. With two clicks she downloaded the data and began to shut the computer down, but stopped. What if something happened to her? The research, all her findings would disappear.

Gillian logged on to the station's mainframe, navigating through the system while racking her brain about the comms instruction she had received.

"Doctor?" Birk asked.

"Hold on." She found the messaging software and located an attachment program before selecting the file. In the corner of the screen, she saw an audio/video symbol and, after a beat, clicked it.

Her own image appeared on the screen with a blinking red dot in the upper right-hand corner.

"This . . . this is Dr. Gillian Ryan. I'm . . . this is a distress call. Our ship has been sabotaged, and there's something wrong with the crew. A . . . a sickness of some kind. We are trying to evacuate and will contact you again soon for a rescue. We need help. Please. We're—"

"Doctor. Someone's coming."

Gillian clicked the "End" button and scrambled for a terrifying second before she was able to attach the video message along with the file.

Her hand shook as she stabbed "Send." She glanced up at Birk, who had shrunk away from the door.

"Who is it?" she whispered.

"I don't know. I just saw movement coming this way."

"Get ready."

She yanked the microdisk from the computer's side and slid it into her pocket as she rushed to the side of the door opposite Birk.

He met her eyes, and she tried to steady him with an encouraging nod, but fear had invaded her muscles, and she was weak. Too weak to fight someone off.

Footsteps approached from outside the door. Paused. Came closer.

Please be Carson.

The door slid open.

Gillian stepped forward, putting as much weight behind the punch as she could, but checked herself as she saw Ander's surprised expression.

Birk grabbed the old man around the neck, and he grunted.

"What the hell's the meaning of this?" Ander asked.

He didn't have any weapons she could see. Nothing in his hands, and his face was turning an awful shade of puce as Birk squeezed tighter.

"Let him go," she said, taking a step back.

Birk released the old man and brought his fists up, their intimidating size barely counterweighing the awkward angle he held them at.

"Lord love a duck!" Ander gasped, rubbing his throat and glaring at them. "What's the meaning of this?"

"Do you have any weapons on you, Doctor?" she asked.

"Weapons? What are you talking about?"

"Birk, search him."

"What—" Ander began, but Birk had already started patting him down, running his hands over the baggy sweater and slacks the physicist wore.

"Don't feel anything," Birk said, stepping back.

"Because I don't have anything! What's happening? I heard an explosion, and when I looked outside, there was burning shrapnel everywhere. Control told me the EXPX had a malfunction and no one knew where its crew was."

"How did you find us?" Birk asked, still looming over him.

"I guessed you'd be here."

Gillian studied him, and after an uncomfortable span, Ander held out his hands, palms up. "What is happening?"

"We think we've found the cause of what's happening to the crew," Gillian said.

"And?"

"Absolute zero isn't absolute. There's still energy loss. We think it's their memories."

Ander's brow crinkled. "Doctor, I really—"

"We don't have time to discuss it now. We're leaving. Come with us."

"Are you insane? Your ship's gone. What are you talking about?"

The door slid open, startling them all. Carson stood there, his gaze locked on Ander. He held something in one hand that he raised and pointed at the old man.

A handgun.

"Where the hell did you get a gun?" Gillian asked.

"From my room," he offered, not looking away from Ander. "Have you told him?"

"Some. He's coming with us."

"No, I most certainly am not," Ander said, straightening to his full height. "And I'm disappointed in you, Carson. Firearms are strictly forbidden. The station—"

"The rounds are composite aluminum. Won't puncture the hull but won't have any problem with a person."

"Then stop pointing it at me," Ander said.

Carson lowered the gun and said to Gillian, "We need to move. Do you have everything?"

"Yes," she said. "Let's go."

"This is ridiculous. Ludicrous. I have no idea what's going on here," Ander said, beginning to follow them into the hall.

"That's exactly why you should come with us," Gillian said, reaching out to take the old man's hand.

He jerked it away and started to say something else when someone stepped out of the elevator ahead of them.

Vernon Figg was dressed in the same uniform he'd been wearing in the biospheres. The stocky man smiled and walked toward them. "There you are!"

Carson leveled the handgun. "Stop there, Dr. Figg."

The biologist's smile faltered, and he halted. "Whoa, what's going on here? Dr. Ander, are you okay?"

"I'm fine, Vernon. Trying to speak sense to these people."

"What are you doing here?" Carson asked.

"Just got here from the surface an hour ago. When the accident happened, I contacted the spheres and had them come up too. I figured that would be protocol in a situation like this."

"The landers are both here?"

"One is, and the other should be shortly. Why?"

Carson shot Gillian a look. "Just checking. If you could step aside please, Dr. Figg."

"Sure, geez, was concerned is all. Everyone in control said they didn't know where you were." He shuffled to the side, holding his palms out. "Thought I'd help look for you." He smiled again.

Carson motioned for them to move, and they started walking again, filing past where Vernon stood.

"Commander LeCroix, I would seriously reconsider what you're doing right now," Ander said, no longer following them. "This will be the end of your career."

"I'm sure it is," Carson said.

"Oh, Commander?" Vernon asked. "I almost forgot. Control said you left this behind. They wanted me to give it to you if I saw you."

"What is it?" Carson asked, turning toward the biologist.

Vernon dug in his pocket for a moment. "Now where is it?"

Gillian saw the tension in his shoulders, the way he was looking directly at Carson as he brought something shining out of his pocket.

"Carson! Look out!" she screamed, knowing at once it was already too late.

Carson tried to bring the handgun to bear, but Vernon stepped forward, grasping his wrist, the muscles in the bullish man's forearms rippling.

Vernon's smile broadened as he swung the scalpel up and across Carson's throat.

Blood fountained.

It flew in a solid arc, spraying Vernon's features and painting a dripping swath across the white wall.

Carson stumbled back, the gun falling from his hand. He scrabbled at the open gash in his throat, eyes bulging, futilely trying to stanch the flow.

"I told you, everyone calls me Vern," Vernon said, turning his gaze upon the rest of them.

Gillian's mind was crippled, the sight of Carson's lifeblood flooding from between his fingers bolting her to the floor. The blood-spattered biologist continued to smile as he approached. Birk pulled her back and stepped in front of her like a shield as she caught movement to the side.

Ander lunged forward, arms outstretched, the movement belying his age.

Vernon received him on the tip of the scalpel.

Gillian saw the short, unbelievably sharp blade slip through the old man's sweater like a magic trick.

Ander's breath came out in a moan.

Vernon twisted his hand once. Twice. And yanked the scalpel free.

Ander clutched the wound and tottered backward, his knees unhinging.

Then Birk was in motion.

The big man leaped over the fallen Ander and drove his fist into the side of Vernon's head.

The biologist saw it coming and slashed wildly, catching Birk on the forearm, but the punch landed solidly.

Vernon staggered back, trying to maintain balance that was no longer there.

He fell to his ass and skidded several inches, the scalpel still clutched in one hand.

And that's what shocked Gillian into moving. Because they were all dead if she didn't.

She ran forward, slipped in a pool of blood, and fell beside Carson, who was sitting up against the wall, still holding his throat.

Her hand grasped the handgun, its grip slick crimson.

Vernon was already on his feet, coming toward them.

Gillian brought the handgun up, yanked the trigger.

Nothing happened.

She felt a small button beneath her thumb and pressed it, knowing if it wasn't the safety, she was dead.

The gun went off, bucking in her hands.

One of the light panels exploded behind Vernon.

She pulled the trigger a second time, and a red flower blossomed on Vernon's right thigh.

He grunted and fell toward her, scalpel extended at her face.

She fired again, rolling to the side, expecting the slashing touch of the blade any second.

Blood smeared beneath her.

Then Birk was yanking her to her feet.

The biologist was stretched out, arms above his head, scalpel lying a foot from his reaching hand. His head was turned toward her, and she saw that most of his lower jaw was gone. His tongue clicked loudly in the ruined hole of his mouth, and one eye stared at her, blinking furiously.

He twitched once and was still, only the spreading pool of gore moving outward around him.

Gillian felt the gun slip from her hand. It clattered to the floor, the sound muted in the wake of the gunshots.

"Are you all right, Doctor?" Birk asked.

"Yeah, he didn't get me."

A gurgling brought her out of the sea of adrenaline coursing through her. Carson was looking at her from where he was propped up. She kneeled beside him, his blood so warm as it soaked through her sodden jumpsuit.

"Oh shit, shit, shit," she said, reaching out to his neck, which pumped a weak stream of blood from between his fingers. "You're going to . . ." She couldn't get herself to say he was going to be okay. And he shook his head anyway, heavy-lidded eyes telling her not to bother.

His mouth opened and closed once without a sound. He licked his lips. "Base . . . level."

Hot tears sheeted her vision, and she wiped them away. "Okay."

"S . . . s . . . sorry. W . . . wish diff . . . different."

"Shhhh, don't try to talk."

Carson dropped his hand away from the wound and reached for her.

She grasped his wet palm, squeezed it hard. The blood was done flowing, and his eyes closed halfway.

He clutched her fingers. Then released.

She trembled with silent sobs, everything red and blurred around her.

"Doctor?" Birk said quietly.

Gillian hitched in a breath and glanced to where he squatted beside Ander. The old man's eyelids were fluttering like butterfly wings.

She gently settled Carson's hand in his lap and moved across the blood-soaked hallway that looked like something out of a psychotic's nightmare.

Ander's eyes tracked her, and he tried to smile. "Getting old."

"You're going to be fine, Doctor," she said, her voice thick. "We're taking you with us."

"No. You were right. There's something very wrong with them. You need to go."

"We can get you out."

He shook his head, and a line of blood leaked from the corner of his mouth. "Find Orrin. Take him. He's a good . . . man. Tell him I love him."

She started to protest again, but he grasped her arm and looked up and to his left. She followed his line of sight, seeing the emergency alarm switch beneath the clear cover.

Ander reached up and flipped the cover open, then let his fingers rest on the switch. "Get away. I can be a distr . . . action."

She shared a look with Birk, whose face had taken on a gray pallor. Ander shoved her away. "Go!"

They stood, and she gave the physicist a last look. "Thank you," she said before they turned away.

Gillian retrieved the pistol and tried not seeing how Carson had slumped farther over, how his sightless eyes stared at them as they passed.

When they reached the elevator the doors opened, and she readied for another fight, but the car was empty.

They stepped inside, and she punched the button for level one. As they began to descend, a shrill alarm blared from the speaker in the ceiling, and a small strobe flashed sickeningly on the wall.

She thought of Carson lying in his own blood, how his hand had felt holding hers before he let go, and her vision swarmed with darkness at its edges. She slumped against the wall, pain radiating out from her shoulder.

"Doctor!" Birk had his arm around her, keeping her upright as everything went black, before the incessant strobe blazed into the back of her brain again.

"I'm okay, I'm okay," she said, grasping a handle on the wall. In the flashing light, she saw dark dots on the floor and wondered if Vernon had cut her. Then she saw the clean slit across the back of Birk's forearm, the steady drip falling from his fingertips.

"It is nothing. Doesn't even hurt," he said as she reached for his arm.

"Bullshit. You need stitches."

"I think we are past worrying about stitches," he said.

He was right. She needed to focus now. The only thing that mattered was getting to one of the landers and getting off the station. Getting back to Carrie alive.

She watched the numbers scroll as they descended.

Level three.

Two.

One.

She took a breath, trying to steady the hand that still clutched Carson's pistol.

The alarm and strobe stopped along with the elevator's motion. The screen read level one, but the door didn't open.

"What's happening?" she said quietly.

The car jerked into motion. Upward.

"Damn it. They're bringing us back up." Gillian looked at the digital display, saw the "Emergency Stop" button, and hammered it.

The car stopped.

"We might only have a minute before they override it. Can you get the doors open?" she asked.

Birk flexed his fingers and jammed them into the seam of the doors. He grunted with effort.

The doors slid apart a half inch. Then his grip faltered, and the gap snapped closed. Birk swore in Swedish and tried again.

The opening reappeared. Widened.

Birk let out a deep cry, and the doors slid fully aside.

And revealed a solid wall.

"Doctor, let's go."

Her head snapped down. There was a two-foot opening between the floor of the car and the ceiling of level two. She knelt and looked out into a vacant hallway.

"Hurry, Doctor," Birk said, pushing her flat to the floor. She eased her legs and lower half out, hanging vulnerably with feet touching nothing. The image of the car starting to move once more came to her, the sensation of being sheared in half so strong she shoved herself free and fell, crumpling hard to the floor.

Birk's feet appeared, and he slithered free, his shoulders and head sliding out as the car suddenly lurched into motion. He hit the floor beside her, staring wide-eyed as the car's bottom vanished and the level's doors closed serenely.

"That would have needed more than stitches," he said.

"Come on. We need to find Lien and Leo." She helped him to his feet, and they set off at a trot down the hall, her attention falling on each camera they passed. Any second someone would step from a doorway and try to stop them, and she would have to use the handgun again.

She swallowed bile as they slowed at a corner and peered around it before continuing. At the end of the hall, there was an alcove, a round port mounted in its center. Two people were sprawled at the bay's mouth, their forms becoming familiar the closer they got.

"Shit. It's Leo and Lien," Gillian said, moving faster.

"Doctor—"

"Come on."

As she neared them, Lien's head lifted weakly off the floor, and she raised one hand, seeing them approach.

"It's okay," Gillian said, stooping beside her, seeing a second too late that the other woman was pointing back the way they'd come.

Birk's bellow of pain flooded her ears as she tried to turn, tried to bring the gun up, but then every nerve in her body was on fire.

Her muscles spasmed in pure agony, and she screamed, the handgun clattering to the floor. She followed it a half second later into darkness.

FORTY-TWO

Muddled sounds.

Frames of pictures Gillian didn't understand. There was a man's face pressed to the floor. Close to hers. One of his eyes was open, the other purple and swelled shut. She knew his name. Except the pain was still receding, keeping most of her thought process at bay.

She wanted to go back to sleep. Let the pain go away and try to wake up again.

She wanted a hydro.

Gillian closed her eyes, and when she opened them, the man was gone.

Leo was gone. It had been Leo lying beside her, such terror and sadness in his one good eye.

She tried putting her hands against the floor to push herself up but could barely move.

"Really knocked them the fuck out, Bob," a voice said somewhere beyond her field of vision.

"That's what happens when you turn these things up to ten. They're out for like five minutes."

"Incapacitato."

"You just made that up."

"It's Italian."

"Bullshit. Help me here, will you?"

There were echoed grunts. The sound of cloth sliding against something.

Gillian tried rolling herself over but managed to lift her shoulder only an inch off the floor. The last hour was coming back to her out of a fog.

The ship exploding.

Their plan to escape.

Carson's death.

She grimaced, smelling the drying copper of his blood. Vernon's blood. Maybe some of Birk's.

Where was Birk?

She lifted her head and was able to glance around the alcove where she was lying.

Two men stood six feet away. One was dressed in a dark security uniform while the other was wearing a space suit minus the helmet. They were standing beside the round port she'd spotted before. There was a small window set in its top, and the one wearing the dark jumpsuit was looking through it, a half smile on his face. And there was a noise, muted but there. It sounded like someone pleading.

The security guard looking through the window reached out and pressed a button beside the port.

There was a long beep and a high screeching that slowly diminished to nothing.

"Holy shit. That was brutal," the other man said.

"Yeah. Needed to be done, though."

Gillian watched them step away from the port, and the one who had pushed the button drew out Carson's handgun from one of his pockets. He ejected the magazine. "Four rounds left. Where the hell did she get a gun?"

"No idea. But he'll be happy we snagged them."

"Most definitely. Glad I saw you when I did."

Strength was returning to her body. She swallowed and blinked, bringing her thoughts into order. The one in the space suit was Guthrie, the pilot who had brought them to the surface. The other was someone she'd never seen before. She looked around quickly.

Where were Leo and Lien?

"Looks like someone's coming around," Guthrie said, staring down at her.

"Pl . . . please," she said.

"Don't worry. Everything'll be fine soon."

"Let's take care of him first," the other man said. "Don't want this big fucker waking up. Took two blasts to put him down in the first place."

"Ten-four."

Guthrie and the guard reached down, and now she could see Birk lying motionless on his back near her feet. They grabbed him beneath the armpits and knees before lifting him off the ground and carrying him to the wall near the port. They set him down, and Guthrie pushed the button on the wall. The same beep issued, and the port swung open.

Birk mumbled something guttural, one arm raising a few inches off the ground.

"Hurry up," the guard said, grasping Birk's legs again. He and Guthrie lifted him up.

Gillian shook her head, lead cobwebs gradually lifting from her mind.

It was a disposal port. For garbage or waste that shouldn't be kept on board. There'd been one just like it on the ship, though much smaller. As she watched, the guard slid Birk's feet and legs inside, Guthrie feeding his upper body in as well.

"Stop," she croaked, leveraging herself up on one arm. She got one leg beneath her and wobbled onto a knee.

"Just relax, Doctor. We'll be with you in a minute," Guthrie said. He struggled with Birk's wide shoulders and finally pushed the big man fully into the disposal. Birk shifted, another mutter coming from him as Gillian made it to her feet.

"Tenacious," the guard said, glancing her direction and swinging the port's door shut.

The door made a hollow thunk and bounced back.

One of Birk's hands was folded over the seal, a half-moon of blood oozing from where the door had struck him.

The guard stepped forward and tried shoving Birk's hand into the port, but it shot up and grasped him by the neck.

"Ah shit," the guard said before he was yanked forward and his forehead connected with the wall.

He fell, slamming to his back as Birk struggled out of the port.

Guthrie rushed forward, but Gillian kicked one of his feet as he passed, and he stumbled to the floor.

Birk slid free of the disposal, his clenched jaw like the prow of a ship. He wobbled once as he took a step. His eyes found hers, and she saw something change in them. Saw them darken.

Guthrie rose onto his haunches and drew out a Taser.

Birk slapped it from his hand and grabbed the pilot's arm. In one motion, he yanked Guthrie to his feet and ran him across the alcove, gripping the back of his head.

There was a loud cracking as Guthrie's face met the wall. Gillian guessed it was his orbital bone breaking, but it could've been his nose too.

The pilot slithered down, a smear of blood tracing his path on the wall.

She caught movement in the corner of her eye as the guard struggled to his feet, the pistol in one hand.

Gillian ran toward him and drove her shoulder into his chest, the impact sending tremendous waves of pain through her skull.

The gun dropped to the floor and danced away, then Birk was there, a Viking immersed in a battle's bloodlust. He grasped the guard by the lapel of his jumpsuit and dragged him to the port, then braced him against the opening before slamming the heavy port door into his face.

Once.

Twice.

Three times.

The fourth swing of the door smashed the top of the man's skull off, and Birk let the body slip to the floor in a wet thud. He was spattered with blood, hunks of something Gillian didn't want to think about clinging to his jumpsuit.

Gillian's gorge rose, looking at the carnage, but just as quickly she stepped forward and scooped up the Taser. But where was the pistol?

Her eyes trailed in the direction she thought it had bounced, and she saw Guthrie pushing himself into a sitting position, his nose flattened sideways and the gun wobbling in his hand.

The barrel's black eye leveled on her.

"No!" Birk leaped in front of her and wrapped his arms around her in a titanic bear hug.

Four reports, the gun beyond loud in the close space, drowning out her screams.

She felt the rounds slam into Birk's back, each one like a hammer blow reverberating through his body into her own. Gillian struggled, but Birk held her fast, arms pressed to her sides.

Slowly he released her. Birk turned, took a step, and fell to one knee. The blooms of red on his back spread quickly, turning his blue jumpsuit black.

She heard a dull clicking and saw Guthrie pulling the gun's trigger over and over.

A sound came from her she didn't recognize, something elemental that welled up from her core.

She took two steps, jammed the Taser against Guthrie's forehead, and yanked the trigger.

There was a low hissing, like an enormous snake, and Guthrie jittered where he sat. A burnt-meat smell wafted up, and when she stepped back, the pilot's scalp was singed black.

He tipped sideways, eyes rolled to the whites in his head.

Gillian turned and dropped to her knees beside Birk, who had fallen to his back, mercifully hiding the bullet holes, but already blood began to spread out beneath him like a blanket of red.

His eyes found hers, and he tried to smile. "Doctor."

She grabbed one of his huge hands in both of hers and denied any of this was happening. She couldn't be seeing this, watching this man die, this wonderfully intelligent young man who had played with her daughter in their yard, had never said an unkind word to anyone, had given up his nights and weekends to further her cause.

And now he had given her everything.

"Oh God, no. No, Birk."

"It is . . ." His voice faded, and he coughed, a horrible wet sound deep in his chest. She ran her hands over him frantically, shaking so hard she could barely stay upright. Maybe there was a chance. If she got him to medical right now, they could do something. She didn't care what they wanted anymore; she'd give it to them.

But this was what they wanted. The crew needed them gone. No record, nothing to expose what was happening here.

"Tell Justin I am sorry, Doctor."

"No. You'll tell him yourself. Get up." She put an arm beneath his head, but he pushed her away gently.

"I think . . . my number is up." He smiled suddenly, blinking against a glaze that was invading his eyes. "I finally . . . finally got one right."

His smile faded, muscles going slack beneath her hands.

Birk's chest rose and fell and didn't rise again.

A sob gripped her so strongly, she was sure it would tear her in half. Gillian slumped forward onto his body, holding him, whispering she was sorry over and over into the hollow of his throat. She could smell his aftershave, sweet and light above the stink of blood.

Gillian sat back. Couldn't process Birk being gone.

A numbness settled over her, and it was like watching the world through someone else's eyes. Everything that had transpired in the last few months had an unreal tinge as if it had happened to someone else.

And, oh God, she wished it had.

A scream tried boiling up and out of her, but she bit down hard on her lower lip. Her gaze traveled from the blood-spattered alcove to the hallway. Around the corner was the elevator, the only way to base level, where hopefully Easton was waiting. Maybe he was dead now too. But she had to try; she owed it to everyone who was already gone.

She grabbed the Taser from the floor and started unsteadily back the way they'd come, then stopped. The elevator wasn't an option. Even if she managed to get on it safely, she'd probably end up being whisked to whatever level the crew wanted her at. Besides, they were likely on their way here right now.

Her gaze flitted over the alcove, stomach plunging at the sight of Birk lying motionless. Beyond him, Guthrie was slumped to his side. Her gorge rose at the sight of the scorched corpse, but not before her eyes lighted on the space suit he was wearing.

It took her the better part of three minutes to get the suit off him, the looseness of his joints and the burnt-meat smell gagging her. She donned the suit, trying to adjust all the straps and securements tighter since it was so large. Where was the helmet, though?

Gillian turned in a circle before stepping into the hallway, hoping to see the helmet on the floor along its length, but there was nothing. She couldn't go on without the helmet. There'd be no point in—

A distant sound filtered to her, and she paused, cocking her head to listen.

The sound of footsteps coming closer. Many sets of them.

She ran.

FORTY-THREE

The hallway scrolled by, endless junctures and doors passing like road signs on a desolate highway.

Gillian turned left, then right at the next hall, stopping to listen over the sound of her panting. Couldn't hear anything over her heartbeat.

They were coming for her. And they would kill her as soon as they caught her.

She hurried on, the suit making constant noise as she ran.

It had to be somewhere close. She'd covered over half of the level, zigzagging through the corridors. Before long she'd be routed back to the central elevator, and she couldn't risk going that far.

A short hall opened to her right, and she skidded to a stop, a burst of elation flowing through her.

The airlock was open, and a row of helmets sat neatly on a shelf inside.

She jogged to them, grabbed the first one, slammed it down, and latched it in place. After reaching inside the space suit's pocket, she drew out her key card from where she'd tucked it earlier and scanned it across the reader to seal the inner door.

Nothing happened.

She waved it again. And again.

Nothing.

They'd shut it off.

"Fuck!" She slammed her gloved hand into the control panel, but the display remained the same. She was about to flee the lock when a thought struck her.

Gillian unzipped two of the opposite pockets before her fingers closed on a familiar shape.

She pulled out Guthrie's key and scanned it.

The display changed, offering her command options. She hit the "Open Airlock" button and stepped back as the inner door slid shut.

Decompression in five seconds, the cool electronic voice said.

She tried slowing her breathing, knowing what was going to happen next.

The outer door opened, the vast emptiness of space interrupted only by a swath of the red planet.

Weightlessness began to take over as she moved to the edge and looked down.

Her head spun with vertigo seeing the lower level and the pocked surface of Mars miles below.

If she screwed up, she'd fall into its gravitational pull, then through its atmosphere, and end up a stain somewhere on the rocky landscape. The only solace would be dying long before she hit the surface.

The hallway outside the lock was still clear. Time to go.

There was a tether line fastened to the station's side that she would hook to in a normal situation with a cable attachment. She dropped the Taser, hated leaving it behind, but none of the suit's pockets would accommodate it. Without a tether, she needed both of her hands free.

She swung herself out of the airlock and grasped the line, holding it so tightly her knuckles ached.

The openness beneath her was all consuming.

Gillian pulled herself downward. Hand over hand.

A support strut impeded her progress, and she had to move to the side to circumvent it. Another ten feet away was base level's airlock. If someone was aware of her location, they'd simply bar her from the lock. And then what would she do?

The thought of floating outside the station trying to find a way in was almost too much. She had no idea how much oxygen remained in Guthrie's tanks, but it would be long enough to go insane trying to gain entry before her air dried up.

Five feet.

Three.

One.

She peered in through the airlock's viewport.

It was empty. The exterior control was to the right side. She followed the tether line over to it and was about to press the "Open Airlock" command when something moved out of a recess into the light.

Leo's corpse floated toward her, swollen and hideous from the ravages of space. His tongue lolled, purple and blistered, and his hands were hooked inward near his chest.

Gillian screamed and lost her grip on the line.

Shit. Shit.

She stretched for the tether, fingers brushing the line as she began floating away. She convulsed, swinging her opposite hand around as she rotated from the station and out into space.

Her pointer finger snagged the line. Came free.

But it was enough to drag her closer, and she wrapped her hands tightly around the line, whispering breathless thank-yous over and over.

She pressed the button, and there was a pause while the inner door shut.

The airlock opened, and she slung herself inside, closing the door behind her. She lay on the floor, trying in vain to push the image of Leo away as hot tears ran from the corners of her eyes. He'd been very much alive when they'd forced him outside and had apparently tried to work his way down to the airlock as she'd done, but never made it. Lien had obviously met the same fate as well. Gillian shuddered, on the verge of being sick. Slowly she gained her feet and moved to the inner door. Pressurization took nearly a minute, and she used it to watch through the window for anyone's approach.

Outside was the "T" of a hall. It took her a moment to gather her bearings, but then she recognized where she was. To the left was the central elevator. The right would take her to the landers' launch area. She hadn't spotted either of the two ships docked below the station on her walk outside, and the fact disturbed her. She should've been able to see them.

Pressurization complete, the system's voice said.

She unlatched the helmet and drew the suit off; it would only slow her down if she needed to run.

Shaking with receding adrenaline, Gillian opened the inner door and stepped into the hall.

There was no one in either direction. She headed toward the launch area. If Easton was still alive, he would be there.

She'd gone only a dozen paces when a weak voice echoed through the corridor, stopping her.

"Help." It was coming from up ahead, near the entry for elevation control. Easton? She moved forward wishing she had some kind of weapon. There was a rasp of fabric, and she could see that the next door on the right was slightly open.

Diver's cell.

Gillian sidled up to the doorway and looked in.

Vasquez was lying on his back in a spreading pool of blood, a ragged gash on the side of his neck. A blood trail led to the small access door set in the glass partition, which was open.

Diver was gone.

Vasquez spotted her as she stepped inside the room, pushing the door the rest of the way open. His eyes bulged as she took a step closer, unsure whether she should help or even if she could help—there was so much blood.

"Door," Vasquez said, and at first she thought he was hallucinating. But then she sensed movement behind her and spun.

Diver was there, his spindly form lashing out from behind the door where he'd hidden. One of his fists caught her on the jaw, and starlight bloomed in the corner of her eyes. She hit the wall and stumbled out of the room, then slipped in some of Vasquez's blood and fell.

Her vision seesawed before steadying, and she tried to rise, but Diver was already there, his fingers finding her hair and yanking her onto her back.

He stooped over her, face inches from her own, teeth yellowed and decaying, breath like a sewer. He screeched, the sound something that could've come from a swath of dense rainforest. The hand with the broken finger, which was wrapped in bright-blue tape, slid beneath her jaw and began to squeeze while the other ran up and down her jumpsuit as he straddled her.

Gillian tried rolling away, but the biologist was too strong. Even in his emaciated state, his grip was like a cable around her throat.

She bucked, the pressure in her head becoming creeping darkness at the edges of her vision. She managed to get ahold of his broken finger and pry it loose.

The bone snapped as she twisted the tape-enclosed digit. Diver bellowed and switched hands, then slammed her head to the floor.

He was going to kill her.

His injured hand tore at one of her pockets, and he drew something out.

Guthrie's key.

Diver looked at the card, something like adoration drifting into his fevered gaze. At the same time, the pressure relented on her throat, and she sucked in a breath, using the respite to shove his chest as hard as she could.

Diver swayed backward but maintained his balance above her. In one motion, he clenched his good fist and drew it back to strike.

Something clipped the top of his skull, and he fell sideways off her, dropping the key card to the floor. Gillian scooted away, untangling herself from Diver as he groggily pushed himself up on one arm.

Orrin wound back with the steel stool he was holding by the legs and slammed the seat into Diver's forehead.

The biologist collapsed to his back and made a mewling growl. Gillian scooted to the wall, rubbing at her neck as she watched Orrin raise the stool again.

One of Diver's hands came up weakly, but Orrin swung above it.

There was the crunch of bone, and Diver quivered and was still.

Orrin's shoulders heaved with exertion, and his face was flushed as he turned to her. "Are you okay?"

"Yes," she croaked. "I think so."

"What the hell's going on?"

"We have to get out of here." She struggled to her feet. "They're killing everyone."

"Who is?"

"The crew. Everyone who's addicted to shifting."

"Addicted?" Orrin shot a look at Diver before jerking his head toward the elevator. "We need to see my father."

Oh God.

Gillian tried forming the words but stopped herself. It would tear Orrin apart.

"We have to get to one of the landers," she said, stooping to pick up Guthrie's key.

"The landers? Why?"

"Easton, he was going to—" She swayed, dizziness sweeping over her.

"Whoa," she heard Orrin say as she stumbled forward. His hands found her shoulders as she fell, and she reached out, fingers snagging the neck of the T-shirt he wore.

There was a roaring in her ears, and her vision doubled before coming back to normal. "Sorry, I—" she started to say but stopped.

A yellow-brown tendril extended up the skin of Orrin's chest toward his neckline. Below it she could see the deeper purple of the bruise's center on his breastbone.

And in that moment, she was back in the ship's airlock, seeing the space suit coming alive.

Kent's rotting face behind the visor, his hands trying to grasp her.

Swinging the steel pry bar around and feeling it connect with his chest.

Gillian shoved herself away from Orrin, barely staying on her feet. "You," she whispered.

His face fell as he glanced down and readjusted his shirt, covering up the place where she'd struck him weeks ago.

"You really weren't supposed to see that," he said, and started toward her.

FORTY-FOUR

Gillian backpedaled, mind reeling.

Something brushed her foot, and she nearly fell on top of Diver's body.

"Gillian, please," Orrin said, walking toward her with his hands out. "Just listen."

She shook her head, eyes flitting to the right where the elevator waited and left toward the docking bay. She feinted to the right and lunged left, but Orrin was already there. Of course, he knew she couldn't go back to any of the levels. There was no one left to help her there.

"Stay back," she said, retreating several steps, surprised when her back didn't meet the wall.

"I want to talk to you."

She was in the entryway to elevation control, the short hall behind her. No way out.

Gillian turned and saw the scanner beside the door, swiped Guthrie's card across it.

"Gillian, don't do this. Hear me out," Orrin said, coming closer. "You don't understand."

The door slid open, and she slipped through.

"There's nowhere to go."

The door closed, cutting Orrin off.

She was in a transition area perhaps twelve feet square. Opposite the hallway entry was another door without windows but plastered with the same warnings she'd seen in the corridor.

Authorized Personnel Only

Absolutely No Metallic Material beyond This Point

She didn't read the rest, only scanned the key again on the inner door.

There was an unbearable pause; then the door whisked open.

She caught a glimpse of something small streaking away from her, trailing liquid, before the pain stampeded up her leg and into her brain, brilliant and blinding.

The titanium plate.

The thought was swept away as she fell screaming through the doorway and landed in a heap. Gillian reached to her shin, sure her leg would be gone from the knee down. It was still there, but her jumpsuit was ripped and wet with blood from where the plate had torn free of her leg.

The inner door slid shut. In a few seconds, the outer door would admit Orrin.

She needed to move.

She rolled onto her hands and knees, getting her left leg under her before trying to stand. The pain was molten as she put weight on the other leg, and fresh blood wept from the cuff of her jumpsuit. She could walk.

The room she was in was round, everything lit by ropes of light strung across support girders twenty feet overhead. She limped along a 360-degree platform with an open center looking down into a pit at least seventy feet across. Below, interconnected veins of glass tubes surrounded what looked like a gigantic inverted top. Pulses of light ran through the tubes intermittently, and it was then she noticed everything in the room was made of either plastic or glass.

Of course. The magnet would pull anything else down to its center, destroying the room. She could feel a strange tugging behind her eyes, like the beginning of a migraine, as she hobbled to a tall plastic cabinet beside the guardrail overlooking the pit.

The door opened, and she caught a glimpse of Orrin stepping inside before ducking behind the cabinet's width.

"Gillian," he called. "I'm just going to talk now. I know you can hear me."

She risked a look around the side of the cabinet. Orrin was standing in front of the doorway, gazing across the magnet opening. Several feet from where he stood was a small puddle of her blood and a spattered trail leading directly to the cabinet.

She ducked as Orrin turned his head toward her.

"I want to apologize for what happened on the ship. No one was supposed to be awake. Tinsel's death was going to be an accident, a malfunction of his stasis unit. But then you were there." There was the scratch of his footsteps, and Gillian gauged the next place she could hide: a lower bulwark of thick glass stemming from the opposite wall.

"I figured I'd have to kill you too, but when I saw you struggling with the hydros, I thought of a way to avert that. And sorry for scaring you in the airlock. I wore the suit in case you saw me. I never intended to run into you. To be fair, you got the better of me. You actually broke my fucking sternum with that bar."

The volume of his voice changed enough so that she was sure he was looking the other way. She hurried as fast as her leg would allow to the bulwark, glancing once over her shoulder. Orrin had his back to her and had taken a step in the opposite direction.

Gillian slid to a crouch behind the thick glass, biting the neck of her jumpsuit as fresh pain rolled up from her leg.

"I thought framing you was kinder than killing you," Orrin said. "I'm not like some of the guys I knew during deployment. Never liked killing."

She could see him through the dense glass, his form distorted and nightmarish.

He turned to look in her direction and paused before kneeling. "Looks like you're hurt. Bet you had some kind of metal in you. From the crash, right? I read about you after our little run-in. Have to say I respect what you're doing. Fighting the good fight."

He rose and started toward her.

There was another cabinet a dozen feet away, and she crawled to it, gasping at the shocks of pain with each movement. Her rosary fell free of her jumpsuit collar, and she silently sent up thanks it was made from wood instead of metal.

"I respect you, Gillian. That's what I wanted to talk to you about. Your daughter. She's dying, right? I'm sorry, I truly am. And I'm sorry shifting doesn't automatically repair damaged cells. Otherwise, we could just run sick people through the machines, right? It would be a miracle."

Gillian tried controlling her breathing. It sounded so loud to her, she was sure Orrin could hear it too. Ahead there was a shallow conduit channel cut into the floor. If she could hide inside it until Orrin passed, then she might be able to get back to the door and out of the room before he could catch her.

"But see, we already have a miracle," Orrin continued, his voice closer now. "What shifting does, it's amazing. You don't know how many days I suffered knowing I could've saved those men. Saved my friends. It was like acid eating away at me from the inside out. Dr. Pendrake helped, but there's only so much someone else can do. I tried pills, booze, fighting, fucking. Nothing kept the memories away."

Gillian clamped a hand down on the wound, trying to stanch the blood, and slithered forward, sliding headfirst into the conduit channel. She fit. Barely. The ridges on the bottom of the channel bit into her stomach and thighs, and she squirmed ahead and tucked herself inside, turning over to her back once she was fully hidden.

"Until I shifted," Orrin said from somewhere very close.

She held her breath. Could he see her? Was there enough blood on the floor for him to see exactly where she'd gone?

"I could tell right away something was different the first time. A little piece missing from the pain. So I did it again and again, and each time I lost a little more of that day."

There was the scuff of his boots on the platform almost even with where she was lying. Sweat trickled across her temples and into her hairline, maddeningly itching.

"Course, you can't control what it takes. I've forgotten things I wanted to remember, like my mother. My fiancée. But I'd do it all over again in a heartbeat. You have no idea the relief of not waking to a living nightmare." His voice broke, and she realized he was crying. "What I told you the other night at the bar? It's like it happened to someone else. There are bits and pieces that seem real, but mostly it's like a dream I had years ago. I was only able to tell you all those details because of my journals and the notes Dr. Pendrake took during our sessions."

There was a long pause, and Gillian felt her entire body tense as Orrin's shadow fell across the railing above her. He was standing only feet away. He knew where she was. He was only toying with her.

"I still remember killing him, though. And Dennis. They were both my friends."

The shadow swayed.

Then receded.

He was moving away.

"But what caused all this is why I'm here. Look at the decisions people make. The Earth is war-torn and polluted to the point we need to leave it forever. I mean, that's insane. They say those who don't learn from history are doomed to repeat it. I say that's bullshit. Humankind has never learned from the past, we hold grudges. We remember, that's why there's violence and hatred. That's why there's wars. It's the most vicious circle ever created."

His voice receded more, and Gillian slowly sat up, peering over the rim of her hiding place. Orrin was nowhere in sight.

"But how can you hate if you don't remember?"

This was her chance. His voice had grown fainter, and if she had to guess, she would put his position almost directly across from the entrance to the room.

She eased her upper body out of the channel, biting back a cry as she bumped the wound on her leg. The room was near silent now. She listened, hoping to hear movement or his voice.

Nothing.

The door was thirty yards away. Go or stay? Run or move cautiously?

Still no sign of him along the grid work that made up the platform.

Gillian ran.

She limped as fast as she could. Each time her right foot came down was a surge of pain. The path ahead was still clear. A glance over her shoulder told her Orrin wasn't there either.

Gillian gripped Guthrie's key card, ready to scan it at the door.

Something snagged her hair.

She screamed, twisting and beginning to fall.

Orrin held her up from behind, wrapped an arm around her throat, and dragged her backward. She flailed, kicking her feet off the ground, but he was too strong. His arm tightened, cutting off the carotid arteries in her neck.

Her vision swam.

Then the pressure eased.

"Your daughter's dying, Gillian," Orrin said in her ear. "She's forgetting you right now. Forgetting everything you are to her. Wouldn't it be easier to do the same?"

Gillian let out a short cry and thrashed again, but Orrin only cinched the choke hold until she neared the ledge of unconsciousness before slackening the pressure.

"Imagine a world without memory. No tragedy would last. Every sin forgiven. Even death would lose its power."

She took several breaths, trying to calm the manic spike of her thoughts. She couldn't get away from him. Not by brute force. There had to be another way.

"You want everyone to end up like Diver out there?" she said finally, trying to work her fingers beneath his forearm.

Orrin made a dismissive sound. "He was a junkie. Weak. Couldn't control himself."

"Everyone else can? It's addiction, Orrin. I know it when I see it."

"That's exactly why I thought you would understand. I didn't do this for the rush of being remade. I did it to forget. You can't tell me you want to remember your husband fading away and dying. When your daughter dies, you'll do anything to forget."

Her eyes burned, and it had nothing to do with Orrin's choke hold. "It wouldn't be just forgetting that I lost my husband or my daughter," she said. "I wouldn't remember what I had with them. And nothing's more important than that." A tear slipped free of her eye and fell to Orrin's forearm.

"I really liked you, Gillian. I hoped you'd see it differently," he said. There was something in his voice that sent a fresh bolt of panic through her. Regret. He was finished talking.

Gillian tried pulling his arm away from her throat, but the choke sunk in deep.

Immediately the corners of her vision frayed. She kicked, her feet sliding out from under her, but Orrin held her steady, slowly applying more and more pressure.

"I'm sorry, Gillian."

Her hand began slipping free of his arm but caught on something draped across it.

The vestiges of her consciousness forced her fingers closed around it.

She gripped the rosary's cross like a dagger and drove it backward over her shoulder.

The closing tunnel of her sight expanded as Orrin cried out and his arm loosened around her neck.

Gillian slipped free of the hold and turned, gagging and coughing.

The cross had caught him on the bridge of the nose and slid to the right, gouging a flayed path to the inner corner of his eye. Bloody tears ran down his cheek, and his opposite eye blinked furiously in response.

Seeing the railing behind Orrin, she staggered forward, gathering speed.

Gillian slammed into him and shoved with every muscle in her body.

Orrin stumbled, and his lower back met the guardrail. His arms pinwheeled, but the momentum was too great.

For a second he balanced on the railing, teetering as one hand snagged hold and he struggled to right himself.

Gillian stepped forward and pushed him the rest of the way over.

Orrin slammed into the other side of the guardrail and spun away, his scream aborted in the shrieking shatter of glass a moment later.

There was the angry buzz of high-amperage electricity and a puff of smoke before the entire room shook. She stepped to the rail and looked down.

Orrin had landed on the interwoven glass conduits far below. His body was already charring, folding in on itself like an insect beneath a magnifying glass. Electricity jumped in ragged arcs from the ruined glass tubes, licking out and across the face of the huge magnet.

The room shimmied again, and she nearly lost her balance.

An alarm sounded, shredding the air.

She ran.

The pain in her leg was secondary now. She expected it, focused on it to keep the panic at bay.

She waved Guthrie's key across the scanner as the floor dropped several inches then rose again. The door opened, and she fell through it. As the inner door began closing, a tongue of crackling electricity wove up and out of the magnet pit like a charmed snake and connected with the ceiling before running outward in an inverted waterfall of light.

Her hair stood up on her head, pulled tight by the static in the air, and the tension behind her eyes ratcheted to another level.

Pulling herself up, she managed to scan the second door, the delay before it opened beyond agonizing. When the hallway appeared, she expected a dozen crew members to be waiting there, but there was only Diver's body and the massive circle of blood around it.

Gillian stepped into the hall, glancing toward the elevator before turning away. There was still a chance in the lander. If she could get inside, maybe she could detach and at the very least get another call for help out.

She made her way down the hallway, hands aching for some kind of weapon as the alarm continued to bleat, a quick tempo matching her heart. As she approached the entry to the decon station, there was a click, and the door swung out toward her.

Without thinking, she dodged sideways and hugged the wall as someone emerged slowly. She sagged with relief.

"Easton," she said.

The mission specialist whipped toward her. His face was coated in drying blood, a long laceration across the side of his scalp still seeping. In one hand he held a six-inch stainless-steel knife.

"Doc, holy shit! Are you okay?"

"I'm fine."

"You're bleeding."

"So are you."

Easton looked past her down the hallway. "Where's everyone else?"

Even in the midst of everything, a lump still formed in her throat. She could only shake her head.

"Everyone?" Easton asked.

She nodded.

Easton visually deflated, his shoulders rounding. "Who did it?"

"The crew. Orrin was the dealer."

"I know. Bastard hit me with a stool. Where is he now?"

"Dead. We need to leave. Something happened to elevation control."

"I know. We're losing altitude and falling into orbit."

"Are the landers ready?"

"They're gone."

"What?"

"They're both gone. Must be on the surface, and whoever left them shifted up from there."

Gillian's heart sank.

The hallway shook, vibrating painfully up through her joints as Easton jerked a thumb over his shoulder. "Listen, from the readouts I saw in there, we've got maybe ten minutes before impact. Elevation control must still be partially functioning, but it won't hold for long. We need—"

Movement down the corridor pulled her attention away from him.

Three men were heading toward them, the one in front holding a Taser.

Gillian stepped back, but her shoulders met the wall. There was nowhere to go. She never thought she'd die like this. So far away from home. From Carrie. The fear was a solid weight in her stomach, and she wondered how much it would hurt.

Easton stood in front of her, turning the knife in his hand so it pointed down. He looked at her. "Doc, you need to go."

She swallowed, dragging her eyes away from the approaching men, and gathered the last of her courage. "There's nowhere to hide. They'll find me. I'll fight."

"No." Easton gestured toward the decon room, and his gaze imparted everything he meant without the time to say it. "Go."

Gillian looked down at the key in her hand and back up at Easton, who nodded before facing the oncoming crew members.

She turned and scanned the door open. The last thing she saw as it closed was the lead man taking aim with the Taser and Easton leaping into motion.

The floor tilted, and she stuck a hand out to brace herself, glass meeting her palm instead of the normal smooth wall.

The teleportation room was empty beyond the barrier, the unit filling up more of the space than she recalled beneath lights that were beginning to flicker. Or maybe it was the knowledge of what she was about to do that made it seem larger, more imposing.

She limped down the hall, then scanned through the next door into the waiting area outside the decon stations. There was a spatter of blood on the floor where she guessed Easton had fallen, along with a digital display blinking a warning regarding elevation and velocity.

Everything was falling apart.

A long bellow of pain came from the outer corridor, diminished through the doors but still heartrending. It was a physical effort not to turn back and try to help him, but it wasn't what he wanted.

Gillian hurried through the mazelike decon chambers, and instead of turning in to the airlock where the landers normally were, she continued on to the next door.

It opened before her, and she stepped into the teleportation room.

There was a falling sensation like coming to the top step of a stairway and thinking there was one more after it. The floor drifted away as the entire station plummeted, and a scream escaped her as gravity relinquished its grip before coming back full force.

She slammed into a rolling cabinet that was passing and spun to the floor, shock waves of agony radiating through her. Gillian gasped at the pain, unable to cry out. Slowly she crawled forward, blinking away tears.

She came to a pedestal secured to the floor a few feet away from the unit's entrance and pulled herself upright. There was a screen attached to the top, an array of four choices highlighted in white on the display.

LOC 1

LOC 2

LOC 3

LOC 4

"Oh shit," she whispered, eyes trailing up and down the list. She had no idea which to pick. One location was Mars's surface, another was Ander's ship hurtling toward the newly discovered planet, and another was the unit at the NASA campus on Earth. But one of the locations was the unit that had been on their ship, which was now pieces of floating wreckage. What would happen if she chose that option? Would she be disintegrated and beamed out into the nether, a signal searching forever for a receiver that no longer existed?

The thought was enough to make her even more nauseous than she already was.

Another tremor ran through the station, and for a moment she felt the free fall of before. Ten minutes. Easton had guessed it would take only ten minutes before they were through the atmosphere and hurtling toward the unyielding surface.

There was no time. She had to decide now.

Gillian reached out and stabbed the first option. It was the soundest choice if the labels had been created in chronological order.

The display asked her to scan her key. She waved Guthrie's card across the eye near its top.

Static came from a speaker overhead, a crackling voice saying something about preparation for departure.

The end of the teleportation unit released and swung open.

Gillian drew in a shaking breath. This was it. Get inside or just wait to die.

She unzipped her jumpsuit and stripped out of her clothing quickly. She began to take the rosary off but stopped, leaving it around her neck. She didn't want to chance the jumpsuit getting mixed up in her own atoms, but there was no way she was leaving the rosary behind.

The broken voice was counting down, skipping numbers, as she moved to the open unit and crawled inside.

The smell overwhelmed her. The decontamination solution was noxious, invading her nostrils until saliva poured into her mouth and she was sure she would vomit.

The room shook again, and she floated inside the tube before slamming back down, flashes of lightning across her vision.

Past her feet, the unit's door swung closed and locked.

It became eerily quiet, except for her breathing.

Blood pounded in her ears.

Would this work? And if it did, what would she lose?

Her eardrums popped, a sense of atmospheric pressure invading the closed space. She glanced down the length of her body, taking in the ugly wound on her leg. If she was wrong, this would be her last few seconds alive.

Lightheadedness overcame her. She felt buzzed. Then drunk. It wasn't unpleasant in the least. There was a strange euphoria as the tube narrowed, becoming a tunnel.

The tunnel, she had time to think as the unit quaked around her again.

She was fading, everything going black. This was death. Nothing else could be like this.

With the last of her will, Gillian reached back, back through the years, and clung to the happiest moment of her life as she fell asleep.

Forever, Carrie. Good night.

FORTY-FIVE

Carrie looked out the car window at the passing palm trees.

She was happy for a second, remembering exactly what the trees were called, but the happiness drained from her almost as fast as it had come. She was going to the doctor, and the doctor was never fun. Auntie Kat said this was a special doctor and that they might be able to help the fuzzies, make them come less. That would be good because they were coming too much lately.

Carrie glanced at Auntie Kat. She looked worried. Her mouth was all puckered up, and it looked like she'd been crying. Carrie guessed that was all right since she cried quite a bit too.

She missed her mom.

Everyone had told her that they would be able to talk on the phone or computer while she was gone. Even Mom had said that. But Auntie Kat told her that they were having trouble getting reception up in the sky where Mom was. She didn't understand exactly what reception was, but she hated it. She wanted to go home to Minnesota. Florida was nice, and she loved the beach and didn't mind going to Uncle Steve and Auntie Kat's church, but it would be fall soon, and she wanted to see the leaves turn colors. Wanted to take their walks around their neighborhood and then have cider when they got back inside.

Uncle Steve cleared his throat again. He'd been doing that a lot in the last few weeks. She noticed he did it whenever he was upset about something.

Auntie Kat turned and looked at her, and for a second Carrie was very scared. Auntie Kat looked so sad. Like she had bad news stuck inside but couldn't let it out.

"How you doing, honey?" Auntie Kat asked.

"Okay."

"Feeling all right?"

"Yeah. Kinda tired."

"We'll be there in just a few minutes. Then I'm sure the doctors will let you have a nap."

"Are you staying with me?"

Auntie Kat's face scrunched up. "Not today. I can't today, but we'll come see you really soon after you get settled in. Isn't that right, Steve?"

"Of course," Uncle Steve said.

Auntie Kat gave her another smile that wasn't really real and looked out the windshield again. Carrie went back to gazing out her window and saw a big sign coming closer on the side of the road.

"NASA? That's where Mommy went, right?" she asked as they slowed down and stopped at a gate.

"That's right. They know your mom here. And . . . and . . ." Auntie Kat turned the other way and quit talking.

A man came up to the side of the car, and Uncle Steve showed him a paper. The man wrote something on it, and then the gate went up and they drove through. After a few minutes, they parked and got out of the car. Auntie Kat took her hand while Uncle Steve got her bag out of the back of the trunk.

"Were you crying?" Carrie asked, squeezing her aunt's hand as they walked toward a big white building at the end of the parking lot.

"No, honey. It's just allergies," she said in her crying voice.

Carrie frowned, looking at her shoes. She remembered her mom had bought the shoes before they came to Florida on the private plane. But she couldn't remember the name of the store or trying them on. The store's name was a word that felt funny to say, but she couldn't see it in her head.

They walked into a lobby, and Uncle Steve gave the paper he was holding to a lady at a desk while Auntie Kat ran a hand over Carrie's hair. It felt good, something her mother had done a lot whenever they were at the doctor.

After a little while, a woman came to get them, and they followed her through a set of doors and down a hallway to another, smaller room where a man with really black skin and a white beard was waiting for them. He was wearing a dark suit and looked like a principal of a school.

"Hello, I'm Anderson Jones," he said, shaking hands with Uncle Steve and Auntie Kat. "And you must be Carrie." He held out his hand, and it was very big, but she was brave and took a few of his fingers in her hand and shook with him just like a grown-up. "I hear you're not feeling well," he said.

"Sometimes," she answered.

"Well, we're going to see if we can do something about that."

The adults started talking, and Carrie listened for a minute, but it was about the fuzzies and not her mom, so she quit listening. There were pictures on the wall of astronauts in space suits above the Earth. The Earth looked so small from way up high, and she wondered if her mom was taking any pictures to show her when she came back.

"We'll take very good care of her," Mr. Jones said before saying, "Carrie, would it be okay if you came with me now?"

She looked from his outstretched hand to Uncle Steve and Auntie Kat. She ran to them and hugged them hard, and her aunt was crying again, and she wondered what was wrong. If this was the doctor's, then they were going to help her. Right?

She asked Auntie Kat, and she said, "Yes, of course they are, honey. We'll be back to visit you really soon."

When she was done hugging her aunt and uncle, she took Mr. Jones's hand and walked with him through another set of doors. She looked back before the doors closed and saw Auntie Kat waving and crying.

"You're a very brave girl, do you know that, Carrie?" Mr. Jones said after they'd walked a little ways down a hall.

"My mom says I am."

"She's right."

"Do you know my mom?"

"Yes. I do, actually."

"Really? Is the reception fixed? Can I talk to her now that I'm at NASA?"

They turned a corner, and Mr. Jones pushed a few buttons on a door before they went through it and climbed down some stairs. She was about to ask him again because she wasn't sure he'd heard her when he said, "I think you'll be able to talk to your mom really soon."

Carrie was so excited, she hopped a couple of times as they stopped near another door and Mr. Jones opened it. She started to ask when she could talk to her mom when she heard someone say her name.

She saw someone coming toward her from across a really white room wearing funny pajamas that were all green and baggy, and it took her half a second to realize who it was in the pajamas running and yelling her name.

Then she was running too because it was Mom.

She took two giant steps and jumped, and Mom caught her. They sat on the ground, and she was crying so hard and holding her mom because she never wanted her to go away ever again. And Mom was saying, "I love you, I love you," and she was saying it back, and she hugged her so tight and promised never to let her go.

Because Mom was finally home.

EPILOGUE

Eight Years Later

Gillian watched the rain.

It swirled and danced with the wind that swept down off the mountainside and through the clearing her home sat in. There was no pattern to it, no rhyme or reason to the storms that came almost every day in the Cascades. The rain just was, and she liked losing herself in its simplicity.

She sat beside the picture window in the two-story ranch-style house and looked at the water running from the corner of the garage across the yard, the pine boughs in the trees beyond speckled and dripping like they'd been dusted with millions of jewels. Like stars.

She looked down at her coffee cup and grimaced. It was empty. Gillian rose and moved to the nearby kitchen from the sitting room, several aching twinges running up through her leg. The heavier storms always affected the old injury like a barometer. Getting older didn't help either. Everything hurt more now than it had before.

The last of the pot filled her cup almost halfway, and she warmed her hands around it, listening to the quiet patter of the rain and the silence of the house. It was hard to fathom that in a week she would have lived here for nearly five years. It still didn't fully feel like home, but rather like she would be moving on soon to yet another location. Of course, it was the aftereffects of having jumped from one medical installation to another for over three years prior to moving to Washington. A U-Haul hangover, Anton would have called it.

Anton Veering. She missed the young, charismatic biochemist more than she would've ever guessed. Missed their late-night talks when neither could sleep and would inevitably find themselves in one of the many NASA-funded labs they shared. The familiar routine of the relationship they'd fallen into so easily had puzzled her for some time before she realized what it was about the thin and lanky man that always caused a fleeting thread of melancholy to run through her.

He reminded her of Birk.

Not at all in stature, but in his sharp intellect and quiet kindness. One early morning in the lab when he'd brought her a muffin and a cup of coffee, she'd had to excuse herself to the bathroom, where she'd sat in a stall and cried into her hands. It had been the first time she'd broken down since holding Carrie after their reunion in the containment area below one of NASA's research centers.

She set the coffee down, her hand trembling slightly as she recalled the two days prior to seeing her daughter all those years ago.

The confusion. The tests. The hours and hours of inquiries and interviews.

And before that, the last seconds prior to passing out in the unit on the station.

The official report was, it had taken her approximately 194 seconds to travel from the teleportation unit on the UNSS orbiting Mars to the unit on the NASA campus in Florida. A little under three and a half minutes. She'd watched the video of her arrival. A protégé of Ander's by the name of Dr. Simon Fletcher had been working at a desk outside the unit's area when there'd been a white flash of light, blinding every camera in the room for several seconds before revealing Gillian lying motionless in the unit's tube. Fletcher had rushed inside and got her out, wrapped her in a blanket, and called for help.

The next thing she remembered was a man standing over her, his dark skin in stark contrast to the white beard he wore. Anderson W. Jones, deputy administrator of flight operations. He'd been standoffish but patient, listening to her story and asking her to repeat it nearly a dozen times for various people he brought to her recovery room. Finally she'd quit speaking, saying only that she wanted to see her daughter before she'd tell them anything else.

And they had given in.

An ember of warmth bloomed inside her every time she recalled the moment she saw Carrie, how fast Carrie had run to her and held her like she was going to slip away.

Gillian picked up her coffee, letting the last of its heat seep into her fingers, which eased the ache in her knuckles. Arthritis, she guessed. Early onset, but then again, she wasn't a spring chicken anymore. At forty-six she looked to be in her early fifties. The stress of the last eight years compounding. But she would take the aches and pains and extra wrinkles she saw in the mirror any day. She was thankful to be alive and even more thankful to hear the sounds in the rooms above.

There was the rattle and bang of a drawer in the upstairs bathroom. A snippet of a song sung quietly. Then the fast thump of young feet in a hurry coming down the stairs.

Carrie stepped into the kitchen and smiled.

She was sixteen now, slated for an early graduation from high school, and was already planning on pre-enrolling in Jefferson College fifty miles away in the foothills of the Cascades, a sleepy school with a great creative-writing program Carrie talked about almost constantly. There was also a shy young man who worshipped her, whom she had begun seeing several nights a week when she wasn't working at the small roadside restaurant halfway down the mountain they lived on.

And she was healthy.

"Good morning," Carrie said, coming to her side. She pecked a quick kiss on Gillian's cheek and picked up the empty coffeepot. "Really?"

"I'm sorry. I'll make another pot."

"It's okay. I'll grab a cup at work."

"I can—"

"Mom . . ." The tone of her daughter's voice encompassed all the discussions they'd had in recent years as Carrie had become more and more independent and Gillian's continual hovering became a topic of contention. It was second nature to protect, to worry, to always dread tomorrow because it had meant another day closer to something Gillian knew she couldn't face.

But things were different now, she reminded herself. She and Anton had seen to that.

Almost immediately after her and Carrie's reunion, she had begun work. Work funded by NASA and partially, she assumed, by the UN in exchange for her silence. There had been a major reordering in the hierarchy of the teleportation project after the disaster and loss of the space station as well as every soul on board. Over a period of several weeks, she was given enough resources to begin splicing her neurological mapping breakthrough with treatment hypotheses. Thankfully, all her findings, which also backed up her account, had arrived shortly before she did, and the leaping-off point for researching a cure had been so much more promising than ever before. With Anton's constant help, they were able to eventually formulate an enzyme that, when paired with the luciferase-luciferin compounds, targeted and dissolved the neurological tangles created by Losian's.

And it hadn't come a moment too soon.

By the time their trials and testing had concluded, Carrie had lost much of her short-term memory capacity. Countless times Gillian had held her upon the little girl's waking, calming her panic-stricken questions about where they were and what was happening. And even as she and Anton raced to a finish line that was promising but promised no certainty, Carrie's long-term memory had begun eroding as well.

The fugues had come more frequently.

The anger and violence a familiar aspect of each day.

But the Lindqvist Enzyme Treatment, or LET, changed everything. Gillian had insisted on naming the breakthrough after Birk. And even knowing the tens of thousands of people the therapy would save, it was a small consolation to everyone who had known him. She couldn't count how many times she'd glanced up as someone entered one of the labs, fully expecting to see the huge man there, to hear him mangle yet another idiom. To see his smile.

Carrie's hands touched her arms, and Gillian came back to the present. "Mom? You okay?"

Gillian smiled, wiping at the sheen of moisture coating her eyes. "Yes."

"I'm sorry. I just . . . I'm okay, you know? You don't have to worry."

Gillian pulled her daughter close and kissed her gently on the forehead. "I know I don't. But that's what mothers do."

Carrie gave her a half smile and turned away to gather a few items on the counter that had spilled free of her overflowing purse, and Gillian caught a glimpse of the stainless-steel port set in the back of Carrie's skull. It was barely noticeable most days, especially when she left her hair down. But when it was wet from a shower or she tied it up on the top of her head, the small injection port was visible.

That was the only drawback to LET. It wasn't really a cure but a treatment.

The enzyme dissolved the neurological tangles and prevented cell death, but it didn't cure the underlying cause of Losian's. Gillian's theory on the disease, concerning several neurotoxins that had an inherent effect on genetic coding, was still being circulated in the medical communities. Most industry leaders were in agreement that the rising air and water pollution was to blame, but the exact poison had yet to be identified.

So the solution was an injection every two years through permanent cranial ports in patients who had the disease. It kept the effects at bay, and though it wasn't what Gillian had hoped for, it was infinitely better than watching the person she loved the most in the world become a stranger.

"Okay, I've gotta go," Carrie said, zipping the bulging purse closed.

"Do you have enough masks?"

"Yes."

"You're sure?"

"Yes. Oh, and Winston and I are going to dinner tonight, so I'll be home late."

"And when exactly is 'late'?"

Carrie rolled her eyes, coming across the kitchen. "Mom, you do know I'm almost an adult now."

Gillian smiled and hugged her daughter close. "I know. But you'll always be my little girl."

They stayed that way for a long time before Carrie said the word Gillian was waiting for. The fact that she wasn't too old to say it, and maybe never would be, created a new wave of warmth in her chest.

"Forever?"

"Forever."

Carrie stepped back from her, giving her a last smile before heading out of the room. "See you tonight."

"Okay. See you then."

Gillian watched out the window as Carrie jogged through the rain to her car and climbed inside. She made a quick turn in the driveway and then was gone in a fleeting flash of taillights.

Gillian busied herself for a few minutes in the kitchen, loading the dishwasher and handwashing several of the larger pans from their dinner the night before. When the chores were done, she stood silently for a moment, listening to the drum of rain before returning to her chair in the sitting room.

Joe Hart

She let her thoughts wander for a time. Traveling over the past like a historian layering events with critical detail. As she relived the last hours on the station, a craving for a hydro rose, expected but also surprising in its intensity. It had been over eight years since she'd had one of the little pills, but the strength of addiction never failed to amaze and frighten her. But she knew exactly what had caused the spike of need. It happened every time she returned to the moment before Ander's machine had taken her apart and sent her across the expanse of space at the speed of light.

Because she'd lost something in that second. And no matter how hard she tried to find it again, it was utterly and truly gone.

Carrie's birth. The happiest day of her life, erased as if it had never been.

She remembered trying to hold on to it as consciousness had slipped away from her in the unit, trying to grasp the best and brightest memory she had in case it was her last chance to do so. But now there was only an empty hole where the day should have been. Looking back, it made some dark, cosmic sense that there was a parallel between her discovery of unlocking the hippocampus through a memory and what shifting took away. One allowed the mysteries of the mind to be charted while the other was payment for trying to break an unyielding law of the universe. She barely recalled the elation of re-atomizing at NASA. What she did remember was severe disorientation, like falling asleep without meaning to and waking up hours later, groggy and bewildered, but tenfold.

Only three and a half minutes, but it had felt like so much longer. Somehow she believed Mr. King had come very close to the truth in his short story.

Maybe more than three and a half minutes had passed for her. Maybe a lot more.

Gillian sighed, sitting forward to rest her elbows on her knees. She shouldn't do this to herself. Shouldn't retrace the steps taken while wondering if she could have done something different, and if she had, perhaps Carson, Leo, Lien, and Easton would still be alive.

Birk would also still be alive.

She let the tears come, let them fall and mirror the rain outside. When they had tapered off, she gazed at the windswept clearing knowing that deep down the guilt and loneliness would never leave. Because in a way, she was still trapped, not on a ship or a space station, but in the web of her choices that had led her here.

Her phones were tapped along with her e-mail. She had to wear dark glasses and a hat every time she left the house and was watched closely via satellite as well as by a UN representative who was stationed nearby with orders to apprehend her if it appeared she was about to break her silence or reveal her identity.

Because that was the tradeoff for her research, for saving Carrie and countless others who had been afflicted by Losian's: her silence. Eighteen thousand–plus people worked for NASA, and most had knowledge of her part in the mission as well as its downfall, but very few were aware she was still alive. If word got out, it would raise countless questions about how. People would learn about Mars and the biospheres and Ander's failed teleportation units and Proxima b. They would know how little time they had left on this dying planet. They would know that the pollution masks and expensive water-filtration systems wouldn't save them. That NASA was decades away from perfecting another method of transporting people the distance to Proxima b, and when it was possible, a "brave explorer," as Ander had put it, would be needed. Someone to take the risk and go there first. So many variables for an indeterminate future. If humankind knew everything, they would realize the end was coming and there was no stopping it.

She only wished she could tell Katrina the truth. Tell her she and Carrie were alive. But revealing the truth would mean the same restricted life for Katrina and Steve and their son, Avery, now a vibrant seven-year-old she had never met. And she didn't have it in her to do that to their family, no matter how much she missed them.

Black energy coursed through her. She stood and paced, walking into the kitchen, then to the dining room, and back to where she'd began.

Her hand hovered over her phone at one point, and she nearly picked it up and dialed her sister's number, nearly threw everything away just to speak to Kat, to hear her voice. But she set it down and moved to the dresser in the hallway, where she pulled the top drawer out and looked down at the object within.

Her mother's rosary. It had shifted successfully as well, and she'd worn it for several years before finally tucking it safely out of sight. It had saved her life, more than once, but now she had other plans for it. She imagined the day, maybe a few years from now, when she'd be able to slip a package in the mail without her tail seeing, away from the prying eyes in the sky. She saw her sister receiving it, observing the lack of return address, and opening the box to find the rosary within. And she hoped Katrina would understand, would still have enough faith left to believe in miracles.

Gillian shut the drawer and returned to the picture window. The rain had tapered off, and she was considering going for a walk on one of the trails that cut through the hundred acres surrounding the house when her phone rang. She picked it up, recognizing the area code.

NASA.

"Hello," she said, not knowing who or what to expect on the other end of the line. It had been nearly two years since anyone from the UN or NASA had contacted her.

"Gillian. It's Jones."

She had to swallow her surprise. The last she'd read, Anderson Jones had been confirmed as NASA administrator by the Senate. He was the last person she'd expected to call.

"How are you?" he asked, filling in her stunned silence.

"I'm . . . fine. Fine."

"That's good. I've been briefed regularly on your and Carrie's status. Are you still enjoying the mountains?"

"Anderson, why are you calling?" she asked, slightly unnerved now for a different reason. Jones had treated her with respect after her sudden appearance in Ander's lab, and she'd learned from several sources that he had been instrumental in clearing her research in exchange for her complicity in the lie the general public was living. The man had always been restrained and composed and conducted himself with quiet, self-assured ease. But now she could hear an undercurrent in the administrator's voice, and if she wasn't mistaken, it sounded like excitement. That or fear.

"There is car on its way to pick you up. A jet will be waiting at Jefferson County Airport." Jones paused for several seconds, and she could hear his quiet breathing. "I have something I want you to see."

♦ ♦ ♦

Gillian was escorted through a back alley to the administration building's wing, her sunglasses and hat firmly in place. Even here, especially here, on NASA campuses, her identity had to be kept secret.

The last four hours were a blur, from the black luxury sedan and silent driver who picked her up from the house to the unbelievably fast flight to the Shuttle Landing Facility on Merritt Island, where she was transferred to another car and deposited in the alleyway to be guided into the building by two men wearing expensive suits. If she hadn't known better, she would've guessed they were Secret Service, but that was an absurd thought since she wasn't visiting the president, only the administrator of NASA.

Her anxiety rose another notch when the suited men escorted her to a small boardroom with only a wide touchscreen mounted in the center of a short table flanked by two chairs. There were no windows in the room, and a single camera watched her from one corner.

Minutes later, the door opened, and Anderson Jones strode inside. He had aged little since she'd seen him, the only sign of the years a speckling of white invading his dark hairline at the temples to match his beard.

"Gillian, very good to see you, and thanks for coming on such short notice," he said, shaking her hand.

"Did I really have a choice?"

Jones smiled without humor. "No, I guess you didn't. But that's the situation we find ourselves in, isn't it?"

She was about to ask if he had to disguise himself whenever he went outside his home, but bit back the comment.

"Please have a seat," he said, waking the screen before them with a touch. "I know you've traveled a long way, and you're probably tired, so I won't delay any longer. What I'm about to show you is completely classified, and to be honest, I had quite a fight on my hands when I voiced my request to have you view it. But honestly, I believe in the coming months and years, we are going to need your expertise. And in any case, I felt you of all people had a right to know."

Jones opened a file, and a video appeared. In an instant, she recognized the room in the frame. It was the teleportation area in the space station. Jones hit "Play," and the video jumped into motion.

Gillian watched herself enter the room and fight against the fluctuating gravity as the station lost altitude. Watched herself make the selection on the unit's pedestal screen and remove her jumpsuit. Thankfully someone had edited the video, blurring her nudity as she crawled inside the tube and it closed. In that instant, she was back inside the tunnel, feeling the station shuddering around her, bleeding, and terrified those were her last moments alive.

"How did you get this?" she asked.

"Automatic data uplink once the space station went into failure mode," Jones said, a grim look on his face.

"I . . . I don't know why you're showing me this," she said.

"Please. Watch."

She saw herself go limp, having passed out from the vacuum created inside the tube.

A second later, the flash. And when the video cleared of its white blindness, she was gone. The time stamp ticked by as the room began to shake harder, a cabinet falling and smashing to its face in silence, the glass barrier between the room and hallway shattering. She was about to ask Jones again what she should be looking for when she saw it

Movement in the lower portion of the screen.

Someone crawling. Leaving a smear of blood behind as they pulled themselves into the room.

Easton.

It was like seeing a ghost.

"Oh my God," she said, bringing a hand to her mouth. "He was alive."

Easton struggled to his feet, swaying as if on the deck of a ship in a tempest. He fell forward and caught himself on the unit's control pedestal.

One of his fingers stabbed at the display, and the unit's door opened.

Easton disrobed, tearing at his clothes, and she saw a line of blood running freely down one of his legs before he crawled inside the tube.

The door swung shut.

The room shuddered, the camera's view jittering violently as static rushed across the screen and ate the last of the video into darkness.

But not before an incendiary flash lit up the entire room.

The video stopped.

Gillian, eyes wide, looked at Jones, who was nodding slightly. "Easton made it out?" she asked.

"Yes. He did."

Joe Hart

"Where is he? Why didn't I see him? He was only a few minutes behind me."

She watched Jones, a million questions swirling inside her until they slowly quieted, a dawning beyond anything she'd ever experienced settling over her.

Gillian sat back in her seat. Stunned. Numb.

"He didn't shift here, did he?" she asked finally.

Jones shook his head and went to work on the touchscreen. "Yesterday at around seven p.m. Eastern, we received this message. We estimate it was sent shortly over four years ago."

Jones touched the screen.

A video began to play.

It was dark at first, only a sullen red glow at the top of the screen before the view flipped suddenly. A distortion, then focus.

Easton's face filled the view pane.

He looked exactly as he had moments before she left him to fight the approaching station crew in the hallway: intense and steadfast, ready to avenge the deaths of his friends.

Easton blinked and looked away from the camera at something past the lens. And in that moment, she could see the person who had told her he was willing to go farther than anyone had gone before. The brave explorer.

"This is Mission Specialist Easton Sinclair, Discovery VI."

Gillian leaned forward, noticing something in his eyes. A reflection.

It was a bright orb, not green and not really blue. She guessed there wasn't a word to describe the color in the human language yet. Not yet.

"Transmitting from Dr. Eric Ander's exploratory ship in the Alpha Centauri system, and . . ."

His voice trailed off as Gillian moved closer to the screen, closer to her friend, catching another clear reflection of the strange new world he was looking at in his wide eyes.

Easton laughed. "And you won't believe what I'm seeing right now."

340

ACKNOWLEDGMENTS

Thanks as always to my wonderful family. Your support allows me to keep doing what I love. Thank you to my editors, Jacque Ben-Zekry, Liz Pearsons, and Caitlin Alexander, for helping find the shape of the book in the block of stone. Big thanks to my agent, Laura Rennert, for always going to bat for me as well as for all the insight and support while *Obscura* was being born. Thank you to Dr. Thomas Edwards at NASA for the excellent suggestions and for injecting some reality into my wild ideas. Many thanks to Sarah Shaw, Mikyla Bruder, Jeff Belle, and everyone else at Thomas & Mercer, who are some of the very best people in the business. Thanks to Blake Crouch, Richard Brown, and Matt Iden for the great feedback while writing. And thanks to all the readers who've given life to my career and the books over the years; your kind words mean more than you could imagine.

ABOUT THE AUTHOR

Photo © 2015 Jade Hart

Wall Street Journal bestselling author Joe Hart is the author of eleven novels that include *The River Is Dark*, *Lineage*, *EverFall*, and the highly acclaimed Dominion Trilogy.

When not writing, he enjoys reading, exercising, exploring the great outdoors, and watching movies with his family. For more information on his upcoming novels and access to his blog, visit www.joehartbooks.com.